THE
WRATH
OF THE
SERPENT

THE
WRATH
OF THE
SERPENT

ALLISON ALDRIDGE

CONTENT WARNING

Blood, intense violence, death, gore, brutal injuries, sexual content, attempted sexual assault, mentions of PTSD, decapitation, poisoning, graphic language, and sexual activities.

The Wrath of the Serpent
Book 1 of the Scottish Folklore Series

IDENTIFIERS
978-1-7332687-7-6 (Paperback)
978-1-7332687-6-9 (Hardcover)
978-1-7332687-8-3 (eBook)

First Edition : 2023
10 9 8 7 6 5 4 3 2 1

Also by Allison Aldridge

Dark Radiance Series
Dark Radiance (Book 1)
Dark Sacrifices (Book 2)

Scottish Folklore Series
The Wrath of the Serpent (Book 1)

Pronunciation Guide
Characters

Arable: Air-a-bull
Seona: See-oh-na
Kol Borthwick: Kohl Broth-wrick
Lennox Elliston: Len-nox Elle-is-ton
Mairead Elliston/Mai: May-read Elle-is-ton / May
Caelen Elliston/Cae: Kay-Lin Elle-is-ton / Kay
Lochlan: Lok-lin
Sylas Nicolson: Sigh-las Nickel-son
Eoghan Montros: Oh-win Mon-tross
Gideon: Gi-dee-uhn
Cailleach: Ka-lee-huh
Ainsley: Anyz-lee
Lorna: Lor-na
Coira: Coy-ruh.
Elara: E-la-ra
Arwan: Aar-wen (Death God)
Demios: Dee-mows
Kenina Elliston: Ken-ni-na Elle-is-ton
Embryss: Em-b-ris
Theo: Thee-oh
Tavish: Ta-vi-sh
Kyar: Ki-ar
Tyr: Teer
Soren: Sor-in
Freya: Fray-uh
Axiom: Ax-ee-um
Cashel: Ca-shell
Morrígna: Mor-gan
Jemma: Jem-ma
Eamon: Ay-Mon

Glossary

Adamore: *Ah-da-more*: Mortal Realm
Draíocht: *Dree-ought:* Fire Night
Sìth: *Sigh-th:* Fae
Aesira Games: *As-ear-a*
Bás Court: *B-a-s:* Druids of Death
Todhchaí Court: *Tow-ha-lee:* Druids of Fate
Cogadh Court: *Kug-ah Court:* Druids of War
Fírinne Court: *Feer-in-yeh:* Druids of Truth
Beatha Court: *Bea-tha:* Druids of Life
Pàidean: *Pie-dean*: Soilder
Ralston Caverns: *Ral-s-ton Carverns:* The Prisons in the Death Court
Sluagh: *S-la-ow:* Demon/Host of Death
"Ní neart go cur le chéile": No strength without unity
Anam Cara Oath: *Ah-num Car-a:* Soul Friend
Leannán: *La-num:* Fated Lover
Scíath: *Sigh-a-th:* Protector
Fear Gorta: *F-ar Gore-ta:* Zombie Like Creature

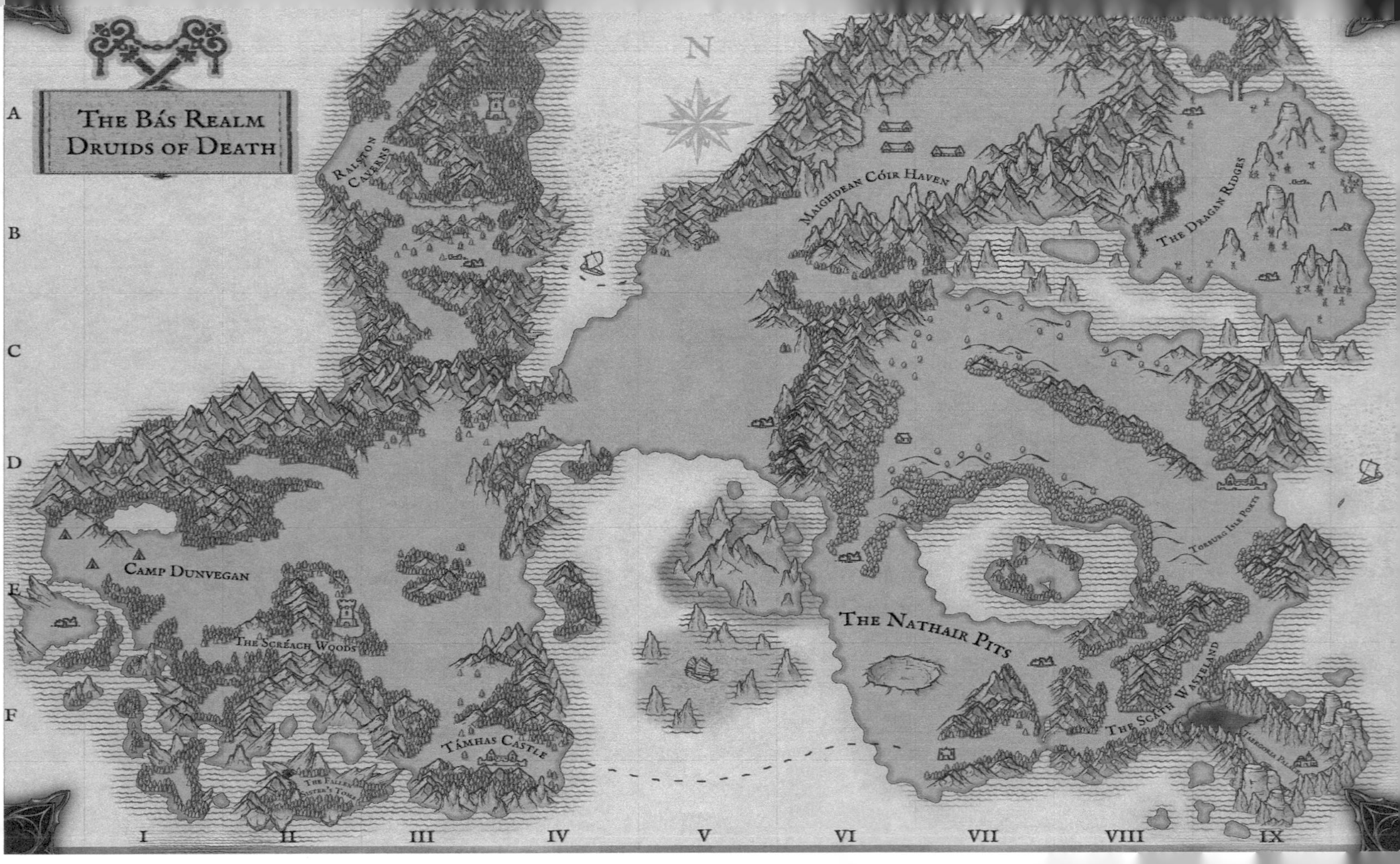

The Bás Realm
Druids of Death
N
Ralston Caverns
Camp Dunvegan
The Screách Woods
Támhas Castle
Maighdean Cóir Haven
The Nathair Pits
The Scáth Wasteland
Torbung Isle Ports
The Dragan Ridges

The Wrath of the Serpent Playlist

MAD WOMAN

TAYLOR SWIFT

LEGENDARY

WELSHLY ARMS

I AM NOT A WOMAN, I'M A GOD

HALSEY

BORN WITHOUT A HEART

FAOUZIA

FOR ISLAND FIRES AND FAMILY

DERMONT KENNEDY

LOVE & HONOUR

CELTIC WOMAN

SNAKE

HALFIVES

EIGHT

SLEEPING AT LAST

POWER OVER ME

DERMONT KENNEDY

BLOODSTREAM

ED SHEERAN

FIND FULL PLAYLIST AND MORE ON

www.allisonaldridge.com/members

For Elijah

There is no one I would rather travel the realms and eat copious amounts of Cheesecake Factory with.

Chapter One
Caelen

Screams filled the night air. They sprung through the burning fields, echoing off the mountains that enclosed the tiny village away from the rest of the world. It was a night of celebration in Adamore, and I could feel the excitement pulsing through the air as everyone scurried around in a joyous panic to ensure the nightly offerings were just right.

Draíocht Night occurred twice a year, the first in Spring to honor Queen Arable, the eldest of the sisters. She brought peace and prosperity to the land after the infamous battle against her sister. Those who still believed in her reign honored her in hopes she would bless the coming season with fruitful abundance. Then, like tonight at the peak of Autumn, just when the leaves began to fall from the trees in a flurry of colors, we honored Seona, the second sister, for her wit and natural talent in battle, in hopes she would protect the village during the harsh winter months. But that talent had also destroyed her, making me question why we choose to celebrate her.

My eyes wandered across the open field, tracing each banner

that represented the five ancient realms the sisters once wielded in the palm of their hands. That was before magic was eradicated from our land, and the door to the realms was securely closed. Each flag, except one, was woven together with brightly colored fabrics.

Purples faded to blues, and a deep maroon color stood out against the fading sun. The final banner was pitch-black with a serpent stitched into the fabric with white thread. As the banner swayed in the wind, it almost looked like the snake was slithering through the endless void of darkness that consumed it. My chocolate-brown hair fluttered in sync with it. The realm the flag represented had always been my favorite. Every time I caught sight of the ancient fabric, a stirring in my stomach began, and a song that felt like home called back to me. My aunt always poked fun at me, insisting it was the wild spirit of my mother flowing through me that pulled me closer to the Druids of Death's court.

"Are you going to just stand there all night and clutch that basket, girl?" a familiar deep voice spoke through the chaos surrounding me. I whipped my head around, playfully glaring at him before a hint of a mischievous smile spread across my face. Kol Borthwick stood nearby, one shoulder leaning against the side of a freestanding wooden archway with a sly grin tugging up the corner of his lips. His sandy-colored hair stuck up haphazardly as if he had just rolled out of bed. No doubt, a female trailed closely behind him.

"What have I told you about calling me *girl*, Borthwick?" I asked, playfully baring my teeth in his direction. He threw up his hands in surrender, causing me to let out a loud laugh. Several locals who were hanging glowing lanterns turned to glare in my direction. I couldn't help but grumble, "The lot of you need to learn how to have fun occasionally."

Kol rolled his brown eyes in my direction. "Come on, you animal, let's finish whatever outlandish errand Aunt Lennox has sent you on. Then you and the birthday girl are all mine tonight."

He slung an arm around my shoulders, pulling me towards a dark pathway. Most in Adamore would shy away from venturing into Hollow Grove. The tree's limbs twisted together, blocking the moonlight from the deserted path, but Kol and I had walked this route for years. We knew each crack in the soil and twist in the trail that ended at a small cottage I called home. In front of the structure was a blooming garden that grew every type of herb, vegetable, and flower my aunt could dream of.

On nights such as this, when the moon was full, and Aunt Lennox had lit the garden's torches, the garden seemed to come alive in vibrant shades of violet and yellow. As a small child, I would hide in the middle of the flowers and stare at the stars while dreamy stories floated around me. When she was alive, my mother claimed garden fairies were responsible for the whisperings. After she died from an illness the medics could not save her from, I asked the fairies to take me back to the dreamland they resided in.

But the fairies never spoke to me again.

Legend says that those touched by death at an early age can't be reached by the fairies, but I think I had lost my childhood spark the night my mother took her final breath. I pulled out of Kol's grasp and launched myself towards the cottage's door. The light notes of a song and the clang of glass filled the home as we stepped into its warmth. A flash of golden blonde hair flew around the entryway before the smiling face of my younger sister, Mairead, came into view. She was always the epitome of a breath of fresh air, with the slight curl to her hair and the soft glow that she emulated when she flashed a smile at you. At just barely sixteen, she held more grace in her pinky finger than I did in my entire body.

"Caelen, you're back!" She bounded towards us. "And you brought Kol!"

"Hello to you too, birthday girl." Kol mockingly bowed towards her, making Mai's face flame red. She let out a slight giggle and mimicked his movements. The two of us were three years apart in age, and I still could not fully grasp that she was no longer a little girl with pink bows in her pigtails and the childish grin who dragged around a tattered doll she refused to part from.

"Where is Aunt Lennox? I brought her…" I paused for a moment, looking down at the basket of mismatched liquid bottles I had picked up from the shops, "whatever these are."

"She is in the kitchen." Mai nodded towards the back of the cottage, where the slamming of glass increased in volume. I raised a questioning brow at her. "I think she was just about to have a fit if you didn't arrive home soon with those. She kept mumbling about the full moon and timing. You know how she is on fire nights."

"We all know how she gets," Kol and I blurted out simultaneously. Aunt Lennox had always been slightly off, which was the nicest way to put it. Most of the local villagers called her "Crazy Len" because she was always going on about the ancient realm kingdoms and the magic that lay dormant in our land. The three of us just nodded along to her rants and allowed her to study her old books if it made her happy.

Stepping around my sister, I made my way into the small kitchen. Kol and Mai followed slightly behind me, their hushed whispers floating around the hall. A long wooden table stretched across the middle of the kitchen, leaving very little room for more than one person to be in the space. Surrounding it were large cabinets and a small fire-lit stove with a pot of greenish liquid bubbling over the top of it. Aunt Lennox had her herb collection spread across every surface of the kitchen. She scurried between them to add to the mixture on the stove. She didn't notice our presence until I spoke over the melody coming from the small music box in the corner.

"Aunt Lennox, I brought you the items you requested from the shops," I called over the noise. My aunt turned around, her wild red hair sticking out in different directions from the bird's nest she had piled atop her head. She peered at the three of us over bright aqua-rimmed glasses, which rested on the bridge of her nose. Clapping in excitement, she reached out to grasp the basket from me.

"Oh, bless you, sweet girl." Aunt Lennox pinched the tip of my chin in her fingertips before returning to her concoction. "I was beginning to think you had run away with that Prince of

Darkness. Silly me, of course."

She turned over her left shoulder to wink at me. It was a comment she had always made to Mai and me, but I was never truly sure what she meant by it. Though I knew Aunt Lennox never said anything she genuinely did not believe could occur, she had been known to prophesize many things during my nineteen years of life.

"No prince tonight, Aunt Len." Kol pushed past me, taking a seat on the bench that extended beneath the table's surface. "Just me. And you know I am only trouble."

"Oh, everyone in the village knows it, dear boy." Aunt Lennox let out a soft chuckle. She popped open a vial with purple liquid in it before pouring the contents into the pot. A puff of smoke erupted from the green liquid before it turned a deep shade of purple and came to a simmer. "And that is why I like that Caelen keeps you around."

She tossed the vial behind her, letting the glass smash into tiny pieces on the counter. I sighed, knowing I would be cleaning up this mess into the early hours of the morning. Mai reached out, running an apologetic hand over my arm. I sent her a soft smile. "Do you need anything else from me, Aunt Len? Kol and I are going to take Mai down to watch the celebration tonight for her birthday."

"Oh yes, it is that time of year again, is it not?" The woman peered out the window before her, staring directly at the full moon. "We haven't celebrated a Draíocht Night on a full moon in over a thousand years. The last one was when the sisters fought against each other on the battlefield. I do feel as though something is brewing in the realms, and we must all be prepared."

"But wasn't I born on a full moon, Aunt Lennox?" Mai's sweet voice called over my shoulder.

Aunt Lennox's eyes glaze over at the memory of my sister's birth, "Why yes, you were, dear. Quite interesting now that you think of it. They refused to celebrate that day due to the storm. Never have I seen that much electricity flash through the sky than the night you were born, Mairead."

A cold chill washed over me as I watched her pace around the kitchen once again, a slight hop in her step as she went. Kol looked to me, one eyebrow raised in question at the statement. I rolled my eyes and nodded toward the hallway. If we left now, she would return to making whatever potion she was brewing, and we could sneak out before the next prediction. Kol stood silently, making his way back into the hallway, Mai following quickly behind him. I turned on my heel and took a step from the room.

"Oh, and Caelen…" Aunt Lennox's voice was fierce as she spoke. I craned my neck to look toward her. Fire danced in her green eyes as she spoke. "Do say hello to that lovely prince for me. I think he owes our family a great deal of explaining."

Her gaze trailed down to the necklace sitting between my breasts. It was a family heirloom my mother gave to me on her deathbed. The pendant that hung at the end of the silver chain was a crescent moon extending into clawed hands that held a bright blood-red gemstone.

The story goes that our ancestors received it from a powerful

Sìth during the war and then sent them away. It is supposed to protect the Elliston family member who bears the burden of wearing it, but Aunt Lennox believes it holds a rare magic inside the stone. She swore that if you watched the gem long enough, one could see the power swirling around the inside, but only the Elliston bloodline could wield its power when the time was right. Personally, I think it is just a piece of jewelry picked up from a traveling witch by our ancestors, who then simply made up a fantastical story to keep the piece interesting.

"Well, you better run along, dear, wouldn't want to keep him waiting." Aunt Lennox turned back towards the stove. I stared at her for a moment longer, her comment making something in my stomach pull tight and snap. My aunt's ramblings usually didn't make me blink twice, but tonight's felt strange. She was right; something about this Draíocht Night *was* different, and I couldn't tell if I was prepared for it.

Chapter Two
Caelen

Mairead, come on, we are going to be late," I screamed down the hall for her. It was Mai's first time going to a Draíocht Night without Aunt Lennox trailing behind her. After days of pleading, Aunt Len had agreed to allow Mai to go with me as long as she kept close to my side the entire night.

The smiling face of my twelve-year-old sister bounded through the hallway, hands haphazardly braiding her hair down her back. I sighed as Mai missed a chunk of blonde locks and tied it off in a light blue ribbon.

"I am ready." Mai smiled at me with a toothy grin. The excitement radiated off her as she hopped from one foot to the other.

"Let me fix that hair of yours." I laughed at her attempt to smooth down the bumps in the hairstyle. "Turn."

Mai did as I instructed, my fingers coming up to untie the braid and begin it again. With one strand over the other in a methodical motion, I managed to master since the passing of our mother when Mai barely had enough hair to pull into pigtails. The act lulled the two of us into a routine silence. I had a theory that Mairead haphazardly did her hair to get these quiet moments alone with me.

"Cae?" Mai's timid voice pulled me from my concentration.

"Mai?" I mimicked her question, waiting for her to respond as she rocked back and forth on her heels. Tying the ribbon back on the tail of the braid, I spun her around. Mai refused to look me in the eye, staring at the wooden door behind me instead. My voice was soft as I spoke again. "Hey, come on, Songbird, talk to me."

Her face relaxed at the nickname, gaze wandering back to meet mine. She sighed. "I'm nervous."

"There is nothing to be nervous about. This will be like any other Draíocht Night, just without as many whispers, because Aunt Lennox is staying home."

"But Isla said that after dark, the travelers prey on those who are easy targets with curses and raise demons with summoning circles to cause havoc." Mai's eyes were wild as she rattled off her fears.

"Isla Thomas is the biggest liar in the village, and you know that." I laid my hands on her shoulders. "You have nothing to worry about after the sun sets. It is mostly just gathering around the bonfire and listening to the old legends. Nothing you can't handle."

She opened her mouth to protest, but I cut off her words. "And if you feel as though it is too much, Kol and I will bring you home."

"Kol is going to meet us there?" Mai's entire face lit up like I had announced she was allowed to bring home a kitten for her birthday. I chuckled, shaking my head at her excitement. She blushed a deep scarlet color, realizing she had just outed her already known crush on Kol.

I threw my arm around her shoulders and pulled her close to my side. "Come on, Songbird, let's go cause some trouble."

People mingled around the large crackling bonfire in the middle of the open field. The steady beat of a bodhran drum mixed with the harmony of a fiddle floated through the night air. The grassy area was packed with bodies. This was one of the few times a year that the locals blended with the transients as we listened closely to their folklore of the Sìth creatures that had once lived amongst us—the two sister queens and a land where magic flowed freely around common folk.

Children sat wide-eyed, watching a woman dressed in a long, cobalt dress with coins hanging from a chain around her hip. The coins rattled as she acted out the story an older man was reciting.

"You see, younglings, magic once filled the very land you sit upon." The old man's gruff voice was as animated as the twinkle in his eyes. "But it was all taken away when the Fairy Flag was lost to all during the final battle between the two sisters. Legend states that the beautiful Sìth Queen, Seona resided in the hills just past those trees."

He pointed back into Hollow Grove with the pipe he was smoking from. I turned to stare at the path I had just stumbled out of with Kol and Mai. Unsurprisingly, the pair had disappeared into the crowd the second we made it to the field. Swiveling back around, my eyes caught the man's. A knowing look shined in the green of them before he continued with the story for the impatient adolescents in front of him.

"She fell in love with a mortal king who was said to have led his people with heart rather than brute force. They united the divide between mortals and those who held magic in their veins in Seona's time in the mortal realms. Not long after, the second sister had a child, but he inherited his father's mortality, and the queen was soon summoned back to her realm by her sister. Our lands fell into a great and terrible war as the two sisters' divide began to surface. During Seona's final moment in the mortal realms, before the legendary battle, she made one request of the king. He was to swear that he would not allow the babe to cry, and his agreement was sworn with an ancient blood oath between the two of them."

I inched closer to the storyteller, my feet moving against my will until they brushed against a chubby toddler sucking its thumb. The child looked up at me, wide-eyed, its arms reaching up for my warmth. I just narrowed my gaze, causing it to sigh in defeat before going back to listening to the story once again. The woman spun in a circle, signifying that our world was in terror as fire-breathing dragons and bloody battles ripped through this very field. I was just about to turn away and go find Kol, when the older man's voice caught my attention once more.

"The babe did cry. Only once when he was left alone on a Draíocht Night, much like the one we sit admiring tonight. His handmaiden had wandered off to watch the shows from the nursery window, but when she returned, she could hear a soft voice singing the child a lullaby. Afraid the child was in danger, the handmaiden raced around the corner and found *no one* was in the room, but the babe was now wrapped in a flag the handmaiden had never seen before. It was worn at the edges and looked to have been used in a battle long before finding its home with the child."

The old man took a long puff from his pipe, exhaling it into the night air. "At the end of the flag was a note which informed the king that this flag would save anyone in peril or win any war if it was waved by someone in great need. But it could only be used three times. After the third wave, the flag would only be what it appeared to be. The note was signed with a simple S at the bottom. Years later, the king's castle was burned to the ground—the mortal sin of greed driving many to seek the power of the flag for themselves. The action sent the realm into terror as Queen Seona sought revenge and many soldiers were slaughtered during the final battle, as Queen Arable tried to contain the power her sister wielded."

My gaze found the man's eyes hardened with anger. I shifted backwards as anxiety began to plague my body. His gaze never left mine as he spoke his next words. "Legend has it that the flag has been waved only twice. Once to win the first war when the King fought against the division of mortal and magical beings. Then, once again, when the realms were threatened by a dark entity that exuded blue electric currents. Now, the flag has disappeared, but those of us who believe in the legends say it is due to turn up one day very soon, and the one who finds it will be tasked with the duty of uniting the realms once again."

The crack of a firework exploding in the sky startled me, causing my body to jump back from the group of small children. They were too enamored with the glittering sky to notice the storyteller and young woman disappear into a cloud of gray smoke. I sucked in a shaky breath before turning on my heels and dashing into the crowd surrounding the fire. The tang of whiskey hung stale in the night air as I maneuvered through a group of drunken men and towards Kol, who stood off to the side. He had a glass of his own dark, amber liquid in one hand, head tilted back to watch the fireworks light up the sky in an array of colors.

"Kol," I called out, bringing his focus upon me. His lips pulled into a lazy grin as I staggered up to him. "Let's get out of here."

"Why? The fun is just about to begin. I heard there was a fortune reader in the tent just beyond there." Kol casually pointed toward the left side of the field. I rolled my eyes at him, turning to look around the crowd for Mai, but she was nowhere in sight. "What has gotten you so spooked, Cae?"

I narrowed my eyes at him and huffed out an angry breath which blew my wild bangs away from my eyes. "Nothing, it's nothing. Just some stupid story that a passerby was preaching about."

"A story, huh? Well, go on, tell the audience what is this story was that has turned your mood so sour." Kol smirked as a deep frown settled on my face, but he continued to wait to hear about the ridiculous folklore.

"It was the Fairy Flag lore." I sighed, running a hand over my face. A thin sheen of sweat had built up on my cheeks from standing so close to the heat of the fire. Kol's eyebrows scrunched together in question. I knew what he was thinking instantly. We had grown up hearing the legend. It was a staple story told at night just before your mother tucked you into bed and you said your evening prayers. "Don't look at me like that, Borthwick. There was something off with the old man telling it. I can't explain it, but it was as if he was telling the story directly to me. Almost as a cautionary tale."

"I think your aunt is rubbing off on you, Caelen." Kol barked out a laugh. "I mean, come on, it is just a story. We hear it every year, and the travelers always believe this will be the Draíocht Night that old rag shows up. But it never happens. And when it does, all that is going to happen is the historians having a field day examining it for their books." Kol tossed the empty whiskey glass over his shoulder, and it disappeared into the dark, but I could still hear the glass shattering against some hard object.

"I really hate when you do that," I grumbled, crossing my arms over my chest.

"Traditions, Cae, it's all about traditions." Kol slung one arm over my shoulder in his usual calm manner. "Come on, let's go find your sister, and then I have something to show the two of you."

"If it involves me almost facing certain death tonight, then count me in. I need an adrenaline rush before the sun rises, and we have to return to our boring lives as the town's misfits," I say, smiling up at Kol.

We began to wander through the sea of people to find Mai. Our feet led us to the back of a small tent filled with different colored gems. The owner of the spiritual apothecary was a young woman named Annie. The pop-up tent was a temporary fix for tonight's festivities, while her shop was just down the road in town next to a bakery that sold the most delicious scones. She claimed to practice the art of reading tarot for clients who requested such a thing, and she had taken a liking to Mai after the first time she read her cards. I never allowed my cards to be pulled, even if Annie was relentless in her pursuit to convince me.

Tonight, Annie wore an emerald robe with yellow suns and moons stitched throughout the fabric. It swayed as she walked in such a way that made her look like she was levitating off the ground. Mai sat in a chair behind the coin counter, a teacup clutched in her hands as she laughed at a younger boy who was shamelessly flirting with her. Through Mai was too oblivious to see the truth.

"Mai," I called out to her at the edge of the tent's opening. Setting down her cup, she excused herself from the boy, a blush tracing his cheeks as she gave his shoulder a squeeze when she passed by him.

"You two look like you are up to no good." Mai gave us a deep smirk, which I matched with a mischievous one of my own. I untangled myself from Kol's arm, reaching out and gripping down on her hand.

"When are we ever up to any good, Mairead?" I winked at her, pulling her from the tent and into the smoky night air.

CHAPTER THREE
CAELEN

A l light drizzle of rain came down as we stepped up to the base of the small mountain just outside of the village. Kol had been insistent that we come explore the abandoned castle that sat at the peak. Fog hung low against the ground, making the structure hold a gloomy aura around it that matched the story, which brought the castle to its ruin. Days before the battle between the two sisters, a rogue group of rebels infiltrated a celebration hosted by the king, and set the entire structure ablaze. Now, all that remains is the broken, charred pieces of a once strong dynasty and the grave of the king who had perished in the fire.

"This place gives me the creeps." Mai shuddered slightly. Even in the low light of dusk, I could see goosebumps beginning to rise on the back of her neck. She wasn't wrong. On most days, this place would just be another abandoned building from the war we explored for fun, but tonight, on the anniversary of the castle's demise, it almost felt wrong to be here.

"Don't you want to know if the rumors are true?" Kol shoved his shoulder into Mai's. He had a devilish smirk plastered across his face, which always meant trouble was brewing. I eyed him slightly, making him roll his eyes in return. "Oh, don't look at me like that, Caelen. I know you, of all people, are dying to see inside that old building. How many times have you heard about the throne that still stands, untouched by the flames from that night?"

"About a hundred." I chuckled. The tale of the burning castle was one of Aunt Lennox's favorite stories that she would rotate in and out of our bedtime routine when we were young. I looked back at the castle. "Okay, come on, you two, let's make this quick. I don't want to get caught in whatever storm is in the air tonight."

My boots crunched against the gravel trail. It twisted and turned in such sudden movements that it was almost impossible to think this wasn't purposely done to keep out intruders. One wrong step, and I would be plummeting off the cliff's edge. I cast a look behind me to make sure Mai was alright and found she was following carefully near me. Kol held out a steady hand behind her, ensuring that he would be there to catch her if she slipped. The trail was short, and we ended up at the top of the mountain just before the sun dipped fully out of the skyline.

Large trees covered the structure's perimeter, and a field of golden wildflowers shone in the fresh moonlight as we made our way toward the castle. I couldn't help but notice the grounds looked well-kept and undisturbed, despite the fact that only adventurous souls like ourselves were brave enough to venture this far.

A large stone archway stood tall in the middle of the field with melted-down hinges on either side of the stone where the entrance had once been and a sheen of moss was now crawling up the sides. Kol was going on about how guests would be announced by their surnames if they held a high enough title in the court's hierarchy.

"And how would you announce us?" Mai swept through the archway dramatically, hands swishing her lilac skirt around in the air. "I do hope it is something poetic."

"Kol, poetic? I highly doubt that, Mairead." I ventured past her and towards the scorched remains of what I could only assume was once a grand hallway. The wind whistled through the planks, and if I listened closely, I could hear the voices of the past chattering back to me. My eyes closed slightly as I breathed in the night air, listening intently to their soothing words.

A girl just older than Mai revealed she was going to the celebrations with the general's eldest son. And there was a man—his voice gruff as he spoke about security plans. But the last voice I could hear was soft, kind, and motherly. It spoke directly to me, whispering my name as it went. The sound of its calling felt right, as if I could merely reach out and get wrapped up in its comfort.

"Caelen, well, she is a hard one to pin down in just a sentence or two, don't you think?" Kol's joking voice ripped me back to reality like a leather cord snapping against my skin. I craned my neck to look towards the two of them. Mai was nodding at Kol's comment as he watched me closely, trying to come up with the perfect snarky remark. Turning in their direction, I waited for him to speak, "How is this? Caelen of House Elliston, the most feared woman in all of Adamore."

"At your service, my lord." I bent down in a mock bow, making Mai giggle. Kol matched my bow with one of his own and cracked a slight smile. "But I think you've got it wrong. Aunt Lennox is the most feared woman in Adamore. She claims she could turn anyone into a common toad if they crossed her."

"She is feared for being in tune with the magic that once resided here, but you, my dear Caelen, are feared for that spectacular show you put on at the knife throwing contest this past summer." Kol wagged his finger in my direction.

I rolled my eyes. The contest he was referring to was one I wished to forget. It was a small event held by the schoolhouse for endurance training. Every male in the village specialized in a skill by the age of thirteen. Kol completed his specialization with a blacksmith who primarily produced swords and knives for soldiers.

The devil himself, Kol Borthwick, had pulled me directly in the middle of a knife-throwing contest with a few other males, who didn't even pay me a look before the games began. To everyone's surprise I landed all five knives in the center of the target. It was the only combat training I had learned from my mother. She insisted that I have some way of protecting myself. The males in the contest were less than enthused to have been beaten by a girl, and rumors about Aunt Lennox hexing the knives swirled almost as soon as I walked away from the field. Now, as I strode through the village, people avoided me like I was the plague.

"That was your doing, and I am still not over how you set me up." I narrowed my gaze on Kol, as he threw up his hands in a surrendering motion.

Turning on my heel, I headed down the hall and into a broken doorway. A breathy gasp broke through my parted lips at the sight before me. At the back of the otherwise destroyed room was a perfectly intact throne. The dark leather of the seat shined as if it had just been cleaned. Its matching metal framework glistened in immaculate condition. Looking at it, you would have thought that the king who once ruled these lands still sat upon it today

"Whoa." Kol's voice startled me, and I jumped slightly. Neither Mai nor he seemed to notice as they stared dreamy eyed toward the odd throne before us. "Why do you think it is still here?"

"The metal must be made out of a material that is resistant to high heat," Mai stated matter of factly. I was never as surprised as others were when my sister relayed her vast knowledge on any subject with such ease. She had always been more book smart than I was. I hadn't given my studies much thought. Kol nodded numbly at her, still trying to wrap his mind around the fact that this item hadn't been looted long ago.

"I don't think I have ever seen you rendered speechless, Borthwick," I teased before striding forward to where the throne sat. A sensual buzz floated around the air as I made my way closer. It felt like magic being pumped into the atmosphere, something in the pit of my stomach beckoning to invite it in.

But that was impossible. Magic was gone, and it would never return to this land, no matter how much Aunt Lennox believed it would.

"What are you doing?" Kol's voice raised in panic as he watched me run one finger along the cool metal armrest. I threw him an odd look over my shoulder before returning to the throne. It was just an old piece of furniture. What was the worst that was going to happen?

Before Kol could tell me to stop, I plopped down into the throne, throwing my legs over the side of the right armrest. As I leaned back into the coolness of the metal, I stared at the two stunned people in front of me. Kol's mouth was opening and closing like a fish out of water, trying to find the words to reprimand me.

"I could get used to this, I believe." I smirked at him. In this seat, even the most humble person would feel powerful. Mai shot me a disapproving look before she began to wander around the room, looking at the broken planks and tiles strewn around. My eyes roamed upwards. The three beams above me didn't look burned or rotted with age. If I stood on the chair, I could touch them. In the middle beam, I spotted a faded piece of fabric sticking out from the side of it. The material must have been shoved there in an attempt to conceal it quickly.

Swinging my legs off the armrest, I set them on the floor and stood. My first foot settled on the center of the throne, and then my other, before Kol began to scold me for stepping on something so valuable. I shot him a warning look. "There is something up here. I want to see what it is. Don't get your knickers in a twist, Borthwick."

Reaching up, my hands traced the fabric ever so slightly. It was rough and stiff, definitely not a blanket or paper material, making me wonder what I was about to pull out. Tugging on it, the material barely budged. It took a few more tries before I pulled as hard as I could. The momentum of the tug, along with the fact that the thing had finally come free, sent me reeling backward and airborne toward the ground. Strong arms circled my waist and caught me before my tailbone hit the ground.

"Thanks," I breathed out, looking up to Kol, who only nodded and set me back on my feet. When I looked down at the object in my hand, I could now see that it was a flag. The edges were slightly frayed, and the color was faded in most spots from the brilliant yellow gold that it once was. In the middle of the flag was a star shape with six different symbols. Each one sat next at the tips of the five-pointed star with the largest of the symbols resting in the middle of the shape. I couldn't distinguish what they meant to stand for, as they were in an archaic drawing method I had never seen before. But the sight of this flag had my mind wandering back to the story told by the old traveler.

"You almost broke your neck for a dusty old flag?" Kol groaned.

"Well, it's more than what you will be bringing home," I hissed. The tone of my voice made him flinch slightly, which wasn't like Kol to do. I knew I was cold and harsh to people who didn't know me, but Kol had adapted to my personality when we were younger. I shook off the action. "Plus, I am sure Aunt Lennox will love to study this."

The sickening creak of wood sent chills up my spine just as I began to move forward. I looked to where the flag had once been wedged and saw a split in the beam. Kol and I made eye contact before we bolted toward the door. I reached out with my free hand as I passed, yanking Mai from the side of the room as the structure began to crumble. Large beams and stone faltered, sending them tumbling down around us. I dodged a massive chunk of marble as it flew in my direction, diverting my steps just in time. Kol was the first out of the doorway, and I threw Mai in front of me, causing her to stumble, before he steadied her. I watched him guide her out to the wildflowers before turning back to look at the throne.

Through the dust and debris, I could make out the shape of a young man, a glistening black crown sitting on his head, and his dark eyes were staring directly at me.

My wild dark locks whipped around me as a freezing gust of air blew in my direction. The man was pointing at me, his silent words screaming orders to no one. I didn't give myself a chance to see what would happen next as I raced from the abandoned castle.

With the flag clutched in one hand, a strange burning occurred in the other. I opened my hand, trying to see if I had cut myself on something while we were trying to escape, but instead, I found an entirely different scenario. In the middle of my palm, a dark black symbol appeared to be inked in my skin, matching the one in the middle of the flag.

CHAPTER FOUR
LOCHLAN

Chess pieces went flying across the strategy room. The rook smashed against the wood paneling and cracked in two. A dark swirl of power encompassed the room as my anger grew. It was uncontrollable, slithering along the walls in smoky tendrils, ready to strike at my command. My champion was a mortal girl who just stupidly stuck herself in the middle of a game she could not win. But what made my anger overflow was the masked figure racing from the throne rooms rubble next to her.

I couldn't see them.

A cloud of black smoke shielded them from my sight. Each time I tried to break through the thick fog, blue currents of electricity would ripple along the cloud, sending my magic into a frenzy. An explosive pain tore through me as the figure's power shocked me into a dormant state. I had never tasted power like that. It rivaled the gifts coursing through my blood. Worse, they made me nothing more than a floundering fool in front of my father.

"You are rattling the entire realm with your rage, Lochlan,"

Sylas purred. I turned my icy glare to the executioner. Her lips curled into a wicked smirk as she brought the wine glass clutched in her hand to hover just in front of it. Deep maroon nails scraped against the wood as she wiped the condensation from the glass onto the desk. Each scratch of her talons drove into my nerves like a viper's strike. Sylas tsked at my stare. "Now, don't be that way, doll. The rules say the team has to win the Games, not the champion. It might be fun to play around with the mortal."

"You would be like a cat toying with a mouse," a new voice stated as they entered the room. Eoghan stepped through the door, eyes trained on the broken chess piece on the floor. "That was one of my favorite chess sets, you temperamental fool."

"General Montros," I growled. He rolled his eyes at the formality, knowing I was using it to get under his skin. It appeared I was the only one concerned about the fact we had to win the Aesira Games in the coming season with a mere mortal by our sides. I would not be the one who lost the crown to a lesser realm because of an insignificant girl. I raked my hand through my dark locks, undoing the style in the process.

"We can use her to our advantage, and you know this, Lochlan." Eoghan pulled out a chair from under the strategy table. He spun it around to straddle it backward. "But the mortal champion is not the only thing causing this foul mood. What has gotten you so worked up?"

"There was another entity in the room with her," I mused, running a hand over my chin, stubble scratching at my fingertips. "But I couldn't break through its protection. The damn thing kept frying my abilities when I tried to coax my way through its fog."

"And what was this thing?" Sylas hissed, her eyes fully alert now that a threat had been addressed.

"Something I have never seen before, but the power it was executing was cold and uncontrolled." I met Eoghan's pinched expression. The veins under my skin still buzzed from the entity's attacks on my nervous system. I had been able to fight back enough that it only incapacitated my power, but if that had not been the case, I might not be sitting up speaking to them now. "It could be possible that our champion is not fully mortal."

"Don't you think you would have been able to pick up on abilities she might possess?" Eoghan asked.

"Not with the other entity sucking most of my attention away from her." I leaned back into my chair, staring down at where the mortal realm was sketched on the map. Turning my attention back to Eoghan, I continued. "Gather Gideon and go retrieve our girl. I want to ensure we prepare her for what lies ahead in the Games."

"Something deadly, I hope." Sylas's dark chuckle filled the silent air.

I flashed her a predatory grin. "Let the sky rain red, my darling."

Chapter Five
Caelen

What the hell were you thinking?" Kol's sharp tone broke my gaze away from the crumbling castle. A large hand gripped down onto my shoulder roughly, spinning my body around to face the furious man. I ripped myself away from his touch and stared him down with the intensity of a thousand armies. The look made the man in front of me falter for a moment, shrinking away from its coldness before transforming back into anger. "You could have gotten us all killed, Caelen."

"Don't lecture me, Borthwick. I am not one of your females who will bend to the slight raise of your voice," I snarled, taking a menacing step forward. Angling my head to look up at him, my eyes raked over every inch of his body to find a weakness. "You'll do your best to remember who you are speaking to."

Kol laughed darkly. "You can't fool me. I know behind all that ice is just a sad and pathetic excuse for a girl. Just because your parents didn't love you the way you needed doesn't mean you can spew that fire towards everyone you cross paths with."

Before my mind even had time to catch up, my hand curled

into a fist and connected with his cheek. I sucked in a sharp breath as the sting of bone met my knuckles. Kol cried out, gripping down on his face as Mai screamed in opposition at the fighting, but I ignored both of them. The force of the punch made him stagger back a few steps, one of those missing its mark on the gravel, and he went tumbling onto the ground. I stalked up to him, my figure towering over his moaning one.

"Speak about my family again, and I will cut your tongue out of your skull," I spat down at him. He narrowed his eyes at me, but I didn't give him a chance to speak again. "Come, Mairead, we should get back to check on Aunt Lennox."

Mai's hand covered her mouth, a saddened look in her eyes. I waited for her to say something about what had just happened, but she nodded slightly before following closely behind me. I stomped angrily down the trail leading to the village, trying to put a considerable distance between Kol Borthwick and myself. Mai was silent as we trudged through the remnants of the Draíocht Night festivities.

The bonfire was still blazing in all its glory, but the only stragglers were a few drunken men and women lounging against a log set next to the fire. Peering down, I noticed the flag was still clutched tightly in my hand, and I let out a sigh of relief. The feeling was odd, I didn't feel any attachment to the fabric, but the dark power of the castle pulsed through it, and I couldn't let that go.

We burst into the clearing, Mai running ahead of me, and I could see the shine of tears streaming down her face. I hadn't meant to upset her. No, that was the last thing I wanted to do, but I had never been the perfect example of self-control. Kol's words roared in my ears once again, and the same anger bubbled up in the pit of my stomach. I tried to shake off the feeling, but it clear it was here to stay for the night. As I walked through the front door, I bolted directly to Aunt Lennox, who was still working on the same lumpy substance she had been when we left.

"Aunt Len?" My voice startled me. It was so soft, and I wasn't sure that even as a child, I had ever spoken in such a sweet tone before. By the way Aunt Lennox whipped around and stared at me with wide eyes, I figured not. Her eyes scanned my body, probably looking for where the damage was, but when she found nothing, her gaze locked onto the flag in my hand.

"What is that you have there, dear?" Aunt Lennox's voice was anxious, and it was as if she recognized the flag.

"Kol, Mai, and I went to explore the old burned castle." My aunt's mouth opened to scold us for such a reckless adventure, but I continued on. "I pulled this out of a beam, and well, part of the castle crumbled. Then this symbol appeared."

Thrusting out my left hand for her to examine, she gathered it in her grasp and brought it close to her face. "Ah yes, I know what this is. Back when magic was prevalent in the lands, wealthy Sìth rulers would brand their valuable items with marking curses. It was a way to spot thieves when they were asked to show their palms face up. This will surely fade."

Aunt Lennox dropped my hand, patting me lightly on the shoulder, and shot me a wink. I gaped at her comments. "But magic doesn't exist, Aunt Lennox, so how is it possible for me to be marked with it?"

"Oh, you know how magic works." She waved her hands in an erratic gesture. I knew nothing about magic besides the basics I had picked up from her incessant rambling throughout the years. "Magic marks those who it lives inside. Someday soon, you will have to realize that you are special, Caelen, and not in the way that every girl in this village believes they are. You have power that you haven't even begun to unlock."

I stared at the woman with wide eyes. Never once had she aimed her magical theories in my direction, but I could tell by the soft glisten of truth in her eyes that she believed every word she was saying. Shaking my head slightly, I thrust out the flag for her to look at. "But the marking on my hand matches the one in the center of this flag. Do you know what it means?"

Aunt Lennox gathered the fabric in her hands, stretching out the crumbled material and looking closely at the symbols. She let out an annoyed sigh towards me. "Of course, I know what they mean, doll. Those are the symbols of the ancient Sìth kingdoms, and that middle one was the most powerful house in their court system."

Blinking once, I couldn't believe what I was hearing. The Sìth were just legends, and I didn't believe for a moment that our land had once been plagued with their cruel intentions. But now, with Aunt Lennox's revelation and the strange feeling I had since seeing the boy prince in the castle, I was beginning to believe it all might be possible.

"Funny how the past comes back to haunt us, isn't it, dear?" Aunt Lennox cocked her head to the side as a thought bubbled in her mind. "My, my, everyone is going to be quite surprised to know the Sìth still lurk through the realms."

Chapter Six
Caelen

Gray-speckled moonlight danced across the inside of the room I shared with Mai. I stared at the ceiling, willing my body to allow the exhaustion to take over and bring on the suffocating darkness that came with sleep, but it was no use. Mai's light snores flowed through the space in a steady stream. I tried to match my breathing with hers, but a crash from the front of the cottage startled the air from my lungs. Pausing, I waited to see if it was just a stray animal who had wandered too close, but the muffled sounds of swearing told me it was no raccoon. I silently slipped from the sheets, careful not to alert Mai to anything.

My lungs burned, begging for air as I ventured away into the corridor. I was too nervous about letting out a breath, afraid the sound might reveal me to the intruder. The hallway was dark, and the cold winter air, which always seeped through the cracks in the walls, made the hall feel like ice.

Listening closely, I could hear two male voices arguing, their words unclear, but the tone was angry. Stepping into the kitchen, I unsheathed a knife from the block. The silver gleamed under the moonlight, and as I turned it from side to side, I could see my face glaring back at me.

The eyes of the girl in the knife's blade were stone cold, and in the trick of the dim light, it appeared as if she winked at me in a taunting "let's play" motion. I winced, pulling the knife down flush against my thigh. The voices were silent now, but I could still hear their heavy footsteps milling around the front of the cottage and what sounded like furniture shifting.

I reached the wall separating the front room from the hall and pressed my spine against the cool brick. Waiting, listening for anything that could give me a clue about who these intruders were and what they came here for.

"It is with the girl." The first male's voice was laced with a foreign accent that I once heard from a wandering sailor who claimed he was from an island just off the coast of the southern highlands. The stranger's odd dialect was only one of the indicators that I wasn't dealing with a local villager attempting to break in for Aunt Lennox's herbs and medicines. Some were hard to come by and I had seen people offer up their own lives to get them when they needed them for a loved one. If it were me, I would fight like hell to save Mairead, no matter the cost.

There was a loud scraping sound before the second voice called out, "Aye, what gave it away, Gideon?"

This male's voice wasn't foreign, and the sharpness in his words sent chills down my spine. There were a few more bangs of furniture being shoved about before the footsteps grew nearer. I held my breath, waiting for one of them to step through the threshold of the hallway. But a creak of the floorboard at the end of the hall stopped them in their tracks. The familiar squeak of Mai's and I's door hinges being pried open filled the silent space before the soft light of a burning lantern appeared in the hall. It illuminated Mai's beautiful pale hair in the darkness, making her look like a princess exploring her castle at night.

Her eyes met mine in the darkness. I lifted one finger to my lips and prayed she would turn back to the room, leaving me to deal with the intruders. Mai's eyebrows scrunched together, and it was clear she could not see my movements. "Cae?"

The footsteps began again, stomping ferociously against the hard floor below them. I twisted from my spot against the wall, swinging out the knife as I went. The sharp tip of the blade nicked the first body that came through the entrance. He screamed out in pain and grappled for me. I moved swiftly, ducking and spinning away from his hands.

"Run, Mai," I cried out as I dodged another attempt the intruder made to grab me. The male's long hair hung limply against his shoulders, and the fire in his golden eyes was unnerving. My elbow landed on target with his abdomen, and he buckled over in pain as an unnerving laugh bubbled out of his lips. I moved to venture farther down the hall when another set of arms wrapped around my waist, hauling me off my feet.

Throwing back my head, it made contact with the second intruder's nose, sending blood spraying onto the wall in front of us. He didn't cry out in pain, though, and only a grunt escaped his clenched teeth as he held on to my squirming form.

"Drop the knife," The male hissed in my ear. This only made

me clutch the blade tighter, and I moved to take aim for his leg, which was left exposed below me. He noticed my movements, and before I could make my attack, my body was thrown against the hardwood floor.

All the air in my lungs vanished upon impact, and I gasped out to gather more oxygen, but the room began to spin in hazy pictures. I could see the knife a few feet in front of me, where it must have landed in the toss. My body crawled towards it, but a hand grasped down on my ankle, and I was pulled back towards the male. The firm grip moved up to my hips, and I was soon on my back, staring up at the male who had just held me.

I floundered for a moment, trying my best to get away from him, but he was straddling me, keeping my bucking hips flat against the ground while his hands held my arms on either side of my head. Long dark hair hung around us. I could tell half of it was tied up in a bun on top of his head, but the rest was like wild smoke filling my senses. Glaring back at the intense dark eyes of my captor, I snarled a bit before fighting his hold once again.

"That's the girl he wants?" The golden-eyed male, who had now recovered from my first blow, spoke. Footsteps neared, and then he was standing over me, observing. "More like a wild beast that one is."

"Gideon," the dark-haired male warned. I could feel his hot breath brush up against my cheeks, making me shiver slightly as he directed his words back to me, "Where's the flag?"

I narrowed my eyes at him. "What flag?"

"You know exactly what flag I speak of, girl." He leaned closer with each word until his nose was brushing against mine.

Girl.

The name set my blood on fire, and I thrust my forehead against his. A sickening crack rang out in the silence, and the moment of shock allowed me to wiggle out of his hold. I bolted away from both males, feet slipping against the cool floor as I flew into my bedroom. The room wavered in and out from the impact of the hit, but I managed to scramble through the doorway before the male could catch me once again. The flag was tucked securely under my mattress where I had planned for it to stay, but if this was what they wanted, I would lead them away from Mai and Aunt Lennox before forfeiting it. A horrifying screech rang out in the hallway, sending me racing in the opposite direction of the open window I had planned on leaping from.

Mai was clutched in Gideon's grasp in the middle of the doorway, with the knife I had used against him pressed up to her throat. A heavy river of tears spilled over her eyes as I stared in horror at the scene before me. The crackling of lightning illuminated the hall, and the gleam of the sky's electric current seemed to make Mai's blue eyes glow in the moonlight. A dark shadow maneuvered around them, coming to stand directly in front of me, obscuring my view of my sister.

"Let her go," I said through clenched teeth. My hand shot out, throwing the flag against his chest. He caught my wrist in his own grasp. I could feel his eyes roaming my figure with a burning intensity that set the hair on the back of my neck on edge. His gaze narrowed on the crumbled fabric pinned between my fingertips and his chest. The male reached down to my other hand, facing my palm towards him as he examined the mark that was still there.

A devilish smirk toyed against his lips as I tried to pull away from him. The hold around my wrist tightened, making me groan in pain. "Did you not hear me? Let. Her. Go."

The words were feral against my lips, which only made his smirk deepen. He craned his neck towards Gideon. "Let the sister go. We have what we came for."

I expected him to release my wrist as Mai tumbled from Gideon's grasp, a small pink line from the pressure of the blade being the only damage upon her skin, but the male did not budge. Pulling once again at the steel grip, I was unable to get away from him.

"Let's get out of here before they send the twins to hunt us down," Gideon called out as he walked from the room, his voice echoing off the walls of the cottage. His partner nodded at the statement and began to follow, dragging me along with him. I fought the movement, only making it more challenging to stay on my own two feet. Mai's wailing cries filled my ears, and my entire being fought to get free and gather her in my arms.

He stopped in the middle of the doorway, causing me to slam into his chest as he peered over his shoulder at Mai with a glare. A ghostly whisper of confusion danced in his eyes as my sister continued to wail in panic. Gideon stepped back into my line of sight, blocking me from seeing the male's expression anymore. Gideon gave me a cheeky look as he thrust a gray wool coat into my free hand. The fabric landed limply against the hardwood, my hand refusing to take the clothing item in my grasp.

"You can make this easy on yourself, Caelen, or very, very hard." Gideon leaned in, causing the stern words to brush up against my heated skin.

I narrowed my eyes at him. "How do you know my name?"

"Everybody knows your name now that you caught that flag."

Chapter Seven
Caelen

Mai burst out of the door of the cottage as we made our way into the middle of the garden. Her movements pulled me away from the man's strange words circling my brain. I turned, sending her a pleading look to return to the hallway, but she stood her ground. She looked like a startled doe staring at us with large, reddened eyes. A burst of lightning shot through the cloudless sky, its electrifying blue color dancing angrily through the stars. Mai took a fierce step forward, mouth opening and closing as her brain tried to find the proper negotiation to make.

"Please," Mai croaked out. My heart shattered for my younger sister. There was nothing more that I wanted to do than to wrap her in my arms and assure her this was all just a bad dream. Though we both knew this was not a dream we could run from. "She's all I have left of a family."

The words smashed into my heart like tiny shards of glass, making it hard to breathe through the pain. It wasn't entirely true; she had Aunt Lennox, but I knew she meant I was the only thing left of our mother. Mai had been too young when she got sick to remember her, and the only memories she could grasp onto were the rose-colored versions told to her by me and our aunt. I averted my gaze, listening to the sobs she could no longer contain.

"Mai, go find Kol when the sun rises. He will take care of you and Aunt Lennox," I said, keeping my tone flat as I spoke. My gaze didn't meet hers again. If it did, I knew I would only be tempted to fight against leaving, and my gut told me that none of us would live another night if I did that.

"Let's go." The dark-eyed male's voice was gruff. He gave me one tug, and I followed willingly this time, head held high as we passed through the remainder of the garden where Gideon now waited. He was fiddling with what looked like a pocket watch that had no clock face.

"You better prepare yourself, girly. Everyone's first realm jump is the most unpleasant one." Gideon gave one last turn to a knob on the side of the device before looking at me directly. "If I were you, I would close your eyes, hold on tight, and pray to whatever Gods you believe in that you have a stronger stomach than most."

And with that, he snapped the device shut, and the world began to spin. The blue electric current that had taken over the skies struck down next to us. Gasping at the sudden surge of power that swirled around us, I threw out a hand, gripping down onto the unnamed male's coat, and fell against him. A strong arm wrapped around my lower waist, securing me tight against his body's warmth. I would have broken his arm in a normal situation, but right now, I felt as if my entire being was being pulled apart bit by bit. The sensation of an invisible hook latching itself into my chest began to rip me in a million directions simultaneously. The stretching feeling was unbearable, and just when I believed my entire being was going to implode into itself, I was snapped back into reality with such a force it made me tumble forward.

Steady hands grounded me, but I pushed out of them and hurled my guts onto a forest floor I was unfamiliar with. Once I was finished, I wiped my mouth with the back of the long-sleeve shirt I had put on for bed, only to find it soaking wet. In fact, my entire body was soaking wet from standing in a downpour of freezing rain. My hair hung around my face in stringy pieces, and I could just make out a pair of glowing yellow eyes watching me from a low-hanging branch of a tree. A soft touch brushed against my back, and I flew up from my hunched-over stance, ready to take on the sudden presence.

"We should get back to the castle. You never know what lurks in these woods at night." The dark-eyed male spoke calmly. I could now see the black eye I had given him as the purpling skin swelled. I stepped away from the male as he narrowed his good eye at me. "Caelen."

It was a warning, but I didn't much care for what he was warning me about. "Why is it that you know my name and I do not know yours?"

"She speaks like a normal human. And here I just thought she could only growl." Gideon jokes, sending me a bright smile that shined like the stars, even in the darkness that surrounded us.

"Eoghan," the male said, bowing slightly toward me as if I was some type of royal. The movement would have made me laugh if I didn't think he was being serious. "Eoghan Montros. But as I said, we really should get out of these woods. I have heard the rain can bring sickness to mortals."

I huffed at his statement. "And what does that make you two? Some type of ancient legend that they tell children before bedtime?"

"No," Gideon barked out with a laugh. "They tell children our tale when they want to terrify them into behaving."

Rolling my eyes at the statement, I waited for Eoghan to confirm or deny this statement, but he just began walking into the darkness of the forest. I didn't wait around for Gideon, who was gazing up at the rain-filled sky, and raced after Eoghan. The walk was long and cold, and I shivered shortly after we started, which prompted Eoghan to drape his wool coat over my shoulders. I gladly accepted the clothing item, and pulled it closer to my shivering form. There was no way I was going to freeze to death in these woods with a male who had stolen me from my home.

"I have a question." I spoke up and waited for Eoghan to acknowledge me. When he didn't, I continued. "Gideon said we were realm jumping. What does that mean?"

"Precisely what he said. We jumped from your realm to ours." Eoghan kept his face forward, not even glancing to gauge my reaction to the news. I simply tilted my head toward him not giving away the panic that was rushing through me at the revelation. Realm jumping was something the travelers talked about when they told tales of a time when holding magic was a common currency for trade, but those were just stories. They described fantastical beings who could leap from one place to another with ease. Mortals coexisted with beautiful beings across the universe until that all crumbled, and the first sister closed the doors to our realm. Or so we thought. I opened my mouth to ask another question, but he cut me off. "You should leave your questions for the Prince. He will be eager to answer anything your heart desires."

When my captors and I emerged from the moonlit forest a few hours later, my eyes caught sight of a castle that could have come out of the novels Mai read. Fog hugged the ground in small patches around a heavily guarded entrance, iron bars locked together in tight reinforcement to keep others out. *Or me in.* I knew that entering through those gates would seal my fate of being stuck here with whatever vicious creatures roamed the halls of this castle. And I did *not* plan to take up permanent residence here. Pulling my shoulder blades together, I glanced back toward the forest for a moment.

"I wouldn't if I were you." Gideon spoke softly. Looking in his direction, I was met with a hard stare, and lifted my chin toward him in a way that told him exactly how much his words meant to me. Gideon scoffed. "You'll end up with an arrow in your back, but by all means, make a dash for it, girl."

I clenched my teeth together. "Do not call me girl."

The fierce tone of my voice made him chuckle darkly. "When you become as ancient as I am, you can decide what you are called, but for now, you are just a girl in a world of very dangerous monsters. Do well to remember that as you step through that gate."

Narrowing my eyes, I watched him move swiftly towards the front gates. His long dark hair swung as he walked. I was puzzled by his words. Though he looked no older than thirty to my mortal eyes, Gideon's dialect was from a time long before my own. Eoghan stood a few feet in front of me, but I could see his eyes sweeping over every inch of the tall brick structure holding the gate together. It was hard to make out the ant-like figures of armed soldiers watching the perimeter at the top of the wall in the dark.

"Come on, both of you." Gideon's voice beckoned us closer. I planted my feet in place, not following Eoghan as he approached the other male. Eoghan's steps faltered, throwing me a glare as he saw me making no movement.

"Don't make me toss you over my shoulder, Caelen." Eoghan's voice was tainted with malice as he spoke. I rolled my eyes at his tone and missed as he stormed over to me. His entire form towered mine, a murderous glare cast down in my direction. I could feel his hot breath against my skin, causing goosebumps to rise as we watched each other. "His Majesty does not care if I bring you in kicking and screaming as long as you make it into that throne room in one piece. Which means you either come in willingly, like a lady, or dragged in, like a wild beast after capture."

"I would like to see you try," I snarled at him. Raising my hands, I gave his body a quick shove, the movement startling him just enough for me to make a dash back toward the forest. My feet zig-zagged as I ran through the thick tangle of grass that covered the ground.

Behind me, I could hear Eoghan's strong voice telling the soldiers above to stand down, but I refused to look back. A hole hidden underneath the grass caught the heel of my foot, sending me tumbling through the air. I landed in a small lake, its stormy waters pulling me under. The coldness of the water washed over me in pinpricked droplets, causing my muscles to spasm in shock. My body flailed, hands trying their best to grapple for anything to pull me up to the surface. Just as my lungs burned from the lack of oxygen, my hand connected with someone else's, and a firm yank flung me from the water.

I fell from my savior's grasp onto my hands and knees as I coughed up the water which had entered my lungs, and a sharp pain began to settle in my freshly twisted ankle. A hand grabbed hold of the back of my damp shirt, ripping me up and into their arms.

"Have you lost your damn mind?" Eoghan's deep voice growled into my ear. I fought against his hold, but it was useless—my body was weak, and I was in no shape to take him on if I got the another chance.

My spine pressed into his chest, allowing me to feel every dip and curve of the male behind me. The angle of his hip bones pushed into me, and it took everything in me not to shudder at the thought of just how other parts of him would feel. Eoghan latched his hand underneath my armpit and began to drag me back to the gate. When we reached the front, Gideon shook his head, body vibrating with silent laughter.

Eoghan looked towards an unnamed guard who appeared to be no more than fourteen. "Tell the Prince his prize has been successfully retrieved."

Chapter Eight
Caelen

"I am no one's prize to be won." I fought against Eoghan's tight hold on me as he marched us along the perimeter of the outer wall of the castle. Eoghan kept his head down ignoring my comment as he pried open a plain wooden door hidden among the foliage and forced me through the entrance. A long torch-lit hall did not give me any inkling of the layout of the true entrance of the castle. I had a feeling Eoghan did this purposefully, given the stunt I had just pulled. He knew I would try to run again the first chance I got.

He ignored my comment, keeping his trained eyes forward as we descended deeper into the castle. My teeth chattered against each other as my soaking wet body came into contact with a chilled breeze. Stringy pieces of dark brown hair hung limply around my face, and I knew I probably looked like some crazed animal. *Good.* Gideon had called me a wild beast, and I would show these creatures what happens when you let a rabid animal loose in a cage full of its favorite prey.

Eoghan's grip tightened as we came upon two grand doors.

Their stark white color stood out against the darkness of the room. Both glowed against the moonlight that shone through the window behind us, making my eyes hurt to look at them. Carved into the wood was an intricate design of swirling black lines that met in the middle to create a pair of ominous eyes that stared back at me. I wouldn't put it past these creatures to have enchanted them to actually spy on those who passed by. Aunt Len had always said secrets were one of the Sith's favorite currencies. They flowed plentifully in places like this. My chest constricted in panic at the thought of being at the mercy of someone with the power to harm the ones I had left behind.

Mairead. Kol. Aunt Lennox.

Their names rattled around my skull over and over again until I felt physically ill. Just when I thought I was going to be sick for the second time tonight, the doors swung open, revealing a magnificent throne room. The entire chamber was a glittering onyx spectacle. Black marble polished to perfection covered the floor. Large pillars accented the space as they held up the grand cathedral ceiling. Decorated with dark jeweled ornaments coiled together at the apex of the roof the perfect image of a snake ready to strike hung over us. Deep ruby eyes of the serpent stared down at me menacingly.

Three thrones sat at the front of the room, the largest in the middle. Its dark color glistened with a devilish wink. The throne was covered in labyrinthine carvings of a language long ago lost to the mortal lands, and wound around each of the sharp pillars was a sparkling snake. The same ruby red eyes curled around the top to peer over the shoulder of whoever sat upon it.

I was ripped forward by Eoghan. His movement were harsh as he heaved me towards the male sitting on the jeweled throne. With each step forward, the throne's snakes appeared to coil tighter against their posts. Throwing me down, I landed on my knees with a thud in front of a small set of stairs, each one covered in plush velvet carpet. I whipped my head around, glaring at the male, my lip pulled back in a snarl. He only matched my gaze with a pointed look, as if to say it was best for me to behave.

Turning back to the male sitting upon the throne, he had dark hair that was peppered with gray from age. His almost translucent skin made him look sickly, and a dark, jeweled crown hung loosely on the top of his head. With his legs draped over one another, he leaned back, curiously watching me. I met his gaze with a scowl, my soaking wet hair obscuring his vision of my entire face.

"This is the champion who found the final flag, General?" The king spoke in a bored tone, as if I was only a minor inconvenience in his daily routine.

"Yes, your Majesty." Eoghan bowed his head in respect to his ruler. "We apprehended the flag from her possession, and she is the same girl the prince described to us. She has the marking as well."

Leaning forward, the king motioned towards me. "Show me your palms, mortal."

I did not move, still processing what the king had requested of me. Eoghan stepped closer, ripping my left palm off the floor and showing his king the deep black ink still on my palm. I stared at it in horror as I could have sworn the marking had deepened in color, making it stand out even more against my skin.

The king only hummed at Eoghan's comment. The sudden clack of boots hitting the marble floor sounded from behind me, and I turned to glance at the new presence in the room. A younger male, who was the spitting image of the one sitting on the throne, approached. He was dressed in tight dark pants with a matching doublet. The first few buttons of the top were undone, leaving it to dip into a deep V. Silver threads weaved through the fabric, creating a beautiful pattern that emulated a lightning storm. A shiver traveled up my spine as my eyes met his. They weren't brown like I had witnessed before on so many others, but instead, they were void of color altogether. Just two pairs of black irises staring intently at me.

The male's lips pulled up at the corners as he approached me. "I see you were successful in finding our little trickster, General."

Eoghan didn't respond as he dipped his head in respect towards the royal, but I did with a deep snarl that only made the male's feline grin deepen. "Oh, you are going to be fun, I can just tell."

"Enough, Lochlan." The King's commanding voice silenced any playfulness in the Crown Prince's eyes. He elongated his spine, making himself seem more regal by just that simple movement. "You failed to inform me that your new plaything was mortal. There has never been a champion in the Aesira Games from the mortal realms, much less a human girl."

"A first time for everything." Lochlan shrugged towards his father. "And how fitting as it is a Millennial Anniversary game.

She will be integrated into my team as our champion as she was the one who found the flag we were tasked to retrieve as the entrance to the Games."

"And if she dies?" The King shifted to his side, letting his elbow lean onto the armrest. His hand firmly grasped his chin as he watched his son for a moment, waiting for his response.

"Then she perishes. The girl is only a mortal, after all. What is one less of them in this world?" The Prince's words hit me in the gut. I cast my glare toward the marble floor to hide the anger bubbling in the pit of my stomach. How dare they decide my future in this new realm. I was no one's prize or champion. The idea of being either made me want to hurl myself back into the lake I had fallen into.

"I don't want to play in any stupid game of yours," I snarled at the Prince. He narrowed his gaze at me before smirking slightly at my statement. "I didn't choose to find a magical flag. You should have hidden it better than in an abandoned castle frequented by the local village adolescents."

The Prince circled around me in long, drawn-out steps. When he arrived in front of me, a single gloved finger flicked out and lifted my chin up to force my gaze on his. He tsked as I flinched away from his touch, then promptly gripped the underside of my jaw harder. "And what fun would that have brought me, *cailleach*."

Lochlan released his hold on me, turning to speak with Eoghan, who had been watching the entire interaction with a stony expression. "She is expected at dinner tonight. Escort her to her maidens and then meet me in my study to brief me on our new guest of honor."

And with that final statement, Prince Lochlan waltzed out into the room, throwing a cheeky wink toward me as he melded into the darkness of the hall.

Chapter Nine
Caelen

I was snatched from my place on the marble floor and onto my feet before Eoghan led me toward the dimly lit corridor the Prince had just disappeared down. Eoghan steered the two of us to the left, his face giving no indication of where we were headed. There was no doubt in my mind that I was going to a four-by-four cell of stone, with little to no light, and my bunkmate would be a dead cricket who had unfortunately taken its last breath in a place like that.

My eyes examined the castle's interior, and it was clear whoever designed it had a distaste for color. The walls were a light wash of white with ornate black molding dividing the dark wooden paneling below it. Every so often, we would pass a large window hidden by the heavy curtains pulled shut, concealing my view from the outside world. The moonlight peeked through the cracks of the fabric's slit, leaving glowing stripes through the corridor.

The pair of us turned down a few more hallways, twisting and maneuvering through passages that all looked the same until we reached the final one. Royal portraits lined the white walls, some smiling, most not. Each gaze in the paintings seemed to follow Eoghan and me as we stalked farther into their territory. I huffed out a sigh, blowing up my bangs that hung limply in my eyes.

"Creepy, aren't they?" Eoghan looked down at me, a teasing smile playing against his lips. I narrowed my gaze toward him as he continued. "When I was just a child, I refused to enter this hall. It's the eyes. They accuse you of all the wrongdoings you have not yet committed."

Ignoring him, I turned my stare back to the path ahead of us. Eoghan pulled me carefully up a flight of stone steps, the temperature dropping with each one as we climbed higher into the sky. I snuck a glance through a carved-out window. A miniature version of the courtyard sat below us. My eyes could barely distinguish the soldiers pacing back and forth between the lookout gate and the slight flutter of the kingdom's flag. Its inky fabric flowed freely in the brewing storm's wind. The breath seized in my throat, eyes wandering straight down to the cobblestone pathway. I was never one to be afraid of heights, but at this moment, the possibility of the brooding king's general tossing me over the side of the edge was high. The action could solve all their problems.

"Afraid of heights?" Eoghan's hot breath brushed my ear. Swallowing down the terror creeping up my throat, I craned my neck to look back at him, driving as much ice as I could muster into my gaze. The stairwell was no larger than the width of a broom closet, causing his large frame to brush against my own in the tight corridor. He observed me, cocking his head to the side as he examined my movements. "I didn't think a wild beast like yourself held any fear in her heart."

"Everyone is afraid of something," I say, my voice coming out in a raspy whisper. Eoghan shot me a narrowed look. "But a creatures intentions lie in what they are afraid of losing and what they are willing to do to keep it from ever slipping from their grasp. That is where the true danger hides."

In one swift motion, I was spun around, my back slamming into the stone wall that was once behind Eoghan. There was a murderous look in his eyes as he stared down at me. He placed his right palm against the wall above my head and leaned into it. My only escape from him would be climbing farther up the tower's stairs. Two fingers snatched the underside of my chin up with such force that I knew there would be purple welts on my pale skin by the morning. I squirmed under his touch, but the movement only made him grip down tighter.

"You have no idea what game you're playing when you speak words such as those, girl," Eoghan growled at me. "Do well to mind your tongue if you'd like to keep that pretty head attached to your body."

I leaned in closer to him, my lips only inches from his own. If anyone entered the stairwell, they would assume we were just two lovers caught in a shadowed embrace. My following words grazed his mouth, a wicked smirk pulling at my own. "I will mind my tongue when males such as yourself show me the same respect they were born into."

Snaking my body away from him, I clamored up the steep

steps again, leaving Eoghan to mull over my words. His heavy footsteps followed swiftly behind me a few moments later, but the Sìth male did not speak to me again. The air around us buzzed with a crackling anger. The thought of getting under Eoghan's skin made me smirk. We arrived in front of a heavy wooden door with a brass handle. I waited for Eoghan to open it, but he just sighed heavily and knocked against the surface three times. There was a shuffle of feet followed by hushed whispering.

The door swung open, revealing a female dressed in a light green gown with a simple apron tied around the front. Her feline eyes were large, taking up most of her face, and she had a permanent scowl across her lips as she stared at the two of us. A mess of black hair was piled on top of her head in a lopsided bun. Two other females with the same large eyes stood just behind her, only illuminated by a single, wick candle.

Eoghan let out a low chuckle as the woman crossed her arms over her chest. "I see you three have taken forms more pleasing for the eyes of your guest."

The woman scoffed at Eoghan. "We were informed not to scare the mortal. Though if this is what you Sìth males believe to be pleasing, the sight of her must drive you mad with lust."

A deep shade of red crept across my skin at her words. My eyes traveled to the floor, avoiding Eoghan's hot stare burning into the side of me. Eoghan coughed lightly, ignoring the woman's words. "This is Ainsley. She is harmless in this form. She and her sisters, Coira and Lorna, will be your handmaidens for the duration of your stay."

Eoghan turned to face Ainsley who still watched him with a

narrowed look. "See to it she is well taken care of."

"I will do as the Prince has commanded. There is no need for the reminder, boy," Ainsley scoffed at Eoghan. She squared her shoulders at the male, nodding once for me to enter the room.

I slowly maneuvered around her, my shoulder brushing up against her. A zing of ancient power shot through me, followed by an acidic taste that settled in on my tastebuds. The sourness constricted my throat as the wide-eyed handmaiden continued. "Now be gone with you, or I will remind you just how harmless we are in this form, General."

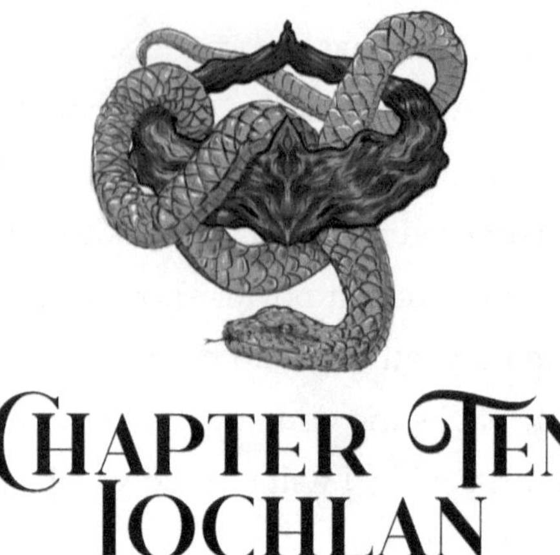

Chapter Ten
Lochlan

Caelen Elliston was not someone who could be tamed, and I had no intention of doing so. Eoghan might believe he could contain her, even break her, but he would soon find out that a mortal woman such as her would not bend to the will of any male.

I strode from the throne room, leaving the general of my father's armies to deal with our champion, pulling the shadows tight around me in my exit. The soft whispers of the darkness curled around my ears, eagerly giving their opinion on the human girl who had just knelt before us. Her blue eyes blazed with fury as I discussed her role in my plan. She would do well to hold tight to that anger in the Games. It will help her survive. Tuning out the hushed voices, I retreated from the dark and into my study, finding Sylas lounging in the chaise by the blazing fire. The deep velvet of the furniture accentuated the crimson-stained fingertips of my executioner.

"How is our champion?" She quirked a questioning eyebrow at me. Amber-colored liquid swirled around a crystal glass as she lifted it to hover just above her lips. "The guards are already placing their bets on how long she will survive the Games."

"Am I not privy to any peace in this realm?" I take the armchair to her left, eyes never leaving the blood coating her skin. "And can you at least try to act civilized when you are in this room?"

"I am always the proper example of a well-mannered female, dear Lochlan." She smirked at the statement, slowly lifting her right hand to take her thumb between her lips and sucked the blood off its surface. With a wicked smile, Sylas batted her eyes at me. "See, perfectly civil. Just as I was when I ripped the rebel's tongue from his mouth when he spoke ill of my crown prince."

"Sylas," I groaned. She had always been one for the theatrics, but in the last century, she was becoming slightly more unhinged in her role. Rumors and tales of her tactics had been circulating the realm just to scare children into obeying. Running a hand over my jaw, the cool nip of my rings caught my skin. "He could have given us a direction to go in when it comes to the unrest brewing at the borders. Right now, we are floundering in the dark, trying to track their movements."

"You are starting to sound like Eoghan, droning on and on about those rebels. They haven't made a move in weeks, and we will be prepared when they do. The boy in that cell wasn't going to tell us anything because he didn't know any more than what we already knew. I made sure to dig far enough back into his mind that even he didn't recall some of the memories I now know about his short life." Sylas watched me with a steady look.

She descended from a long line of powerful Seers. Her

mother had been auctioned off to a high-ranking general in my father's council when she came of age, but the Seer linage had won out against the shadows in Sylas. Her ability to comb through a person's memories with only a single touch had been seen only a handful of times within the prophets. The experience was an unpleasant one, to put it lightly.

We sat in silence for a long while, just basking in the presence of each other and listening to the embers crackle in the hearth. My mind continued to wander back to the dark-haired champion. I could feel a power radiating from her, but it was not the same as the one I had felt in the vision when she had captured the flag. That power sizzled and cracked through me, as if all of my nerves were set on fire while Caelen's rolled off her skin in soft burning waves. My thoughts were cut short as the study's door slammed against the wall, shaking the bookcase near it. A few leatherbound copies toppled from the shelves as Eoghan bounded in, his face red and chest puffed up in frustration.

"That girl is the most infuriating mortal I have ever come in contact with." Eoghan's voice echoed off the walls. He let out a defeated breath before throwing himself down in the armchair across from my own, letting his shoulders slump. "She will never be able to be trained."

Sylas grinned. "I think I might need to come to training tomorrow morning."

"Don't antagonize him," I grumbled, flicking a piece of fuzz off my pants. "Caelen will fall in line. She just needs the right motivation."

"Motivation? And not being slaughtered in the Games is not

enough motivation?" Eoghan asked, throwing his hands up at the idea.

Ignoring his rant, I leaned my head against my left hand. "Who else was there when you found her?"

"A sister. No older than sixteen." Eoghan's eyes darken at the statement. "She appeared harmless, but I am not sure. There was a presence that clung to her. The girl didn't even understand what she was wielding, but whatever the power is, it tried to protect her from Gideon and me. It's dark, and the feeling that accompanies it feels like…."

His words trailed off, eyes glassy as he remembered his encounter with this presence. Sylas reached out, laying her still bloody hand on his shin to pull him back to us. "It felt like what, Eoghan?"

"The moment just before death."

CHAPTER ELEVEN
CAELEN

The door slammed behind Ainsley, leaving Eoghan alone in the hallway. I could hear his footsteps descend the stairs before the three females began to shuffle around the space once again. The stone walls curved around the reasonably large room. One wall held a small fireplace which warmed the space surprisingly well. Straight across from the fire was a bed that surpassed the child-size mattress I had at home. It was covered in an oversized wool knit blanket that stretched across the silky surface of the tan sheets. Mismatched colored pillows were piled high against the wood-carved headboard.

"Well, don't just stand there." Ainsley's shrill voice broke me from observing the room. She stood hunched over a steel table in the corner of the room, eyes staring daggers at me. Ainsley waved her hand lightly and pointed to a chair next to her. "Come, sit, so I can get a good look at what we are going to have to work with."

Scrunching my nose at her remark, I advanced towards her. A pair of soft hands gripped down on my shoulders as I settled into the chair. The woman was short with wide eyes that held a wonder-like sheen compared to her sister's. I admired her hair, which shifted from pale pink to purple as she swayed around me. She was dressed in a pink dress that matched her hair, skirt floating behind her with a personality of its own.

"Well, she is a pretty one, isn't she, Lorna?" She spoke her voice like bells in the wind. The last woman in the room appeared next to her sister. I gasped at the bright blue hair billowing down her back in lavish waves. Lorna took my chin in her grasp, turning my head side to side before simply nodding at Coira.

A shiver traveled up my spine as the three cat-eyed women stared intently in my direction. Aunt Lennox had spun warning tales about creatures who served and worshiped the Sìth royals. But under their manipulated beauty, the creatures were cruel and unwavering in their ways. The stories of wraiths venturing into towns and leveling them were legendary. The three women's beauty never reached their eyes, revealing a coldness only found in a soulless creatures.

"You two should begin, or she will never make it to the feast." Ainsley's eyes broke away from mine as she threaded a needle through a piece of dark blue silk. Lorna didn't speak a word to me as her long fingers firmly grasped my arm, hauling me to my feet and into a bathing chamber. Her touch was cold as ice, and I ripped myself from her grasp as the door to the room shut tightly. She waved her hand, causing the gold metal faucet to turn lightly until water began to flow from the pipe. I jumped back into the marble countertop, startled at the sight. A metallic taste took a hold of my tastebuds as the sickly-sweet aroma of magic filled my nostrils. Lorna only narrowed her eyes at me like I was a child being quietly reprimanded.

I didn't fight her as she bathed me in oils that smelt of vanilla. Not even when her meticulous fingers began to pluck all the stray hairs from my body while she mumbled what I assumed were insults in a foreign tongue. I was left to my own devices as she swept out of the room. In the silence of the space the anxious feeling that had been quietly gnawing at my insides was now suffocating. I rolled my shoulders back cataloging every creature and story that had once been myths into my memory. There wasn't time to loss my cool, when just beyond the bathroom door was a world of nightmares that could easily kill me. For now, my one goal was surviving long enough to get back to Mairead. Ainsley stepped into the space this time. The scowl that had once been plastered across her features was now replaced with a concentrated look. Her eyes raked over me once before nodding slightly toward a gray dressing bag.

"Come now, let's get you dressed, so we can fix that hair of yours," Ainsley said, her voice softer than the tone she had used with Eoghan. I shifted uncomfortably as she unzipped the bag to reveal a deep crimson dress. The corset was structured at the top, embroidered flowers and jewels covering the entire bodice, stretching down to embellish the top half of the skirt. As I stepped into the garment, Ainsley guided it around my body.

The gauzy material of the skirt pooled over my legs, and I swayed back and forth with it, making the tulle swish around like a storm cloud in the sky. It had been years since I had worn a dress, and they had never been this high in quality. Something like this would take years to scrounge up the funds for, and I had never been one to waste coins on frivolous items such as this.

Not when I knew what it felt like to not eat for days. It was a gnawing feeling that pulled at your insides until you felt as if your body was going to cave in on itself. But better I experienced the pain rather than Mairead. Money had always been tight, and though I tried hiding just how bad it had gotten at times, I am sure Mai had known. Droughts in Aunt Lennox's business forced me to take drastic measures at the local pub at night. Sometimes I came home with more than enough money to get us by for the moment. Others, I left with nothing, slipping into the darkness with red-rimmed eyes and a laundry list of regrets.

The tight tug of the corset strings caused me to suck in a slight gasp. I threw a glare over my shoulder at Ainsley. She only pulled tighter before tying the ends and tucking them into the skirt.

"I pray that Coira can work some type of miracle on this." Ainsley flicked a limp piece of hair over my shoulder. I followed her as we returned to the bedroom, taking a seat in the same chair I had earlier. Coira flitted towards me, light hands brushing from my scalp to the ends of my hair. Closing my eyes, I let the coolness of her touch lull me into a peaceful state. At some point, the feeling of a brush found its way to my face, but I didn't budge until the sisters were entirely done.

"She is one of the prettier mortals that I have seen in this court." Coira's dreamy voice broke me from my rest. Peeling open my eyes, I found all three wraiths staring at me with an odd look of pride.

Lorna grasped my necklace in her hands, letting the pendant rest in the center of her palm. She looked up to her sisters. "Does this stay or go?"

"Stays," I blurted out. The females watched me curiously. "It was my mother's. I never take it off."

"Well, it is not the ugliest necklace I have ever seen." Lorna sneered down at me. I opened my mouth to reply to her jab, but a knock on the door caused me to swallow my words. I shoved the necklace into the dress to hide the piece from other prying eyes.

Ainsley rushed over to the door, throwing it open to reveal the Prince leaning against the doorframe. Lochlan had changed from his previous attire into an onyx color suit that reflected the style males in Adamore wore. I stood from my seat, smoothing down the dress as I went. The Prince cocked a challenging eyebrow at me as he peeled his body off the wooden panel.

"Your Grace." Ainsley bowed deeply towards him, and her sisters followed suit. I refused to move an inch, not even when Ainsley hissed at me in the same foreign tongue Lorna had used earlier. Narrowing my eyes at her, I elongated my spine to prove my point. There was no realm in which I would bow to my captors.

"Are you ready, *cailleach*?" Lochlan asked, drinking in my appearance with greedy eyes. I scoffed at him, causing his grin to deepen. "Try to behave yourself, dear. I would hate to lose my best chance at winning because of your sharp tongue."

Chapter Twelve
Lochlan

Moonlight illuminated the halls as I guided Caelen in the direction of the throne room. I walked in long, drawn out strides, my shadows snaking tightly around my wrists in their typical slithering motion. Casting my gaze towards the mortal girl, I could now see her prominent cheekbones and ice-colored eyes that one of the sisters had painted with a black liner for tonight. Caelen's gaze met mine, brows pinched together as she took me in.

"I must apologize for my previous behavior." I spoke over the soft click of her heels against the marbled floor. "My harsh words were not ones I find joy in spewing, especially for new guests of our court."

"Which part are you apologizing for, exactly?" Caelen eyed me suspiciously as we rounded the corner and came upon the throne room's door.

Joyous laughter filtered into the hall as the court gathered for a celebratory dinner, every subject unaware that the named champion they were eager to lay their eyes on would be a human girl. Caelen scanned my figure before continuing. "Are you apologizing for claiming my life is of no value to you unless I am a pawn in whatever game you're playing or the idea that mortals are somehow beneath you?"

I sighed, running my gloved hand over my jaw. "Both, I suppose. It may not appear so, but I am truly apologetic for your treatment this evening. It was not the first impression I desired you to have of me."

"Then why was it?" Caelen's voice was full of venom as she turned to face me head-on—not an ounce of fear as she spoke to me like I could not have her hung for her attitude. My shadows halted, waiting patiently to see what punishment I would enact for the disrespect.

I only chuckled at her stupidity. "My father, the King, does not do well with weakness, and you, my dear cailleach, are a significant weakness for him."

Stepping forward, I reached out and took one of her hands in my own. She stiffened under my touch, eyes intently watching the lone shadow that intertwined our wrists, locking her in place. The shadow drank in her fear like a glass of the sweetest wine, momentarily causing my mind to go fuzzy as the euphoric taste overtook me. Tilting my head down, I met her stare. "Each of us has a role to play in the courts, and mine is not always kind, as you witnessed earlier this evening. I do hope you see past the charade I put on for my father and listen to my proposal about the Games tomorrow morning."

Caelen's lips parted, but no words rolled off her tongue as the throne room's double doors swung open. I dropped her hand smoothly, a sly smirk pulling at the corners of my lips as I peered over my shoulder at the guards making their way into the hall.

"Gentlemen, see to it that our guest of honor finds her seat next to mine this evening." I ordered, the smooth, bored drawl of my words filling the corridor. "I have a pressing matter that I must attend to."

I placed the palm of my hand on the small of Caelen's back and led her forward into the grasp of the expressionless guard to her left. She looked back at me as I stepped away from her, and retreated into the hall, still facing the group.

"Oh, and do see to it that she is announced," I called to the males before pulling the darkness around me as it transported me into my study, where I knew Eoghan was waiting. He was leaning back in a chair, legs propped up onto the desk before him. His eyes were glazed over as he was lost in his thoughts. I cleared my throat, causing him to jolt and turn toward me.

"You are missing your favorite accessory." Eoghan narrowed his gaze at the top of my head. I sneered at him for the comment. We both knew I loathed the jeweled crown I was shackled to.

"Remember, I could have you punished for a comment such as that, Eoghan."

Eoghan barked out a laugh. "I would like to see you try."

I would, too. We both knew neither of us could command the other. Our bond went deeper than the roles we played in the court. Eoghan had been at my side for every crucial moment of my life. And I for his. There was an unspoken agreement between us that tied us to each other.

"We are late for the festivities." I rounded the other side of the desk, sitting on the chair behind it. Eoghan rolled his eyes, tossing back the dark liquor in his glass. I poured myself one. "Or are you not attending tonight?"

"I will be there, but I need to prepare myself," Eoghan grumbled. "I keep having these visions of the sister. Is it possible that the power which surrounded her followed us back?"

"It is improbable," I mused, swirling the glass around once before bringing the drink to my lips. Hissing at the burn of liquor sliding down my throat, I continued. "It is more likely that Caelen has a similar power of her own that has been sparked by bringing her into our realm."

"No," Eoghan argued. He swung his legs down, feet now firmly planted on the carpet below him as he leaned onto his knees. "I am not arguing that Caelen is not powerful. I can feel it pulsate off her, but the sister. I think we need to be very aware of the young girl."

"And why is that?"

"Because if others are made aware of what we left behind, *they* will go looking for her. I haven't felt power like that since they graced these halls."

"Are you insinuating we could have another tyrant on our hands?" I asked, mind whirling with the memories of the two sisters who almost destroyed us all.

Eoghan observed me for a moment, a dark look overtaking his features. "I am saying we need to be vigilant that the supposed mortal girl we just welcomed into our ranks could be the demise of us all."

Chapter Thirteen
Caelen

Follow me this way," a guard to my left said softly, his green eyes creased with pity as he guided me to a line of people who waited to be announced to the court. Each name ticked by, but I did not register any of them as my mind swirled with the whiplash the Crown Prince had just given me. Which was the true persona of the strange, shadow-covered male? And could I trust him and his general? I stopped in front of a steward who stood before a heavily drawn velvet curtain.

The short man was squinting down at a long roll of parchment that was tossed over his shoulder and extended onto the floor. He examined each carefully inked name on the paper with such precision that I was positive he already knew every one by heart.

"Announce her." The green-eyed guard spoke gruffly to the steward. It took all the willpower in me not to laugh as the man stared up at him with a displeased look. The steward's ears turned a light shade of pink in annoyance as he took in my presence.

"She is not listed," the steward sneered and returned to the parchment. "It would be improper for her to be announced."

"The Prince has commanded it," the other guard, who stood a few feet behind us, growled out. "Now announce her, or I won't hesitate to hang you from the flagpole once again, Gerald."

Gerald jumped at the threat and turned to poke his head around the side of the curtain to whisper to someone. When he came back around the cloth, the two guards made themselves scarce, and Gerald straightened up to prepare for the announcement.

The ruby curtains flew open at the sound of a trumpet, revealing the throne room that had been transformed into a dining hall. Large oak tables were placed around the room, each decorated with crystals and candles as centerpieces. An aerialist was strung up in the middle of the chamber, effortlessly maneuvering down the silk in a sensual twist. Somewhere in the distance, my name was called by the steward, but I was too busy gaping at the beauty the room had become. My eyes wandered around in amazement at the twinkling lights filling the space. I barely felt the light touch against my shoulder that pulled me back to reality.

Every soul in the throne room was watching me. Some held curiosity, but most were disgusted that a mortal would come into their court and dare to be announced. A woman with white-blonde hair gathered into an extravagant updo, held together by purple pins to match the diamond-encrusted dress she wore, glared at me. She leaned over to whisper to a male next to her, eyes never leaving mine. The pair giggled at the comment.

Suddenly the entirety of the space felt incredibly too small for this many people. I took a step back, spine brushing up against the now-closed curtain. Throat constricting, I began to panic, but saw no way to escape their scrutiny. The room was starting to close in on me, heating to an unbearable temperature. I frantically searched for an exit but instead, caught sight of a pair of soft, hazel eyes.

Eoghan stepped into the room through a side entrance near the middle and watched my panicked movements. A deep crease folded between his eyebrows as he took in my state. I stepped forward, ready to make my way toward the General, who was dressed in a formal uniform. Medals, patches, and pins adorned his jacket, showing how accomplished he was in his role. He was the only familiar face in a room full of strange creatures that would like nothing more than to dig their talons into me.

"Caelen." A soft voice spoke from beside me. I tore my gaze away from Eoghan to meet the prince's deep, onyx stare. He now wore a crown on the back of his head. It wobbled, but never fell from its resting place. "I apologize for leaving you, but I forgot the most important accessory of this outfit."

Lochlan shot me a crooked grin, holding out his hand for me to take. I placed my palm in his, and he directed me through the crowd. Whispers about the mortal girl were like cannons going off in my ears. I kept my eyes down, trying my best to get to where we were headed without being sick.

"Now, where is that fire that amused me so much earlier?" Lochlan leaned down, his words brushing up against the shell of my ear. I shook my head, not trusting words to come out. He chuckled. "If you let the court bully you now, they will never give up trying to destroy you. Trust me, some of these creatures are ruthless with their pursuit of destroying threats, but no harm will come to you tonight in my care."

"And what if they are right?" I questioned, voice wavering slightly from the nerves. "I don't belong here in your world."

Lochlan focused on me, "You might be surprised at how wrong you are about that, Caelen."

We arrived at the head table where two seats were purposefully left vacant next to the king and a woman in a soft gray dress. Her red hair was tied tightly behind her in a slick bun, not a curl out of place. I sat in the chair Lochlan pulled out for me. "Thank you."

"This must be the girl who found your flag, is it not, Prince Lochlan?" The woman's voice was soft and silky, bringing you in and wrapping around you like a blanket. But the glint in her dark green eyes told me she could be deadly when provoked.

"The one and only. Isn't she marvelous? Elara, this is Caelen Elliston." Lochlan took his seat beside me, picking up a goblet filled with a deep red liquid. He swirled it around before bringing it to his lips. "Elara is my father's lead advisor."

Elara's lips pulled into a slight grin. "The pleasure is mine."

I nodded slightly at the female who was observing me. My hand shot out, taking the goblet in my hand and bringing it to my mouth. The liquid inside burned the back of my throat, causing me to cough.

Lochlan leaned in, "My apologies. I should have warned you that the wine is quite strong compared to what you might be accustomed to."

I shook my head at his comment. "This tastes like what I imagine breathing fire would feel like."

"You become used to the sensation," Elara remarked. She leaned back in her chair, allowing a young boy to place food in front of her. It was a simple meal. Potatoes and a steak that was garnished with basil. She reached down, picking up a knife, gaze never leaving mine as she began to cut into the bloody meat. "So, Caelen, is it?"

"Yes," I responded directly to her for the first time, my voice coming off more timid than intended.

"How did you come about the flag in the first place?" She brought the meat up to her mouth, watching for any signs of deception on my part.

I gulped down my fear and rolled my shoulders back. "It was wedged between a few planks in the old, abandoned castle in my village. Not the best hiding place, if you ask me."

Food appeared before me, causing my mouth to water with anticipation. It had been years since I had a good meal just for myself. I reached for the utensils, holding myself back from shoving an entire potato into my mouth with only my fingers. I may have been starved, but they didn't have to know that.

"The Elders hid those flags." The King spoke in a bored tone. "There must have been a reason for them to decide on a place such as that."

"It was fate." Lochlan pointed his fork in my direction. "I believe she was meant to find that dusty rag."

"You have always been one for theatrics," Elara laughed softly. I lifted my fork to my mouth, suppressing a moan of delight at the food. The meat was cooked to perfection, and the potatoes were seasoned with just the right amount of garlic to make me want to eat them every day for the rest of my life. The movement allowed my necklace to come loose from the dress and fall against my chest. Elara eyed the piece. Her stare was lustful as she drank in the swirling red within the stone. "Such a beautiful necklace you have there. Where on earth did you get it?"

"It was my mother's," I mumbled, the lump in the back of my throat rising as I said the words. Setting down the fork, I was suddenly not as hungry as before. The rest of dinner went on without any interruption. Conversations swirled around me until the King finally rose and brought the attention onto himself.

"As you may have been made aware, we have a mortal guest amongst our court this evening," The King announced into the silent room. I sat up straight, not allowing myself to slump deep into the chair to hide. "The Aesira Games that will secure the throne for our realm for another century are once again upon us, and as you are well aware, this year is special for many reasons. Your prince has accepted the champion who acquired the final admittance flag this evening. Her name is Caelen Elliston. She will be a guest of honor in our courts."

The room exploded with commotion. A cacophony of outrage rang in my ears. I could not gather what was being done. There were too many voices speaking at once. Then, the shattering of glass fell over me. Gasping, a burning sensation began to overtake the back of my arms. Wine dripped over my shoulders, leaving a sticky trail as the droplets traveled into my corset. I felt my body being pulled up by a hand that directed me out of a back exit. I could still hear the screams of rage as whoever had me rounded the corner into another hall.

"I think she is in shock." A male's voice spoke in hushed tones. "Female mortals are easily upset, I have been told."

"Excuse me?" I whirled around to see Eoghan and Lochlan whispering to each other. They both turned to look at me, eyes wide with fear. "I'll have you know that female mortals are not easily upset. I was just processing the fact that I have wine dripping down my back from a glass that was thrown at my head. All because I became a champion in a game I have no idea how to compete in. Let alone, agreed to."

"When you caught the flag and the magic inked your palm, that was your agreement to play in the Games." Eoghan motioned toward the black ink staining the inside of my clenched fist. It felt like the symbol was burning into my skin as he stared at it. I ripped my hand from his view, hiding it behind my back. "You agreed to the terms. It would be the only way you would be able to play."

"How did I agree to them when I didn't even know any of this existed?" I glared, pointing one finger towards Eoghan in a warning. "And if you claim it to be fate or magic, I just might throw myself out of that tower tonight."

"Well, it is a good thing we have bars on the windows, isn't it, sweetheart?" Eoghan hissed, taking a menacing step toward me. Lochlan caught him by the chest, stopping him in his tracks.

"I am not sure how you unknowingly agreed to the Game's

terms. Never has there been a champion chosen by the flags magic from the mortal lands. But you caught the flag, meaning it wanted to find you, or it would not have revealed itself," Lochlan explained. He clamped one hand on Eoghan's shoulder. "Make sure someone is standing guard by her room tonight until the uproar of my father's announcement has died down."

"Of course." Eoghan nodded at his prince.

Lochlan began down the corridor, melding himself into the shadows. "Training begins tomorrow, Caelen. I would prepare yourself."

Chapter Fourteen
Caelen

The whizz of metal flew by my head. I threw my body down against the firm mat underneath me and twisted away from the blade as the male above me stabbed it to the surface. The sun still hadn't even risen before the General pulled me from my bed to begin training. No one else had graced us with their presence, and I was starting to believe Eoghan would have me running around the training pad all day until I bested him. Another slash and the sword rested at the base of my throat, Eoghan's devilish smirk watching my reaction.

"And you meet your demise, yet again." He pulled the blade away from my neck, thrusting out a hand to help me onto my feet. I glared up at him, arms crossed in defiance. Eoghan rolled his eyes. "Fine, be a child and pout on the floor. It won't make the fact you are unprepared any less true."

"Unprepared for what?" I placed my elbows underneath me, leaning on them as he approached a rack with various weapons. "I still do not understand any rules of these Games, and yet you have paraded me around this training ring like I am to be the next prized soldier in your legions."

"You would not last a day beside the soldiers in my legions," Eoghan scoffed at me.

I opened my mouth to argue, but Lochlan's voice called from behind me. "Eoghan, stop baiting the poor mortal girl. Caelen will be able to hold her own and then some soon enough."

"You didn't just watch me almost take her head off because she cowered from the blade." Eoghan threw a cheeky grin at the Prince.

I shot up. "I do not cower from anyone or anything."

"There is the fire I so desperately wanted to be lit last night. Perhaps you just need the right person to get under your skin for it to come out." Lochlan strutted around the ring, coming to stand to my right. I sent him an annoyed look. "Oh, lighten up, Caelen, we are all friends here."

"Friends? I do not remember a time when a 'friend' threatened my life by kidnapping me and forcing me to be a part of a game I still do not know how to play."

"All in due time, my dear. Remember you chose to be a part of the Games by signing the contract with the flag," Lochlan said, the boredom in his tone evident. My eyes lingered on the ink still imbedded into my palm. No matter how many times I tried to scrub my hands clean, the mark still remained. Lochlan motioned towards the entrance of the training ring. "Ahh, here she comes."

A tall and curvy female walked into the space. Her long blonde hair swayed in the slicked-back ponytail she wore. The black armor hugged each indent of her body, leaving very little to the imagination. I met her bright blue eyes as they examined me further.

"Caelen, this is Sylas Nicolson. She is my strategist, among other nefarious titles she has earned within the court." Lochlan introduced the female. She eyed me closely, taking note of the fresh bruises that were beginning to bloom on my skin.

"She is clearly not very gifted in combat, Loch," Sylas countered Lochlan's introduction.

"Sy, watch it," Eoghan chided, his back facing the weapons rack as he placed the sword he was previously working with in its home.

"I am just stating facts, Eoghan." Sylas clicked her tongue and began to circle me. My face burned as she slowly maneuvered to view every flaw she could find. When Sylas returned to face me head-on, she spoke, each word dripping off her tongue like the sweetest honey. "So, Caelen Elliston, what are you skilled in?"

I narrowed my gaze at the blonde. "I have exceptional aim with hand knives."

"Eoghan, if you would." Sylas cocked her head in his direction. The General pulled a set of knives from the rack. Each gleamed like it had just been shined. Eoghan moved forward, handing one of the blades to me. I grasped the wooden handle in my palm, taking in the weapon's weight in my hand. Sylas pointed towards a painted target at the other end of the ring. "Hit the center, and we will be the ones to decide if you are an exceptional shot."

I grumbled slightly, stepping away from Lochlan and Sylas to reach the center of the room. Breathing in once, I remembered what my mother had taught me.

"Center yourself and let the blade become an extension of your arm, Caelen."

My gaze zeroed in on the red-painted wood board, taking a swift step forward before spinning around once and chucking the knife in Eoghan's direction. There was a roar of anger from Lochlan as the weapon flew through the air, but for me, time slowed. The glinting metal twinkled under the rising sun, a beauty in motion. A thud set time into place as the knife landed directly above Eoghan's skull.

His challenging eyes stared into mine, and I raised a defiant eyebrow. "Hold a blade to my throat again, and it won't land above your skull."

"Duly noted, sweetheart." Eoghan let the pet name linger on his tongue as he drew out the syllables.

"You are absolutely insane," Sylas called out to me. I turned towards the blonde. Her hands were on her hips, and she had a wicked smirk plastered on her face. "She will fit in nicely with the rest of our misfit team. Don't you think, Loch?"

Lochlan's expression was a mix of anger and pure amazement as he looked at the knife embedded above his friend's head. "Yes, she will, but I think that is enough training for the two of you. Wouldn't want someone to lose a critical body part over a harmless spar."

"I might actually like to witness that if Eoghan was the one losing the eye." Sylas rocked on her heels. "You would look devilishly handsome with an eyepatch, General."

"You think you are hilarious, Sylas, but you couldn't last

two minutes in the ring with me." Eoghan barked out with a loud laugh.

"Pick up a blade, and remember who you are dealing with," Sylas challenged. Eoghan picked up two swords, tossing one to Sylas, who caught it effortlessly. My eyes barely registered her movements. Aunt Lennox mentioned that the Sìth had enhanced mobility in strength and speed, but seeing it in action was terrifying.

Lochlan's hand landed in the center of my back, steering me away from the duel that was beginning. "I think it is time to share with you the rules and history of these Games you are to win for me."

The castle's gardens were thriving with life. Reds, yellows, and violets melded together as the flowers interlaced themselves into a beautiful bloom of color. Sprites were attending to the plants, their bodies giving off a shimmering aura according to the specific jobs they were given.

A pang of sadness washed over me as an image of Mairead's smiling face flashed through my mind. She would be ecstatic to get her hands dirty in a garden this grand. Hours would be spent here before Mai would bound into whatever room I was holed up in with dirt dotting her face as she begged to show me the budding flowers that were beginning to bloom. A blue water sprite whizzed by me with a giggle, splashing water onto my face.

"They like you," Lochlan said, a soft smile appearing on his face. I wiped off the droplets from my skin. "If they didn't, you would know. As a boy, I angered a fire sprite, and the little bugger lit up my arm hair."

I laughed. "How could you have possibly angered it that much?"

"I honestly have no inkling of what I did. Sprites are temperamental." Lochlan smoothed out the black tunic he wore as he spoke. "But that is not why I brought you to the gardens."

"Are you finally going to tell me what these Games I am to play in are?"

"Yes." Lochlan watched me from the corner of his eye. "In the simplest terms, it is an endurance game of capture the flag through the different realm courts' manipulated arenas. Each task is set to weed out a court until only the two strongest teams remain. My court is the Bás Court, but we are often referred to as the Druid Court of Death in your archives. We have reigned champions for centuries."

"So, no pressure, right?" I gulped down the fire burning in my throat.

"The realm court who wins the Games gains the power of each court, allowing them to rule until the next Games, which happen every one hundred years. My father holds a small percentage of all five courts' power to wield if needed. But wielding that much power never ends well. On a regular basis he chooses to specialize only in his court, given power and the prophet abilities of the Todhchaí Court." Lochlan explained. Our steps led us farther into the depths of the garden. "This is the first year I have been given the opportunity to lead a team to victory as my duty to succeed my father for the crown comes closer."

"And how do I fit into all of this?" I asked, my gaze traveling to my feet. We stopped in front of an archway of roses, their thorns poking out in all different directions, threatening to stab those who get too close to their precious ruby petals.

"You found the flag, and that means something to all of us. The Elders place flags in locations that will bring the most power to the Games." Lochlan studied my reaction. "And you must carry a spark of magic in your lineage for you to have been able to make a deal with the flag."

"Magic doesn't exist in Adamore. It hasn't been there since the battle between the two sisters, which was hundreds of years ago, and the story is practically fiction at this point," I sputtered out, throwing my hands up at his accusation. It was like talking with Aunt Lennox, which sent a sharp pain into my heart. "Plus, I still don't understand the parameters of the rules of these Games."

"Technically speaking, there are no defined rules. Teams must capture the flag designated to them no matter what obstacle gets in their way. The Games are brutal and dangerous. Many have died for their courts, and we honor them each year during the opening ceremonies. The Elders decide the best course of action if an issue arises. Each team is given an entry flag, and the one who retrieves it is named the champion, which would be you, cailleach. The courses are determined by the Elders and the assigned court leaders. All will be different and deadly at that, but they are never the same. The only goal is to get to your team's flag before the others can capture their own. Teams advance by ranking, fall below the line, and you are eliminated."

"Seems complicated." I shook my head.

"It can be, but Eoghan, Sylas, and I will prepare you the best we can. It is not only a physical game but one of wit too, which I believe you have, Caelen." Lochlan grasped my hand in his. I stared at his fingers as they interlocked with mine, his thumb absentmindedly brushing along the tops of my knuckles.

"It's not like I have a choice in the matter," I whispered. "I was named champion, so I assume that means I have to play."

"Yes, the deal you made with the flag cannot be undone. Also, it is unfortunate, but my father knew if he named you our champion, you would not be able to return to your lands until the Games were concluded. It would be a scandal if our champion did not participate." Lochlan caught my gaze. "I am truly sorry for that, Caelen."

Nodding at his apology, I pulled my hand from his. "I will need to know everything about the druid courts and their realms if we are to stand a chance of winning."

"Yes, you will." Lochlan winked. "My mother was one of the first champions in our realm when the Games were just in their beginning stages."

"She was?" I stared at him in shock. "But that must have been thousands of years ago."

"The aging of the Sìth is almost nonexistent in comparison to a mortal's life span." Lochlan chuckled as I tried to wrap my head around the concept of living that long. "We do age, but only until we are fully grown in the physical sense, which is typically just after our twenty-fifth year, but that does not mean the mind has developed in suit. That takes longer to mature."

"Clearly," I grumbled, my fingers coming up to brush the scarlet rose petals in front of me. Their silky texture rubbed between my fingertips, practically crumpling under my harsh touch. "And how old might you be, Prince Lochlan?"

"I stopped counting after my 700th birthday," he confessed, brushing a curl that had fallen from my braid behind my ear. "Let me walk you to your chambers so you can clean up and eat before we dive into our studies."

Chapter Fifteen
Caelen

A breakfast that could feed ten people was piled in my chambers when I left Lochlan in the hallway. Fruits, scones, and jams made my mouth water in delight. Ainsley directed me right into the bathing chamber, insisting I wash up before even thinking about food. The heat of the tub's water steamed around my naked body, soothing the sore muscles I had obtained from only a single training session. I knew tomorrow I would feel as though I had been run over by one of the prince's prized mares.

Peeling myself out of the water as it grew cold, I dressed in the simple ivy-colored gown Ainsley had laid out for me. The skirt fell just below my knees, while the bodice clinched into place, hugging my upper body tightly. I let the long sleeves pool around my arms in a soft wave of green. Ainsley slipped into the bathing chambers, not saying a word as she began to comb through my tangled mess of hair. The gentle tugs lulled me into a comfortable silence with the creature as she weaved my hair into an intricate bun at the base of my neck. Coira stepped forward, a soft smile pulling at her lips as she pulled out a few curls in front to frame my face.

"You will do." Ainsley admired her work in the mirror. I let my eyes roll to the back of my head and accepted that wraiths could never give a compliment without a snide remark. "Now, off you go to eat. The Prince is waiting for you in the library, and we do not want to keep him waiting."

My ears perked up at the mention of a library. Rows of paper bound together that whispered stories through their pages made my stomach warm with a sense of familiarity. Ainsley shoved me lightly towards the door and out of my daydream. I stumbled into the room and sat in a plush chair that was pulled up to the table. Lorna piled food onto my plate, setting it directly before me and watching as I took a strawberry between my lips. The fruit was the perfect ripeness. I suppressed a groan in delight as the juices dribbled out of the corners of my lips. Kol would have fought me for the delicacy if he were here. They had always been his favorite.

Every year I would save a small number of coins for his birthday and venture into the village market to pick up a batch of the red fruit. Each time he scolded me for spending the little money we had on him, but I knew Kol looked forward to the present. My heart ached. We had left our friendship in a mix of curses and violence. I could only imagine what he thought when Mairead burst into his family's home in the dead of night, claiming I had been kidnapped by two strangers. There was no way that girl waited for the break of dawn to go to him. He was likely up, the strange sense of doom overwhelming him.

Kol and Mai always had a particular way of knowing when the other was in emotional distress.

"You look sad," Coira said softly, her fingers carefully threading a needle through a light-colored tulle fabric. I picked the sugar crystals off the scone in front of me, and suddenly the idea of anything sweet turned my stomach over. Coira spoke again, leaning into the table to get closer to me. "I understand, being pulled from everything you have ever known. The pain will dull, but it never fully disappears even after a century of busy work."

I looked into her cat eyes, the color swimming with a deep sadness that was sincere in her attempts to relate to me. "This is temporary. Once I win the Games for the Prince, I will be going back to my home, and my sadness will fade."

"Time is a funny thing. It does not flow equally through each of the realms." She went back to pulling the thread through the fabric, this time a little more forcefully, making her stitches sloppy. "You could be taken back, and that sister of yours could be wrinkled with age in her last moments."

I sucked in a shaky breath. Lochlan neglected to inform me of how the flow of time between the realms differed, but maybe it was because I had not asked the correct question to understand that what I would be returning home to after the Games. I pushed away from the table and pitched toward the door. "I have to meet the Prince."

"We know. The library is on the third floor. You'll know you have arrived when you reach the golden doors," Lorna called gruffly towards me. I didn't acknowledge her help, just slipped out into the hall and fumbled down the steps.

My breaths came in short, shallow spurts as I entered the hall of portraits. I stopped, digging the heels of my hands into my eye sockets. Tears were beginning to pool in the corners of my eyes as I tried to remember the exact color of Mai's and the joyous sound of Aunt Lennox's voice explaining how to keep the moles from eating through her prized garden. Quickly I swiped at the few lone tears that trickled down my face. I couldn't allow anyone in this court to see me in this state.

Emotion was a weakness, and the Sìth's intentions were clearly nefarious. I wouldn't allow another Elliston to be pulled into this world just to be driven mad. My mother's crazed eyes, in her final moments, flashed across my vision. I clutched the necklace, letting the strange warmth radiate through me with every passing second. Swirling images of my mother hunched over a worn book, quill clenched between her teeth as she read, swam through my mind.

Staggering down the hall once again, I turned the corner and into a tall, slender body. My mind snapped back to reality as Elara steadied me on my feet. "Caelen, what wonderful timing. I was just about to come and see if you had a moment to speak."

"I am to be meeting the Prince in the library, but I seem to have lost my way through the maze of halls," I lied. She cocked her head to the side, clearly knowing I was trying to evade her. I smiled. "But if this can be discussed while you guide me there, I would love to speak."

"Of course. We wouldn't want to keep the young prince waiting. Follow me." Elara shifted around, beginning back down the hall she had come from. I scurried after her, holding my head high as we maneuvered through the castle. "Are you finding your chambers and handmaidens to your liking?"

"Yes, the King has been most accommodating to me," I said, keeping my gaze on the hall in front of me.

Elara hummed, "And the Prince? Has he explained to you what is at risk if you are to not succeed in the Games?"

A silent threat hung in the corridor from the king's second. The air was stale as we reached a torch-lit hallway, the golden doors of the library at the end of it. The embers lit up the two of doors. They shimmered under the blazing heat like a pair of glittering stars in the night sky. I turned to Elara. "Yes, I am well aware of what you and the court stand to lose if we are unsuccessful in winning."

"You stand to lose just as much, dear. What is it that the Prince calls you?" Elara reached out, gripping a piece of lint off my dress and forcefully plucking it off the fabric, "Cailleach, is it? Do you know what that means, Caelen?"

I shook my head, not trusting my voice to not betray me. Elara smirked down at me. "It is from a legend that tells the story of the Fate Spinner. She was a powerful witch in our court who could weave the past, present, and future in the palm of her hands. With just a flick of her wrist, she could map out a creature's entire lifespan and then warp it to match her own desires. Most know her as the Second Sister. You're familiar with the legend, correct?"

"Yes," I said, my words feeling like sandpaper on my tongue. The sister's cleverness and ability to weave fates were what had given her such an advantage on the battlefield.

"Then you know how the tale ends." Elara narrowed her eyes at me. "The Prince believes you to hold something special in that mortal body of yours, but I see directly through the fraud you are, Caelen Elliston."

I stepped away from the female. "What are you insinuating, Elara?"

"Nothing at all. It is my job to ensure that you are aware of what you risk losing if it does, in fact, come out you have deceived the Prince and this entire court," Elara's voice was deadly quiet, a certain fire glowing in her eyes. I sucked in a shaky breath at her unsung threat. Elara was dangerous and had the King's ear. She could have me removed just as quickly as I was brought into this realm but in a much more permanent capacity.

"Caelen." Eoghan's voice echoed in the hallway. I whipped my head towards the sound. He stood just outside the golden doors, arms crossed over his chest as he watched the interaction occurring. "Lochlan and I were afraid you had gotten lost."

I breathed deeply. "Elara saved me from my wandering."

"I am glad we could have this little chat, dear." Elara plastered on a sick smile. She turned towards Eoghan nodding once at him. "General."

"Elara." Eoghan matched her tone. She observed him for a moment longer before vanishing around the corner. Once she was out of sight, I raced toward the golden doors, allowing Eoghan to guide me into the room. I crouched down, letting the weight of the king's second's words plummet through my mind in a raging loop. The light touch of a hand on my shoulder sent me reeling back and away from it. I stood, looking toward Eoghan with a wild gaze.

"Are you alright?" Lochlan's voice was distant as I stared at the General's knowing look.

"Elara cornered her," Eoghan explained to him. I stepped back, spine hitting the wall behind me. "Caelen, what did she say?"

"She insinuated I was a fraud, and once she had the proof, I would no longer be here to threaten the courts," I whispered and closed my eyes to take a few deep breaths as the two males began to argue in hushed voices.

"Elara must believe she has been sent by the brewing rebellion circling the outer realm's regions to allude to such a thing. She wouldn't dare question my father's decision to allow her to reign as champion, but she would question mine. You and I both know how against Elara is to my father stepping down from the throne," Lochlan spit out. "It would still not explain how Caelen could catch the flag in the Adamore if she didn't have an ounce of Sìth blood running through her veins. It took more magic out of Gideon than he has used in centuries to realm jump there, and that is coming from one of the most skilled jumpers there has been."

"We both know Elara hasn't been right since she..." Eoghan's voice trailed off. I opened my eyes to see both males staring at me.

"What?" I scowled at them and straightened up. "I don't see either of your lives being threatened. Give me a moment to process, or is that too mortal of me to do?"

Lochlan barked out a laugh. "No, not at all. I am impressed that you were able to keep it together in front of Elara. She can be horrid and brutal. I have experienced it firsthand."

"I could call her many other names that should not come from a lady's lips." I chuckled lightly. Although I still did not fully trust the two males in front of me, they seemed to need to keep me sane for their own benefit. At least I knew that my being alive was more to their advantage than my death. Granted, Eoghan had a rough way of showing it, but I knew he was fiercely loyal to the Prince, and that was enough to confirm he would not harm me. "So, if you are going to teach me thousands of years worth of history before the Games, I suggest we begin."

Chapter Sixteen
Lochlan

Eoghan occupied Caelen's time in the mornings, and I held her attention in the evenings as she learned as much about our lands as she could before the opening ceremonies. There was just enough time for the poor girl to sleep and eat if she was lucky. Tonight, I had conjured a pot of tea that would refill and heat itself when it grew low. A steaming cup sat in front of both of us as the moon rose higher into the sky. The room was filled wall-to-wall with ancient books on crown-molded shelves. Three floors circled the main chamber in a masterful swirl. I had spent hours in between the rows in my youth as I tried to consume every story and any piece of information about my lands.

Six druid kingdoms for the six Gods who had bestowed their unique powers on the Sìth royals who descended from their bloodlines. The Sìth courts had been created at the beginning of time when the atoms exploded, and the Gods blessed the land with the realms. After the battle of the two sisters, Caelen's realms' magic was banished, and the Gods saw no need to use it to their advantage any longer, leaving only five remaining realms for them to wield. All who were left to dwell there were now mere mortals as the magical bloodlines faded quickly.

"Currently, I am here." Caelen reached out, placing her finger in the center of the map before us. "This is the Bás Court, or as the writings have also referred to your people as the Druids of Death."

Her eyes watched me hopefully as she waited for my confirmation. I nodded once. "Very good, you are finally catching on. And what gifts did the God of Death, Arwan, bless his people with?"

Caelen's gaze widened as the wheels in her head began to spin. She stammered a second longer before answering, "Shadow magic."

A shadow snaked around my shoulder, beginning to slither around my throat. I smirked. "Correct again."

"How does it work? Your shadows? I have not seen any other wielders in the courts." Caelen leaned in, examining the movements of my shadow closely.

"The Elders consider our type of ability to be dark magic. Many shadow wielders keep their shadows hidden, such as my father. Mine seem to have a mind of their own. No matter how hard I try to contain them, one of them always slips out to make their presence known."

"But when you want them to, they will listen to your commands?"

"Yes." I smiled. Her eyes were filled with a childlike wonder I had never experienced when speaking of my abilities. "We can also take from the darkness surrounding us and manipulate it for our own gain or travel through it to another destination without having to realm jump. I am one of the only few shadow wielders who can manipulate mine into physical objects such as weapons, dark entities, or even a self-heating teapot."

Caelen's gaze shot to the teapot next to us. "You can make them create anything?"

"Within reason." I shrugged, leaning back into my chair. "Sometimes they have to put their foot down and tell me no."

"I didn't think you knew what the meaning of the word *no* meant, being as you are a prince." Caelen shot me a devious look as she picked up her cup and sipped the contents down. Her eyes looked over the black pentagram star drawn out in a book in front of her. "Your mother was not from this realm."

It was a statement, not a question. I nodded numbly. "My late mother married into this court. She was from the Cogadh Court. The union between my father and mother was a very powerful one at the time. Death and War go hand in hand, but never once had they ruled together."

"What magic did she possess?" Caelen asked, thumb absentmindedly running over the left point of the star where my mother's court was displayed.

"Curse magic. She could conjure hexes, send someone in a lust filled frenzy or bouts of insanity accompanied by unstoppable rage. The unhealing wounds were always the worst to see. Sometimes I wish I had taken to her power rather than my father's," I said with a playfulness that was always in my voice when I spoke of my mother. "And she was the best there was."

A pang of sadness radiated through the room as I mentioned her, but the feeling was not coming from me. I had long since come to terms with her death after the rebel attack on the castle. She had always sworn to protect her people, and that night, she did exactly that. Thousands of lives would have been lost if she had not conjured her final hex. The bright glow of her green light had shot through the lands in a heated flash, and sometimes when I close my eyes, I can still see its faint flicker.

Caelen reached over, placing a hand on my shoulder. I looked up, meeting her stare. Sadness glimmered in her blue eyes. "I am sorry you lost her, Loch. Truly. I know how hard it is to lose the one person who loved you unconditionally without question."

"She was magnificent and had a fiery personality like yours. The two of you would have enjoyed each other's company." I smiled as she perked up at the comment.

"If she is anything like her son, I am sure I would have enjoyed meeting her as well." She shot me a soft smile, then settled back into her position over the map.

I chuckled before pointing towards the court on the star's point beside my mother's. "The Todhchaí Court is where our elders reside. The Druids of Fate are the prophets and can tell you the timeline of your life as the tides change."

"Sounds horrible." Caelen's face twisted up in disgust.

"Oh, they are, but the Elders are essential to the survival of the realms."

"What about the Fírinne Court? Who are they?" Caelen

questioned. At the top of the star's point, the name was etched into the paper in dark ink.

"They are the Druids of Truth." I brushed my hand across my jawline. "Annoying as hell due to it as well, and if they get ahold of even a drop of your blood, they have the ability to control your mind. You'll reveal everything, only being able to speak the truth, even the ones you were unaware of while under their control."

Caelen groaned at the thought. "Remind me to keep my blood far away from them when they are near."

"Have secrets you don't want to share?" I flashed a mischievous grin at the mortal.

"Don't we all?" She winked at me, evading the question entirely as a devilish smile tugged at the corner of her lips.

"The final realm is home to the Druids of Life, who reside in the Beatha Court. They pull their magic from their surroundings." I nodded to the last point on the pentagram. Caelen cocked her head to the side, examining the name.

"They harness earth magic?" she asked. I nodded once at her statement. Caelen slumped down into her chair, arms crossing over her chest. "Okay, and each court gets to gather a team to participate in the Aesira Games in hopes of ruling the courts?"

"Yes, and no. The ruling court is just a title that comes with the crown. What they desire is the power that is granted to each court. The crown ruler has the ability to dip into each of the court's magic, if need be, but the consequences of manipulating that much power at once will cost the caster more than just their life. Even my father, as power-hungry as he is, has never once desired to wield all five court's abilities at once. He has chosen to specialize in the seer's abilities with the guidance of the Elders, along with his birth-given powers. The First Sister was the only person who could wield all the court's powers without fatally harming herself."

"Queen Arable used them to defeat her sister. I know the story." Caelen rolled her eyes.

"Do you? The battle left both sisters powerless. Arable contained not only her sister's powers within a glass crystal but also the power of the God who had blessed the mortal lands with his gifts. It has been lost for centuries." I swirled the tea around my cup, watching the liquid tremor under my touch. "The sisters helped ruled your lands together before their selfish nature destroyed it."

Both of our gazes locked on the burned center of the star where the mortal's land's true name had once been etched into the parchment. Even I could not remember the name of the land. The Elders had made sure that was been wiped from the histories and minds of the Courts. Whispers of the true name had filtered through the realms, but they were only rumors. Nothing was confirmed. Caelen's home had once been viewed as the pinnacle of power to the courts.

A yawn escaped Caelen's lips, eyes drooping slightly from exhaustion. I reached out, flipping the leather-bound book shut. "I believe I have filled your brain with enough stories for this session. It is well into the night, and soon Eoghan will be pulling you from your bed to train."

She hummed at my statement. "He is truly a brute."

"Eoghan can be a little overbearing in his training methods, but he has produced the best soldiers in our legions." I laughed as her face twisted in annoyance. "And I have no doubt that you will be his best creation."

"I will not be described as some type of experiment, Lochlan." Caelen turned to me, anger pulsing through the air.

I held up my hands up in surrender, "My apologies. That was not my intent."

"Then what was your intent?" Caelen spoke through clenched teeth.

"It is not important at this point."

Her eyes rolled to the back of her skull, and she stood from her chair to make her way toward the door. Placing one hand on the metal handle, Caelen turned back to me. I watched her closely, the torchlight shadows dancing across her face. The room appeared to darken as she spoke. "Do not underestimate a woman whose soul craves power. It will be your demise, Prince."

"If power is what you crave, dear cailleach" — I matched her gaze, my shadows appearing around me in a cloud of a pitch-black void. She sucked in a shaky breath as they rippled across the room toward her, halting only an inch from her ankles — "I can give you every last drop if you only ask."

The clank of dishware echoed around the terrace the following morning at breakfast. The sun's rays broke through the clouds, sending its warmth onto my skin. I relished the feeling. Across from me, Caelen sat looking absolutely exhausted. Dark bags hung under her eyes, and I wondered if she had ever gone to bed before stumbling into the training ring.

Her gaze met mine, a single curl falling into her eyes from the braid that pooled down her back.

I quirked an eyebrow up at her. "Rough night, cailleach?"

"You are insufferable," she whispered under her breath, fork coming down to impale an unsuspecting egg in front of her. A low chuckle sounded from the other end of the table as my father watched the interaction.

"How is our champion advancing in her training, General Montros?" he asked, swirling around a crystal glass of dark red liquid. Caelen's movements paused, the egg now hanging limply in front of her lips as she waited for Eoghan to respond. From the corner of my eye, I watched Elara's reaction, her face remaining neutral, but her eyes burning with envy. I tracked her line of sight to the necklace hanging against Caelen's chest. The red pendant shone in the morning rays, showing off its swirling insides in all its glory.

Eoghan cleared his throat, setting down his cutlery. "Caelen is a quick learner. She will have no trouble in the Games, Your Majesty."

A lie.

Eoghan didn't so much as hint at the fact that yesterday morning he had bested Caelen in all of the combat training rounds he had forced her to participate in. I had been observing away from their eyesight, cringing every time Caelen had been slammed into the mat underneath her. We were running on so little time, and she needed to be ready to take on the deadly opponents trained since birth to represent their courts in the Aesira Games.

Eoghan relaxed as he leaned back into the chair. Caelen sighed beside him, finally placing the food in her mouth as he continued, "The Prince was right in his decision to include her in the team. She will make a perfect addition."

"Would you agree with General Montros's assessment, Caelen?" Elara asked. The jealousy that had once been contained in her eyes was now rolling off her scent. Her hands gripped the knife in her right hand, and I flicked my eyes toward Eoghan. His eyes glazed over the same way they did when he was examining a battle plan. Elara desired for our lies to be outed in front of my father. Her goal was not to drive the point that mortals were inherently greedy and schemed against all else, were not to be trusted. Rather it was to ensure the king would never trust the heir to his throne again. Elara had made it perfectly clear that my innate fascination with the mortal realm showed that I was not fit to take the throne any time soon.

Caelen nodded slowly. "Yes. I am being well prepared by both the Prince in my studies and General Montros in physical training."

"How wonderful." She grinned, letting the words slide from gritted teeth.

Breakfast continued, the silence filled with my father and Eoghan discussing the current uproar in a war camp just outside the forest limits. The General would have to make an appearance if we had any hope that the strife building between the ranks, would end in little to no bloodshed. Eoghan dreaded his visits.

He had left the war camps long ago, but the haunted look in his eyes when we discussed visiting told me enough to know that it was painful to enter them once again. His past was well hidden from others, but you cannot outrun your own traumas, no matter how hard you try.

A young boy scurried over to me. His scrawny fingers wrapped around a stark white envelope. I plucked the item from his grasp, turning it over to see the burnt orange wax seal of the rebellion melted onto the letter. The scorpion stared back at me, its poisonous tail arched over its large body, piercing through the belly of a serpent. The creature laid limply in the air like a trophy for the predator. It was a clear threat from the rebels. I slowly turned my calculating stare on my general, signaling we needed to handle what I had just acquired.

"I must respond to this correspondence immediately." I excused myself from the table. "General, if you would follow me, I must discuss this with you."

We both stepped away from the table, Eoghan bowing slightly in respect to my father before departing down the hall. The blood in my ears pounded with each step we took until I could not wait any longer. I turned to Eoghan, causing the male to come to a halt. The envelope felt like an explosive I was trying to disarm as I peeled open the wax seal.

There was only a single feather inside. The bottom soaked the pure white surface in crimson blood. They had made it to the mainland, where the hawks of the north migrated once a year. They were due to travel back to their nests in the coming days as our land was overtaken by the winter's chill. It was a taunt and a warning that the rebels were closing in on us.

"They have advanced onto the mainland, Eoghan," I gritted out, words coated in venom. Tossing the feather and envelope into Eoghan's chest, the contents fell to the hardwood floor. "If the rebels press any farther in, they will infiltrate our villages again. You recall what occurred the last time that happened, do you not, General Montros?'

"Of course I do, Lochlan." Eoghan glared at me. A deadly rage rippled through him as he remembered what had occurred so many years ago. The ones we had lost. "We have been monitoring their every movement. If they moved inward, I should have been informed."

"Clearly not." I scoffed at his comment.

"Lochlan," Eoghan warned, anger lacing his words. "I think it is best if I visit the camp once again and see why the commanders neglected to inform their general about this pressing information."

From the corner of my vision, a lemon-colored fabric flashed around a doorway cove. The same yellow color that Caelen had been dressed in at breakfast. I tipped my chin in the direction of the door. Eoghan craned his neck, smirking slightly as he heard the rustle of her dress, moving around in the darkness. I opened my mouth, ready to inform her that she had been caught, maybe even throw a snide remark out about her needing to have a session with Sylas in the art of spying, but the sound of Caelen's screams made the words on my tongue vanish.

The smell of burnt flesh infiltrated my nose. Eoghan raced ahead of me, reaching Caelen as she pitched backward out of the darkness and plummeted to the ground. He caught her easily, arms weaving under her shoulders and lowering her to the floor. Caelen's head lulled back into his chest as her breath became erratic. I hovered over her, eyes raking up and down her body to find the source of her pain.

"It burns," she panted out, gaze lowering to the necklace that was now glowing against her breastbone. Caelen's eyes rolled back into her skull, allowing the pain to overtake her. Eoghan's muffled voice called out to her, a hand coming up to brush the stray hairs away from her sweat-coated face. I bent at the knee, batting the pendant away from her skin. The piece flopped over her shoulder and onto Eoghan's jacket.

"Holy Gods," Eoghan murmured, eyes wide at the red skin bubbling from the heat. I narrowed my eyes at the symbol as it sizzled under the cool air in the hall. Burned into Caelen's chest was the pentagram that represented the realm courts. In the center of the star, the ancient name of a God long since forgotten in the mortal lands was glowing orange. "Does that say what I think it does?"

"Indeed, it does." I ran my finger over the name, drinking in the power that pulsed through it. *Demios.* My shadows whispered the name over and over again. "And here she thought she did not the hold the power to play in the Games. What else are you hiding in that necklace, Caelen?"

Chapter Seventeen
Caelen

Searing pain bloomed across my chest as my mother's necklace pulsed. I could feel my lips moving, responding to the two males above me, but I could not hear what I was saying. Eoghan's pained expression hovered over me through my hazy vision until I let go and let the fiery darkness consume me.

A field painted in blood. Droplets glistened off the pale grass, shining like rubies underneath the harsh sun that beat down. A pair of cold hands dug their talons into my bare shoulder as they pulled me deeper into the chaos surrounding me. Destruction scattered across the palace grounds as people frantically tried to find a place to hide.

Flames burned brighter by the second, even as the guards tried to contain the fire. Villagers tried to force themselves out of the palace walls, but the drawbridge that once kept them safe was blocked by a feline beast. It hissed and swatted at the guards, who managed to get close enough. They soar across the field like birds flying through the air. Everyone was sitting ducks, just waiting for the beast to snatch them into its wide grin.

Strangers dressed in matching rags of dark orange stood out in the crowds. Bodies marching to the rhythm of a war drum played miles away from the attack. The horrid laughter intermingled with the cries of Lochlan's people. Their eyes were wild with revenge as they slaughtered innocents. Rebels. This was what Eoghan and Lochlan were terrified of occurring, and instead, the rebellion had closed in on the palace. Seeing the destruction that was littered around me, I was sure the villages were just smoldering piles now. My feet carried me forward as I raced through the crowd, no one seeming to notice my presence as I pushed into the throne room. I stood in the middle of chaos, just watching the scene play out for me.

The beautiful dark marble columns surrounding the throne room burst into dust in an almost musical way. Tattered pieces of the realm court's flags lay amongst the rubble crumbling around my feet. I watched in horror as a column fell towards me as it broke a part and threw my hands over my head, blocking the downfall of debris. Peering back up, I observed the rebels relish in the death toll they continued to rack up as they moved through the throne room. I silently counted the dead.

Royal subjects were now only blood smears across the marble floor. Bits of rubble and color continued to fly around my head, and I tracked each pebble as they connected with the hard floor. The tiny substances sounded like bombs detonating in my mind every time one struck the hard surface. Each scream that echoed through the room sent an electrifying sensation through my body. Heat sizzled through my arms and into the tips of my fingers. The warmth mixed with the coldness of the deceased latched on to me as they got their first taste of death.

Something hit my foot with a thunk, causing a warm, sticky substance to squish between my bare toes. Slowly I peered down at the object, and as a gut-wrenching scream escaped my lips, I lost my footing on the slick floor. Falling forward, my body landed in a pool of crimson that surrounded me. The warm liquid soaked the thin white dress I wore, dying it a deep rust color. Clawing my way back on the floor, I gawked at the scene in front of me, unable to wrap my head around what I was seeing. Blood pooled out of a decapitated head that had been rolled across the hall by a laughing rebel. It was like a sick game of knock-over-the-pins the children in my village played. The head wasn't just a head but the severed head of the Crown Prince. Lochlan, the male who had become a confidant between the swish of pages and tea leaves, now stared up at me with lifeless eyes. His dark jeweled crown still hung against the top of his head.

"Lookie here, boys." A fair-haired rebel with a sword dripping in liquid the colors of rubies leaned down and plucked the crown from the skull. "I am now the Druid Prince of Death."

Their sick laughter surrounded me as the scene melted into a mess of colors and lights.

I flew up, my forehead colliding with a hard surface. Groaning, I gripped my skull as the pain began to radiate through the bone, but it was nothing compared to the searing sting on my chest.

"Caelen?" Eoghan's voice called out to me in the distance. I cracked open my eyes, looking directly up at the male. His hands hovered over me, trying to find which wound to attend to. Slowly the world around me came into focus, and I noticed my head was lying in his lap. My eyes widened, and I scrambled to my feet as Eoghan protested my movement.

"Eoghan, where is he?" I asked frantically, words coming

out hoarse as they scratched against my throat. I must have screamed my vocal cords raw. Eoghan stood with me, a wild look on his face.

"Where is who, Caelen?" he asked, stepping towards me. I could see he was unsure if I should be standing on my own as he stretched his arms out to catch me if I plummeted toward the floor once again. I scoffed, not caring to be coddled by the General. Not after the horrors I had just witnessed in my vision. Not when the Prince's blood had soaked every inch of my skin as his head was made into sport. I shuddered at the thought, my skin crawling with the reminder of what felt to be so real just moments ago.

"Lochlan," I called out in a panic. "Where is the Prince, Eoghan?"

"Look behind you." Eoghan threw a hand in the direction in an aggravated motion. "Has she gone mental?"

I whipped around to see Lochlan standing just behind my trembling figure. A concerned look laced his features as I scanned him for an indication that he had been harmed. I let out a sigh of relief. His head was still attached to his shoulders. Running a hand over my chest, I groaned in pain as my fingers made contact with the raised skin under my pendant.

"Let me have a look at that." Eoghan maneuvered around me, carefully moving the necklace out of the way to get a better look at what lay beneath. I gritted my teeth, trying my best not to pull away from his touch. His fingers traced the underside of my chin. "Look up for me."

I did as I was told and waited for him to make his assessment.

Lochlan was the first to speak. "Should we be concerned about the fact that the necklace branded her?"

"Probably." Eoghan's touch hovered over the center of the brand, sending goosebumps across my skin. He didn't seem to notice, or if he did, he was keeping his comments to himself.

"I will have a salve we use on the soldiers in the camps sent up to your chambers." Eoghan pulled away, and I tilted my chin back down to glare at him. His eyes darkened, matching my intensity. "A bit of gratitude would be appreciated. I could just let the damn thing get infected."

"Bite me, you brute," I hissed, teeth clamping together to prove my point. The muscles in his jaw popped as he showed some restraint with his words with the looming presence of the Prince behind him. I would regret it in our next training session when he had me running laps around the castle in silence. That's one time I could look forward to in our training—the quiet. Eoghan held himself to a high standard when it came to readying a "soldier" for war. No more quick banter like the first session that Lochlan and Sylas interrupted. No jabs were thrown between the two of us. Just corrections and orders. I preferred it be that way anyways.

Eoghan turned towards the prince. "I think it is best that we keep this incident contained, and I will escort Caelen back to her room for the rest of the day."

"I believe that is best as well. Inform Ainsley and her sisters that, until the brand has calmed, to dress her in something that hides it." Lochlan nodded. He pulled a white piece of parchment out of his suit jacket's pocket. "I must attend to this, but I will come to you once I am finished, cailleach."

Lochlan pushed through the door behind him and disappeared. I began down the hall of portraits, leaving Eoghan to follow. I didn't need an escort back to my rooms. I knew the way. The journey up the stairs made my lungs burn as we made our way toward the door in rushed steps. Once we reached the entrance of my room, I was drained of any remaining adrenaline from the vision. Eoghan broke the silence surrounding us as I reached for the door handle.

"Why were you so concerned for Lochlan when you came to?" he asked, leaning up against the stone wall next to the door. I traced the golden handle, letting the cool metal kiss my fingertips as I went.

"You wouldn't believe me if I told you," I whispered.

"Try me," Eoghan pushed. I craned my neck towards the male, eyeing his stoic face. The only crack in his cold demeanor was the crease between his eyebrows as he took in my exhausted state.

I shook my head. "The thought of reliving what I saw makes me want to throw myself out the windows of my chambers."

"Good thing we had bars placed on them when you arrived." Eoghan smirked at me.

"You already informed me of that." I rolled my eyes, gripping down on the doorknob. I wanted nothing more than to curl up in my bed and chalk this morning up to a bad dream, but Eoghan caught my hand, pausing my movements.

"You may not trust me, Caelen, but if the prince is in danger, I need to know." He spoke softly to me as if I was a child that scared easily. He was right—I did not trust him. I resented him for taking me away from Mai. Hated him for the fact that when I returned to her, she would not appear to me with the same youthful flush to her cheeks. I should be just as angry with Lochlan, but there was a fondness I held toward the Crown Prince, an understanding that we had silently come to that night when he spoke of his late mother. His apologies spoke volumes over the General's constant ridiculing. As if I were the dangerous one in this palace. No, Gideon had been right that first night outside the castle—I was merely a mortal girl in a land of creatures all ready to slaughter me the first chance they got. Eoghan had stolen my future with my sister away from me, and now for once, I had the upper hand against him.

"Why would I reveal anything to someone who so willingly destroyed my life?" I let the words roll off the tip of my tongue, a hint of sadness coating them. Pulling my hand from his grip, I laid it on the cool wood of the door before speaking again. "I will tell you and Lochlan what occurred when the time seems right, but for now, I have to process what I saw."

"Then I will be waiting for your call." Eoghan stepped away from me and began descending the staircase. He paused momentarily before he rounded the first spiral. "I see why Loch is so enamored with you, Caelen. You can be much more than the beast that you hide behind. Under all that spite and venom you throw at me, I can see you are loyal to a fault. I may not have your ear, and it is clear we both have our reasons for disliking each other, but I do enjoy seeing the crack of humanity you keep hidden from me."

I slammed my hands against the door, the surface smacking into the stone wall behind it. Racing into the room, I noticed it was dark, and all three wraiths had clearly gone to handle their daily tasks outside of the chambers. A soft chuckle echoed in the hall, making my blood boil. I pushed the door shut, leaving the General in the stairwell.

Making my way to the bathroom, I stood before the mirror to assess the damage the pendant had left. In the center of my chest, a star matching the one the Prince and I had previously studied in the library was burned into my skin, leaving the bright red skin raised and bumpy. Scrawled across the center, a name I did not recognize was etched on the surface of my skin.

"Demios," I breathed out. The red in my pendant glowed slightly at the name, the liquid inside swirling and fighting against itself to break free of its cage. I grasped it in my hand, shielding it from my view. My blood ran ice cold as the deep voice of another entered my mind.

"I am the destroyer of worlds. The one they fear above all else. But you, dear Spinner, do not fear me. No, you crave my power. Interesting."

CHAPTER EIGHTEEN
CAELEN

H ave you ever heard a songbird sing?" Kenina Elliston's voice broke through the overgrown grass she rested against beside a rushing river. Mairead toddled across the lush grass between my mother and me, her golden hair shining in the morning light. Bright purple wildflowers were clutched in her chubby hands as she bent to pick them from their homes in the fields. "Caelen, are you listening to me?"

My eyes shot up, taking in the unapproving gaze of my mother. I shrugged at her. "I have heard the birds sing in the mornings. They are quite annoying."

"This isn't a game, Caelen." My mother shot forward, gripping my forearm and pulling me toward her. I toppled into her, landing awkwardly on my hip. Mai let out a gleeful squeal as a hummingbird repeatedly buzzed around her head in a figure eight.

I zeroed in on the motion, watching the animal swish and sway in an inhuman way. The sunlight spotlighted my sister and the bird, glimmering rays of rainbow dots dancing in between her fingertips. And then I saw it, the tiny green body of a person with iridescent wings flittering behind it. I went to stand, but my mother held me in place, her gaze on the same creature as it continued to play with her youngest child. A smirk twitched at the corner of her lips. "You must protect her, Caelen, no matter the cost. The power that surges through our veins is not of our land, and those who are desperate for power will seek to find you both."

"People? What people, Mother?" I tore my eyes from her face and back to Mairead, her fingertips mere inches from touching the fairy. The winged creature paused, sinking closer to her touch, entranced by the strange human toddler.

Mai let out an excited shriek as she stroked the fairy's skin, and the world around us suddenly went cold. It happened so quickly that I thought I might have imagined the incident, but the fairy began to fall from the sky, its skin a sick grayish color as it went. It landed in a heap of limbs on the meadow's flowers, eyes desolate as it stared up at the darkening sky. Mairead huffed at it, annoyed that her newfound playmate was no longer entertaining her.

I craned my neck to the horror-stricken look of my mother. "Trust no one, Caelen, not even the softness of that Crown Prince you have grown fond of. He is just as much of a serpent as the rest of them and has the wrath that could destroy worlds. The royal bloodline is after one thing and one thing only."

"What is that?" My voice shook slightly as I asked the question. My mother's eyes glazed over, her demeanor melting into a passive one as she looked toward Mairead once again.

Kenina Elliston's voice was not her own as she spoke again. "Have you ever heard the songbird sing?"

A sharp knock ripped me from my dream. My heart hammered painfully against my ribcage, breaths coming in shallow spurts. The moon had reached its highest peak in the night sky, shining its rays across my sweat-covered skin in haunting waves. I swiveled towards the sound as it broke through the room once again. Placing my feet against the floor, the biting cold of the stone shot through the soles, and I suppressed a hiss of discomfort. The temperature in the room was like standing in the middle of an ice storm. I could see my breath in front of me. Reaching the door, I cracked it open, coming upon the Crown Prince. His dark eyes seemed to be an endless void tonight. My breath caught in the back of my throat, my mother's haunting warning ringing back in my ears.

"I didn't wake you, did I, cailleach?" Lochlan's lips pulled into a cunning grin, eyes glancing at the unmade bed before finding my gaze again. I shrunk behind the wooden door, shielding my body from his eyes.

"No, I was up." I pulled the door open farther, making room for the Prince to enter the chambers. "Would you like to come in, Lochlan?"

The smirk he wore deepened as he stepped through the threshold. "Do you often invite males into your chambers this late at night?"

"Only the ones who are annoyingly charming." I rolled my eyes at the comment before turning away from Lochlan to make my way to one of the chairs placed in front of the fire. Sinking down into the velvet cushions, I watched the male standing just in front of the door. "Is there something you need, Lochlan?"

"Eoghan was droning on about a vision you had earlier in the hall. He claimed it left a haunted look in your eyes." Lochlan pulled his lip between his teeth at the thought. I rolled my shoulders back as he took long, drawn-out steps in my direction. "I thought you might want to discuss it with someone other than him. He can be quite harsh at times."

"The General can be more than harsh," I grumbled, leaning back into the chair to try and appear unfazed at the General's concern. The comment made the pit of my stomach altered between being sick from the fact that he cared and intrigued by the notion.

Lochlan dragged a chair from the table in front of me and spun it around to sit on it backward. His eyes softened as he spoke the following words. "Now, what was in that vision that scared you so much?"

I sucked in a shaky breath, the images flashing across my mind as I tried to find the correct words to articulate them. "There was so much carnage, and it felt so real. As if I could reach out and touch the destruction piling up, but I was just a mirage. And you…"

My words stuck in the back of my throat, blurred vision locking with the Crown Prince. He waited patiently, a pitched expression that I could not read entirely coming over his face. I let my next words roll off the tip of my tongue like a poisoned wine. "You had been assassinated by rebels who laughed at your death. They viewed you as nothing more than a figure they had to cut down in their crusade for revenge."

The fire popped, sending a crackling burst of embers into the air. A darkness encompassed the room as Lochlan's shadows began to deepen into a color as black as night. I sucked in a ragged breath, "Do you think it could be an omen? Or something trying to warn us about the rebels you and the General had been discussing in the hall?"

Lochlan never broke my gaze, "It was just a vision, nothing more and nothing less."

"A vision doesn't leave its mark unless it is important," I whisper, my hand tracing the burn underneath my necklace. The skin was still sensitive to the touch, even with the salve that Ainsley had carefully slathered onto it before bed.

Lochlan's eyes wandered to the fire, it bounced off the deep void of his black eyes. "No, I suppose it does not, cailleach."

"Should I prepare to defend myself not only in the Games but also in the walls of this castle?" I whisper, letting my concerns hang in the stale air.

"You are safe under my protection, Caelen," Lochlan growls out, a frenzy of shadows swirling around him. "Never think you are not."

"But the rebels cou- "I sputter out, but Lochlan's sharp look silenced me. Biting down on my bottom lip, I peeled my gaze away from his.

"Keep your mind trained on the Games, cailleach, and let Eoghan and I handle the rebellion." His words were a gravelly whisper that made the anxiety coiled tight in my stomach spread through my body. I simply nodded, not wanting to argue with the angered male any more tonight. But I knew as soon as my eyes closed, the sickening roll of his skull, and the horrid laughter of the rebels would be the only thing that would consume my dreams.

Chapter Nineteen
Caelen

Tomorrow night is the opening ceremony, and you have yet to show me you have the ability to survive even a second in the Games," Eoghan taunted me as we circled the mat. The sun was beginning to rise over the training ring, letting the morning heat beat down over the stone walls. Squinting through the sunshine, I ducked as Eoghan's sword slashed towards me, glistening. I brought up my own weapon, the clang of metal echoing in the silence.

I panted, holding his sword with my own blade in place over my head. "I don't know what else I can do. You are Sìth. I am mortal. No matter how fast I move or how hard I try, your kind will always have an advantage unless I have a knife in my hand."

Eoghan paused, letting his blade fall to his side. "You give yourself so little credit, Caelen."

"I haven't once bested you," I cried out at him, throwing down my sword. It slammed against the mat, bouncing a few times before settling. I gripped the roots of my hair and exhaled a frustrated breath. Eoghan was watching me with a stony expression. I sneered at him, "I don't need your pity. My fate is sealed. Just promise me you will inform my sister of my demise when the time comes. She deserves to know what happened, not be left wondering for the rest of her days."

"You are not being sent back to her in pieces, Caelen." Eoghan crossed his arms over his chest. "Stop feeling sorry for yourself and pick up that sword again."

I leaned down, snatching up the weapon. Even after weeks of holding it the blade still felt foreign in my hand. "It is no use."

"Why?" Eoghan crossed the ring and towered over me. I tilted my chin up at him, glaring at the arrogant gaze that stared down at me.

"This is not me," I said, motioning towards to weapon. "I can't control it like I can control my throwing knives."

"Loch has ensured you are to have at least one knife on your person before you enter that arena, but you cannot rely on just them to protect yourself in the Games," Eoghan pushed, "not when you are unable to wield magic like the rest of the champions."

He sidestepped me, pressing into my back. I froze, not used to him being this close to me. Biting down on my tongue, I swallowed the shaky breath that threatened to escape. Eoghan's fingers hovered over the hilt of the sword where I gripped it, knuckles turning white as he came even closer. I could feel his heated breath on the back of my sweaty neck, making the hair stuck to it rise. Suppressing a shiver, I waited for his next move, but we were both frozen in place.

Eoghan cleared his throat. "Think of the sword as an extension of your arm. Let the movements become natural."

Bringing my arm up with his, Eoghan guided my movements slowly. The blade swung down in one fluid motion with my limb before rotating back up to block an imaginary enemy.

"Now you try by yourself." Eoghan stepped away from me, coming back to stand in front and observe my movements. I did as I was told, mimicking the actions he had guided me through. The blade became lighter with each slash as Eoghan circled me, my eyes tracking him went. "Plant your feet. You are leaning too far into the heels of your boots. That is what gives me the advantage of overpowering you."

"Is that what it is, General?" I cocked an eyebrow at him. Eoghan froze, his back muscles flexing under the dark armor he wore. I admired him, waiting for him to lash out at me, but all he did was turn his gaze over his shoulder, meeting my challenging one.

"One more attempt to best me in a fight. If you win, I will give you the ability to see your sister," Eoghan said as the breath hitched in the back of my throat. I opened my mouth to ask how that was possible, but he cut me off. "But if I win once again, you will be coming to the war camp with me today to train with the witch twins."

I could only nod in agreement at his offer. If there was a possibility of seeing Mai and ensuring she was still alive, then I would take it. Eoghan reached down to where his sword lay and began to advance. I planted my feet like he instructed me to. Eoghan swung at me, meeting the end of my blade as I maneuvered away from him. As we danced around the arena, Eoghan twirled the blade with confidence. I rushed forward, engaging in the first swing I could manage. He blocked me, twisting until I almost lost the grip of my weapon.

Huffing out a shaky breath, I kicked out my foot and connected my heel with his ankle. He cursed at the impact giving me just enough time to shift and get my sword away from him. Taking the blade around my head, I slashed down in one last jab, the top of the sword landing just above his heart.

"I think that makes me the winner." I smiled victoriously.

Eoghan shook his head at me. "Oh, Caelen, so naïve you are when it comes to battle."

My feet were swept out from under me, slamming me onto the mat. Eoghan's blade was held against my throat, his body hovering over me. I cursed, closing my eyes, and waited for him to move the blade from my throat. Slamming my head against the mat, I dug the heels of my hands into my eyes, the feeling of tears beginning to burn at the corners. I had been so close to getting a glimpse of Mairead. The sting of the loss burning deep inside my chest.

"You were resting on your heels again." Eoghan's voice loomed above me. "But for what it is worth, that was the best I have seen you move around this ring since you have arrived."

"I don't need your praise," I snapped. Standing up from my spot, I stomped over to the rack where the weapons were stored and slammed the sword into place. I turned on my heels, ready to race back to my room, and shut myself in the darkest corner until the ceremonies were ready to begin tomorrow night.

Eoghan caught my upper arm, reeling me back toward him. "Where do you think you are going?"

"Remove your hand from me," I spat out through a clenched jaw. Eoghan narrowed his eyes at me, but did as I asked.

"Meet me at the front gates in an hour," Eoghan commanded. I began to walk away, but he called back to me, "And tell Ainsley you will need a coat for the journey. Can't have our mortal champion getting frostbite."

***

Eoghan stood near the castle's entrance, sternly speaking to a guard when I arrived. The biting wind of the afternoon flowed through the courtyard, nipping at the underside of my nose. I stepped up to the General as the soldier scurried away.

"You are late," Eoghan reprimanded, making me smirk.

"Blame Ainsley. She had a fit about winter wardrobe when I informed her of my little adventure I would be taking."

"She will live," Eoghan said, beginning to walk towards the stables just off to the left of the courtyard. Two horses were saddled up, Sylas standing next to one. She stroked the mare's dark mane, letting the animal knock its head against her own with a soft neigh.

"Are you joining us?" I asked when we got closer, though I knew she would have been able to hear me from across the yard with her enhanced hearing. Sylas turned, a bright smile stretching across her face.

"No, just came to visit an old friend." Sylas caressed the horse once again. She turned her attention to Eoghan. "Loch threatened that if you don't bring her back in one piece, he will string you up in the courtyard for the crows to feast upon."

"Loch said that? Or is that your interpretation of what you would do at his command?" Eoghan met her mischievous eyes.

"A little bit of both, General." Sylas winked at him. "But please do not let either of the twins have too much fun with the little mortal. We still need her for the Games."

"They will be on their best behaviors," Eoghan assured her. He stepped forward, pulling out one of the throwing blades I had used in training earlier this morning. It was now secured in a leather knife sheath attached to a holster that concealed the sharp blade away. An intricate design of two blooming flowers connected by a swirling vine stood out against the deep leather coloring. The holster's loop looked as if it had been weaved like the baskets, I had seen the shop owners in my village once create. Eoghan bent at the knee and gripped my inner thigh, causing me to suck in a harsh breath.

I tried to pull away from his touch, but he held me in place to strap the knife on the outside of my leg, constricting my thigh as he tightened the leather cord. Straightening, Eoghan retreated back and made his way over to his horse. He stepped into the stirrup, swinging one leg over to sit comfortably on the saddle. Eoghan nodded to me. "You know how to ride a horse, right?"

"No." I shook my head, eyes widening with terror at the idea.

"Well, no time like the present to learn," Sylas said. She held out a hand to help guide me into the saddle's stirrups. I stepped in and hoisted myself up onto the metal piece, following the same motion Eoghan had just done to get on the animal. The mare began to neigh, backing up at the motion of me getting on to it. I gripped down tightly to the reins, hoping it didn't start to buck. Sylas stepped back, soothing the horse softly. "Shh. It's alright, girl."

I sighed heavily when it calmed to Sylas's words. Looking down at the Prince's strategist, I asked, "Now what?"

"Stop stressing, for one thing. You are upsetting Nova," Sylas scolded me. "And just let her guide you. She will follow Eoghan like a lost pup. She has been trained to stick close to the General on these journeys."

"If you two are done," Eoghan's bored voice called to us, "I would like to get to camp before the sun sets."

"We aren't coming back here tonight?" I asked, turning to look at the castle.

"Remember that first night we ventured through the woods?" Eoghan asked. I turned back to him, nodding slightly. His eyes grew dark. "We don't want to get caught after dark in this part of the forest. Owls will be the least of your worries."

Chapter Twenty
Caelen

The trees had eyes. Every single one of them watched as we trotted through their woods. Eoghan was silent for most of the journey, leaving me to my own thoughts. He had been anxious about the rebel's moves inward on the borders in his conversation with the Prince, and that worry was embedding itself in the fold forming between his brows. My eyes wandered through the trees surrounding us. Even with the sun shining bright above them, the woods were dark. I could only imagine what lurked behind the branches, camouflaged by the endless void.

"Why are we going to meet these twins?" I asked Eoghan. Nova trotted quicker, coming up even with Eoghan's steed. The Sìth kept his gaze trained ahead, lost in his own thoughts. I took my foot out of the saddle and reached over to nudge his calf. Eoghan's eyes snapped to mine, and my mouth pulled into a crooked smile. "I asked you a question, General."

"Don't call me that." Eoghan scowled at me. "It sounds dirty coming off your tongue."

"Hmm, I could call you other names with this tongue," I teased. Eoghan's entire face flamed a deep scarlet color at the insinuation, only pushing me to continue. "Or I could do other things with it?"

"You act like a menace." Eoghan shook his head angrily at me. "Has anyone ever told you that?"

"Many people have told me that, but I do not care to entertain their judgments." I turned back to watch the path ahead. It twisted and dipped, making the ride unsteady. "You, in particular, like to remind me."

"Just to ensure you do not forget." Eoghan's voice was playful. It was the first time I had noticed him loosen up around me. Out of the corner of my eye, I could see that the typically brooding and serious general now sat, relaxed. His shoulders hung loosely, and there was a twinkle of amusement playing in his hazel eyes.

"Are you going to answer my question?" I asked.

"The Twins will be joining the team," Eoghan explained. "In the previous Aesira Games, the teams were only granted four members per realm, including the court's champion. This time, due to it being a millennial game, the Elders decided that teams can be as large as six. It appears to be a last minute decision."

"Why would they do that?" I asked, brows scrunching together in confusion.

"More contestants mean more power to wield in the Games," Eoghan explained, turning his head slightly to meet my gaze. "The Elders believe that not only should the games choose who rules for the next century, but also act as a celebration for the realms. They want as much entertainment as they can have for this year."

"So, we are just playthings for the courts to be entertained by?" I mumbled. Eoghan's eyes narrowed at my comment, his heightened senses catching every word of my hushed tone.

"If that is the way you wish to view it," Eoghan said, turning his attention back to the path. Up ahead, I could see the break of light between the trees signaling that we were coming out of the dark woods.

"How do you see it?"

"I see it as an honor to represent my realm." Eoghan's statement was clipped. His face remained stony, trying to hide the lie behind it, but the words did not meet his eyes.

"An honor or a burden?" I asked. Eoghan's head whipped towards mine, ready to scold me for my bluntness, but a high-pitched whistle broke him from his words. My eyes scanned the tree line, searching for source of the sound.

"Come to play with us, General?" A light and airy female's voice floated around us. A chill ran down my spine, causing me to sit straighter than before, but Eoghan still lounged back in his saddle. "We both missed your constant brooding."

"Embryss," a new male's voice scolded. "Don't taunt him."

"But what else am I to do?" Embryss whined. Nova was still walking at a leisurely pace through the gravel path, not stopping as a dark figure rounded a large elm's trunk. They ran a single nail along the rough wooden surface in a taunting motion. "Eoghan likes my games, don't you, General?"

"Your games always end with me injured, Em." Eoghan

shook his head at the figure, letting a low chuckle pass through his lips. The shadow turned, leaning itself against the tree in a sensual way that I knew I could never achieve. Eoghan halted his horse just in front of the figure, and Nova followed suit. "Why don't you let us see that beautiful, deadly face of yours?"

"Stop stroking her ego," the male's voice chastised from above us. I threw my head back to see if I could find him, but the shadows were even heavier in the leaves. "She already thinks herself to be the most beautiful creature in this realm. I grow tired of stopping at every puddle she stumbles upon for her to stare at herself."

"Brother," Embryss warned. "Do not test my patience today."

A whoosh of wind gathered up dirt and leaves, pelting me lightly as they went. I brought my arms up to shield my eyes from the debris. Eoghan sighed at the commotion, clearly used to whatever was occurring enough to not bother intervening.

"Are you done with the temper tantrum, sister?"

The air stilled, and then everything was calm once again. Slowly I peeled my arms away from my eyes, staring directly at a male who lounged on a low-hanging branch in front of Eoghan. The shadows that were just covering him dissipated, allowing me to catch sight of his deep brown skin and short buzzed hair.

His head lulled back against the tree, right hand balancing a pear between his fingertips as he examined it under the light. The ends of his dark jacket hung loosely over the branch like shadow hands reaching out to grab me. He reminded me of the jungle cats described in stories who would wait for their prey above the rest of the world, only to strike at just the opportune moment. I let out a shaky breath making him turn to gaze at me, my lungs constricting as it landed on me. The male's eyes were striking, the right a bright blue and the left a glimmering amber color. He narrowed them at me, a sneer painting his handsome face.

"What is the mortal doing here?"

Eoghan rolled his shoulders back as if he was preparing for a fight to break out. "Lochlan thought it best to get introductions over with before we are in a war zone."

The male scoffed at him, but Embryss chimed in over his words. "I think she is rather pretty, don't you, Theo? Shame that pretty face will most likely be destroyed by the end of this."

"Pity." Theo's voice was bored. He kept eye contact with me, bringing the pear up to his lips and taking a bite from it. The juice ran down his chin as he chewed on the food. He quirked an eyebrow up, turning back to the forest's darkness. "Will you come out now, Embryss?"

There was a high-pitched giggle before the shadows disappeared, finally revealing the female. She had the same dark skin as her brother though her eyes were opposite to his. Embryss was dressed in a revealing silk green dress that dipped low on her chest in a pool of color. The slit cut up the planes of her legs, landing just below her hip bone that was pushed out due to her stance. A blade was strapped to her outer thigh, glistening in the little light that shined on her. She was breathtakingly beautiful. There was no doubt that when she claimed to be the most beautiful in the realm, she was not lying.

"Hello, pretty little witch." Eoghan drew out the words, a sly smile gracing his face. A strange burning radiated through me as he drank in her beauty. It began in the pit of my stomach, bubbling up until I could feel the burn of rage on the back of my neck. Embryss pushed herself off the tree and sauntered over to us. There was a light skip in her step as she pranced over to Eoghan, laying a single hand on his mare's head to pet the animal. The horse nuzzled into her hand, letting out a satisfied snort.

"I missed you too, girl." Embryss spoke softly to the animal. She paused her strokes, turning her eyes on me. A sly smile played on her face as she spoke to me. "You must be the mortal I have been hearing whisperings about from the trees. I am Embryss, as Eoghan has stated. That brooding thing on the branch is my twin, Theo. It is a pleasure to finally meet the Prince's champion."

"The pleasure is all mine," I spit out as I ground my teeth together. She shot me a knowing wink.

"We will meet you back in camp," Eoghan explained. "And please try to refrain from bringing your wicked attitude with you."

"But how am I to leave it behind when it is the prime reason for my sparkling personality," Theo droned on as he flicked a bug from his shoulder. I rolled my eyes, waiting for Eoghan to signal to his horse we were venturing forward. Nova followed lightly, passing under the male's branch as she went.

Theo's taunting voice traveled with us. "Remember your place, little mortal."

Camp was bustling with soldiers when we arrived. The sun was at its highest point in the sky now, leaving me to believe it was coming close to mealtime. Eoghan stood a little taller as we traveled through the masses. The troops kept their eyes downcast as we passed. I couldn't tell if it was because they feared or admired Eoghan. Possibly a bit of both, causing them to rush back to their posts. Multiple tents were set up to my left, their bright shades meddling together in a mess of color. Patches were stitched into their roofs, indicating the ranks which slept under their protection.

Eoghan led us to the edge of camp, dismounting his horse and handing it over to a young boy who took the mare from him. I swung my leg away from the saddle, balancing on one foot as I came down. The momentum of my swing propelled me backward, and I grappled for the edge of the leather seat. Strong hands caught my hips, guiding me down to the ground and onto my feet.

"Thank you." I turned around, my chest brushing against his own. My heart pounded rapidly against my ribcage. I looked up into Eoghan's caramel-colored eyes, watching them grow darker the longer we stood like this. His hand shot out, gripping Nova's reins, and he stepped away from me. I blew out a breath, letting my nerves settle as Eoghan spoke to the handler a moment longer before returning to me.

"Come on," Eoghan beckoned me towards him, voice rough and gravelly. He stalked ahead of me, leading the way to a faded blue tent. The doors were held open, strapped into place with a bit of twine rope, revealing a large oak table in the center. Four males surrounded the piece, looking down at a map of Bás lands.

"Eoghan, my boy." Gideon's bright voice welcomed us into the warmth of the space. He stood behind the table, hunched over the map as he marked a dot in the middle of the ocean. Eoghan rounded the table, the soldiers parting away from Gideon for their general to stand next to the male. Gideon clapped him on the back. "Good to have you back in camp, if only for a moment."

"It is good to be back." Eoghan leaned into the map, a hushed whisper summoning a male with red hair to him. "Have you located the mole in your legion, Commander Tavish?"

"Yes." Tavish nodded. "He is being held in the bunker. We were awaiting your direction."

"I want to speak with him." Eoghan's eyes flicked toward me before returning to the commander. "Ensure the bunker is secure and clear out the area for my arrival."

I gulped back the bile in my throat. There was a darkness coming over Eoghan as he sent the male away. It stuck to him in sticky globs that refused to leave. The soldier had allowed the rebels to infiltrate the shorelines, and I knew the General would not be arriving in the bunker for a friendly chat. I had seen Eoghan in action, even if that power he held was well hidden under hand-to-hand combat. When I sparred with him, I could feel the hot and sensual touch of his magic under the swings.

"Caelen." Gideon's voice broke me from my haze. "Has the Prince managed to tame the beast inside you?

The corners of my lips tugged upward. "Only in his wildest

dreams."

"That's my girl." Gideon winked towards me. A warmness filled me at the comment. I ventured forward, leaning over the other side of the table to get a closer look at the map, but my body was jerked away from the surface. Throwing an elbow back, it caught my attacker in the gut giving me the advantage. I unsheathed the knife Eoghan had strapped onto my thigh before we left the castle grounds. Reaching out, I gripped the soldier's red hair, yanking it up to expose his neck, and crashed him into the wooden pole holding the tent together. The structure rattled above us as I slammed the blade up against the male's throat; it dug into the skin just enough for him to hiss out in pain.

"Did you teach her that, Eoghan?" I could hear Gideon whisper. Tavish's green eyes bore into mine with the rage of the entire army around us.

"No." Eoghan chuckled in amusement.

The male tried to move, only coming to terms that he would meet the blade's sharp end no matter how he maneuvered. He barked out the following words like an order to one of his soldiers, "Release me, or you won't like what occurs next."

"You seem to forget who is holding a knife to who's neck." I grinned at him, batting my eyelashes in mockery toward him.

"Let him go, Caelen," Eoghan's voice called to me. I dug the blade slightly deeper, hoping to draw blood in the process.

Craning my head back towards Eoghan, I sent him a wicked smile. "But he is so fun to play with."

"Caelen." Eoghan's harsh tone warned me not to take this any further. He was watching me closely under his furrowed brows, eyes raging with my insubordination.

"Well, since you asked so nicely, General," I teased, turning back to the male and quickly pulling the knife from his neck. With my grip still on his hair, I forced his head down, the male's nose meeting my knee in a sickening crunch before I released him. Stepping back, I smiled at the sight of the blood trickling down his face. He reached up, swiping his fingers under his nose and pulling back to see the sticky red substance coating his fingers. With a growl, he lunged for me again but was dragged back into place by another male.

"I won't forget this, girl," he snarled at me. "Watch your back, Prince's champion."

Chapter Twenty One
Caelen

Embryss sat on a stool in front of me, twirling the blade Eoghan had taken away from me after my altercation. Her long hair was now in a tight bun at the back of her head, and she had changed into a set of skintight body armor. The black scales glistened under the evening light, similar to the ones Eoghan always wore in training. Her twin, Theo, was sulking in the dark corner of the tent, unamused with the instructions to watch me from his general.

"Why does Eoghan call you witches?" I asked. Embryss turned to me, eyes wild with amusement.

"Because we are," Theo bored voice called out, ignoring his sister's glare.

"We inherited a special set of skills from our mother's side. Skills that can be quite deadly to those who upset us." Embryss snickered at my expression. "Don't look so horrified. You are safe as long as you serve a purpose for Prince Lochlan."

"And then what?' I asked, gazing at her different-colored eyes that danced with devilish mischief that drew me in. "You kill me?"

Theo chuckled darkly. "Oh no, little mortal, we play with you."

"So, torture is your thing." I leaned forward, throwing him a wink.

"Torture? That is such an asinine way of play." Theo's curved into a slight smile, picking at the dead skin near his nails. "Our playthings are brought to the brink of insanity and then stroked back down in such a way that they never want to leave."

"It is all quite personal." Embryss smirked, letting her blood-red lips curl up in a sinister grin. "I wonder what would drive a pretty little mortal like you mad?"

"You'll never get the chance to find out," I fired back. The tent's flaps billowed open as Eoghan stormed into the space. His feet hit the gravel under us with intense emotion that, if possible, could send tremors through the entire camp. Eoghan rounded the table to hover above me, body shaking with rage.

"You are unbelievable," he shouted, a single finger poking the middle of my chest.

I swatted the hand away, rising to my feet, standing tall against his towering frame. "Unbelievable? Would you have rather I allowed a Síth male to overpower me? I thought we were training for scenarios just like that."

"We train to ensure you can stand on your own in the Games." Eoghan's voice rose an octave. "Not for you to endanger the lives of every soldier in that tent. Do you even know who you were threatening with that blade?"

"A high-ranking official, I presume, by his inflated ego." I smirked at his seething eyes.

Eoghan snatched the underside of my chin, dragging me into him until we were only a breath away from each other's lips. I could feel the vibrations of the words come off them as he spoke. "He is the leading commander when I am not in this camp—meaning that a Pàidean is a step below my rank. He would have your head on a spike for your actions today if you were not a vital piece to the Prince's game strategy."

"Unhand me." I tried to pull back out of his touch, but Eoghan gripped harder on the skin, causing me to hiss in pain.

"You will fall in line, Caelen, if only for the time we are in this camp." Eoghan's hot words sent goosebumps down my arms. The burning world around us seemed to fade away as the two of us glared at each other. Every sound became a distant muffle as Embryss began to ramble on about something to her twin. My breath was hitched as I stared into Eoghan's eyes longer, the hazel swirls coming together in a magnetic brown color.

"The General, interesting choice, Spinner," a deep ancient voice echoed through my mind. Its menacing tone continued to speak, but this time in a language I did not understand. Something deep in my soul rumbled, warning me to pull away from Eoghan, but his intoxicating scent of cedar and mint drew me farther into him. I let out a light gasp, the sound sending Eoghan flying across the tents forest floor to put distance between us. We both watched each other, my shallow breathing the only sound I could hear. His eyes flicked down to my necklace in confusion.

Eoghan turned his attention toward Theo and Embryss. "Entertain her while I am gone."

"And how do you suppose we do that?" Theo's eyes wandered between the two of us with a knowing look.

"Show her the magic you two are always so smug about, but do not let her leave your sight. I will be back in an hour to collect her," Eoghan instructed and turned to retreat from the tent.

"Oh, this is going to be fun." Embryss's sing-song voice floated around me. Eoghan exited the tent, my uneasiness vanishing with him, only to be replaced by a hollow feeling deep in my chest.

———

The Twins radiated power. It misted around them like silver wisps, sending sparks of fear through those who dared to play with them. I sat on a tree stump, observing as Embryss maneuvered around her brother. She had explained that though they could perform most of the same spells, the Twins had taken a liking to very different sides of their magic. She specialized in the manipulation of the mind. Embryss could make you see, hear, or feel anything she wanted and then take it away entirely, sending you tumbling through a dark void until she released you. She described it as paralyzing the mind and molding it into a puppet she could toy with. On the other hand, Theo was the oracle, with the ability to see into every dark fear a person had ever had for his twin to use against their prey. The two of them were truly a terrifying duo.

Theo had begrudgingly explained that being an oracle meant he could see every path that could be taken by a person. All except for me. I could see by the deep furrow of his brow this angered him immensely. Embryss admitted she had not tried to use her power against me as it would upset Lochlan. It appeared she had a strange need to please everyone around her, and I couldn't tell if it was for her own gain or just a personality trait of the beautiful narcissist.

"I haven't got all day, sister," Theo hissed, his eyes held a glassy sheen to them as he flipped through her next moves. Embryss flashed a bright smile at him, continuing her prance around the trees. Theo rolled his eyes. "No, that scenario is just cruel, seeing as you were the one who tormented me enough that I gained that phobia."

"Just because you are my brother, does not mean I have to go easy on you." She giggled. Theo paused, turning to look at me and then back at his twin, who was grinning like a cat. Embryss cocked her head to one side, "Do you think he would be angry with me?"

"No," Theo hummed. "Not if it was for training purposes, and she agreed to it."

"Agreed to what?" I stood from my seat, watching both with a curious gaze.

"Would you please let me show you what I can truly do?" Embryss begged. I went to speak, but her shrill voice cut me off. "I promise not to be too hard on you. Plus, Theo can't even tell me your deep fears!"

"Way to rub it in, Em," Theo grumbled, throwing his hands up as he stormed away to hide in the tree's shade.

I blinked at Embryss as she watched me with joyous eyes. "Okay, but nothing that will maim me."

Embryss's smile deepened. "Maim is a harsh word. I like to

say my gifts give character to those I use them on. Now hold still."

My body went rigid as her bright eyes darkened, zeroing in on every part of me. I couldn't speak, my throat constricting, causing breathing to become obsolete. She released control of my limbs, and my hands automatically reached up to clutch at my throat. Black dots were beginning to float around my eyes as the air in my lungs disappeared. Fingers clawed deep into my skin, drawing blood as they went. The warm liquid did not travel far as I smeared it around my skin in my attempts to gain control again. My legs wobbled once before they buckled, and I hit the dirt floor in a heap of myself. There was a faint call for Embryss to stop, but she kept going, never blinking as my world wobbled in and out of view.

A firm tug in my chest grounded me to the earth, even as I so desperately wanted to fade into the comfort of the darkness. A large figure stepped in front of me, breaking Embyrss's control and bringing the world back in raging color.

"What the hell were you thinking?" Eoghan's voice boomed over the clearing. I fell forward, hands catching me, and I sucked in a ragged breath. The grassy floor squished between my fingertips, grounding me to the earth I had almost let fade away. Eoghan's voice continued on. "Embryss, are you even listening to me?"

"It wouldn't let me go." The female witch's voice shook. I turned my gaze up to watch the interaction in front of me. Theo had stepped up behind his twin, a comforting arm bringing her close to him as he whispered something in her ear. Embryss was shaking. "There is something protecting her. It was fighting against my magic. I couldn't escape its grip until you broke my line of sight. I was only going to blind her momentarily, but it was as if I couldn't run from that intoxicating voice."

"Voice?" I croaked out, still gripping tightly to the earth beneath me. Whispers of the sensual voice which had caressed my mind nights earlier echoed in my ears. Eoghan turned, eyes scanning me for injuries that were not gained from Embryss's magic. He neared me, stooping low to examine me further. I locked eyes with him, concern lacing their honey color. He reached out gently, stroking the side of my face causing my eyes to flutter shut. The feeling of panic subsided, replaced by an overwhelming sense of calm. It was like jumping into a river on a hot summer's day.

"It was coming from your necklace," Embryss's whispered, pointing one finger at the object. I groaned as the piece's metal hit my skin, the necklace beginning to grow hot as we spoke. The sizzle of skin was the last thing I heard before Embryss whispered, "It is back, and that kind of power is dark, girl. Do not let it consume you."

CHAPTER TWENTY TWO
LOCHLAN

Fire light danced on the mahogany bookshelves late into the night. Eoghan's panicked words rang in the back of my mind as I ventured farther into the depths of the library. The soft sound of rain pelted on the window Caelen sat near. She and Eoghan had returned from the camp rather unexpectedly last night, following an incident with Embryss. The sun had not even risen into the sky but with the heavy storm I was certain the rays would not be bestowing their warmth on to us for a while. The small reading nook was cut into stone, with a window that allowed the guest to see the mountainscape of the palace's land. On most nights, the visitor could barely make out the bats as they swirled around the peaks in the dark.

A leather-bound book laid open on Caelen's lap. Yellowing pages crinkled under her thumb and forefinger as she flipped through the fairytale book my mother had once read to me before bed. I shifted slightly, causing the oak flooring beneath me to creak. Caelen's head shot up, eyes finding mine in the dim light.

"Enjoying yourself, cailleach?" I asked, the question pooling from my lips in a sensual tone. Her eyes scanned my figure, landing on the book clutched in my grasp. I trained my gaze on the water droplets running down the windowpane behind her head. "Eoghan informed me of what happened at the camp."

Rolling her eyes, Caelen slammed the book of fairy tales shut. "Which part? The part where I threatened a soldier with a blade, or the incident with the witch twins?"

"I was informed of the Twins, but now I am dying to hear about the soldier who dared to cross you." I smirked, eyes slowly trailing down to meet her stare. "I am sure that was a sight to see."

"Eoghan was not happy with me," Caelen mumbled. She turned away, looking out of the window to avoid my eyes.

A deep chuckle rumbled in my chest. "Eoghan is never happy with anyone. You will get used to it."

"Not likely." She shrugged toward me. I stepped away from the bookcases, strolling over to hover over her. Placing a hand on the windowpane, I leaned forward, caging her into the reading nook.

"My mother would read me these stories here when I was a child," I hummed softly. Caelen looked up at me. A warmth gathered in my core as I reminisced on a happier time in my youth. "Those moments came to be my favorite spent with her."

"Loch-" Caelen whispered, unable to find the words to comfort either of us at the moment. A similar pain circled around her irises that I knew swam in my own. I could only reach out, letting my hand rest on hers which gripped tightly onto the book in her lap, knuckles turning white as she did. Her eyes flicked down to my touch as I absentmindedly stroked my thumb back and forth against her pale skin. We froze in this position for a moment more before I pulled away, the ghost of a smile tracing my lips.

"Come." I motioned her to follow me. "I have something I would like to show you."

Setting the book to the side, Caelen followed swiftly after me. My long strides made it hard for her to keep up as we maneuvered through the shelving, finally coming upon the restricted section, which was gated off. The metal hummed with the magic protecting the reading material behind it, making the hair on the back of my neck stand up straight. I breathed in the ward's powers, something deep inside me feeding on the energy that pulsated off it.

Reaching out, my fingers traced the underside of Caelen's braided hair and plucked a hairpin from the chocolate locks. She watched as I jabbed the metal into my skin and let the ruby liquid pool to the surface of my pointer finger. I placed my finger against the head of a serpent that coiled around the flattened lock, my blood soaking into the creature. It hissed before unlatching itself, and a spark of golden rays shimmered off the gate, letting the magic drain from its surface. Caelen sucked in a breath, eyes wide with wonder at the enchantment that rained down in front of her.

"Embryss has been quite fascinated with that necklace of yours since she was bewitched by it. I can't lie and say I have not been curious about it as well," I called towards her as I crossed through the threshold of the gate. The shuffle of feet followed behind me as Caelen raced after me.

"It is just a necklace, Lochlan. Nothing more, nothing less."

Craning my neck, I peered over my shoulder at her. "Are you sure of that, cailleach?"

My voice was void of emotion. She halted at the question, cocking her head to the side to examine my next move. I was aware of the legend of a necklace that had been lost to the first sister, hidden away from the hands of those who wanted to wield the power within it. Caelen claimed the piece had been handed down to the eldest daughter in the Elliston bloodline once the previous wearer had passed on. It was rumored to be a protection device for the wearer. But what was inside that swirling red encasing was powerful enough to wield itself outside its bound walls.

"Yes," Caelen replied bitterly.

"You are stubborn, I will give you that." I shook my head at her. "Eoghan and I believe that somewhere in these books, there will be something to assist us in finding where that necklace hanging around your neck originated from. I could feel the power pulsing out of it the moment you turned to me in the throne room that first night, but after Embryss explained her experience with it, I think we need to get a handle on it before it overtakes you."

"Overtakes me?" She scoffed. "It has been in my family for centuries, and not every woman that has worn it has never gone mad."

"They died an early death, though, have they not?"

Caelen sucked in a sharp breath, eyes roaming wildly around the room as she recalled a distant memory. "Yes."

"Magic does not always drive one mad, but instead drains the wielder if they do not understand how to harness its power."

Caelen met my gaze with a dark look. "Then show me where to start."

CHAPTER TWENTY THREE
CAELEN

My ribs cracked together as Ainsley yanked the corset strings tighter around my body. I gasped, both hands gripping down on the backside of the metal bed frame, stabilizing myself from toppling back into her. Ainsley huffed at me in annoyance, pulling once again before tying the strings together and tucking them into the light linen skirt she had put me in. I was dressed in a dark blue color that, in some lights, could be mistaken for black. Standing straight, the fabric shimmered with golden flecks in the dim lighting.

"They clean you up well," Eoghan's deep voice called out behind me. I turned to see him standing in the middle of the room. All three wraiths had conveniently made themselves scarce. We had not spoken since the strange, intimate moment I had felt at the camp, and I would be lying if I had said it had not been replaying in my mind on a loop. Now standing before him once again, the air around us held a heated desire that was begging me to step closer to him. I rolled my shoulders back, driving the delusional feelings out of my mind. He was nothing more than the male who had stolen me from my land and forced me into this one.

I shook my head at his comment, letting the loose curls that Cora had framed my face with fall in front of my eyes. She had kept my hair minimal, pulling it into a half updo with the top section snaked into a bun that rested in the middle of my skull.

Eoghan cleared his throat. "We should go. The team is gathering in Lochlan's study before the opening ceremonies begin."

"Okay," I breathed out, letting my feet carry me toward him. His ghostly touch traced against my spine, sending a buzz of electricity rattling through my veins. I inhaled sharply, cursing myself for reacting to his touch in such a way. Eoghan trailed behind me as I began my descent down the stairs, calling out over my shoulder tot the General. "You've been avoiding me."

"I have been patching up your messes."

I threw a glare over my shoulder, meeting his playful glance. "My messes? I think you should be thanking me for the entertainment I graced you with."

The cheeky smile slid from my face as my foot got tangled up in the hem of my skirt, sending me tumbling down the stairwell. Eoghan's firm grip caught me around my hips and pulled me into his chest. I heaved out a couple of breaths letting my head fall back against his shoulder. Eoghan's hot breath brushed against my neck, but the only thought I could think about was tracing the pattern of him against my hip bone. We both were frozen in the moment. My eyes wandered down to the jagged stone steps that I almost managed to impale myself on.

"Thank you," I breathed out. At the sound of my voice, Eoghan's grip tightened before loosening altogether, letting me step away from his warmth.

"There you go again, throwing yourself into danger." He chuckled, but the sound was void of any emotion. "If you wanted me to save you, there is no need for the dramatics, *sweetheart*."

My heart jumped at the pet name. I licked my lips, turning around to throw him a narrowed look, but I am sure the Sith male could hear my thundering heart with his enhanced hearing, although if he could, he did not lead on.

"I don't need saving," I growled out.

Eoghan shook his head. "So next time, I should allow you to break your neck on the stone?"

"Shut up." I whipped around, picked up my skirt, and descended the rest of the stairs. The irritation that accompanied me when he was around washed away any bubbly feeling I had previously felt. Eoghan followed lazily behind me. I could feel his eyes burning into my exposed back. We rounded the corner into the portrait hall, and I halted at the fork in the hallway.

"It's this way." Eoghan maneuvered around me to take a right down a dimly lit corridor. I paused for a moment, letting him get slightly ahead of me before I followed. The entire team would be in the Prince's private study, a first for us, and the thought made me nauseous.

On top of the twins despising me, I knew that the other realms were not fond of Lochlan choosing a human champion for the Games, which made me a target. I could put on a show, one that implied I was unbothered by the whispers that had been flitting through these halls but deep down, the pressure of what was at stake for the entire team was starting to affect me. My nights were filled with tossing and turning, allowing little time to rest. I knew Lochlan had taken notice of my lack of appetite at meals as well, his knowing eyes watching as I picked at the food in front of me. I could not fail. If I did, Lochlan would lose his crown, and I would never be reunited with my sister. My feet carried me forward as Eoghan reached the end of the hallway.

Eoghan grasped down on the door's handle, twisting it to reveal Sylas lounging on Lochlan's desk, a burgundy liquid swirling around an ornate glass while the Prince was sprawled out in a chair behind her. His lips wrapped around a matching goblet, taking a long drink, eyes meeting mine as I passed through the study's threshold. In the corner farthest from the door, the Twins stood, talking in hushed whispers to each other. Theo watched me with a hardened look, keeping his sister's attention away from my gaze.

"Cailleach." Lochlan's smirk deepened as he watched me through dark lashes. I rounded the desk to greet to him, taking the cup from his hands and bringing it to my lips. Lochlan's hand wrapped around my wrist, holding the cup steady against my mouth. He quirked an eyebrow. "I wouldn't if I were you, Caelen."

Raising one of my own brows, I gave in, allowing him to pull the cup away from me and back onto his lips. Sylas leaned back, golden hair spilling onto the dark wood of the desk, "It's not for mortals, you beautiful fool."

"Will it kill me if I were to drink it?" I watched the now-empty glass in front of me.

"No," Sylas purred. "It is Sìth wine and has been used to seduce mortals into doing what we please with them for centuries. Addicting little drink but quite entertaining."

I hummed at her answer, meeting Lochlan's dark eyes. He turned towards the others in the room, setting down the glass in front of him. "Caelen and I will meet you all at the ceremonies. I want an audience with our champion. Alone."

Sylas leaped from the desk and sauntered out of the room with the Twins following close behind her. Eoghan stood rigid, still in the doorway, as he watched Lochlan with a narrowed gaze. His lips were pursed slightly, studying each move the Prince made. Lochlan nodded towards him. "Don't worry, Eoghan, I will be on time this year."

"You are never on time, Loch," he said, lips pulling into a ghostly smile before he turned out of the room, doors coming closed after him. I swiveled back to the prince, but his eyes were still watching the doorway from which his General had just retreated.

"You wanted an audience with me? Why so formal, Lochlan?" I asked, my voice playful even as my nerves began to reveal themselves.

"Habit, I suppose." Lochlan leaned back in the chair, his eyes raking over my appearance. I resisted the urge to squirm under his scrutiny. One hand came to his mouth, resting the knuckle closest to his thumb on his lower lip as he continued to stare. Dark eyes pierced into me as if he was determining how to take out an enemy. The room chilled with the buzzing of his power. Where Eoghan's was a searing caress on my skin, Lochlan's power was suffocating, reeling me in and stealing the air from my lungs as it pulsed through the room. He sighed, pulling me out of my trance. "You should take a moment to prepare yourself for what you will endure tonight. The courts are vicious in a normal game, but you seem to have ruffled quite a few feathers this year. Once you are officially announced to the rest of the realms' tonight, every creature will be praying to the Gods for your downfall."

"I can handle myself," I lie. The courts could wield power that could eliminate me with only a blink of an eye.

Lochlan chuckles. "Oh, I am sure you can with that smart mouth and training Eoghan has begun with you. Still, I must ask you to be on your best behavior unless otherwise provoked, Caelen."

"What constitutes as being provoked?" I asked, one side of my lips quirking up in a devious smile.

"You will know if the time comes." Lochlan's eyes were glowing with determination. "Once we leave this room, everyone on the team will take on their chosen persona that we feel most comfortable displaying to the other competitors. We cannot show an ounce of weakness. It will be exploited in the Games, if given the chance."

I meet his gaze with a glare of my own. "And I am a weakness, Lochlan?"

"No." He stands, bringing up a hand and lightly stroking down the side of my face. "The other realms' champions may be dangerous, but you, dear cailleach, are more powerful than anyone gives you credit for."

"I am mortal, Loch. I have no power."

Lochlan's touch traveled down to my collarbone, picking up the swirling red pendant. "I wouldn't be so sure of that, Caelen. This necklace may be the same one born of legend, which ensnared one of the most powerful Sìths in our histories. You wouldn't be able to contain it if you didn't have an ounce of Sìth blood running through your veins. I know it. Eoghan knows it. And I think somewhere deep down, you know it as well."

I stepped away from him, watching his attention linger on the jewelry piece. My heart skipped a beat as his words rattled around my brain, but I couldn't deny how the pendant now pulsed against my skin in rhythm with my heartbeat as Lochlan complimented it. Complimented whatever was trapped inside.

Without skipping a beat, Lochlan bowed his head toward me and rounded the other side of the desk. Just as he was about to exit, his voice called back toward me, "Good luck tonight, my mortal champion."

***

Enchantments and smoke hung heavy in the air as I stepped through the castle's grand entrance. The doors were held open independently, allowing me to see the festivities occurring across the stone walkway. A large fire engulfed the burn pile in the middle of the field that I had once run from Eoghan in.

There were hundreds of creatures swarming the grassy area, but the Sìth lords and ladies were the ones that grasped my attention immediately. Each one of them held themselves like Gods who graced us with their supernatural beauty. Blurs of color circled the field where each of the realm's flags waved in sync with each other. I was to meet the team under our own, but the dark color sent a wave of emotion through me as I watched the snake slither in the breeze.

Pulling my gaze from it, I returned my attention to the path in front of me. At the end of the stone walkway, a woman with electric teal eyes that resembled an eel leaned sensually into a male with bright red hair. He lounged up against a large column as he sipped from a goblet. My eyes caught his, the woman's words losing his interest as he zeroed in on me. Shadows and bright colors began to swirl in my vision as I met the male's gaze directly. Silent words spilled from his lips as he drew me into his spell. I stepped forward, falling into the male's calming gaze. One single finger beckoned me in.

The pulsing thrum of the necklace jerked me back, causing me to stumble through the entrance of the castle. A large hand steadied me from toppling over in my attempts to run and hide. I turned, meeting the hazel eyes of Eoghan, his hardened stare watching me closely. Words failed me. My lips opened and closed like a floundering fish on the land, but nothing came out. Lifting my hands to my throat, I gripped down, pleading with Eoghan to help me.

A guttural growl ripped through the air. "Enough, Tyr."

The redhead male's low chuckle echoed in my ear before a rush of air reentered my lungs as his hold released me. Eoghan gripped down on my shoulders, holding me in place. I craned my neck to peer over my shoulder at Tyr, a deep smirk plastered across his face as he reached up to condescendingly wave in my direction. I lunged for him, the promise of being on my best behavior slipping from my thoughts.

My spine slammed back into Eoghan. His angry breath brushed up against the column on my neck as he spoke. "That is enough from you as well, sweetheart."

"You don't control me." I squirmed against him, trying to slip from his grip, but it only tightened.

"No," Eoghan groaned as my heel met his shin. "But right down in that field is a prince, who is counting on the both of us to make it there in one piece. Now straighten out your skirt and get the wild beast inside of you in check."

"Fine," I growled out. Eoghan removed his hold on me, and I shot forward towards the grassy field. Turning to look at the General once more, I threw him a gesture that made a woman with dark purple hair gasp in shock before I slipped into the crowd, ignoring his glare. Amongst the creature's beauty, I stuck out like a sore thumb. I ducked my head, masking myself with the smoke that traveled around the bonfire and ventured farther to the black flag.

The Prince's back was towards me as he spoke with his second. Sylas twirled a curl around her finger, looking bored with whatever he was speaking of.

"Your General is on my last nerves, Loch." I stomped around him. His amused eyes met mine, waiting for an explanation. I poked his chest. "Remind him that next time one of these beasts decides to take control of my sharp tongue, that he has no right to stop me from cutting theirs from their head."

"I will remind the lot of you again that I am in love with this mortal girl." Sylas leaned back, racking her eyes up and down my body. I flushed at her admiration.

"Aren't we all." Eoghan's voice dripped with disdain from behind me. "She is the life of every gathering."

"Leave her be, Eoghan," Lochlan countered, rolling his eyes at our antics. "The ceremony is about to begin. Once my father concludes his speech Eoghan and I will escort Caelen to be announced. Then the lot of you can find whatever nefarious acts that please you for the night."

Brilliant light burst through the sky as the fire sprites dashed into the stars in a synchronized dance. They twirled amongst each other, creating patterns of sparks in their path. It was the most fantastical display of the Sith's version of fireworks. I stared in awe, the light thump of drums beginning to play around us. The pulsating beat of the instruments echoed through the fields and into the heels of my feet. Closing my eyes, I breathed in the night air, savoring how the fire's smoke burned slightly against my lungs. It reminded me of Draíocht Night. It reminded me of home.

Peeling my eyes open, I met Eoghan's curious ones. He watched me take in the ceremonies with a particular childlike wonder. A tug in his direction caused me to step toward the General, but the booming voice of the King halted me midstep.

"Welcome to the Millennial Aesira Games." Lochlan's father stood on a large stage made of stone, Elara at his side in a midnight blue dress that cut down low. He was dressed in a matching-colored suit, and a flowing cape lined with fur billowed behind him. A black jewel-encrusted crown sat upon his head.

It gleamed under the sprite's light. "The Bás realm is honored to yet again to host the opening ceremonies for such a pivotal game. We honor those who have fallen and each of the realm's sacrifices over the last thousand years. Your contributions have not gone unnoticed."

A shiver traveled up my spine as his eyes met my own. There was a wicked gleam in his gaze that made my blood turn cold. His eyes left mine, turning back to the eager ears of the realms. "Our champions have shown true strength in their quest to capture their realm's flags. This year's lot is exceptional in power and wit. In a few moments, we will reveal each of them to you. Enjoy the Games but remember not all is as it appears in them."

Elara stepped away from the King, her hands wrapping around a flaming staff. Returning back to the King, he grasped a strong hand around the wood and descended the stone podium until he was in front of a crystal bowl filled with bright orange liquid.

"Let the Games begin," he shouted before dipping the flames in the orange substance appearing to extinguish the fire. The bowl shook, a crackling sound rattling around us than a large bird covered in flames shot from the crystal. I gasped, staggering back from the sight as everyone around me cheered with glee. The creature spread its wings, twirling before it transformed into a glowing woman, her bright orange hair shining in the moonlight.

"That is Kyar," Lochlan's voice whispered into my ear. "She is a phoenix, one of the last of her kind."

"A phoenix?" I kept my eyes glued on the flaming girl, her glimmering fire spinning like a turn top in the stars as she continued her show.

"They are very rare, but their ability to heal is coveted widely through the realms," Lochlan explained. I peeled my gaze from the girl to look at him. "She is magnificent in her true form."

"She is." I grinned at him. The sounds of cheering melded into a euphoric beat of the drums and fiddle as they began to play into the night air.

Lochlan's palm traced down my spine, landing in the small of my back and guiding me forward. "Come, we must take our places in the lineup."

Four other champions and their companions stood near the stone platform the King had just exited. I could feel their searing stares turn toward Lochlan and me as we arrived at the end of the line. I stepped back into a hard body, knowing immediately that it was Eoghan.

"Hold your head high, Caelen." His words tickled the back of my neck. I rolled my shoulders and tipped my chin up slightly. "Just like that, sweetheart. Don't let any one of them see your fear. Show them the wild beast that I would love to tame."

Before I could respond, the red-haired male from earlier stepped toward Lochlan. His teal eyes met mine as he shook the Prince's hand. A predatory smile spread across his lips. "This must be your mortal champion that everyone is so fascinated by. Is it, not Lochlan?"

"This Caelen Elliston." Lochlan's left hand reached for my own. I placed my palm in his and allowed him to guide me forward. "Cailleach, this is Tyr, the Crown Prince of Cogadh."

"Yes, the Druids of War," I hummed. Tyr bent to lift my right hand in his, laying a single kiss against my knuckles. His lips lingered for a moment, taking his time to brush them against each knuckle before slowly rising to tower over me.

"You have taught her well, Lochlan." Tyr eyed me with curiosity. "Though her manners meeting royalty could use some work. It is customary to bow when in the presence of a prince, starlight."

I ground my teeth together. "And when I see someone worthy of bowing to, I shall do so."

Lochlan's hand gripped down on mine tighter, waiting for the War Prince to strike against me, but Tyr only let out a bellowing laugh that echoed through the air, causing the other champions to turn in our direction. "She is a wildcard, Lochlan, be sure to keep her under your thumb, or I might sweep in to have her for myself."

Tyr waltzed backward, taking me in as he bowed in a dramatic fashion toward me. "I look forward to competing against you in the Games, starlight."

CHAPTER TWENTY FOUR
LOCHLAN

Delightful screams flitted through the air as the court jester ensnared the crowd with a dramatic show as he recounted a story from a past game. His brightly colored costume sparkled under the firelight, sending rays shining onto the stage in front of him. He slammed his hands together, consuming himself in pitch black smoke as he disappeared from view, only to appear once again sat upon one of the large wooden poles at the right corner of the stage.

A raven-haired beauty from the Todhchaí, the Druids of Prophecies, stepped onto the stage. She was dressed in a bright orange dress with sheer long sleeves that were littered with iridescent stones. Her irises were white, glowing against the duller shades around them as she menacingly gazed down at the crowd. A male with pale hair stood behind the female with his hands clasped in front of him. An untrained eye would assume this meant his guard was down, but I could see the shimmering wave of a protection shield wrapping around the two of them. Turning my attention to Caelen, she had her head cocked to the side, taking in the first champion of the night.

"That is Soren." I leaned down to her, speaking softly in her ear. "Her mother holds the Todhchaí throne."

"And her father?" Caelen kept her eyes trained on Soren as the female stepped from the stage with the help of her male companion.

"He is an Elder," I stated. Caelen shot me a narrowed look, and I shook my head slightly. "She has no advantage over any of us. Her father does not claim her. I feel as though this might be her way of telling him to piss off if she was to win."

She chuckled, allowing Eoghan and I to guide her forward as the line to the stage moved. Tyr waltzed onto the middle of the stage next. His chest was puffed out, arrogance dripping off him. The crowd drank it in, females tossed wildflowers onto the stage, and males chanted in the ancient Sìth language over and over. Tyr stretched his arms out, spinning in a slow circle as he took in the praise. His attention turned to Caelen, and he bowed lightly in a condescending way.

"He's a favorite," she mumbled, earning a snicker from Eoghan, who still stood behind me. She craned her head back to stare up at him. "As much as you annoy me, you will never compare to that."

"Duly noted, sweetheart." A wicked smirk spread across the face of my General as he spoke.

"I would remember this face if I were you, Caelen." I pulled her attention back to the stage. A female with chestnut brown hair and lashes to match stepped onto the platform. Her shimmering blue gown clung to her like the ocean as it washed onto the land. She appeared timid as the crowd began to clap for her, but she shot a dark glare toward the creatures below. A few of the smarter ones shrunk away from her stare, their clapping faltering as they went. Rolling my shoulders back, I watched as she scanned the crowd, memories of her ruthless tricks floating across my mind.

"Your cousin is looking rather deadly tonight." Eoghan's voice dripped with sarcasm.

Caelen whipped her head around to gauge my reaction. "Cousin?"

"My mother's youngest sister was betrothed to the Prince of the Beatha Realm." I made a nonchalant gesture towards the Princess of the Druids of Life. A low bun sat at the base of her neck and accentuate the back of the blue dress as it dipped low down her spine. "One thing led to another, and Freya came to be. She has been a thorn in my backside ever since."

"She has a liking for ripping out the hearts of those who wrong her with a spiked vine," Eoghan mused. "Murderous little thing."

"Gives a new meaning to putting your life in someone else's hands." Caelen's words sliced through the air. Freya's gaze caught mine, her eyes like daggers piercing into my heart. I nodded in acknowledgment, making my cousin sneer at me. Caelen's throat bobbed slightly. "I think she heard me."

"She wouldn't dare get on Lochlan's bad side this close to the Games, Caelen." Eoghan shoved me forward lightly. There was one final champion before us, making his ascent of the stage's stairs. I closed my eyes, listening as the jester named off the Fírinne's, the Druids of Truth's champion. Axiom was a large male with muscles that rippled down his body like a God. Golden tattooed skin peeked out from a rolled-up tunic shirt. I had very little knowledge of Axiom, but Sylas had reported that the newest champion to this century's Games had been trained in the depths of the Ralston Caverns.

Ralston was a place of nightmares, where every creature that haunted you lurked behind caged bars and shadowed whispers. Why the Elders would allow a prisoner a chance to capture the Fírinne's flag was a mystery that even Sylas, who had once resided in the caverns' walls, could not answer.

"I think I am going to be sick," Caelen mumbled next to me. I glanced at Eoghan, who stood relaxed behind her, eyes rolling into the back of his head.

"Well, don't lose your cool over Axiom," he groaned, throwing a hand toward the male. "His size may be the only advantage he has over you."

She opened her mouth to respond, but I interrupted her. "You can continue your lovers' quarrel later."

I placed a foot on the first step, holding my hand out for her to grasp. "Come now, cailleach, let's give them an introduction they will not forget."

She took my hand, gulping down her fear as her face morphed into an emotionless void that even I could not read. We climbed the steps together, the blinding lights of the stage shining down upon us as we reached its center. In the distance, I could hear the jester announcing Caelen's name, but my eyes were zeroed in on my father. He sat on a jewel-encrusted wooden throne in the center of the field. Less ornate thrones for the other realms' rulers sat on either side of him. He raised a single brow at me, waiting for me to crack under his stare.

"Do you trust me?" I asked Caelen softly, eyes never leaving my father's.

"Yes," Caelen responded, a smile pulling at the corners of her lips as she drank in the crowd's cheers.

My shadows began to pool near our feet, slithering around us until they became a cyclone of smoke that spun in time with the beating drums echoing through the lands. Caelen's breath caught in the back of her throat as they stole the light from the sky, leaving the two of us in pure darkness. I took a breath in, summoning them to do as I had instructed them earlier this evening when I spoke with Ainsley about Caelen's wardrobe for the night. As I exhaled, they rushed away from us quickly and into the crowd. The dark wave washed through the creatures before us, their screams of terror soon turning into delight.

Casting my gaze on my mortal champion, her once plain dress had transformed into a glittering gown. The leather bodice hugging her upper half was adorned in deep ruby jewels that coiled around her figure in a swirling pattern, ending with the head of a serpent that rested on her left shoulder. Its onyx eyes glimmered in the light. Gauzy red and black material pooled around her legs, a slit following either side of her hips, leaving a single panel of fabric to cover her.

Without missing a beat, Caelen stepped forward, eyes staring directly into Elara's as she rounded my father's throne to watch the spectacle I had orchestrated. I held my breath as

Caelen dipped into a deep curtsy, arms extended outward as she did. Her head was held high, watching the King's second with a fiery look before standing tall once more and descending the stairs.

Chapter Twenty Five
Caelen

I raced down the front steps of the stage, the skirt of the dress that had materialized from Lochlan's shadows swishing against my heated skin. Footsteps followed close behind me as I rounded the fire and descended the hill back toward the castle. A hand caught my upper arm, halting me in my path.

"You aren't angry with me, are you, cailleach?" Lochlan's voice was playful, but his sad eyes gave him away. I shook my head at him, not sure if I would be able to keep down the bile that was rising in my throat if I opened my mouth to respond. Lochlan sighed, releasing my arm and running a single hand over his chin. "Good."

"Why does she get the pretty dress, and I have to be forced to wear this old thing?" Embryss's musical voice floated around us. I let out a light laugh as she came into view. Her deep purple dress shimmered in the firelight as she moved closer. The neckline was cut down her body, almost reaching the center of her slender stomach. The female could wear a burlap sack, and she would still outshine me any day.

"You, my little witch, could have any jewel in this kingdom." Lochlan turned to wink at her. "But jewels have not been what you have desired for quite some time."

"No, they haven't." Embryss pouted, her bottom lip sticking out slightly. "It's really just the thought that counts, Prince Lochlan."

Lochlan chuckled, shaking his head slightly. A few dark curls fell into his face, giving the Prince a boyish charm that was typically hidden away. "And what can I do to make it up to you, Em?"

"Dance with me." She thrust out a hand as the rhythm behind her picked up.

Lochlan smiled at me. "Will you be alright if I indulge her for a few dances, Caelen?"

"I think I can manage," I said, my voice coming out stronger than I had anticipated. Embryss let out a happy squeal as she reached forward and pulled the Prince into the throngs of people spinning around the moonlit field.

I turned back around, feet guiding me toward a small table with glasses filled with dark liquor. I snatched one up, tossing the drink back, ignoring the burn that followed. After a few moments, I lost count of how many of the small goblets I had drunk, but the warmth that was consuming my body now was overpowering the anxiety I felt when I fled from the stage.

My hips began to sway in time with a fiddle, hands roaming the planes of my body as I tossed my head back to stare at the moon. Its bright light appeared to be casting a spotlight on me, and I reveled in its cool touch. A foreign hand caught my hip, pulling me back into its figure. I sucked in a sharp breath as whoever was behind me moved with my hips, finding my rhythm and matching it. I tossed my head back against their shoulder, letting the stranger kiss down the side of my neck. My breath hitched as they found the sensitive part at the crook of my neck. Slinging up my right arm, I raked my hands through their hair and let out a giggle.

As fast as we had begun our dance, it was over, my body flying away from the stranger and into another's arms. I turned to look over my shoulder at my dance partner, coming face to face with the male who had accompanied Soren this evening.

A low hiss broke through his clenched teeth. "We weren't finished with our dance, General."

I stretched my neck to see Eoghan watching the fair-haired male with a deadly look. He clenched his teeth, jaw popping in and out as his grip on my arm tightened. I moaned in pain, but he ignored it.

The blond male smirked. "I have never tasted mortal blood, but I have heard it is like pure gold. Would you like to share a taste?"

Eoghan pushed me behind him. "Threaten to harm her again, and you will not make it to the first task in one piece."

Holding up his hands in mock surrender, the male backed away. "Don't worry, little mortal, your blood will be mine soon."

I shuddered at the thought, watching as he disappeared into the crowd. The pure ecstasy I had been feeling moments ago was gone, and now, just having my eyes open made me want to be sick. I bent at the knee, letting my dress pool around me before I sat on the grass beneath me.

"What are you doing?" Eoghan barked at me. Ignoring him, I placed my head in my hands, trying to get the world around me to stop spinning. I could feel his looming presence towering over me. "Caelen, I asked you a question."

"I am sitting to ensure I do not hurl on you," I called up to him. A light hand on my knee jolted me out of my position. Eoghan was now crouched in front of me, anger still licking the golden flecks of his eyes. I smiled, reaching out to place a hand on his cheek. "You have pretty eyes."

"Did you drink the wine?" Eoghan's gaze flicked over to the table. "Sylas warned you not to touch it."

"Sylas isn't the boss of me, and neither are you," I scoffed. Eoghan narrowed his gaze at me. Waving a finger toward the goblets, I added, "Also, how was I to know it wasn't what we drink at meals? It all appears the same to me."

"You should have gone inside after the ceremony," Eoghan scolded. My vision flashed red, and I shot up from my spot. Was he insinuating that I needed to hide away in a tower like a helpless creature?

I hovered over him. "I didn't need you to save me tonight."

Eoghan rose slowly, his nose brushing up against mine as he went. "Do you know what Cashel is?"

"Sith?" I responded with a roll of my eyes. Eoghan snatched the column of my neck, forcing me to look up at him. I tried to pull away, but his grip only tightened around my windpipe.

"Cashel is a Slaugh." Eoghan leaned in, his breath tickling my cheeks as he spoke. "A demon hidden behind a powerful enchantment spell to ensure he blends in tonight. Cashel enjoys feasting on his victims before stealing their souls. Would you enjoy spending eternity in the clutches of a demon, Caelen?"

"I can protect myself," I growled out. My foot shot up, connecting with Eoghan's shin. He hissed out in pain, and his grip on me loosened. I darted away from him, racing across the grounds of the castle. My feet pounded against the stone walkway as I swung around the courtyard and into a hidden entrance of the gardens. A pair of hushed whispers floated in between the flowers. I strained my ears to try to hear what they were saying. A hand wrapped around my face, silencing the scream that rippled through me as I was yanked back into the large rose bushes. Their thorny stems protruded outward, just begging to draw blood from their next victims.

"Do not make a sound." Eoghan's hushed voice was urgent. I breathed through my nose, leaning back into him as we traveled deeper into the shadows of the garden's hedges. The leaves shielded us from the intruders lurking in the maze of flowers.

"Spread out," a deep unfamiliar voice called out in the silence. "I want the mortal champion found and brought to me."

Eoghan's grip around my hips tightened, grounding me to him as my knees buckled. I closed my eyes, trying to match my breathing to his as the sounds of running echoed around us. His hand traveled down, softly grasping at the column of my throat and tugging me closer. We both stilled, but neither of us moved to pull away from the other. I cursed myself for enjoying the feeling of his hand wrapped around my throat in such an intimate way. For noticing how his fingers flexed lightly as he dug them into my skin. The light prick of pain sending a swelling heat across my body. I focused back on the garden and noticed it was silent.

Not even the flutter of the sprites' wings could be heard. The eerie silence only lasted a moment longer before the rumble of an explosion in the distance rocked the earth beneath us. My eyes flew open, looking towards the sky that was now covered in orange smoke that resembled the same symbol that had stained the letter Lochlan had been delivered. A large scorpion lit up the night air making my stomach twist in fear. Then the screaming began.

Eoghan shoved me from our hiding space. I stumbled out of his grip before turning toward him. I didn't have a weapon on me, but I could see Eoghan had come prepared with a small dagger he pulled from his boot. Reaching into his jacket pocket, he pulled a vial full of fluorescent green liquid and turned towards me.

"You need to get back to your room. When you arrive, use this to create a line behind your door. No one but Lochlan or I will be able to cross the threshold once this is in place." Eoghan shoved it into my palm, closing his hand around my own. "Oh, and try not to get it on your skin."

I shot him a crazed look. "What about you?"

"What about me?"

"You can't just go down there into that madness," I shouted over the ricochet of explosions happening in the field.

Eoghan chuckled darkly. "It is my job, Caelen, and besides, a few rebels will be easy enough to eradicate."

Opening my mouth, I almost told him to be careful, but clamped it shut immediately. I didn't care. I couldn't care. Nodding numbly, I spun on my heel and raced toward the garden's glass doors. Flinging them open, I bounded into the hallway. My feet slipped on the slick hardwood floor, sending me skating around until I managed to get a hold of the wall. There was a bang at the end of the corridor as rebels entered the castle. Gathering my skirts, I hiked the hem above my ankles and ran as fast as I could toward the hallway of portraits. The pounding footsteps behind me beat in time with my racing heart.

"You can run from us, mortal champion, but you can never outrun your destiny," a lone rebel voice called toward me as I reached the edge of the staircase. Taking the stone steps two at a time, I made my way to the landing in record time. My door was open, and I could hear the sound of someone shuffling about as I approached. A flash of auburn hair floated around the bed as I entered. A set of polished silverware was dumped across the floor, and I shot forward, picking up a knife as the rebel noticed my presence. Slowing, the female turned to face me, eyes widening as she scanned my body.

"Oh, my, aren't you a prize." Her eyes zeroed in on the necklace, a greedy look coming over her face. She lunged forward, right hand swiping out to grasp the chain around my neck. I leaned back, her nails scratching across my chest. Gasping in pain, I blindly swung the steak knife at the rebel's face. The blade connected with her cheek, and blood began to pool down her pale skin. She clutched at her face as she roared, "You bitch."

Her fist swung out, connecting with my jaw. Blood filled my

mouth, and my vision began to waver as she came at me again. I ducked, just barely missing the blow. The momentum of her punch made her stumble forward, and I took the opportunity to connect my knee with her gut. She wheezed, falling onto her hands and knees as she gasped for air. I spun around, raising my foot and slamming it down into her spine.

The sickening crunch of her face hitting the hard floor below her echoed through the room. My hand latched onto her shoulder, rolling her body over and meeting her bloodshot eyes. Stepping over her, I bent at the knee, straddling either side of her hips as she struggled underneath me. I leaned forward, grasping both of her wrists in one hand and hoisting them over her head as I held them in place.

"What were you looking for?" I asked through clenched teeth. The female spat, little spit droplets splattering across my cheeks. Slamming the knife against her windpipe, I dug the dull blade into her skin. "Are you feeling more talkative now?"

"You awoke the Gods when you arrived in the realms." She smiled up at me, her teeth covered in ruby liquid. I grimaced as it began to trickle out the corners of her mouth. A sickening laugh broke through her lips as she continued. "Have you ever heard the songbird sing, little mortal?"

"What did you just say?" I growled, the words of my mother flashing across my mind. The blade dug deeper into her skin, making my captor choke on her own laugh. Dark liquid was beginning to soak through the blade. The feeling of it squishing between my fingertips made my skin buzz with energy.

"Caelen," a familiar male's voice called through the thick

fog that was beginning to coat my mind. Boots covered in mud came into view as they stood next to the rebel's head. "I can take it from here, sweetheart."

I slowly peeled my eyes away from the female and trailed up the long legs of the voice's body. Eoghan's hazel eyes blazed with fury as he examined my face. I sighed, lifting the weapon away from the rebel's throat, and handed it to the General. He folded his fingers around the handle of the knife, pulling it away from my hand. Eoghan reached out, offering me his hand to take. I hesitated, gaze wandering back to the female underneath me.

"I will give Mairead your love when I see her again." The rebel's smile deepened. Without hesitation, I slammed my elbow into her eye socket and stood from my place as she writhed in pain.

"Dispose of this filth as you see fit, General," I spoke, voice void of any emotion that would give away the anger that was currently coursing through my veins before turning on my heel and heading into the bathroom. Slamming the door behind me, I gripped the edge of the countertop, an angry scream ripping through my lips.

Pulling my stare from the marble, I met my own glare in the mirror. A ghostly smile tugged at my lips, the pulsing red jewel hanging on my chest, making the room glow. "What have you gotten mixed up in since I have been gone, Mai?"

CHAPTER TWENTY SIX
CAELEN

Morning sun beat down on my skin. I leaned my neck back, basking in its warmth as I tried to not vomit all over Eoghan's shoes as he spoke to Sylas in a hushed tone. I was ushered out of my bed this morning by the sister wraiths in order to arrive at the entrance of the stables before the first task began. Ainsley had tried to shield my view of the blood of the rebel, which still stained the hardwood floor, but it was no use.

The events of last night had rattled me, and now I felt as if every creature in the task today would be able to smell the nerves pouring off of me. Rolling my neck back and forth, I tried to relax the tension in my muscles. Heavy boots crunched over the gravel as they approached us. I peeled open my eyes to meet the sneer of Theo. Embryss was nowhere to be seen, which I found odd.

"Where are the others?" Sylas asked. She rounded Eoghan, a light jump in her steps. Well, at least one of us was excited about the blood bath we would be facing today.

"Lochlan was pulled away by Elara. She wanted to discuss

our plan of action for today's task." Theo picked at his fingernails, tone bored with the simple question.

I snorted inwardly. "We have a plan? That's news to me."

"Yes, the team has a plan." Theo narrowed his eyes at me. "But when all you can only offer us is a messy throw of a knife as support, we saw fit that you were excluded from the knowledge."

"Theo," Eoghan growled in warning. "I would watch your tongue if I were you. She handled herself perfectly fine last night during the attack."

"I would hardly constitute that as an attack." Sylas chuckled darkly. "They came to fight but ended up being picked off one-by-one. There wasn't even enough blood to stain the grass."

My stomach churned, my mind traveling back to the blood that squelched between my fingertips as I dug the blade deeper into the female's throat. A sick realization overcame me. I enjoyed the harm I had inflicted. It made me feel powerful. Turning my gaze away from the two of them, I met Eoghan's pinched expression, eyes darkening with anger as Sylas continued about the events of last night.

"Go find Embryss." Eoghan cut through Sylas's words, silencing the female. She nodded at him before she began pulling Theo along after her to find his twin. I let out a shaky breath as they descended the hill towards the castle.

"I thought you would like some time to gather your thoughts before Lochlan and our transporter arrive to bring us to the arena," Eoghan mumbled as he turned his back on me to stalk into the stables. I followed him, a question burning at the back of my throat. The same one that had kept me up all last night.

"My thoughts are the furthest from the arena at the moment." I eyed him, taking in his relaxed demeanor. "How can you be so composed after what occurred last night?"

"I assume you think a small rebel attack would rock me." Eoghan lifted an eyebrow at my narrowed gaze. "It is a common occurrence, and there were no deaths other than their own."

My jaw slightly hung open at his words. "But weren't you and Lochlan worried about the rebels infiltrating the lands not that long ago?"

Eoghan's expression darkened. "The rebels you experienced last night are the outliers, the ones she sends when she knows they will not return. The rebels Lochlan is threatened by are far more sinister. They have tainted their magic with an ancient power long since banished from our realms. It consumes the wielder until they are nothing more than a bloodthirsty monster."

"Do you know how the rebel in my room knew who my sister was?" I questioned as we arrived in front of Nova's stall. The horse leaned forward, knocking her head on my shoulder. I placed a hand against her snout, rubbing lightly.

Eoghan watched me with the animal. "I think Sylas might have some competition of who Nova likes more."

My strokes paused, causing Nova to let out a frustrated neigh. "You are avoiding my question, Eoghan. I thought leaving Mai in the mortal lands and coming here would keep her safe. But now a rebel knows who she is and has spoken to her. What was the point of coming to compete in your Games if she is now mixed up with this world?"

"Your sister must be dabbling in a type of ancient magic that could call upon creatures of all kinds." Eoghan's hand came up to rub the back of his neck. "She is lucky she only got the attention of a group of rebels."

I narrowed my eyes. "Mairead would never be that stupid to toy with darkness like that."

"Would you do it for her if she was in your position?" Eoghan's intense stare met my own. My heart thumped erratically against my chest because he knew the answer already. I would sacrifice my life for my sister if it came down to it.

Opening my mouth to respond, my words were cut off as Lochlan bounded into the stables. He wore a similar black armor as Eoghan and me. The gleaming scales of his chest plate glistened even in the low lighting of the space. There was no sign of the glittering crown that normally rested on his head. He eyed us suspiciously, clearly picking up on the heated air around Eoghan and me.

"Our transporter has arrived. If we don't want to be docked points for arriving late, we need to leave now." Lochlan flashed a feline grin at me. "He has requested to transport you first, cailleach."

Lochlan backed away from us, humming a light tune before rounding the corner with a lazy swing of his arms. I shook my head at his giddy excitement. My nerves bundled tighter in my core as Eoghan and I followed the prince. A male stood with his back toward us. His shoulders shook slightly as he laughed at something Embryss said. As we exited, the figure turned, and the familiar face of Gideon came into view.

He flashed me a dazzling smile. "Are you ready for today, Caelen?"

"No," I stated plainly, my shoulders slumping slightly.

Gideon, having none of my pity party, rolled his eyes and beckoned me closer. I dragged my feet toward him, allowing him to pull me under his arm. "Sure you are. And you getting maimed slightly will not make you any less beautiful."

A laugh broke through my lips at the comment. "Thank you for whatever type of messed up pep talk that was, Gideon."

"Anything for my favorite mortal beast." He squeezed me closer, my shoulder digging into his ribs before he released me. Clapping his hands together, Gideon began to rub them together, golden sparks flying from them. I stared in awe at the flecks of light as they floated around my face like stars in the night sky. They swirled around quickly, forming a funnel that he reached inside of and produced the pocket watch he had used the first night I met him. Gideon flipped open the device. "Now I can transport two at a time. Who would like to go with Caelen?"

Lochlan waved a hand at him as he spoke quietly to Sylas, their faces pulled taut with irritation at whatever the topic of conversation was. "Eoghan can accompany her. We will follow shortly after."

"Alright." Gideon began toying with the pocket watch. "Step up, you two. Hopefully, you have built up a stronger stomach than before. We would hate for the other competitors to see you unload your contents onto the floor right before you enter the Games."

I had decided that I despised that pocket watch of Gideon's as we landed in the middle of a fire-lit tunnel. My stomach swirled with the temptation of vomiting the second I steadied my feet, but I swallowed down the feeling. Gideon left without another word, traveling back with a pop for the rest of the team. I turned around, resting my forehead against the cool stone as I tried to get the room to stop spinning.

Eoghan leaned against the wall, his shoulder beside my head. "You are taking that time better than your first jump."

"Am I? Because I feel as though I am going to pass out while simultaneously getting sick this time," I whispered, my voice echoing off the wall in front of me.

"You will get used to the feeling." Eoghan chuckled. "I have something for you."

Turning my head, I let my temple rest where my forehead had just been. "You got me a present, General."

"Think of it as a training ribbon." Eoghan reached down to his hip, where a throwing knife was sheathed away in his armor. He held it up, the shiny metal blade showing me my reflection as I took in its beauty. The handle was a deep brown color, with runes carved down the center. It was the most breathtaking weapon I had ever seen.

I reached up, running a single finger over the carvings. "What do they mean?"

"Ní neart go cur le chéile," he whispered, the words rolling off his tongue like a lullaby. "There is no strength without unity. I know it is cliché, but in the Games, the team will be the only ones you can trust."

Wrapping my hand over the one that held on to the blade's handle, I peered up at him through my lashes. "It's a beautiful reminder. None of us can win this without each other. I couldn't have prepared for this without you, Eoghan, and I know I still have many more sunrise lessons before I have the ability to fully hold my own against one of you. Thank you for not giving up on the stubborn mortal."

Eoghan nodded, his throat bobbing. The popping sound of Gideon returning had me flying back from the General's touch, putting some distance between us. Sylas and Embryss stepped away from Gideon, both looking as if the jump had not phased either of them in the slightest. I pursed my lips at that, folding my arms over each other in annoyance.

He reached forward, pulling at the knife sheath attached to my armor's left hip, and slipped the weapon into its new home. Clearing his throat, he turned his attention to the two females in front of him. Sylas grinned, the corners of her lips stretching from ear to ear as she watched Eoghan and me.

"They do look cozy, don't they, Sy?" Embryss purred, throwing an arm over Sylas's shoulders and leaning into her. I rolled my eyes at them as their gazes narrowed on me. The final pop sounded around us, revealing that Lochlan and Theo had arrived in the tunnel. Gideon's booming laugh rattled the stones around us. He lifted one finger, pointing at both females in an accusatory way.

"You two are plotting." Gideon winked at Sylas as she bared her teeth at him. "Wicked little things, just how I like them."

Lochlan rounded Theo's figure and approached me. He blocked my view of the antics happening behind him. I peered up at him. "Now what?"

"An Elder will come to collect the team soon and escort us to the entrance of the arena," Lochlan explained, his eyes wandering to Eoghan's. "Did you catch any whisperings about what we will be facing in this task?"

"No," Eoghan grumbled. "The Elders have kept what they are planning close to the vest."

"Are we just expected to walk into their trap?" I questioned, my gaze flickering between both. Eoghan shook his head but did not respond.

"Each realm's magic is very specific. Everything in the Games will depend if they have chosen to insert us directly into the action or if we will remain physically here, but" — Lochlan's hand reached up, tucking a loose strand of hair behind my ear — "mentally, you will be within the Games."

"Perfect," I groaned. A shadowed figure appeared at the end of the tunnel. It floated forward in slow movements. The gray cloak it wore was tattered at the bottom, the stringy pieces brushed up against the stone flooring. Holes littered the garment, and the figure's hood was drawn close to their face, shadows masking any facial features from being seen. Through the holes in the billowing sleeves, I could see a stark white color of a bony arm, no flesh marring the area. I sucked in a breath, looking toward Lochlan, who was now standing taller than before. It was clear that this was the Elder that would bring me to my fate in the arena.

The figure moved past us, never acknowledging us, but Lochlan gripped my forearm and dragged me to follow them. I stumbled slightly before getting my bearing and matching the pace he was traveling. Blood pumped loudly in my ears as we made our way closer to two wooden doors. The surface had long scratch marks embedded into the wood. My breath hitched at the sight. A mirage of ghostly figures came into my sight line as they left their marks, and I could feel a dark power pulsating off the surface of the door. Their screams rang around the tunnels, echoing in my ears, making my stomach twist in a sickening way that I had only ever felt once before in my life when I had been trapped as a child in my mother's wardrobe.

Lochlan halted, pulling me to a stop as well. The vision in front of me dissipated just as quickly as it appeared. The Elder stepped forward, painting a rune in a deep ruby liquid that I was almost positive was not paint. It dripped down the wood, the excess pooling on the floor in large puddles. Before I could question what was occurring, the doors flew open, revealing a swirling night sky of blues and purples. White stars twinkled in the distance, shooting across the sky in magnificent arcs. I took in the sight, mesmerized by the beauty I was beholding.

Lochlan leaned down, his lips brushing against my ear. "The champion is required to enter the arena first."

"And how am I to do that?" I questioned, watching him in the corner of my eye as what I assumed to be the North Star flashed brighter than the others.

"You jump." Lochlan's words were void of emotion. "The portal is the entrance into the Games. Once you leap into its depths, it will bring you to the first task."

I nodded numbly, my gaze traveling to my left where Eoghan stood. He was watching our interaction with a fierceness that made something deep inside me spark alive. I stepped forward, the coolness of the night sky brushing up against my skin.

"Oh, and Caelen," Lochlan called my attention back to him. I craned my neck to stare into his dark eyes, "remember, we only need you to capture the flag. Leave the rest to us."

My brows pinched together at the comment, but I shook

off the uneasy feeling coming over me and turned back to the portal. A bony hand gestured me forward as the Elder pulled away from the doorway. Moving closer to the edge, my toes hung off the threshold. Just as it had done the night the flag had marked me, the symbol in the center of my hand began to burn.

I sucked in a painful breath as I brought my palm up to see that the black ink was now glowing orange as the pulse of ancient power recognized me as a chosen champion. I could feel the magic beckoning me to make the leap. Its cold talons traced the edges of my ankles as I debated my fate for a moment longer. Turning my head, I met Eoghan's hardened stare.

And then I blindly jumped into the Games.

Chapter Twenty Seven
Caelen

The humidity hit me first. I groaned, peeling myself from the damp earth, and stared up at the reddened sky above me. A blazing heat beat down on my back as the sun sat at its highest point in the sky. The swish of water meeting a shore in the distance collided with my ears as I gathered my bearings.

Large trees surrounded me, their smooth trunks and tangle of vines canopied over me. Standing from my place, I peered over my shoulder to see if any of my other teammates had managed to make the jump into the arena. As I stepped farther into the jungle, my boots squished into the black sand underneath me. A thump behind me stilled me in my tracks. Slowly, I turned to face the newcomer, eyes finding a pair of hazel ones. Eoghan had landed on his feet, sending a burning feeling of annoyance through my body.

"Perfect," he sneered at the surroundings. "I hate the beach lands."

"Can't swim, General?" I smirked, turning to face him fully. "And here I thought you could do it all."

"Now is not the time to throw jabs at each other, Caelen." Eoghan eyed me before peering down at his weapons belt. He appeared to be counting the items, taking inventory of what he had brought in with him. I swiveled toward the tree next to me, watching as the condensation dripped down its bark. Eoghan spoke again, this time, his voice less hostile. "The Games will not begin until all teams' members are in the arena. I would prepare yourself."

"I thought that was your job to do before this moment," I shot back, eyes still watching the droplets.

"I hate that jump," Sylas's sensual voice announced as she arrived. Peering over my shoulder, I watched as she unsheathed a sword from its home on her back, its metal shining under the sun's rays. "I wonder what the Beatha wielders have conjured for this task."

Embryss materialized next to her. "Well, it couldn't be worse than last time. I am still growing back my hair from the acid rain they produced."

My eyes bugged out for a moment. Acid rain? I was almost positive mortals would not just lose hair from being drenched in that. Gulping back bile, I brought my hand up to my necklace, toying with the piece. It warmed at my touch, beginning to pulse with my every twirl.

"Caelen." Lochlan's deep voice pulled me from my motion. All the members of our team stood, watching me with intense stares that made me want to turn and hide in the thick foliage of the jungle. Loch narrowed his gaze at me, opening his mouth to speak but a glowing orb of orange shot up from the black sand.

Pebbles rained down on us, pelting me as I shielded my face from their attacks. The orb pulsed three times before a woman's shrill voice sang from it.

"We sing our songs of splendid seas to lure men forth to their knees. For we have captured five flags from thee, now come retrieve them past the depths of our seas."

A wicked giggle followed the poem before the orange globe of light shot up and out of the tree line. The arena's earth shuddered as a gong rang out, signaling the beginning of this task. My eyes widened, and I looked toward Lochlan for direction.

"Sirens," Lochlan groaned. "You know what that means, right?"

Embryss frowned. "The water wraiths will follow suit."

"Like Ainsley and her sisters?" I asked, voice cracking with fear.

"Except uglier." Eoghan pulled a blade from his hip. "And nastier. These creatures have never left the company of their waters. They will be ruthless, and if given the chance, they will drown you for the sheer pleasure of the act."

My blood went ice cold. The shuffling of feet sounded behind me, and I rushed forward, placing myself between Eoghan and Theo. The latter sneered at me, but continued to lazily lean against a tree. I gripped my knife, not pulling the weapon just yet. A slither of shadows pooled out of Lochlan's palms, forming a barrier of pure darkness in front of us, blocking our view of what was descending upon us.

"It's playtime, little mortal." Sylas chuckled darkly, the tip of her sword pressed into her pointer finger as she twirled it. Blood trickled down her palm, but she didn't seem to notice or care. I glanced in Eoghan's direction as he rolled his neck, the bones cracking as he went. Then, without a word, the team began to run, leaving me behind.

I scrambled forward, my boots catching on the damp sand. Lochlan's wall of darkness followed after us at a rapid pace. My pulse quickened as it nipped at my heels. We wove through the throng of vines, Theo slashing through them with a hatchet to create our path. The air around us was heavy with moisture, causing a slick sheen of sweat to cover my skin. I sucked in a ragged breath, the cool air burning my lungs as I pushed on after the Sith in front of me. Suddenly, the team screeched to a halt, but my feet were moving too quickly for me to stop.

I slammed into Lochlan's back, the two of us toppling down a hill with the force. We twisted and turned, taking hits of branches as we went. My back slammed against the jungle floor, knocking the air from my body. I wheezed, pulling myself onto my hands and knees as I grappled to compose myself. A hand gripped the back of my shirt, ripping me up and slamming me back onto the ground. Tiny black dots danced in front of my eyes as I tried to focus on my attacker.

Dark hair pooled around me like tiny wisps of smoke. Two hands came down around my windpipe, squeezing with as much force as they could. I clawed at their hands, but they were unwavering. Two pure white eyes caught my gaze, pulling me into their depths. If I could have screamed, I would have, but someone began to dig through my mind with a fine-tooth comb. Each memory they produced sent an excruciating pain ricocheting through my entire body. It felt like every nerve in my body was exposed and on fire. I ripped my hand from my attacker's wrist and swiped at their face.

A female's voice cried out in anger, releasing me from their grip on my throat. Before I could regain my senses, a fist swung in my direction, and I felt time slow as I swiveled to the left. The attacker missed their mark, landing the blow in the sand beside my head. I swung my elbow back, taking them by surprise and knocking them off me. Getting back on my knees, I began to crawl like a child who was just becoming accustomed to maneuvering on their own. A slim hand wrapped its way around my ankle, yanking me back to them. A scream finally slipped from my lips as I went, echoing off the trees and sending a flurry of birds scattering over us.

Turning on my back, I came face to face with the wicked grin of Soren. Her piercing eyes filled with a bloodthirsty glint. She swung again, this time her punch landing as it crashed into the underside of my chin. My head snapped back, pain blossoming as I bit down hard on my tongue. Blood began to pool in my mouth, and I spit toward the female, red dots spraying across her pale complexion. Soren reached down, pulling a five-pointed throwing star between her hands. I pushed myself back as she took her first swipe at me.

"Caelen, your knife," Eoghan screamed down at me. Without taking my eyes away from Soren, I reached into the hidden holster and retracted the knife from it. Another slash came my way, but I blocked it with the edge of the blade.

Soren smirked, her voice coming out in a hiss. "The mortal champion knows how to fight, does she now?"

She put more of her weight into the blade, causing me to buckle slightly, my spine nearly touching the sandy surface once again. I sneered, "And she doesn't play fair, I am afraid."

Slamming my foot up, it connected with her cheek. She shrieked, and I took my opportunity to swing my knife down, the blade embedding itself in her thigh. Crimson rained over me as I ripped it from her skin before getting to my feet and assessing my surroundings. A male team member of Soren's was withering under the tightening of the shadows Lochlan lazily controlled. His captured prey was beginning to turn blue as he squeezed tighter. I watched the male's eyes widen before his body dropped from lack of oxygen. At the realization that his plaything was no longer struggling, Lochlan dropped the male, letting him flop to the ground like a rag doll. His limbs were bent unnaturally, but I could still see the rise and fall of his chest.

Lochlan let a guttural growl rip through the space around us. "Duck, cailleach."

The powerful command in his voice was one I had never heard before. It was the voice of a ruthless ruler, the one his father and Elara had tried to mold him to be, but Lochlan rebelled at every chance he got. The trail of shadows did not pull away from his feet as they slithered around him. There was a darkness in Lochlan's eyes that convinced me that he felt as omnipotent in this form as the Sith were legend to be.

I did as I was told, crouching down. The bitter sting of my muscles made me hiss out in pain. A lone shadow of Lochlan's shot forward, forming as it moved into a single arrow that whizzed across the arena. I tracked the weapon as it flew over my head and embedded itself into the shoulder of Soren, who was trying to slip away from us. She went down with a thud, a shrill cry breaking through the air.

"Damn seers," Lochlan grumbled. With one hand extended, he strode forward, offering me help to my feet. "One team down, four to go. Am I right, cailleach?"

Chapter Twenty Eight
Lochlan

Caelen looked like she was going to fall off the side of the mountain's cliff we were currently hiking up. The encounter between Soren and her counterpart had taken a lot out of my mortal champion, but I needed her to find the strength within herself until we had the flag in our possession. I had concluded that we needed to make our way toward the beach, where the sirens spent their time lounging on rocks and drawing in their next victims. The twins would be useful here. The creatures had always found quite a liking for the witches.

"It's been too quiet," Sylas hissed through clenched teeth. I narrowed my eyes at her statement, but my gaze never caught on her wild one as it roamed around. She was taking in every piece of land surrounding us, trying to find the deception the Elders always placed in our path during the Games. She ground her teeth together harder. "Whatever they are conjuring has to be catastrophic."

Caelen's ragged breathing pulled my attention away from Sylas. Eoghan stood just behind her, eyes trained on every movement she made to ensure she didn't plummet thousands of feet down if she tumbled over the edge of the cliff. Loose gravel caught under the sole of Caelen's shoe, causing her to skid forward slightly against the narrowed path. She let out a shriek, grappling for the side of the wall to her right.

The Twins had weaved together a thick rope of vines to create a makeshift climbing line which required us to walk in a straight line as we maneuvered around the mountain. The line snagged, its force pulling at me, but I dug my heels into the ground just as Eoghan hooked his arm around her middle, swinging her into him. Her stare caught my own as her chest heaved up and down in panicked gasps.

"If you ever"—Caelen gulped down the fear that racked through her body—"sign me up for these Games against my will again, Lochlan. I will have your head."

"Are you threatening the Crown Prince?" Theo growled out as he turned to glare at the mortal behind him. I craned my neck to find Embryss trying to nudge her brother forward and away from the altercation he was inciting.

"Oh, piss off, Theo," Sylas grumbled, reaching around Embryss and shoved him harder than his sister. Thunder struck above us as dark clouds rolled through the sky. Theo's eyes were trained on Sylas, not daring to advance against her knowing that neither would walk away from a fight with all their extremities intact. But his magic was bubbling to the surface as the wind began to pick up.

"That is enough, Theo," I snapped at him. He glanced my way before turning his attention to the swirling sky above us. A sickening feeling filled the pit of my stomach as a bolt of electric blue lightning lit up the clouds. Theo was not the caster of this storm. Turning to my General, he held Caelen tighter in his grip. "We need to get off the edge of this mountain before we are blown from it."

I pushed my feet forward, leaving the two of them behind. Dirt and debris were beginning to kick up in the wind, making the path in front of us almost impossible to see. I could hear the shuffle of Eoghan and Caelen gaining on me. If I wasn't careful, I would be trampled by them or crash into the three in front of me.

Embryss' ear-piercing scream shattered my concentration, halting my movements. A few seconds later, the vined rope snagged forward. The weight of Caelen's body slammed into me, the force throwing me forward into the rocky surface of the mountain. I scrambled into a sitting position, digging the heels of my boots down into the earth with all my strength. The vine in front of me was hanging over the cliffs edge, and as I peered over, I could see the twins and Sylas suspended in the air. The high-speed winds swung them violently before slamming them down into the jagged surface of the mountain.

"Lochlan! The vine!" Eoghan's voice hollered over the wind. I reached out, gripping the makeshift rope hanging at my legs, and tugged. The braided vines pulled taunt, and I could hear the cracking of the piece hanging over the cliff's edge slowly breaking apart. My shadows slid around it, trying to mend the vine themselves, but it was useless. Each crack of the rope sent a sickening shudder through my entire body. I would not lose any members of my team today.

A forceful yank from behind me ripped me from my morbid thoughts. I craned my neck to see Caelen pulling at the rope, most of it resting on her shoulder as she tried to use her mortal strength to help the three below us.

"Caelen." Eoghan's cold voice was the same as when he stepped onto a battlefield. It had been a long time since I had heard that tone coat his words. Caelen paused, peering back at him with a worried expression. He gripped onto her piece of the vines. "You need to untethered yourself from the rope and then begin working on Lochlans'."

She did not question him like she normally would have, just went to work unknotting the rope tied around her hips. The vines fell away from her, and she dove forward onto her knees. Her hands shook in violent tremors as she pulled at the intricate knotting, I had secured myself in. She let out a choked sob as she pulled at the vines, part of the knot not budging under her efforts. Caelen's chest heaved as she started to panic.

"Look at me," I whispered for her ears only. Her tear-filled blue eyes met my own. I took in her swollen lip and the cut above her eyebrow that was still dripping blood down her pale skin. A single shadow weaved its way through her hair as it tried to comfort her. "Take a breath and try the knot again. Panicking is only going to make this worse for all of us, cailleach. You can conquer this."

Caelen released a shaky breath, nodding as she returned to the rope. Her fingers found a small loop of the knot, quickly untangling it from itself. She stepped back, allowing me to carefully remove myself from the vines as they slid down my body. Gathering the excess rope, I wrapped it around my hand to get a better grip.

"If the lot of you could hurry it up," Sylas screamed below us. I shook my head at her. Of course, she was not phased even a bit by the fact that she was hanging by a vine slowly beginning to break apart. Peeking my head over the edge, I shot her a bright smile. Her eyes narrowed on me, and I knew she was imagining all the different ways she could inflict pain on me if given the chance.

"I am not going to just stand here and not help, Eoghan," Caelen's shouted over the howling wind. Turning back to them, Eoghan was now standing in front of Caelen. Her eyes blazed with anger, the shine of tears now long gone as she tried to pull a piece of the vine away from him, but he was not budging.

"You will only get in the way or kill yourself by trying to help. Let the trained warriors handle this, sweetheart." Eoghan flashed her a condescending smile.

Caelen scoffed. "Let the warriors handle this? Because accepting help from a female is just so beneath you, is it, General?"

A dark chuckle slipped through Eoghan's lips, and I braced myself for the quip he was going to throw at Caelen, but an ear-shattering scream jolted the three of us back to the others. The vine quickly slipped through my fingertips, the slack tumbling over the edge of the cliff. I flung my body forward, scrambling to gather it in my hands.

It snagged, sending a sickening crack through the air as the vine began to break apart. My abdomen skidded against the rocky surface, sharp rocks cutting into my skin. I yelped out in pain. A firm tug on my ankle stopped my descent off the cliff. I peered over my shoulder and found Caelen looking back at me. Her teeth ground together as she held my body weight in place. Eoghan reached down in front of her, taking the small bit of rope he had left into his hands.

Turning back, I let my shadows retreat from me, trying my best to mend the vine to be strong enough for us to pull three fully grown Sìth over this ledge. A single bolt of lightning ricocheted through the sky, its electricity flickering out into the blackened clouds. I sucked in a shaky breath as the feeling of untamed power ripped through the air. Its metallic taste filled my mouth, and I resisted the urge to gag. Then it struck again, shooting down from the skyline and hitting its target. Blue sparks shot from my shadows as they absorbed the new power that mingled among them.

A pained hiss slipped through my clenched teeth as the blue light licked at my forearms, frying any control I had over my shadows at the moment. Their wispy figures made frenzied circles in front of me as they tried to find their way back to me, but it was no use. My body was drained of any power that it had just moments before.

"If you don't start pulling that vine, I am going to knock you over the cliffs edge," Caelen's voice growled out from behind me. I obeyed the mortal, pulling at the vine. The wind swirled around us in violent howls, and the only indication that our efforts were working was the rope that I could throw behind me as we got closer to our teammate's positions.

A single hand latched itself over the edge of the rocky surface, its ruby-painted nails digging into it. I latched mine with the other as it swung over the edge and pulled Sylas up. Her body landed next to mine, both of our chests heaving up and down as Eoghan helped Embryss and Theo onto the ledge.

"Well, you know what they say…" Sylas smirked in my direction. "Surviving a lightning strike is a sign of good luck."

"Who are *they*?" Theo hunched over, hands bracing himself against his knees. He quirked an eyebrow at the golden-haired female.

Sylas's smirk deepened, eyes trailing down to my forearms that still stung from the electric shock that had radiated through my shadows. "They, me, what is the difference, really? But it appears our Prince is in for a trove of good fortune."

My eyes tracked hers, coming upon my newly marked skin. The same electric blue color feathered across my arm, perfectly matching the lightning strikes pattern. Dragging one finger across the marking, the pulse of unbridled power still radiated from it, as if the wielder had wanted me to keep it close until they came back for it. My stomach rolled as I continued to stare. This marking was not a sign of good fortune, but instead a warning of the chaos that would rain down on us when this entity chose to take back what they had left within me.

CHAPTER TWENTY NINE
CAELEN

Stark white sand squished underneath my boots as we descended on the beach. The dark waters swayed menacingly against the shore, almost as if they dared us to be brave enough to enter its depths. A single island sat in the middle of the water, each realm's flag waving haphazardly in the wind, waiting to be obtained by its team.

"How are we supposed to get to the flag?" I eyed Lochlan. His face had been set in a deep scowl since we retreated off the mountain, and his shadows had not returned to cling to his sides as they had the entire time in this task. Something had been off since the lightning had hit the cliff's edge. The tension rolling off both him and Eoghan was making me queasy. A shoulder knocked into me, causing my feet to stumble forward. I snarled at Sylas, who just flashed me a bright smile that challenged me to test her patience.

"Careful there, little mortal." She tsked. "Wouldn't want to ask the wrong questions and end up at the bottom of the seafloor."

"Are you insinuating that one of us has to swim to the flag?" I glanced back at the island. The shore must be at least 100 yards from where we stood. My stomach twisted more at the thought. I had only ever swum in the small lake just outside of town, and it had been shallow enough that I could still reach the bottom on my toes. I shifted my eyes back to the fair-haired female as the whizzing sound of a weapon filled my ears.

The air was knocked from my lungs as I hit the sand. A body was draped over mine, shielding me from harm. Looking around, a pure gold arrow was embedded into the sand inches in front of me. The sun's rays shone down on the stark white feathers at the top, blinding me with how bright they were.

"Dammit, stop gawking at the arrow, Caelen, and crawl toward the water," Eoghan's voice yelled into my ear. I did not argue as he peeled himself from me and began in the direction of the dark blue sea. My fingers dug into the sand, clawing into the surface and pulling clumps of the wet substance up as I dragged myself after Eoghan. Grains of dirt shifted under my armor, scratching at the delicate skin underneath it. Another arrow flew toward my head, this time clipping my left ear. I cried out in pain but continued on.

Warm liquid pooled down the side of my face, mixing with the sweat that was coating my skin from the humid air. I reached the water's edge and pulled myself onto my feet, waiting for Eoghan's next command, but he was suddenly nowhere to be found. Standing quickly, I searched for him, but it was as if he vanished into thin air.

The violent surf crashed into my shins, sweeping me off

my feet and dragging me into its depths. I gasped, accidentally swallowing the salty water into my lungs as it slammed into me. It burned going down, and I had to force my mouth closed as I tried to cough it up. The waves sent me tumbling around in the water, making it impossible to decipher which way was up or down.

A swish of inky hair floated around me. Whipping around, I tried to follow as it disappeared into the darkness underneath me. There was no telling what was living down there, but I knew one creature that would not be merciful with me if they got me in their clutches. My head broke the water's surface for a moment, allowing me to gather just enough air to keep me going before I was floundering again.

Mustering enough strength, I tried to push forward into the water in an attempt to get back up to the surface. A horrid screech reverberated through the water, stopping me in my tracks. I clutched at my head, trying to muffle the cries, but the screams crept through the cracks of my fingers. A creature from my worst nightmares shot in front of me, its jagged teeth snapping and hissing as it neared.

Suddenly the three wraiths who dressed and bathed me daily seemed to be child's play compared to their sibling. The creature's gray skin was almost translucent as it moved through the water. Dark stringy hair floated haphazardly behind it. The soulless black eyes that stared menacingly at me made my hands tremble in fear. I kicked out, landing one solid hit in the middle of the wraith's chest before the thing lunged for my throat. My lungs were burning again from the lack of oxygen, tiny black dots beginning to gather in my vision as it wavered in and out.

A strong pull thrust me toward the surface once again and away from the wraith's anger. It held me up, not allowing the sea to swallow me again. My eyes stung from the whipping wind. I bobbed up and down as I got the handle of the treading water.

"Thank y-" I gasped out to the person beside me. A dark chuckle broke me from my semblance of safety, and I turned to meet the teal eyes of Tyr. I pushed myself back, water splashing against his tanned chest. The water droplets shined under the setting sun as they slowly trickled down him. My gaze flicked up to his, the corners of his mouth pulling up to settle into a patronizing grin.

"I hate for us to meet like this, starlight." Tyr winked in my direction, his right hand coming out from the water, revealing a glimmering blade as he twirled it in the light. "But I can't let a mortal win the first task. That would look bad for everyone involved."

In the distance, I could see Axiom dive into the sea with perfect form and begin his descent on the small island that sat to my left. Out of the corner of my eye, I made out the blurred colors of the flags waving wildly in the wind.

"I'll give you a head start before I gut you like a fish, starlight," Tyr taunted me. A shiver traveled up my spine. There was no way I would be able to out swim him, and from the looks of it, none of my other teammates had made it into the water after me. "Start swimming, little mortal. Ten."

I dove under the water, kicking madly to get as far away as possible from him. Breaking the surface, I gasped in a shaky breath.

"Six," Tyr's voice rang out into the air before the water drowned him out again. My heart beat wildly in my chest as I shot forward once again. The darkness of the water left me wondering if I was headed in the right direction. I swung one arm up and out of the water before it dove quickly back down with such force that my skin stung with the contact. I continued the motion with the other one, trying to emulate the way Kol had swum in the lake back home. He had always made it look so effortless. Tyr's counting continued. "Three."

The shore was only a few yards away, but I wasn't going to make it before time ran out. I took in one last gasp of air, gathering as much I could into my lungs as Tyr roared and began his hunt. Diving into the water's depths, I hoped the darkness would mask me from his view. A swarm of wraiths circled close to the sandy shoreline, predators hiding just below the surface for their prey.

One caught my movement, hissing out the same ancient tongue Ainsley spoke in. My blood turned cold as the slash of a blade swooped through the water, missing me by just an inch. The ocean swallowed the scream that tore through me. Swinging my fist, it connected with the underside of Tyr's nose. Dark red liquid pooled around him. The wraiths took notice of the blood in the water, and I pushed myself back as they descended on their meal. Their sharp teeth gnashed together, dark tongues licking Tyr's blood into their mouth. A deadly glint flashed in the eyes of one who had just had her gaze set on me as she lashed out at the male, catching him under his chin with her long, talon-like fingers. I didn't wait around to see what they would do to him and swam as fast as I could to the shore.

I clawed at the sandy surface, pulling myself onto the island, landing cheek first onto the beach. My chest rose and fell in rapid movements as I tried to recover. The sound of a cannon made me shoot up and scramble to my feet. A glittering Owl lit up the sky, its broad wings stretched out in victory as it soared through the sunset. Time seemed to slow as I turned to see Axiom waving his team's flag in the air in victory, the matching owl symbol stitched on its surface. I stumbled forward, watching as Freya's hand reached out and grasped the moss-green flag in front of her, ripping it from its pole in triumph. I didn't even look up as the second cannon shot off to see the Beatha deer that was surely prancing across the clouds.

My feet moved quickly, picking up pace until I was sprinting toward the black flag on the opposite end of the beach. The muscles in my legs screamed in opposition at the movement, but I pushed forward, determined to get to the prize. Skidding to a halt, I almost ran directly into the brass pole that held up the billowing black fabric. With one swoop, I snatched the black flag into my grip, letting myself drink in the sudden surge of power that shot through my body with it now in my possession. My necklace hummed in pleasure as the prickle of magic reached it. I let my head lull back, eyes closing slightly as the third cannon rang clear into the twilight sky. The sizzling of the cannon was soon replaced with the roar of cheers.

Opening my eyes, I came upon a crowd who was celebrating the three champions standing before them in a large stone arena.

Axiom and Freya were egging on the crowd, but I couldn't find it in me to care much for their praises. My gaze zeroed in on Lochlan, who leaned lazily on a wooden column holding a swooping banner decoration. Striding forward, I slammed the flag into his chest, catching the Prince off guard. He coughed slightly at the impact, waving Sylas off as she lunged to grab me.

"Next time, capture it yourself, Lochlan," I bared my teeth at him. We were so close our noses brushed up against each other.

His eyes narrowed at my tone. "Do not give me a reason to show you how truly cruel I can be, Caelen."

The cold touch of his shadows slithered over my shoulder, slowly wrapping around my neck, and I almost dared him to command them to make the killing blow, but a soft touch landed at the base of my spine.

"Let's take this away from the audience behind us." Eoghan's words brushed up against my ear. I eyed him from the corner of my vision. A dark purple bruise was beginning to bloom on the underside of his jaw, but other than that, he looked untouched. He scanned my face, eyebrows pinching together in concern.

I pushed out of his touch, still keeping my glare on him. "No need. I do not wish to speak to the Prince any longer than necessary tonight. Plus, I am sure he has a female in the crowd to impress. Be sure to remind her who you are when you bed her tonight, Your Majesty."

CHAPTER THIRTY
CAELEN

Gideon had retrieved me and escorted me back to the castle grounds. The cheerful screams of the arena still rang in my ears as I limped up the stairwell. Exhaustion plagued my body with each step, and I wondered how much longer I would be able to go on for. Every nerve on my skin felt raw and exposed as the air brushed up against it. I gritted my teeth to hold in a groan of pain as I made it to the final step. Reaching out, I braced a hand against the stone wall next to my door as my vision wavered in and out.

"Caelen," Eoghan's commanding voice called out to me, but I didn't turn to look toward him. His heavy footsteps clamored up the steps. I could see his mud-caked boots to my left. "You need to have your injuries cleaned and bandaged."

"I don't need your help," I snapped. The words slid off my tongue in a low hiss. Pushing off the wall, the force almost had me stumbling back, but I managed to steady myself and swing open my chamber's door. My feet carried me toward the bathing room, letting the door slam against the wall. The mirror rattled in its frame as I turned the dial of the faucet on.

"Let me see it." Eoghan was behind me, his golden eyes meeting mine in the mirror. They held an uncharacteristic softness tonight. It made my stomach turn in disgust. I tracked his eyes as they cataloged each cut and bruise coating my body.

"I'm fine." I spoke in a short, clipped tone, but it didn't stop him as he advanced to take a closer look at the cut above my eyebrow I had acquired from Soren. Spinning around quickly, I held my arms out, trying to stop him in his tracks, but it only caused my spine to dig into the marble countertop.

"Let me-"

"I'm fine!" I yelled with more force this time. My chest heaved up and down as a new pain pulsated from my ribs on my right side. I choked out a strangled gasp as I tried to catch my breath. Eoghan's hands found their way on either side of my hips.

"Come here." He spoke softly as he lifted me off my feet and set me on the countertop next to the running sink. Eoghan caught my gaze. "Do not move from this spot."

I nodded in acknowledgment before he disappeared back into the dark room. My mind whirled with images from the Games, and I shuddered at the thought of Tyr being attacked by the water wraiths. I knew he was going to kill me, but my gut twisted at the thought that I had caused his demise. Eoghan returned moments later with a pile of gauzy fabric in one hand and a bottle of dark amber liquor in the other. He set both down beside my thigh before beginning to methodically soak one of the fabric pieces. A darkness coated his stare as if he was reliving every time he did this to a soldier in his legions.

Eoghan turned toward me, parting my legs as he stepped between them. My breath hitched in the back of my throat. I was suddenly very aware of his hand gripping my thigh and the thumb that was absent-mindedly stroking up and down. Each one caused the hammering of my heart to pick up as I imagined it rising just an inch higher to where I now desperately wanted it. I was almost positive Eoghan could hear it as well, but there was no stopping the thundering beat now. Clearing his throat slightly, he hovered his hand over a cut near my bottom lip as he spoke. "This is going to burn."

He lowered the cloth to the cut, letting the liquid seep into it. I groaned and tried to roll my head away from his touch, but the hand that had just rested on my thigh stopped me. Eoghan's fingers gripped the base of my head as he flashed a smug smile. "Not so fast, sweetheart. I wasn't done with you."

Eoghan dragged me toward him until I was barely sitting on the edge of the countertop. I rocked forward, letting my chest rest against his as he continued to dab at the cut until he was satisfied. The light touch of his thumb grazed my lip, and I had to swallow the moan that threatened to slip from the back of my throat. I peered up at him through my lashes, his control of the situation slowly slipping as a guttural growl rumbled through him.

Then I was back in my original position on the counter, my back hitting the mirror behind me as he flew out of the bathing chambers, mumbling that he would send a healer to look over my other wounds. I sucked in a shaky breath, letting the fog that had just clouded my mind fade away and replacing it with a seething anger at myself. How could I be so stupid to let him touch me like he had done it a thousand times before? Eoghan, who had stolen me from my home, and even though I trusted him to protect me in the Games, it did not mean I wasn't still resentful for his actions.

But even with that resentment, my bottom lip still burned in the most delicious way from only a simple touch, and I knew I could not indulge in Eoghan's touch again. I was already prepared to chase that feeling that had consumed me down to my core. Slipping off the counter, I began peeling the leather armor from my body, leaving a trail behind me in small piles. I slipped into bed, letting the comfort of the silk sheets lull me into a sleep that was filled with golden eyes and fiery touches.

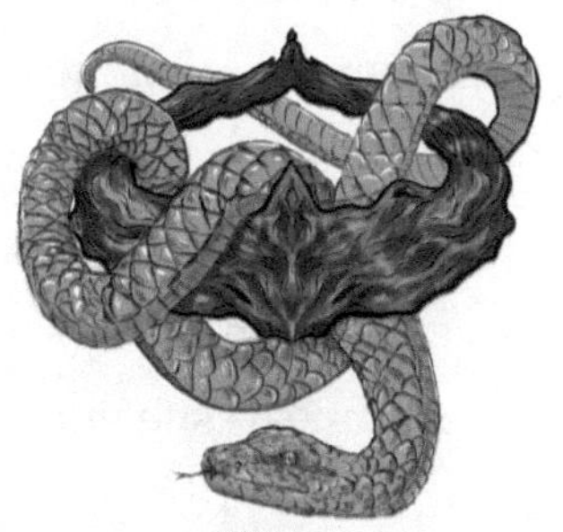

CHAPTER THIRTY ONE
LOCHLAN

The sounds of dishware hitting porcelain made the pressure building behind my eyes feel as if it was going to explode. The thought of my father's second's face when she was told she would have to scrape the Crown Prince off the royal table made me chuckle. Caelen's eyes caught mine at the sound. She was dressed in a powder blue linen dress, and the injuries that had covered her face just last night were almost nonexistent from the healer's careful hands. Her gaze narrowed on mine, returning to her breakfast in front of her. My little mortal champion was angry at me, and I would allow the attitude for only a short while longer. Let her believe she had won whatever game she was playing at.

"The healers forgot to heal your arm," my father's gruff voice called out to me. I peered down at the electric blue lines that scattered from my fingertips to the middle of my forearm. Flexing my hand lightly, the lines appeared to move in flashes, the same way the lightning had lit up the storm clouds in the Games.

"They said their salve would be of no use," I grumbled. "It appears the markings are here to stay until they come up with a solution."

"How is it you acquired the injury, Prince Lochlan?" Elara's light and airy voice flitted through the space. I resisted the urge to roll my eyes at her sweet tone as she watched me closely from the chair sitting to my left.

"A lightning strike," Caelen responded for me. Her blue eyes stared down Elara, who had turned to look upon the mortal. Something flashed across Elara's gaze that could only be described as disdain. Caelen reached for her glass, bringing the drink to her lips to take a long sip before returning the glass to its place. "It was during the tropical storm portion of the Games."

"Tropical storm?" my father questioned her.

Caelen was taken aback by his acknowledgment. "Yes, we were on the side of a mountain, and a storm had been conjured as an obstacle for us."

Elara eyed her suspiciously. "There were no tropical storms conjured by the Elders for this first task. You must be mistaken."

I leaned in, ready to remind her of the evidence on my skin that sat just inches from her, but one of my father's advisors stepped up to the table. He leaned down, whispering something quickly in Elara's ear before disappearing from my view.

"We are needed elsewhere," Elara stated plainly. She stood from her spot, her slender frame towering over me. Shadows emerged from the underside of the table as they crawled over the surface in front of me. Their deep color sends warning bells through me. Elara appeared to notice them as well, cocking her head to the side as they continued to snake around a fruit bowl. "You are not needed in this meeting Prince Lochlan."

Turning my attention to my father, I waited for him to object, but his eyes were glazed over as he watched Elara give the command. He stood from his seat, the trance-like state continuing as he marched from the throne room, Elara close on his heels.

"That was weird," Caelen whispered. "Wasn't it?"

"Yes." I kept my eyes on the doorway they had just exited from. My father was not one to allow Elara to exclude me from an advisor meeting. In fact, he had been more adamant that I attend them in the past few months leading up to the Games. Slowly, I peeled my gaze off the door and back to Caelen. "My study. Now."

———

Eoghan had met us shortly after I had sent correspondence to him. He stood in the farthest corner from Caelen. She appeared to be trying to hide in the depths of one of my velvet chairs to avoid eye contact with him. I flashed Eoghan a curious look, but he didn't so much as blink in my direction.

Eoghan rolled his shoulders back, scanning the room once before speaking. "Where are the Twins and Sylas?"

I rolled my eyes. "I wouldn't be able to summon Embryss or Sylas from their dalliance if I tried."

He scoffed at the statement. "I will not be putting out another fire the caused by the two of them again. Do you not remember the last time?"

"I think the entire realm remembers." I chuckled, twisting

the metal ring around my pointer finger. "Elara said something interesting at breakfast."

"He would have known if he had the decency to show up," Caelen stated with a pinched expression.

"Caelen," I warned. She tossed her hands in the air, signaling her defeat. Eoghan was watching her with a look I couldn't quite place. "Is there something going on here that I should be made aware of?"

Eoghan's head snapped toward me, "No."

"Absolutely not," Caelen replied at the same time as my General.

I leaned back into my chair and eyed them suspiciously. "Are you sure?"

"You were about to inform me of Elara's comment at breakfast." Eoghan ignored my second question. He rested a shoulder against the wall next to him, picking at the sleeve of his shirt.

"She claimed the tropical storm was not conjured by the Elders. But if that were true, how do you explain this?" I held my arm up, letting the fire light play against the markings.

"Elara must be misinformed," Eoghan quipped back.

"Or could someone else have conjured it without understanding what they were doing." I let my gaze travel toward Caelen's necklace around her.

"Me?" Caelen squeaked out. "No, I didn't do that. I would have known if I was creating a tropical storm."

"Not if you were unaware of the feeling of power flowing through you," I pointed out, "Your adrenaline could have masked the feelings, making it possible that you were the wielder of the storm."

"No. I know what it feels like when this thing decides to use me as a vessel." Caelen turned her entire body toward me, the red jewel of the necklace gleaming in the low-lit room. "It becomes hot, and everything in me feels as if it has been lit up like a freshly set bonfire."

"It has used you as a vessel before?" Eoghan's tone was the same one he used when interrogating one of his soldiers.

"I guess that is the only way I can describe the visions it gifts me, but other times it is just a voice that speaks to me." Caelen shrugged like it was customary for magical objects to speak to the wielder. "I didn't cast that storm. It had to have been someone else."

"The sister?" Eoghan breezed right past the voice comment as he looked toward me.

"She hasn't left her estate for decades. Why would she venture this far out to cast a storm in the Games?" I asked. The First Sister had made it clear that she wanted to be left alone after her sister was handled. She had isolated herself from any creature ever since, and those who dared to try to make contact were rarely heard from again.

"Maybe she is curious about Caelen."

Caelen shot to her feet. "Would you both stop acting like I am some sort of amazing find? I'm not. I am a mortal who has been thrown into a game that almost killed her. Gods, it still might."

"Your necklace says otherwise," I taunted, one finger

pointing toward the glowing piece.

She clutched at the piece, and I waited for her to try to rip it from her neck, but she just shook the object at me. "Exactly. Anything special about me comes from this Gods forsaken necklace. I am tired of being treated like something I am not. Just admit it, Lochlan, you chose the wrong mortal for this task."

"Caelen." I tried to soothe her rant, but she stepped around the velvet chair, hands slapping against the hard top of the desk.

"Don't *"Caelen"* me," she seethed, eyes blazing with a deadly vengeance. "I had no prior training or ability to fall back on. I was almost killed seven different times in the first task, but all either of you are worried about is the storm that conjured itself."

"We will continue our training sessions. No soldier has ever stepped out of a handful of sessions ready for battle," Eoghan explained as he took a step forward.

"I'M NOT A SOLDIER!" Caelen screamed, whirling on him. "I am a mortal, that is all, and yesterday proved I am not cut out for this."

She sucked in a shaky breath, letting her head bow forward. I could smell the salt of her tears as they began to run down her face. "I failed both of you."

Before either of us could respond, she shot forward and out the door. Eoghan watched with sad eyes as the door slammed behind her. Silence encompassed the space around us as we both took in Caelen's statement. I sighed, resting my forehead in my hands.

"I'll go talk with her," he murmured as he made his way out of my office.

"For once, can you just admit it, Eoghan?" I called out to him. He paused in front of the door, hand hovering over the wood.

"What am I admitting to, Loch?"

"That you care for that girl. You may think that you don't deserve to feel for someone like her, but it is written all over your face that you care for Caelen in some capacity. Stop torturing yourself because you believe you must repent for crimes that are not your own."

Eoghan stood rigid, taking in every word I said, and for a moment, I thought he might confirm it, but just as quickly, he pushed the door open and exited.

CHAPTER THIRTY TWO
CAELEN

Tears cascaded down my face in large droplets. They hit my linen dress, causing the light blue color to darken. Blood pounded in heavy beats in my ears. It felt as if my heart was going to break from its cage in my chest as it thumped in painful spurts. My chest heaved up and down as the corridors of the halls began to waver. Placing my shaky hands on the wall, I rounded a corner, trying my best to remember the way out into the gardens. I had to get out. I couldn't stay in this damned castle any longer, couldn't look at the same dark walls and portraits day after day. There was too much riding on the Games, and every painting's eye that caught mine reminded me of the legacy that I was about to fail. The image of Lochlan's smiling face danced across my vision and I couldn't help the sob that shook my body as I realized that he had become important enough to me that I didn't want to disappoint him.

I stumbled through two iron doors, their ornate metal design wove together in beautiful swirls. My knees hit the soft padding of the grass that covered the ground below me. Scrunching it between my hands, the blades scratched the pads of my fingers. I cried harder, my chest growing tight as bile rose in my throat, threatening to spill out. In this moment, the weight of all five realms felt like it had been placed upon my shoulders. Not because Lochlan had commanded it to be, in fact, he had always stated the opposite, insisting that we would win the Games as a team. But I had failed. The team had come in third, and I knew that would not be good enough going forward. I had no business competing against ancient creatures who could conjure life in the palms of their hands.

A watery laugh broke through my lips at the thought of Lochlan's face in the study as he divulged his theory of me being able to conjure that storm. My laughter continued like a mad woman as I sat up, letting my body slump to the side and bask in the morning light. My hand trailed upward to the necklace hanging against my chest, the matter inside the stone pulsating at my touch. I sighed, letting its energy travel through my arm, the tingling sensation flowing through me like the most sensual caress.

Peeling my eyes away from the sky, I found that I was not in the floral gardens that I frequented most days. Instead, sprawling herbs sprouted from pots that hung above my head. Their chains were hooked to a glass ceiling that made the sunlight send glittering dots of rainbows across the plots of dirt below. Each row of plants was labeled with tiny wooden plaques indicating what grew in the garden.

"How did you get in here?" a male's voice asked in an urgent tone. I turned to where Eoghan stood in the doorway, a shocked look plastered across his face.

Shrugging at him, I replied, "The gates just opened for me when I pushed them. You know how to open a gate, do you not?"

"Yes, I know how to open a gate, Caelen," Eoghan said, his lips turning downward at my joke. "But this is Elara's private garden. Most of the herbs in here could kill you with a single touch."

"Well, it's a good thing I didn't plan on frolicking through them now, isn't it?" I smirked at him. Eoghan rolled his eyes before holding out a hand for me to take which, I refused. "I am fine here."

"Elara won't be happy with this intrusion. The gates are normally locked by a spell that can only be undone by her." Eoghan motioned again for me to take his hand. Sighing, I laced my fingers with his and allowed him to pull me to my feet. I drew away from his touch, dusting off the front of my skirt which was now stained from the grass and dirt.

The light sound of voices approaching sent my stomach plummeting. I lifted my gaze to meet Eoghan's hoping he would just reassure me it was only a guard, but the intense look in his eyes told me that was not the case. His hand gripped down on my upper arm, yanking me toward the back corner of Elara's greenhouse. He weaved in and out of the plants, carefully making sure I avoided any of them touching my skin. A large green plant stood tall in its pot, leaves sprouting from all angles of its stem, giving us coverage to hide behind. Eoghan pushed me into the corner, my back pressed up against the glass paneling of the building. He stepped forward, arms coming up to cage either side of my face. I sucked in a breath as the space seemed to heat around the two of us.

Eoghan's normally golden eyes were dark as he looked down at me. I kept eye contact with him, not able to break away from the intensity of his gaze. The voices were closer now, and I could hear Elara speaking to another person. Her musical tone was gone as she explained to the advisors they were no longer needed, and she would take care of the problem herself. The shuffle of feet exited the greenhouse, but Elara still stood just in front of the plant hiding Eoghan and me.

"The question still remains," the King's voice echoed off the glass walls. "Do you trust the mortal girl?"

The air in the space disappeared, and I was no longer breathing. I peeled my eyes away from Eoghan, peering to the side where Elara stood. The ruby dress she had worn to breakfast now stood out in against the dull colors surrounding us. A single hand played with one of the plant's leaves as she spoke. "No, but I trust her anger and need to prove that she is trusted enough to return to her sister."

My attention snapped back to Eoghan. He eyed me with a warning that told me not to make a sound. The crunch of boots pacing against dirt had my anxiety spiking. One of Eoghan's hands shot down to my chest and I made a move to swat it away, but he was quicker than me as he gathered my necklace in his hands as the stone began to glow. The pulsating color was mostly contained between his fingertips, but some still shone through the cracks. Reaching up, I placed one hand on top and the other on the bottom of his, hiding the light even more.

"So, we eliminate her? If she were to win the Games that is." The King's voice was distant now.

Elara moved, her face fully visible to me through the plant. An evil that I had never felt filling the air. Her eyes met mine in the dark, but she didn't make a move to show that she had seen Eoghan or me as she spoke her next words. "We are to kill her no matter if she wins the entire kingdom's favor. She is a deadly fire that cannot be left to burn."

<hr>

Eoghan and I did not moved for a long while after Elara and the King had exited the greenhouse. I didn't know if I was in shock, but I let Eoghan's closeness soothe me for a few short moments. The rest of the day consisted of me in the library, paging through more books that only relayed the same information in different ways through their text before giving up and making my way to the training ring. There was no one wandering the halls at this hour to question my intentions as I made my way up the few steps and peeled open the ring's door.

The full moon hung bright in the sky, and I took in its beauty. I had planned on working off some of my frustration but now all I could bring myself to do was lay in the center of the mats and stare up at the clear sky. My eyes tracked each glowing star as they winked down at me, and I connected the constellations with the tip of my finger as they appeared in my view. Mai and I had done this thousands of times. She loved to point out her favorite stars and make up her own constellations as she went. Each new name she spouted out made me laugh harder than the last.

"What are you doing out here, cailleach?" Lochlan's voice broke through the silent night air. I turned my head to the side to see him standing just in front of the entrance, a ghostly smile pulling at his lips. A lone shadow danced across the mat to me. I laughed at it as it nuzzled into the side of my face.

"Isn't it obvious? I am mapping out the stars." I giggled as he shook his head. He sighed, walking forward, and laid in the spot next to me. Our shoulders were touching, as we both took in the beauty of the sky in silence. A rogue star shot across the sky, and I gasped out in delight. Turning towards Lochlan, my hands flailed slightly, knocking into his shoulder from my excitement. "LOCHLAN! Did you see that?"

"I did. The legends say that if you see a shooting star you must make a wish." He chuckled lightly as he closed his eyes, making his wish. I studied his face as he did. Lochlan looked so peaceful here, and I imagined this is how he must have always looked when he was a boy who did not have the weight of an entire kingdom counting on him to win their crown back. He cracked one eye open. "You're not doing it correctly, Caelen."

Turning back to the stars, I closed my eyes to make my wish. My mind wandered to Mai, her bright smile reflecting off the afternoon light in the garden. She had a speck of dirt splattered across her nose and her blonde hair was haphazardly sticking to her forehead. Cracking open my eyes, the stars above me were now blurred from the tears that were collecting in the corners. My heart ached at the images of my sister, and if the Gods were kind, they would return me to her without much time passing. But time and time again, I was proven that the Gods were not kind to people like me.

"You didn't fail me. I hope you know that." Lochlan's spoke in a hushed tone. I turned my head to look at him, but he did not return the gesture as he kept his eyes trained straight ahead of him. "If anyone failed, it was me. I failed you, Caelen."

"Loch," I breathed out, not sure what he was referring to. His shadows pooled around us. They were so dark in color that it was hard to see the ground below me. Their wispy tendrils swirled together, making a bed of clouds around us as Lochlan's anger rose to the surface.

"Don't," he objected, face contouring to a pained expression. "Don't try to reassure me that I didn't. You are not from our world, and I let you fend for yourself in the first task."

I let out a laugh that filled the training ring, reverberating off the stone walls that prevented us from plummeting off the side of the castle. "You didn't fail me, Lochlan. I think we were all out-matched this round."

"We really had no chance." He joined me in laughing. I rolled over when a sharp pain shot through my side as I continued to laugh harder. Lochlan reached up, running a finger under his left eye. "I mean, three of our teammates fell off the side of a mountain and we let them hang there for far too long."

"I fear for the revenge Sylas has planned for us." I shot him a smile. Finally, Lochlan turned his head to meet my eyes. The dark color of his were filled with a joyous sparkle now, rather than the regret from moments earlier. Propping my elbow on the mat below me, I rested my head in my palm. "There has been a question that has been gnawing at me since this morning, though."

"Does it have to do with Elara and my father?" Lochlan

groaned out.

"So Eoghan told you about that?" I asked, watching as he nodded slightly. It wasn't that I was surprised that the General had told the Prince but I couldn't help but chuckle at the two of them. Shaking my head, I continued. "No. I knew she did not care for me and wanted me dead in the end, so it is not very surprising that she would voice that opinion to your father."

"Eoghan and I would never let her harm you," Lochlan assured me. I nodded at his statement, a warm feeling flooding through me as Eoghan's name rolled off his tongue. There was something deeply wrong with me. Maybe it was the lack of sleep, because I should not be reacting to his name in this way. But despite that, my heart began to pump faster as my mind wandered to last night in the bathroom. To the light touch of his thumb running up my thigh as he tended to my wounds. Lochlan cleared his throat, pulling my attention back to him. "What was your question, cailleach?"

My face burned red in embarrassment with the knowledge that Lochlan could tell who my mind had wandered off to. In my recent studies, I had learned that Sìth could scent certain emotions if they were strong enough to exude an aroma. I directed my attention to the ground before speaking. "What did you mean by the First Sister never leaves her estate?"

"The First Sister, Arable, has a large piece of land on the edge of the Bás Realm's borders. My father, the Elders, and the other prominent monarchs of the time agreed she could live her days without any interference from the outside world after the battle between her sister occurred," Lochlan explained. "This was early in my studies with the advisors and the terms were kept between the parties who signed the agreement. Arable hasn't made an appearance in court since the day she left the castle grounds."

"You knew Arable?" I asked in a shocked tone.

Lochlan chuckled lightly. "I knew both Arable, and her sister, Seona, very well. They visited our court often and though my father has never admitted to it after what occurred, but there were rumors that I was to wed Seona to unite our realms."

"You and the Second Sister? I don't know if I could imagine you with someone so wicked." I shuddered at the thought. Lochlan gave me a pointed look that told me I was stepping over a boundary he did not wish to cross. "Don't look at me like that. She wanted to destroy the entire mortal realm because her sister told her she could not continue on with the human lover she had. It makes sense now if she was already betrothed to another."

"Is that what the story has become now?" Lochlan gaped at me. I shrugged lightly, waiting for him to correct me. "Seona and Arable were closer than any sisters I had ever met; they loved each other more than anyone in the realms. They had taken the Anam Cara Oath with each other." I shifted slightly, and eagerly waited for Lochlan to continue. "An Anam Cara is your bonded pair. You can have more than one, but it is rare to be even graced with one. The bond gives you a direct line to each other's thoughts and feelings. When Arable had to eliminate her sister because Seona had become a threat to everyone, it destroyed her. The bond ripped a piece of her soul from her, and she was never the same. It was as if I was looking at a shell of the queen she had been before when she bid her farewells for the final time."

I studied him for a long moment as I tried to wrap my head around what he was saying. My heart ached for Arable. If put in her position, I would never be able to stand up against Mairead. "But if Seona was Anam Cara with Arable, why did she choose to duel with her?"

"It was dark times. The realms were in shambles as war raged through the lands." Lochlan's eyes were glazed over, his mind taking him back to that time. "Seona and her followers had begun to become unpredictable. They were no longer targeting our armies, and instead they began to massacre villages of mortal woman and children. There was no pattern, no reasoning behind each one. Seona wanted to make a point that she could inflict chaos with just a few pulls of a string in hopes that we would surrender."

"So, what? Seona did all this for a mortal love she would one day outlive?"

Lochlan scoffed. "Gods, no. Seona loved the mortal king and he had made her his Queen, but it was not enough just to have the title. She was already a sister queen in her own lands. Seona wanted the magic of the mortal realm to accept her as the true ruler. You see, she did not want to share the throne that was her birthright with her sister and made it her mission overthrow the mortal realms. But the realm's magic rejected her, and Seona was the one who unknowingly killed her Leannán in her crusade for that power. But she blamed Arable for the burning of the castle."

I let the true story swirl around my brain. We had gotten it so wrong for centuries. It had never made much sense to me that Seona would need to be put down because she loved the mortal King. Now knowing that she was driven mad with lust for power, every riddle Aunt Lennox spouted out my entire life began to unravel for me. I paused, thinking back to a specific phrase Lochlan had casually rattled off during his tale.

"Leannán?" I questioned, the word sparking a giddy feeling in the center of my chest as it rolled off my tongue. "I have read that somewhere. It is the equivalent to a soulmate in my realm, correct?"

"In the simplest terms, yes. A Leannán is the rarest and most sacred bond that someone can obtain in my world. They are each other's perfect mate, equals in every way, and the ones great wars have been fought to avenge. To find you Leannán is to find the most intimate parts of yourself and place them in the hands of another without fear they will drop it."

Lochlan's words resonated with something stirring in my soul. The thought of finding another who was wholly yours in every sense was what everyone dreamed of. Rolling back over onto my back, I stared up at the sky. Clouds had now filled the sky covering my view of the stars. My voice cracked as the words spilled over my lips. "I hope the Gods bless you with a Leannán one day, Loch."

"To say I have not prayed every day of my existence for that, cailleach, would be a lie." Lochlan's soft voice lulled us into a peaceful quiet for the rest of the night.

Chapter Thirty Three
Caelen

Cold air nipped at my nose the following morning. My muscles burned as they tightened from the chill breeze that whipped around me. Our team stood side by side, waiting for the small male in front of us to grant us access through a gold-plated door. I tugged at the shoulder strap of my leathers, trying to busy myself from thinking too hard about what horrors we would face behind it.

"What do you mean, only two of us will be competing in this task?" Lochlan questioned the guard. The male squeaked as Lochlan's shadows crept up around him in the form of a dark snake. They coiled around their master, a long tongue lashing out to hiss in the guard's face. A low rattle rumbled through the shadows causing the male to blanch white and scramble for the right words.

"I was instructed that only two members of each team will be permitted into the Games' arena space. One must be your champion, and the other will be decided through the pool of fate." The male's eyes were wide, taking up most of this face.

His mousy hair flopped to the side in stringy pieces as if he had not washed it for days. I scrunched up my nose at the thought. Eoghan's elbow rammed into my side, drawing my attention to him.

"We are to play with fate, you say?" He kept his eyes on mine. I should have wanted to look away, but the pull to him was still as strong as it had been the night after the first task. Eoghan's gaze flicked towards Lochlan's. "Sounds like we are dealing with the Todhchaí tricks this round."

"Their charades are always grand," Theo stated plainly. I turned to look at the male, and he sneered at me. "Sharpen your mind for this one, little mortal. Fate is such a fickle thing, and I am getting the feeling yours is dwindling right before my eyes. Pity."

I lunged forward, hands reaching out to lock around Theo's throat. My fingertips barely traced his skin before I was ripped back into place. A low snarl slipped through my lips as I glowered at the now-snickering male before me. His one blue eye glowed with an impish glint, the whispers of a challenge I would not fall prey to settling in the air around us.

"Enough." Lochlan's command sent shivers down my spine. I settled back against the figure behind me, crossing my arms over my chest as I continued to watch Theo. Eoghan stilled at my relaxed demeanor, but he did not make a move to push me from his chest. For some odd reason, the action felt natural for the two of us, even if we were normally at one another's throats. Theo picked at an invisible piece off lint of his gleaming armor, tossing it in my direction with a smirk. After a few more moments, the golden door swung open, revealing a pure white room behind it. The light bouncing off the space made me squint at the brightness cast into the hall.

"You may enter now," the mousy guard instructed. He took several steps back, allowing Lochlan to pass through the space where he had just stood. Sylas and the Twins followed quickly after their Prince, but I stood planted in my spot with Eoghan.

"Who do you think fate will decide to compete with me in this round?" I asked, my meek voice just above a whisper. If I had my pick, my choice would be him. Eoghan had proven that he was willing to help win these Games and keep me alive until Lochlan secured his throne.

"It depends on what the task entails. The Fates will choose the best fit and most entertaining competitor to go in with you." Eoghan let out a low laugh. "Let's just pray to the Gods that it isn't Theo."

"You don't mean the actual Fates, do you?" I turned to look at him over my shoulder. He nodded once, confirming my question. I scoffed. "Great, that is just perfect."

I pushed forward, allowing my feet to carry me in the direction of the open door. Eoghan followed close behind me. "I wouldn't upset the Phantom Queens. They can be quite ruthless if insulted."

"I think her presence, in general, is going to upset them, Eoghan," Sylas called out to him. Rolling my eyes, I passed through the threshold of the doorway, coming upon an endless white void. There were no walls or ceiling, just a never-ending stretch of nothingness for miles. A stone water basin stood tall in the middle of the space. Three women were carved into the side of the column holding up the grand crystal bowl at the top. Each held on to a long string of rope. It twisted and turned around their bodies, binding the sisters together as one. Their menacing eyes followed my every movement as I staggered farther into the room.

Above the Fates' heads, a magnificent dragon curled around the crystal bowl, large wings fanning out as it held up the gleaming glass under them. Each scale upon the creature's back shone under the stark light of the room, and I could have sworn they fluttered slightly as each team member took their place around it.

Embryss ran a finger over the gilded lip of the bowl. "It's been a while since I have given my blood to the Scrying Bowl."

"Let's see which of us is lucky enough to compete alongside Caelen." Sylas smirked before reaching into her leathers and producing a short dagger. She brought the blade down against her palm, slicing open the fragile skin underneath it. Large droplets of blood pooled from the wound and off either side of her hand, staining the pristine floor beneath her. She wiped the dagger on her pants, leaving a wet trail on them before passing the weapon to Embryss, who eagerly sliced her own palm. I watched each team member repeat the action, ending with Eoghan. A flutter began in the pit of my stomach at his blood, and if I didn't know better, I would think I actually cared that he was bleeding just mere inches from me.

"Wish us luck, cailleach." Lochlan winked at me before each member of the team dove their blood covered hand into the bowl's clear liquid. The dragon holding the crystal let out a deafening roar, spouting flames from its open mouth. The fire caught the underside of Eoghan's arm. He let out a hiss, stepping away from the creature to miss the next bout of flame that shot from it.

My eyes widened as the entire space began to spin. I grounded my feet, trying my best to stay upright as the room began to pick up speed. I could only guess this is how getting caught in a storm cloud would feel. The movement was unyielding, trying its best to whip me around in every direction, but I held my own against its force. Squeezing my eyes shut, I begged it to stop, afraid that if this continued any longer, my racing heart would explode in my chest. Another roar ripped through the air, and then suddenly, everything was still.

I peeled my eyes open, coming upon a room full of golden strings. They crossed over one another in a tangled web of glowing beauty. Musical voices floated through them, their words not making sense as they spoke over one another, but they calmed me. My necklace shined on the threads in front of me, casting a beautiful red glow upon them. Stepping forward, my finger traced one of the strings, sending a zing of power through my arm. I sucked in a shaky breath as I plucked the string. A high-pitched note reverberated through them. The noise bounced in a musical game from one golden thread to the next.

A warmth grew in the pit of my stomach as I watched the strings respond to my light strokes. But just as quickly as they sang for me, silence enveloped the space. The string I had just been toying with began to change in color. Underneath the tip of my finger, the once golden color was now turning black. The deep onyx spread like spilled paint on either side of my touch. I ripped my hand away with a gasp. Slowly, every thread of gold was overtaken by the darkness as it spread like a disease.

"What have you done?" Theo's voice growled out. I tore my eyes away, noticing now that he was the only one left standing next to the crystal bowl. His face was furious, eyes tracking the color-changing strings until they landed back on me. His eyebrows shot up. "What are you?"

"I didn't mean to, I swear," I sputtered out.

"You shouldn't be able to play with the fate lines." Theo pulled away from the bowl, stalking towards me. He pointed an accusing finger at me. "Let alone eliminate them."

"Eliminate?" I squeaked out. Frantically I spun around, coming upon room now full of blackened strings. My stomach dropped, and an overwhelming sadness washed through me. The same sadness I had only ever felt on the day my mother had passed.

"You just changed the course of someone's fate. Let's just hope it was an insignificant creature and not your own," Theo snapped. He stalked forward, snatching my wrist in his hand and pulling me in the direction of the golden door we had entered not long before. "Come on, we need to find the flag."

I ripped myself away from his touch. "Don't command me like you have any authority here. You are here to serve me in this task, not the other way around."

He chuckled darkly. "Well, lead the way then, princess, but

remember, nothing in this dreamscape will be reality."

Pitching forward, I snatched the door handle in my grip and wrenched it open. I turned back to look at Theo as the darkness behind the door revealed nothing of what we were getting ourselves into. He bowed dramatically, hand swaying towards the emptiness in front of me to urge me forward. I stepped through the entrance, the toe of my boot clipping the lip of the door, sending me tumbling into the dark.

My hands met the coolness of freshly watered soil. Firelight danced over the ground, golden hues mixing with the rich brown. I pushed myself into a sitting position, eyes locked on the violets and yellow flowers that blossomed in the garden under the moonlight. My heart swelled at the sight. I was home. The cottage's stone was now covered in ivy. It crawled up the sides, rooting itself in the cracks of the structure.

"Do you even know what that does?" Mairead's musical voice floated from the open window of the cottage. I sucked in a ragged breath, tears brimming my eyes. Her voice had matured in the short time I had been gone, but Ainsley had warned me that this would be my reality. Her laughter broke through the air, the sound shattering my already fragmented heart.

"No, but I am assuming it is important if Aunt Len keeps it on the top shelf," Kol teased my sister. Standing from my spot, I took a clumsy step closer to the home. I could see them through the front window. Mai leaned into Kol, her nose scrunched up as she continued to laugh at his antics. A bright green liquid sloshed around a capped bottle as Kol shook it back and forth. A river of tears was now pouring down my face.

They had moved on without me. Mai's baby face had slimmed down from age. I could see the now prominent cheekbones turn rosy at Kol as he whispered sweet nothings into her ear. I leapt toward the door, but a hand halted me in place.

"It's no use." Theo's usually harsh tone he used with me was now a mere whisper. I looked into his soft gaze, my eyebrows pinched together in question. He trained his gaze on Mai and Kol. "They are using them as a way to distract you. We only have a short time to get to the flag. If I were to guess when the sun begins to rise, we must have retrieved our flag."

"Please. I have to speak to my sister. If only for a moment," I begged. Theo turned to look at me, eyes filled with pity, and I knew he would stop me if I tried to bust through the cottage doors. Then reality hit me like a ton of bricks. "They wouldn't be able to communicate with me even if I tried, would they, Theo?"

"I'm sorry, Caelen." His words were clipped like the statement physically pained him to say.

"Come on." Mai's voice pulled me back to her. "I want to show you the lilies that have bloomed in the garden."

The shuffle of footsteps sent Theo and me racing away from the cottage. We neared the edge of the trees, their thick branches enveloping us both in darkness. I turned one last time to see Mai exit the cottage. She wore a pale pink dress, the edges of her skirt marked with dirt, indicating she had been sitting in the garden for hours today. It swished in time with her as she took the front steps two at a time. Mai turned toward where I stood, and I could have sworn her eyes met mine in the dark. Her brows pinched together in confusion, and she cocked her head to the side.

"Caelen, come. We don't have much time," Theo called from the path behind me. I took her in one last time, capturing the picture of her standing on the porch, the wind blowing through her golden hair for memory, before unwillingly tearing my eyes away from my sister.

I felt numb as I followed after Theo, feet mindlessly carrying me forward. We made it out of the trees and into the clearing where I had last seen the blazing fire of Draíocht Night light up the area. Tonight, it was quiet, not a soul passed through the grasslands as we ventured farther into the village.

I paused for a moment, letting Theo get slightly ahead of me. "I don't understand, shouldn't there be obstacles or at least a puzzle we need to decipher?"

"Well, I just helped with the first challenge the Elders placed in your path, did I not?" Theo grumbled. He scanned the village, taking in every shadow that danced under the moon with hawk-like precision.

"I would have left eventually," I scoffed.

"Eventually would have been too long for us."

Stalking forward, I rammed my shoulder into his and continued down a cobblestone path. As I approached Annie's shop, my marking burned. Groaning at the sensation, I glared down at the black ink. The snake symbol of the Bás realm was now glowing green as it coiled around the star's point. The creature hissed, its long tongue directing me into Annie's shop.

The shop's front door was ajar, inviting me to step through. I moved forward, footsteps falling silent as I maneuvered around the cobblestone. Theo did not question my actions but instead stepped around me, a throwing star spinning between his thumb and forefinger as he pushed the door open farther. A single purple light glowed in the back of the shop, illuminating the small space. Annie was nowhere to be seen. I motioned for us to travel deeper into the shop, the symbol pulsated as we did.

"Does this mean we are going the correct way?" I whispered, jutting my hand out for Theo to see. He let out a conformational grunt, eyes continuing to track the space around us. A gust of wind blew through the room, slamming the door as it went. I whipped around, frantically pulling at the door handle, but it didn't budge.

"Perfect," Theo grumbled. A high-pitched whistle sounded in the farthest corner of the room. I slowly turn, waiting for whoever hid in the shadows to emerge, but they never did. The whiz of Theo's throwing star rang through the room. A bony hand shot from the dark, catching the weapon between their blackened fingertips. I unsheathed my dagger, waiting for the creature to throw the star back in our direction.

"Have you ever heard the songbird sing, mortal champion?" the shrill voice of a female asked. Goosebumps covered my skin at the question. The star twirled between the female's fingertips, the purple light of the space sending shimmering dots across the silver metal. "She has a lovely voice."

"Come out and show us your pretty face," Theo purred, a deep smirk pulling at the corners of his mouth. He crossed his arms over his chest. "Since we are breaking the rules, it is only fair that I get to take in your beauty again, Morrígna."

The spinning star paused momentarily as the creature took in Theo's request. My lungs burned from the lack of air as I realized I had stopped breathing when the female emerged from the corner, finally coming into the light. Her deep auburn hair flowed down her back in waves. Two small braids framed her angular face, and her bright eyes shone like emerald jewels.

Her red-painted lips quirked up at Theo, drinking in the male's appearance. "Hello, witchling."

"Did you three miss me?" Theo taunted, taking long, drawn-out steps toward her. I squinted, trying to see where the other two he referred to were, but no one else was there.

"Yes," Morrígna breathed out. "We wish you would take our offer and stay in our company for eternity."

Theo quirked his head to the side. "Why are you really here?"

"The Fate Spinner called upon us." Morrígna's eyes flicked to me, gaze trailing down to my necklace.

"I am sorry, but I am not who you think I am." I gripped down harder on the handle of the dagger. The female tilted her head as if she was trying to figure out a puzzle. And then she was right in front of me, her black-tipped hand latched around my throat. The force of her slammed my head against the door, sending a sickening crack through the room.

Stars danced in my vision as I tried to focus on the creature in front of me. Morrígna snarled in my face, a dark mist pooling from her lips and coating my skin. I tried to cough at the smoke, but my lungs rejected the action. Instead, I inhaled the taste of salt and greed deeply, filling my mouth with its assault.

"Do not move, Caelen." Theo's voice called somewhere

in the distance but I couldn't take my eyes off the creature's emerald ones. They hypnotized me in their stare, dragging me further into my mind as they prodded at memories I had buried deep into my subconscious. A scene of my mother's face flashed across my vision as she tossed an infant me in the air. Her bright eyes filled with joy and wonder, but what I found strange was that our family necklace did not hang against her breastbone. I could not remember a time that the red gem didn't accompany her wherever she went.

My thoughts were slammed back into reality as the creatures' nails swiped across my throat. Blood splattered onto her pale skin in bright red droplets. My hands scrambled to the three deep wounds stretching diagonally across my throat. I applied pressure to them, my breathing panicked as my knees hit the hardwood floor.

Theo had the creature in his grasp, a new throwing star held against its throat. The thing began to change, features taking the ones of my mother. First, her eyes cold and unwavering as they watched me grapple at my bleeding neck. Then the once red hair melted into a deep brown color, curling as it went at the ends. I closed my eyes, the urge to fall into the loving hands of death overwhelming me.

"Keep your damn eyes open, little mortal," Theo shouted, his voice harsh and commanding. I snapped my eyes open, now coming upon the full mirage of my mother.

Her full pink lips quirked up. "You always were pathetic."

I coughed out a sob, a dribble of blood trailing out the corner of my mouth. My mother sneered at me and struggled in Theo's iron hold. "You, Caelen Elliston, are a fool. All you are to them is a mortal girl stuck in a game with those who are only hungry for the power hanging around your neck. And once they rip that from you, you will be worthless to them, just as you were to me until my dying breath."

Her words hit me like a tidal wave. Their harsh truths breaking apart any bit of control I had over myself. My tears ricocheted off the floor, each one mixing with the deep rust-colored stains underneath me. Blood pounded in my ears, blocking out the words pouring out of Theo's lips.

"I'm sorry," I whispered into the void, praying to the Gods the message got back to Lochlan. That's all I wanted now, for him to know how sorry I was for failing him. I sucked in one last staggering breath and gave in to the darkness clouding my vision.

Chapter Thirty Four
Lochlan

Madness erupted through the stone colosseum when Theo landed in a heap in the center of the arena. His back faced Eoghan and me, but no one could miss Caelen's dark locks pooling over his arms. Theo's shoulders were hunched over her, shielding her body from the prying eyes surrounding us. I shot up from my seat, a shudder wracking my body. A lone blood-coated hand slipped to the ground. Its impact in the dirt rattled something deep inside me.

"Caelen," Eoghan's gruff voice roared. He was already on his feet, rounding the barrier in front of us. Time around me slowed as I watched his feet hit the gravel, small pebbles flying up at the force of his steps. The taste of salt stung my lips, but I couldn't do anything but stare at Caelen's limp hand. Her palm was facing up, and even through all the blood, the marking the flag had given her stood out.

As Eoghan skidded to a halt in front of Theo, time slammed back into place. His face was grief-stricken as he gathered Caelen out of Theo's arms and into his own. An intense pain consumed me. It boiled up from my stomach until I felt like I would explode from its fire. My shadows' screams shattered the air as grief and anger tore at my chest.

Numbly I made my way towards them, feet carrying me forward without thought. Embryss now sat knee to knee with her twin, trying to pull him back from the trance he was in. Eoghan's free hand shook as it assessed Caelen's throat. Three dark scratches stretched from Caelen's right ear to her collarbone. Blood still gushed from them, coating the scales of her leathers.

"We need a healer," I screamed out. The arena had gone quiet, and my crazed eyes wandered the space, trying to find anyone who could help. My gaze caught on my cousin's. Tears leaked from Freya's crystal eyes, her hands wringing the flag as she tried to control her emotions.

"Come on, sweetheart, open your eyes." Eoghan's soft words filled my ears. He placed a hand under her chin, pinching at it as he tried to get her to come to. "Dammit, Caelen, don't do this to me. You can't leave us that easily."

A ragged cough sputtered from her lips before she was groaning in pain. I shot forward, bringing up a wall of shadows to hide us from prying eyes. Caelen rolled closer to Eoghan's warmth, hissing at the movement. Eoghan tossed back his head, breathing out a deep sigh, prayers of the old language spilling from his lips.

"Never." My knees hit the ground as I spoke. I reached out, taking Caelen's hand in my own and squeezing. "Ever, do that to us again, cailleach."

A hoarse laugh broke through her chapped lips. "Does this

mean you care?"

Caelen's question was directed upwards at Eoghan. I shook my head in amusement as his eyes narrowed on her, but it quickly changed as her face paled, eyes rolling back into her head once again.

"Not so fast, sweetheart. Keep those pretty eyes on me, and I'll let your smart comments go for the time being," Eoghan commanded. A sly smile traced her lips as she watched him. My shadows began whispering amongst each other, eager to observe the general and their mortal champion as Eoghan stood and started towards the healer's tent at the other end of the arena.

"Do you think he doesn't see the bond, or is he ignoring it?" Sylas stepped up to stand next to me.

I kept my stare trained on Caelen and Eoghan as they disappeared through the tent's flaps. "Eoghan will never view himself as deserving of Caelen, just as she will never submit to him as a bond that sacred asks of her. I give them one more task before they give in to each other's desires."

Sylas brought a thumb up to her bottom lip, tugging at it as she thought. "And when they do, it will be felt across realms."

Chapter Thirty Five
Caelen

Three light pink lines scarred the delicate skin of my throat. They were the only physical reminder of what happened in the second task. Eoghan and Lochlan visited me daily, but neither would answer any of my questions about what would come next for our team. I hadn't captured the flag because of the changeling that had interfered, which meant our team should have been eliminated from the Games. Lochlan had explained that the Elders were furious with the Todhchaí realm. They had allowed the creature to slip through their wards, endangering every team in the Games.

I laughed at the statement. The entire idea of the Aesira Games included every possibility of death one could imagine and then a few more. But apparently, this had never happened before, because an outside source to attack a champion the Elders were considering disqualifying the Todhchaí Champion instead of our team.

A cream envelope had been delivered to Ainsley earlier this morning. It was an invitation from Elara to have tea with her in her private study. I knew the request was not optional, which is why I was now staring down the King's Second as she stirred a sugar cube into her tea.

"You seemed to have recovered well." Her eyes tracked the lines. I resisted the urge to shift in my seat. Elara's gaze flicked back to mine, bringing the teacup to her lips and taking a long sip.

"Yes." My voice is breathy. Elara quirked a brow at me, and I smiled slightly. "The healers were able to repair all the damage sustained from the changeling."

Elara chuckled. "General Montros and the Prince have taken quite a liking to you as well."

Instead of responding, I lifted my own teacup to my lips. The lavender tea was warm against my throat as I sipped it down. When Elara realized I would not give her any insight into my relationship with either male, she leaned back against the deep oak chair she sat in. Licking her lips, she surveyed my calculated movements as I set the cup down.

"The Elders were very kind to reinstate our spot in the Games." Elara's eyes were blazing with fury that was not shown in her poised face. "Shame about the Todhchaís, though. Soren was a promising champion."

Nodding once, I placed my hands in my lap. "She put up quite a fight in the first task."

"Yesss," Elara stated, dragging out the *s* in the word like a snake. Standing from her chair, Elara rounded the table slowly. "And you still understand how important the next tasks are? Currently, our realm sits in the second spot, with the Beatha realm in the lead and Fírinne just below us. The Elder's based our placement on your advancement through the arena. If there had not been an interference the likelihood of you obtaining the flag was far higher than when the Axiom captured his."

I nodded, taking in her words. Freya, Lochlan's cousin, would be out for blood in the following rounds, and her need to prove a point to a father who never claimed her as his own would make her that much more dangerous. Axiom would also be hungry to outrank us and remove us from the Games as the Elders began to dwindle the numbers down for the final tasks.

Elara stepped behind my chair, her chilled hands laying on the tops of my shoulders. I gritted my teeth as a shiver traveled down my spine. She leaned down, words low and threatening. "Are you a hero or fool, dear girl?"

The question startled me, and I tried to turn to meet her gaze, but she held me in place, forcing my back against the chair. A single finger trailed down my collarbone, brushing up against the red stone nestled under my dress.

"Heroes are the fools," I breathed out. Elara's movements paused as she waited for me to continue. "They destroy everything good about themselves over events they had no control over."

"And if you were to be given a choice in saving the one who called to the darkest parts of your soul and your sister, you would simply do nothing to save him?" Elara questioned, her talons digging into my flesh. My vision flashed red at the mention of Mairead, but I kept my composure as she continued on, words brushing up against the inside of my ear. "Some would think of you as a villain then."

"Then I am the villain, because you could put a knife in his heart, and I would not weep a tear," I growled out, but my mind flitted through images of Eoghan in the training ring, a bright smile plastered across his face as we sparred under the rising sun. Why was I thinking of him? He was no more mine than I was his, and I never would be. But the deep calling that tugged me toward him when we were near was growing stronger as the days continued. And he knew if it came down to another's life and Mai's, I would always choose my sister's.

"But you would tear the realms apart to feel something remotely like his warmth again?"

"Precisely."

<hr>

Wild wisteria hung in bouquets of purple off a garden arc. The floral display canopied the entrance of the grand Garden of Life. Daisies of all colors dotted the stones underneath my feet. I was enchanted by the garden's beauty as Lochlan led me into its depths. In honor of their placement, the Beatha realms were awarded the night to host the other champions.

Orbs of light floated in a small pond in the center of the garden party. Large lily pads mingled between each of them. The soft sounds of a violin drifted through the night air. A young female passed by Lochlan and me to offer us both a flute of sparkling pink liquid. I looked towards him, waiting to see if this drink would give me the same effects that these creatures' wine had.

Lochlan chuckled, picking up two glasses and thanking

the female before handing me the drink. "It is safe for you to consume, just a simple champagne for tonight's festivities."

I sipped on the pink drink, the bubbles burning as they slid down my throat. My face twisted up in disgust. Eoghan's booming laugh echoed from behind me before plucking the drink from my hand. "Not a fan of the elixir of life, sweetheart?"

"I don't blame her." A calming voice cut off my quip. I turned, coming upon Freya. She was even more beautiful up close. Her chestnut hair was braided off to the side, pearls and iridescent crystals littered throughout the style. She was dressed in a pale orange tulle dress that cinched at her waist. The bodice accentuated her curves as it was pulled tight by a leather cord between her breasts. Freya dipped her head in acknowledgment. "Eoghan. Cousin. And you must be Caelen."

"It's a pleasure to meet you." I smiled slightly at her.

She giggled, shaking her head at my pleasantries. "There is no need to be so formal. I wanted to come over and welcome you to Beatha."

My eyes wandered around the garden once more. Butterflies the size of my palm soared through the sky, spinning in figure eights before diving into the flowers. "Your home is gorgeous."

"Thank you." Freya's stare was locked on the three pink lines. "I am glad that you have recovered from the attack."

Shock shot through my body at her words. It would have never occurred to me that the other champions cared for my well-being. Freya's shoulders shook with silent laughter. "I may be ruthless in the Games, as I am sure my cousin has told you, but I do still have a heart."

"Freya," Lochlan warned, but his tone was playful. "Leave the poor girl alone. She doesn't understand the dynamics of life at court."

"I apologize." Freya winked at me. "Please enjoy yourself tonight. Lochlan, if I could have a word with you for a moment."

She motioned behind her slightly. Lochlan nodded, placing a hand on my shoulder and then looking toward Eoghan, who just nodded at the silent request before strolling after his cousin. I sighed, breathing in the crisp scent of watered soil. Although I did feel a sense of home in Lochlan's realm, I would not argue against spending all my time lounging in the Beatha gardens day after day.

"How are you feeling?" Eoghan's voice pulled me from my daydream. I turned, finally taking in his appearance tonight. Instead of his standard leathers, he was dressed in a pair of dark pants. The long sleeves of his shirt hugged his arms perfectly. He had let the top two buttons of his shirt lay open, letting the dark ink of a tattoo peek out.

"Fine." My voice was clipped. I wasn't entirely sure why I was being short with him, but my conversation with Elara had stirred something inside of me that I was unwilling to delve into. It was better to keep Eoghan at an arm's length, physically and emotionally if I had any hope at getting back to Mairead.

"Come, I want to show you something." Eoghan's palm landed in the center of my back, pushing me forward slightly in the opposite direction of where Lochlan had just gone. Allowing Eoghan to guide me, we weaved through the gathering without being noticed by anyone. Eoghan nodded toward a footpath.

"This way."

The sounds of the party became distant as we ventured farther into the wildflowers that surrounded us. Thick branches towered over us, winding through one another and blocking out any light as their weaving became tighter.

"Eoghan," I called out, utterly blind to what was in front of my face. The soft touch of his hand moved down my exposed back. I shivered under his touch, causing his hand to pause mid-stroke.

He cleared his throat. "Just a few steps farther."

Continuing with Eoghan's guidance, I waited patiently to see what we could be doing traipsing around the darkest corners of the gardens. Eoghan's footsteps traveled away from me, sending my heart racing in a panic, but as I was going to call out to him, the space around us began to glow. Teal and purple lights danced around me as they lit up the cherry blossom trees surrounding us. A river of electric blue ran through the center of the trees, its incandescent glow drawing me in as it ebbed and flowed.

"It's magnificent," I whispered, eyes wandering around in amazement. A bright green dragonfly buzzed in front of my eyes, giggles spilling from my mouth as its wings tickled the side of my cheeks. I could feel Eoghan staring at me, sending heat to my cheeks. We stood like this for a long while — me watching the wonder around me and him watching me. Finally, I turned to meet his golden eyes. "Thank you for bringing me here."

"This is one of my favorite places in the Beatha gardens." He reached out a hand, beckoning me forward. My heart raced at the gesture, and I hesitated for a moment before taking it. His fingers curled in between mine as he pulled me into him. My breath caught in my throat.

Everything in me wanted to run as far as I could away from this male, but there was a sliver of hope deep down that begged me to give in. The intensity in Eoghan's gaze as he looked down at me sent a ripple of butterflies fluttering around my stomach. His thumb traced the raised skin on my neck in one long sensual stroke. Eoghan leaned me back, his lips now brushing down the center of my windpipe. I swallowed down the moan that was threatening to escape my lips as he whispered into my skin. "Please never scare me like that again, Cae. I can't explain to you the terror I felt when I saw your limp body in Theo's arms."

Tears brimmed the corners of my eyes as a mix of emotions slammed into me. I gasped, "Don't lie to me, Eoghan. You have wanted me dead since the moment you stole me away from my home."

Eoghan's thumb paused. "Is that what you really think?"

"It's what I know." I pulled away from him, taking a few steps back. His shoulders were hunched, face dropped down in defeat as he watched me retreat. "You came into my world and destroyed it, but now that I was bleeding out after being attacked by a creature from your world, you suddenly care? Suddenly want to make me feel for you in a way I have never felt for anyone in my life?"

"You are so much more than the confines the mortal realm places you in," Eoghan growled, words coming through gritted teeth.

"I was happy there!" I screamed. My feet shuffled forward, hands landing their first blow on his chest to try to push him back, but he stood his ground against me. "Did you know where I was dropped in the second task? Who I saw?"

Eoghan stayed silent, eyes burning with anger as I landed another blow. "Mairead. Kol. They moved on without me while I am stuck here. With you."

Venom coated my words as I lashed out again, but this time, Eoghan caught my hands in his own, pulling me into him until our noses brushed. Our angry breaths mingled together as we both heaved out our frustrations. Eoghan leaned down, a ghostly whisper of his lips tracing mine.

"I can't," I mumbled, my voice cracking at the end. His grip loosened, and I took my opportunity to turn away from him. Gathering my skirt in my hands, I raced away.

A sob broke through my lips as I rounded the corner of the path. I stopped, hands reaching out to steady myself on a tree trunk. Heart wrenching sobs racked my body. I couldn't stop them as they continued to come in waves. A sharp pain radiated from my heart as I tried to catch my breath.

"Let me take you back to the castle," Lochlan's soft tone suddenly pleaded with me. I looked up at him, but he was only a blurred mess of colors as he helped me to my feet. I threw my arms around him, burying my head in the crook of his neck. Lochlan's fingers raked through my hair, soothing my cries as his shadows enveloped us in darkness.

CHAPTER THIRTY SIX
LOCHLAN

The thunk of metal hitting wood echoed through the training ring. I knew Caelen needed to release the pent-up emotions she had been repressing. Her hysterics in the garden's tonight were the first indication to me that my mortal champion was toeing a very dangerous line in her mind. The constant pull of who her heart had she left behind and who it found in her time here was beginning to way heavy on her. I sat back, thumbing through a book that Embryss had retrieved for me from the restricted section after Theo and Caelen had survived the second task. Theo had not spoken much about the altercation between the changeling and Caelen, but he had mentioned the creature had called her a Fate Spinner. My heart had raced at the term, thinking back to the dark eyes of the last spinner I had encountered.

Seona had wielded her power with such ease, changing the life path of so many Sìths who had not believed in her plan to rule the mortals as their true queen. It had been so simple for her. A snip of a lifeline there. A twist in their fate path here.

Seona held every creature's life in the palm of her hand, and we had all known it. That was until her sister had cut off her control in the Todhchaí realm by ripping the heart out of Seona's lover. Well, he believed she was his lover, but to her he was just a means to an end. Caelen heaved out a frustrated scream as another dagger left her hands. Peeling my eyes off the book's page, I quirked up an eyebrow at her.

"No, I don't want to talk about it," Caelen sneered at me. She reached down, fingertips tracing the mat before realizing she was out of throwing knives. Her boots hit the ground in anger as she stomped up to the wooden board. Caelen ripped a blade from the target. "Talk to me about something else. Anything else. Just distract me."

I chuckled. "You are really wound up after tonight, cailleach."

"Don't start with me, Lochlan," she snarled, knuckles turning white as she gripped onto the blade's handle.

Sighing, I stood from my spot and flipped the book back open to the page I had been scanning. "Do you remember much about what the changeling said to you during its attack?"

Caelen blew up her bangs, and they floated limply in the air before dropping back in her eyes. "It's all a blur. One moment, I was watching Theo taunt the thing, and then it had its claws wrapped around my throat."

"Changelings are tricksters at their core. They take on the form best used to manipulate their prey," I explained, my finger tracing the dark ink against the white page. "But it called you something that Theo took notice of."

"It called me a Fate Spinner," Caelen stated simply and

turned fully towards me. She reached out, placing the lone knife on top of the target before stepping closer to me to read over my shoulder. Her eyes scanned the ancient text, eyebrows scrunched together in confusion as she tried to decipher the words. Huffing out a frustrated breath, she continued. "I can't read this damn thing, which means you better start explaining."

"So bossy tonight," I chided with a small smirk. Caelen rolled her eyes at the comment but waited for me to continue. "I have been looking deep into Fate Spinners, but there is very little text about them. Most of it was destroyed in the war because people grew to fear their kind."

"Were they horrid?" Caelen sucked her bottom lip in between her teeth.

"No," I assured her. "Seona was a Fate Spinner, and a damn powerful one at that. If I had to place bets on it, Seona was the most powerful Spinner the realm had ever seen. There is a reason she is so often referenced in our texts as the Goddess of War. Her magic was breathtaking, the way she could wield the Fates' powers with just a wave of her hand and cast warnings to those who were teetering between the land of the living and death. She was smart and cunning, which made her a good leader during battles."

I could feel Caelen's dark gaze scan over my face. "Seona almost destroyed the realms and you are trying to tell me that Fate Spinners aren't awful?"

"Seona was an outlier. She had too much power for her own good and that power warped her brain. She destroyed villages just for the pleasure of hearing the screaming that echoed through them, but that does not mean every Spinner in history was a reflection of her." I peered at her from the corner of my eye. Caelen's face was beginning to turn a light shade of pink as anger rose through her body. "You are not the Second Sister, Caelen, but I do believe that her power is hanging around your neck."

Caelen flew back, placing as much distance as she could between us. Her hands clenched and relaxed down by her side repeatedly as she tried to ground her emotions. "Where did you get that idea from?"

"Only a true Spinner would be able to keep that much power contained." I stepped forward, eyes trained on the angry female in front of me. "There is a reason all the Elliston women die an early death. Your realm was suffocating your birth given magic and that much power would begin to drive the wielder mad before it slowly started to poison their body. But since you have been here, your magic has been able to creep to the surface."

A shudder wracked Caelen's body as she shook her head back and forth, denying the truth. "No. It's not possible."

"You can't hide from this, Caelen." I took another step toward her, which she matched with backwards step of her own. "Your mother knew the truth. There is a reason she passed the necklace housing the Second Sister's magic and something much darker to her firstborn before her death. She knew you would keep it safe until it was time to be dealt with."

Caelen's fiery glare landed on me. She lifted one finger, pointing directly at me. "Do not speak of my mother like you know anything about her. My mother did not wield magic. She was mortal and died a mortal death."

Her words came through clenched teeth as she spit them at me. Turning on her heel, she began to make her way toward the exit. I called out to her just as she was about to descend the first stair.

"There is a reason why her and her sister were Anam Cara. They weren't just bonded by blood but also by their abilities. Without one, the other's power would falter, and yet here you are, wielding unharnessed power. If you do not learn how to control it, one day, it will overtake you. I do not want to be the one to put you down, Caelen."

Chapter Thirty Seven
Caelen

Rain pelted against the castle's windows. Good. I hope Lochlan had gotten caught in the storm and was now soaked to the bone. There was still a deep burning that radiated in the center of my chest. It wasn't anger, though, that fueled my veins, it was sheer annoyance that maybe the Prince of Death had a point.

"Damn him," I whispered out. My feet paused midstep in the dark corridor as the crash of thunder rumbled through the sky. The vase sitting in an alcove shook violently as the storms wrath rippled through it. I ran both hands through my hair until my fingertips were grasping at the roots.

Lochlan was right. I shouldn't be so stunned at the realization that I was not fully mortal, seeing as Aunt Lennox has always told me the truth, even when I thought she was mad. Another crash of thunder had me jumping in place. A high-pitched shriek slipped through my lips just as the one person I did not want to encounter stepped into the hall.

Eoghan stared at me from the end of the corridor, a single

eyebrow raised at my sound. Ripping a hand from my hair, I slapped it over my mouth as I watched him, wide-eyed. His deep chuckle filled the silence. "Thunder? That is what I should have been threatening you with in training?"

Gasping at his comment, I dropped my hand. "I am not scared of storms!"

"It sounded like you were." Eoghan mimicked my squeal as best as he could. A genuine laugh sprung from my lips. The joyous sound melted away the annoyance that had just held me in its grasp. Maybe Eoghan wasn't the monstrous creature I had weaved him to be in my mind. It had been a long time since I had felt actual happiness. Not even Kol had been able to make my darkness fully dissipate with his ridiculous jokes.

Eoghan's bright smile shined in the moonlit patch that poured out of the curtains. "Come. I'll make you something to calm your nerves from the storm you aren't afraid of."

He started forward, venturing farther down the path to the left of the hallway and through a wooden door. I hesitated to follow him. How could he be so calm after what I said to him in the garden? I had outright told him that he wanted me dead. The hurt that had flooded his hazel eyes had cracked a piece of me that I didn't know cared. Before I could turn to run in the opposite direction, a light shove sent me stumbling forward. Whipping my head around, I caught the tail end of a wispy black shadow as it skittered behind one of the velvet curtains.

I narrowed my gaze at it. "Stop meddling in my business."

The shadow appeared to peer out from the curtain to watch me. I glared at it before turning to follow behind Eoghan. The temperature dropped as I made my way through the door. Following the long stone hallway, it twisted and turned, veering off every so often in another direction. I could hear the sound dripping water coming from somewhere off in the distance. This was an entirely hidden system behind the castle walls. I could only assume this was how my handmaidens were able to make themselves disappear so quickly. The glow of a soft light at the end of the beckoned me further into the darkness of the hall.

I finally reached my destination, the smell of spices and fresh baked goods wafted through the air. I inhaled deeply, taking in the scents that reminded me of Aunt Lennox cooking in our tiny kitchen. Behind the bench, a kettle whistled over an open flame. Eoghan stood behind a large wooden prep table. The dark wood stained with patches of flour from earlier prep.

"Peppermint or cinnamon?" Eoghan held up two glass jars for me to see. One held a generous amount of peppermint leaves, their bright green leaves glowing off the glass as it shone in the fire light. The other was filled with cinnamon bark. I could smell the sweetness even through the closed container. Two teacups sat in front of Eoghan, chipped in a few different places.

"Cinnamon." I nodded toward the dark sticks. "And make it sweet too."

"As you wish, sweetheart." Eoghan mockingly bowed in my direction and began to open the jar. I shook my head at him, a ghost of a smile pulling at the corner of my mouth. Eoghan turned, his hand tracing the top of the iron kettle as he lifted the lid to place a generous number of cinnamon sticks into the boiling water. Their warm scent filled the kitchen as I ventured farther into the space. Running a single finger over the wooden countertop, I felt its smooth surface dipping in certain areas from knife divots. I could feel Eoghan's intense stare watching my movements. Peering through my lashes at him, I watched as the tips of his ears grew red.

"Do I make you nervous, Eoghan?" I asked, voice low and gravelly as the words slipped off my tongue. He shook his head in my direction, the blush now venturing down the side of his neck and across his cheekbones. I rounded the tabletop, standing at the corner, just a few feet away from him.

Eoghan turned, back digging into the edge of the counter as he leaned against it and crossed his arms over his chest. His eyes were trained on the kettle as he waited for the spice to finish seeping. I sighed, craning my neck to peer out of the large window that sat just behind me. The rain continued to pour down in large droplets, mixing with the moonlight to create a dreamy scene. My mind wandered back to the garden, and how the male who stood stoically across from me had held me. His hot breath tracing my lips with a tempting featherlight kiss. I had wanted to give in. Gods, even right now, I would not object to him splaying me out across this kitchen bench and devouring every inch of me until my mind was hazy.

Eoghan inhaled deeply before clearing his throat, and this time it was my cheeks that burned scarlet. I kept my eyes down, too embarrassed to meet his dark gaze. "What did Lochlan do to put you in such a foul mood?"

"He was right," I grumbled, wringing my hands together nervously. The whistle of the kettle filled the silence. Eoghan reached forward, pulling the pot from its hook and bringing it back to the counter. He poured the now amber-colored liquid into the chipped cups and placed the kettle on an iron saucer on the tabletop. Striding to a wooden cabinet, he opened the two doors and removed a small glass canister before returning to his spot once again. Sticky golden liquid pooled into one of the cups as Eoghan turned the jar to its side. Placing the honey to the side, he stirred in the sweetness with a golden spoon, then pushed the cup in my direction.

Picking up the cup between my fingertips, its warmth flowed through me. I hadn't even realized I was cold until I brought the cup to my lips and the heated liquid slid down my throat. Eoghan raised a brow. "Is it sweet enough for you?"

"Yes." My words were breathy, mixing with the steam coming off the drink. He nodded and waited for me to elaborate on my previous statement about the Prince. I set the cup down on the table. "Lochlan explained to me what Seona was and why I can bear my necklace. Why my mother and every woman before her in the Elliston family died at such an early age."

I swallowed down my emotions, but one lone tear fell down my cheek. Eoghan stepped forward, abandoning his teacup and closing the space between us. The pad of his thumb caught the tear, calloused skin swiping it away from my face. I sucked in a shaky breath, our eyes meeting in a fervid stare. My bottom lip wobbled as my fears spill from them. "I don't want to be a monster."

"Seona was not born a monster. She carved that path herself when she chose power over the ones who would have died for her," Eoghan explained. His hand slid under my jaw, cupping the side of my face as he continued. "That is the difference between you and her. She would have slaughtered her sister without so much as a thought, but you would end worlds to ensure yours was safe."

A sharp pain radiated through my heart as the image of the older Mai I had seen flashed across my mind. I turned out of his touch and gripped down on the sides of my cup. Eoghan's hand dropped limply by his side, but he stayed in place as he leaned his hip against the counter. I brought the teacup to my lips, the liquid now cooled as I drank it.

"I am sorry." Eoghan's voice was gravely, filled with an emotion I could not place. I froze in place, the edge of the cup now hovering near my lips as he continued. "For stealing you away from your life and your sister. I had not taken into account my actions until tonight. I thought I was following orders and nothing else mattered at the time. Then, this wild beast of a girl came flying into our lives, and I realized she was as loyal as they come. I don't think I even realized that I actually cared for her until she was lying limp in another male's arms."

It made sense now. Why he had never shown any remorse for his actions. Eoghan was a soldier to his core, and he was following the orders of his Prince, not his friend. I had held this male to a mortal standard that he was not raised to uphold. Flinching slightly, my harsh words rang in my ears. I placed the cup back in front of me and gathered the courage to turn back to him. Eoghan's golden eyes watched my every move, his jaw clenching as I placed my hand on his chest. "Thank you for apologizing. It means more to me than you know."

Pink splotches pricked Eoghan's cheeks as he took in my thanks. I stepped back, eyes heavy and begging for sleep. Following the same path I had walked earlier, I headed towards the door. Before leaving, I turned back to Eoghan. He still stood in the same spot, watching me leave. The corners of my lips pulled up into a sleepy smile. "Goodnight, Eoghan."

A warm feeling bubbled in the center of my chest as I made my way into the tunnels. Before I got far, I could hear Eoghan's soft voice call after me, "Goodnight, sweetheart."

Lorna pulled a thread of lavender through a matching colored skirt. I watched her movements, taking in every stitch with heavy lids. The three sisters had been in my room waiting for me when I arrived back from the kitchens. They were gathered around the fire, whispering to each other like a bunch of schoolyard children. Coira brushed through my tangled hair, the action reminding me of the nights my mother had done the same. Casting my gaze on the eldest, Ainsley, was shifting through a basket of buttons. She plucked a deep burgundy one out, holding it close to a shirt before returning it to the basket and looking for one to satisfy her.

"Have the three of you always served the King?" I asked. Three sets of wide teal eyes met mine. Lorna's lip pulled back in a snarl, and I sank back in my seat, but Ainsley held up a single hand, silencing the middle sister.

"No," Ainsley stated plainly. "Lorna and Coira have always served in the palace, but I was appointed a position elsewhere before the war."

Placing a hand under my chin, I rested my elbow on my knee and leaned into it. "You served another realm before this?"

"You ask too many questions, girl," Lorna hissed at me. I narrowed my gaze at her, waiting to see if she would show me just how vicious she could be outside her waters. Ainsley turned away from the shirt and exited the room. The needle and thread Lorna had been holding slammed against the floor as she threw it down. Standing, she followed her sister. "Mortals will never learn when they need to keep their mouth shut."

I flinched as the door slammed behind her. Coira pulled me back against the chair, beginning to comb through my hair once again. We sat in silence for a few minutes before she spoke. "Ainsley does not like to speak of her time serving the Second Sister."

I turned to face Coira, her large eyes swimming with sadness for her sister. "She served Seona?"

The youngest wraith hissed, "Do not speak her name. She was a vile creature, one even more dangerous than us."

"I'm sorry," I sputtered out. "I don't mean to upset you, it's just…"

"You're curious." Her eyes softened. Setting the brush down, she smoothed out the front of her black dress. "Ainsley's time with the second sister was filled with horrors that neither Lorna nor I could pull out of her. She will not speak of some of the acts she witnessed, but it has left her with invisible scars. I hope one day she will entrust us with that hurt but until then we do not pry. And I ask you do not either."

I nodded at her, understanding that it was not truly a request. There was a hidden threat under her soft tone, one that I did not want to endure. Coira pulled me up and ushered me off to bed. Before she blew out the candlelight, she spoke. "Ainsley knew you were special the second the general brought you to us. Please don't let the power blessed upon you warp your mind. I don't think my eldest sister would be able to recover from another spinner tormenting her."

Chapter Thirty Eight
Lochlan

Blood filled a small vial as a young female squeezed my pointer finger. I watched the red liquid fill the glass, knowing this could only mean one thing. The Fírinne realm had control over this task and none of us would be able to hold back our true feelings in the arena. For a team that bickers as much as ours did, we were in for a difficult time. The female set my blood on a glass table behind her before moving on to Caelen.

"Once in the arena, you will have an hour to retrieve your flag." The Fírinne female laid her hand out, gesturing for Caelen to offer up her finger for the pricking. Caelen hesitated, eyes meeting Eoghan's, who leaned up against the stone wall behind him. He nodded once toward her, answering the silent question that only the two of them were in on.

Caelen sucked in a shallow breath before she handed the female her hand. She wasted no time, jabbing Caelen with the long iron needle with very little care. As she forced the blood to flow faster into a new glass tube, she spoke again. "I would warn you to watch your tongues, but you won't be able to do that unless you want to cause yourselves immense pain."

"Perfect," Caelen grumbled. The female continued on through the team, gathering a vial from each member and then disappearing out of the room.

"It is a good thing I always speak my mind freely, or I would be terrified of what secrets I would reveal," Embyrss's airy voice called toward me. Turning a playful glare towards her, she merely giggled and shot me a wink. Theo stood a few inches behind her, eyes cast downward. My shadows floated around me, their constant chatter suddenly silent as they tried to manage their worry for the oldest twin.

Theo had been keeping to himself for days, and it was as if I was staring at a shell of the witch he had been. Embryss had come to me in the early morning hours, eyes swimming with tears as she begged me to help her brother. She could feel the misery and despair that was overtaking his very being. Embryss felt as if she was choking on the feeling, and couldn't imagine how her brother was surviving it.

Sylas eyed Embryss with a look that could only mean trouble for the rest of us. She hummed slightly. "Not all your secrets are out in the open, Em."

Embryss's entire face flushed at the statement. Before she could respond to Sylas, the female from before returned to the room and beckoned us through the door. "Follow the gravel path until you get to the glittering stone wall. A guard will relay further instructions when you arrive."

I stepped around her, my shadows brushing through her light brown curls, making the female let out a small squeak.

Eoghan's deep chuckle could be heard behind me. Apparently, my shadows were either in a mischievous mood today, or whatever she had done with our blood was affecting them before the rest of us. The crunch of my boots against the dirt path filled the silence as we maneuvered our way to the meeting point. After a few minutes, a gray wall came into view. Its stones shimmered a faint purple hue, indicating to me that there was heavy enchantment cast over them.

"Portal?" Eoghan asked, taking his position to my right. His arms were crossed over his chest as he examined the space around us. A single guard stood close to the stone wall with his back facing us. Caelen stepped up, taking the empty spot to my left and settled her hands on her hips. Tilting her head to the side slightly, she took in the shimmering hue. There was something different about Caelen today. Her eyes were brighter, almost as if she had a weight lifted off her shoulders. A certain confidence radiated off her skin, causing my shadows to buzz around her feet, feeding off the exhilarating feeling.

I rolled my shoulders back and answered Eoghan. "Possibly, or a mirage they are using to hide the arena."

Three chimes sounded around us, and the guard finally turned around to address us, "The champion must lay their hand against the stone."

Caelen stepped forward, taking long, drawn-out strides toward the wall. Eoghan followed closely behind her. I chuckled slightly at the action. My General was in so much trouble with that one and he didn't even know it. Sylas and the Twins replaced them next to me. Theo toyed with a metal clasp on his leathers, counting the throwing stars he had placed in the hidden pocket earlier. The guard had made himself scarce as Caelen closed in on the stones. Reaching her tattooed hand out, she placed it in the middle of the surface. A hiss broke through the air and the purple glow intensified, pulsing three times before the world went dark.

A cry shattered the peace around us as the floor under my feet disappeared. We were tumbling through an infinite void, with no end in sight. I tried to gulp down the stagnant air, but nothing soothed the burning that was building in my lungs. My shadows were lost in the free fall, and no matter how hard I pulled, they did not return to me. A flare of violet light flashed across my vision, blinding me momentarily.

The sound of birds chirping filled my ears as my vision returned to me. The blinding light of the moon filled the forest around us. I scanned the grassy hill we had been placed on, counting each of my team members slowly. They were all here, unharmed, and in the exact places they had been before the floor was ripped out from under us.

"You know that idea came from Conall," Theo grumbled, brushing off invisible dirt from his pants. "Bastard."

Four sets of wide eyes watched as Theo gathered what he said about one of the oldest Elders. He slapped his hand over his mouth, eyes panicked as he remembered who was running this task. Embryss's high-pitched laugh bubbled in her chest. She laid a comforting hand on her brother's shoulder as she tried to contain her amusement.

"What is it they say again?" Sylas bumped her shoulder

against mine. "The truth speaks even if the tongue is dead."

"Something like that." I rolled my eyes at her, turning my attention to Caelen. "Come, we only have an hour to find the flag and we have no direction in this forest."

Striding forward, I pushed through the tree line, Caelen's hurried footsteps following close behind me. I trained my ears to listen to our surroundings, trying to see if the other teams were close enough to us to be a threat. I scanned the forest floor, thick branches melded together, making it difficult to see in the darkness. A single shadow maneuvered its way over my shoulder. I nodded, wanting to venture forward and survey the land for danger. It slithered through the greenery, taking in every shift in the wind as it went. Veering off to the left, I tried to find a break in the trees. The flags would be in an elevated location and wandering around in circles would get us nowhere.

"Loch, look out!" Eoghan's voice called out, but it was too late. The tip of my boot caught on a tree root, which had grown above the soil. The force sent me tumbling down the side of the hill, my body seeming to catch every jagged rock and stick that was in my path. I saw the water before I felt it. Pond water filled my mouth as I gasped out in surprise. Flinging myself back to the surface, painful coughs racked my body.

"What in the hell was that?" I rasped out, unable to keep my thoughts to myself. Caelen, Sylas, and Eoghan made it to me first, their shoes brushing against the pond water. Sylas burst out laughing at the sight of me, a sheen of tears coating the corners of her eyes.

"That appears to be a pond," Embryss answered innocently,

her wide eyes took in my soaking form. "I would get out. There are probably snakes in that water."

"The only snake in the vicinity of this water is Caelen." Theo's normal taunting rose to the surface as he prodded at Caelen.

Caelen whipped around, glaring at the male. "How is this my fault? I didn't push him into the water!"

"Knock it off and someone help me out of here," I grumbled, throwing out a hand for one of them to grab. Eoghan's grip locked on mine, helping me to my feet. I stepped from the pond, boots squelching on the muddy bank.

"You look a little wet there, Lochlan," Sylas sputtered out through laughter. Eoghan coughed slightly, trying to hide his own chuckle, but it didn't work.

"Are you done?" I asked them. Water dripped down my armor as I tried my best not to pay attention to the uncomfortable feeling that was beginning as the material began to slowly dry.

Caelen stepped closer to me. "I think we need to split up."

"No," I commanded. "The last time the team split up, you almost died. Do you not remember that? I could give you a reminder."

"Stop being such a grouch," Eoghan reprimanded, "You fell in a lake, Lochlan. You will survive being wet for an hour."

"You will survive being wet for an hour," I mimicked him, my voice growing an octave higher. Caelen reached out and shoved me lightly. I shook my head, coming to my senses, as the fog of the Fírinne's magic cleared. "Sorry. Their damn magic is stronger than normal today. Is it stronger for either of you?"

Eoghan shook his head. "I don't seem to be feeling the effects. Maybe they forgot to drink my blood today."

"They drink our blood?" Caelen's face blanched a ghostly shade.

Sylas sneered. "Of course they drink our blood. How else would they be able to have us under their control? I am actually jealous of their need to drink the blood of their victims. One sip and they are able to get them to talk. I have to resort to playing with my food."

Embryss's face twisted up in disgust. "I love you dearly, Sylas, but you are twisted."

"Thank you." Sylas smirked at the comment.

I shook my head at them. "We are wasting time."

"Which is why I think we should split up," Caelen stated. "There is a better chance of us finding the flag if we can cover more ground."

"The mortal makes a good point." Theo flicked a bug from his shoulder. "For once."

"The rules do state that we just have to catch the flag." Eoghan eyed me. "That doesn't mean that Caelen has to be the one to catch it."

"Fine," I snapped. Turning to the Twins, I added, "You two take the east. Sy and I will take the west and you two can take the north."

Caelen nodded, turning her back to me, and began walking with Eoghan toward the northern quadrant of the arena. Before she made it back into the tree line, she turned back to me, eyes locking with mine. "Be safe. We will see you after this is over."

Chapter Thirty Nine
Caelen

We walked in silence, my shoulder brushing Eoghan arm every so often as we descended farther into the trees. After his apology, something inside me released the grudge that I had been holding onto, my anger dissipating little by little with each moment that passed. Now the pull that I felt toward the General felt natural to tug on. We arrived at a fork in the path—one side leading through more forest terrain, while the other veered down into a cluster of mountains. Their angled tops towered over us as they slowly began to rise into the sky, the farthest mountain peaks disappearing into the cloud banks.

"Do you think we are going the wrong direction?" I sighed, running one hand over my sweat slicked face. Even though it was night in this arena, the muggy air had my body overheating. I turned fully toward the General. "And that is why we haven't seen another team wandering the woods?"

"No." Eoghan kept his eyes trained toward the sky, almost as if he was waiting for something to soar through it. "We are headed in the right direction. Did you bring your dagger?"

My hand traced the edge of the dagger he had gifted me in the first task. "Yes."

He peeled his gaze away from the clouds and stared at me in the eyes. "Good. Don't forget to watch the skies as we make our way toward the flag."

"Why, because a giant bird is going to get me?" I teased, stepping around him to head down the second path. Eoghan's hand stopped me in my path, gripping down on my upper arm and pulling me back toward him. I spun into his chest, hand landing a hard blow just above his heart. "Don't touch me."

"Caelen," Eoghan warned, the golden flecks in his hazel eyes darkening as he narrowed them on me. "I will not hesitate to incapacitate you if it means keeping you safe. These creatures have been trapped here for a long time, and they will not think twice about ending your life. They are running purely on instinct now."

A deafening roar echoed through the mountain, shaking the trees' leaves as it reverberated off of them. I stepped farther into Eoghan's warmth. "Gods, what was that?"

"Dragons." Eoghan's eyes were lit with wonder. A large grin captured his face. "I haven't seen one since I was a child. My mother helped hatch an entire litter of babes. They are sensitive and stubborn creatures, if you offend them, they will not forgive easily. But to gain one's trust is a divine act from the Gods."

I smiled up at him, watching as he reminisced about his childhood. Eoghan's face dropped slightly as he finally realized what had slipped through his lips. "Do not repeat that to anyone, Caelen. I do not speak of my mother anymore. Not after her death."

"I promise," I stated, the truth magic not allowing me to lie, even if I wanted to. Eoghan nodded once at my statement. He dropped my arm and stepped around me as he made his way down the slight decline of the path. I sucked in a deep breath and silently prayed I would get through this task without embarrassing myself in front of the male in front of me. Turning on my heel, I followed after Eoghan quickly. The temperature began to drop as the mountains enclosed us in their shadows. Even from here, a light dusting of snow was visible on some of the peaks. The bright white substance glittering off the moonlight. I could see my breath in the air as I let out a shaky breath.

Every shadow that danced on the rocky surface had me on edge. Was it just as it appeared to be, or was there a creature following our every movement waiting for the perfect moment to strike? I couldn't stop myself from calling toward the General, fear lacing my words. "Eoghan?"

"Scared, sweetheart?" Eoghan's taunting voice echoed through the rocks. I could practically see the sly smirk tracing his mouth, even with his back facing me. He turned his head slightly to look back at me, the darkness of the night masking part of his face. "Don't worry. I won't let the dragon steal you away from me."

Scowling at this comment, I leaned forward and shoved his shoulder slightly. The action only made him bark out a bellowing laugh. "I don't need you to save me, and would you keep it down. Whatever or whoever is hiding in these peaks is going to hear you and then what is your plan?"

"Protect your honor, of course, sweetheart." Eoghan turned, walking backwards as he taunted me. I couldn't help but notice the relaxed nature that he had adopted. Normally his emotions were coiled so tight that I was afraid he was going to explode under the pressure. It was nice seeing this more playful side of Eoghan. It made the pit of my stomach fill with a nervous glee that I had never experienced before.

I glared at him, throwing up an obscene gesture. "Piss off, Eoghan."

He rolled his eyes and hummed lightly. "Such a crude mouth attached to that beautiful face."

I bit down on my tongue, silencing the words that were trying to force their way out of my lips. My feet shot forward, leaving Eoghan behind as I began up the uneven cliff side. Large boulders were stacked on top of each other and I had to jump slightly to haul myself onto the first one. My throat felt like it was on fire, and I was biting down on my tongue so hard that the metallic taste of blood was filling my mouth. I gulped down the liquid as I began my ascent up each rock, a rush of excitement mixing with apprehension filling me as I made it farther into the cloud bank.

The jagged peaks towered over me, their snowcapped tips glistened in the moon's glow. Craning my neck, I peered at the rocky landscape below, where the large trees and dry grassy area were mere dots below me. I gulped down the bile that was beginning to rise in my throat.

"Don't look down, sweetheart," Eoghan's calming voice called up to me. I closed my eyes, trying my best to ignore the fire building in my esophagus as I fought against the truth magic. "Keep your eyes up and make it to the cliff's ledge. You are almost there."

Turning back to the cliff, I gripped the top of another rock, hauling myself up with my upper body strength. The high altitude was starting to affect my breathing, leaving me gasping as I fought to pull the crisp air into my lungs. I could see the plateau of the mountain just above my head. I would need to take a running leap for me to grip the edge and hoist myself over it.

I stepped back, letting the heels of my boots hang over the edge of the boulder. If I leaned back even for a millisecond, I would be tumbling backwards. My heart pounded against my chest as I raced forward and propelled myself up toward the cliff. My left hand latched tightly onto the rocky surface. I looked down at Eoghan, who stared at me with a wild look. Below him, the sheer drop made me let out a high-pitched squeak.

"If you don't pull your ass over that cliff right now, Caelen," Eoghan screamed at me, a twinge of fear in his tone, even if he was trying to hold back in showing it. I swiveled back, reaching up and placing my other hand on the edge's surface. Sharp shards of gravel dug into my fingers, causing me to let out a low grunt. I tried to focus on calming my breathing down, but the fear coursing through my veins was overpowering any other thoughts. I had grossly overestimated my ability in pulling my entire body weight up.

Every second hanging there felt like an eternity as I desperately searched for a way to get myself to safety. There was a divot in the walls' surface, where a rock had once been embedded. Swinging my leg up, I dug my heel into the surface and used the ledge to push myself up. My elbows hit the mountaintop's surface first, chest heaving as I scanned the area. Four multicolored flags stood tall on metal poles on the other end. They swayed in the wind, but the overwhelming sense of dread filled me. This was too easy. Why were there no other teams fighting their way to the top of this mountain?

A scream spilled from my lips as the ground underneath me began to violently shake. I held on for dear life as a large, clawed foot slammed down in front of me, bits of gravel flying out from under. The creature's razor-sharp talons dug into the mountains surface. I knew they were deadly, and capable of tearing through even the strongest steel as if it were a piece of parchment. Iridescent scales shimmered under the moon's light, their deep red color like a thousand gemstones. My eyes traveled upward, tracking each menacing feature as I went until my eyes met the bright yellow ones of a dragon. It snorted out an angry breath, and I could feel the heat of it wash over me.

"Caelen," Eoghan's deep voice called up to me. I did not make a move to respond, not wanting to make any sudden noises or movements that would anger the dragon above me. "Do not make eye contact. It will take that as a challenge."

"Too late for that," I whispered out, eyes still locked on the dragon. It cocked its head to the side, examining me like I was something it had never seen before. Dragging one long talon across the dirt, it created a deep line in the earth. The dragon leaned down until its eyes were level with mine and let out a deafening roar that echoed through the mountains. I threw my body over the edge, chest hitting the ground as the dragon's fiery breath scorched the earth where I had just been.

Ash and embers flew around the air. I dodged them as I pulled myself up and rolled under the creature's belly. Another wave of flames burst forth from the creature, lighting up the night with a brilliant orange glow. The heat of the fire was intense. I could feel it radiate off my skin. Crawling on my belly, I dodged the swing of the dragon's spiked tail as it slammed onto the ground, sending shock waves rippling though the earth.

"CAELEN!" Eoghan shouted over the chaos. I stumbled away from the dragon, eyes locked on the dark flag in front of me. Pain radiated through my side as the dragon's tail caught me, throwing me across the mountain. My back collided with the stone wall, and I let out a low groan.

The creature turned its sights downward as Eoghan climbed up the edge of the cliff. I reached down, hand wrapping around the smooth gray stone. With as much strength as I could muster, I pulled my arm back and chucked the stone toward the dragon. It flew through the air, nailing the creature directly on the back of its thick neck. It whirled around, as Eoghan pulled himself fully over the side of the mountain.

Leaping to my feet, I moved away from the stone wall, the dragon stalking toward me. My heart thudded rapidly with fear and adrenaline. Its massive jaws snapped open, revealing rows of teeth. I reached down, fingertips flipping open the flap of my knife sheath. My hand gripped the handle tightly, preparing to take on the dragon with only a knife and the very little training I had.

Eoghan's eyes met mine from across the land, and he nodded once in approval, readying himself as well as he pulled a gleaming sword from its place resting on his back. I charged forward, heat licking my backside and fear prickled my skin as flames erupted from the creature. Eoghan's sword clashed against its scales, sending sparks flying in every direction. The dragon roared in anger, its yellow eyes blazing with fury as it tracked my footsteps. Throwing out my knife, I slammed the blade between the soft spot of the dragon's scales and talons before retreating closer to where Eoghan stood. We continued to clash, moving around the creature in a synchronized dance, both of us targeting the dragon in different spots. Ducking, Eoghan's body shielded mine as heat blast over us.

Anxiety seized my legs as I stand back up, feet stumbling backward as the dragons teeth snap inches from my face. Swiping my blade toward the creature, the tip of the weapon nicked just below the creatures eye causing it to release a howling roar into the sky. It's long neck stretching endlessly above me as the creature throws it's head back in pain. The moon's light glimmered against the dragon's scales, sending a rainbow of colors dancing across the grassy mountain. My lungs burned as I rounded back again to my original spot as the dragon arced back down, eyes now sad, filled with a pain that I recognized in myself. I staggered back as a strange pain radiated through my veins. It pulsed in time with the dragons ragged breathes.

"Stop." I paused, letting my knife fall from my grip in the process. Eoghan looked between my weapon and me, eyes wide with fear as the dragon began to move forward once again. It dipped its head down low, bowing toward me in the most regal way a creature of its size could. On pure instinct, I slowly lifted both hands up by my head. They shook slightly as I eyed the dragon once again.

"If the dragon doesn't kill you I will," Eoghan's gruff whisper floated around the space but I ignored him, keeping my full attention on the creature in front of me. Wide yellow eyes blinked slowly at me, the movement felt as if had lasted a lifetime. I tore my eyes away from it's stare and took in every inch of the dragon in front of me. Scars littered the creature's skin, and I couldn't help but wonder if they had been intentionally given or if the dragon had obtained them in battle. A burning rage bubbled in the pit of my stomach as my gaze locked on the thick gold chained collar shackled around the creatures neck. It was clamped so tight that dried blood had begun to cake on to the shiny surface. With every slight move the dragon made the metal dug deeper into it's neck and reopened the same wound every single time. A swirling circle insignia sat in the center of the collar and I could feel the dark lick of magic that radiated from it.

Fear rippled through my veins as its hot breath brushed my skin. I stepped forward, one foot in front of the other, watching for any sudden movement from the dragon. My left hand reached down, landing on top of its snout. I began stroking the dragon's thick scales, their coolness soothed my heated skin. With each stroke I inched closer to the collar until my fingers latched onto the buckle that held the device in place. In one quick movement I unfastened the collar and pulled it away from the dragons neck.

A zap of power shot through my left arm as the magic which had just held the dragon under it's spell lashed out at me. The golden chains clanked against the hard ground as I threw it to the ground, shaking out my arm to quell the pain.

The dragon began to make a sound I could only compare to the purring of a cat, a deep rumble coming from its chest as its eyes fell closed and bumped it's snout against my cheek lightly. Eoghan's jaw hung open at the reaction. I know he had fully expected that we would have to kill the magnificent creature. I spoke softly. "You're a beautiful girl."

A snort of approval caused me to giggle at the creature. It was nothing more than a big lap dog that wanted love—minus the fire breathing and sharp talons that could shred me to pieces in seconds. I ground my teeth together at the thought of those who had chained the dragon to them. If I could make them pay for their actions I would ensure it was a slow and agonizing way death. The sounds of cheers could be heard coming from the other end of the mountain. I turned my head, catching the sight of Freya, who was beginning to make her climb.

A guttural growl broke through the space as the dragon realized we would soon be interrupted. I stepped back, allowing it to stand tall, wings stretching out to their full width. Below the red scales, the wings were bat-like. Thick skin and structured bone stretched under the moonlight. Black tendrils ventured through the skin in sporadic patterns that reminded me of the lightning strike on Lochlan's arm.

With a powerful flap of its wings, the dragon launched itself into the air, its massive body soaring effortlessly into the night. I stared in awe as the creature made a loop, shining scales sending rays of light down onto the dirt in front of me before taking a dive in the direction of Freya.

"How did you do that?" Eoghan's voice pulled my attention

from the creature. I turned my gaze to meet his shocked one. He strode forward quickly, placing both hands on my shoulders. "You just bonded with a dragon, and it let you."

"Bonded?" I shook my head at him. "No, I think it was just lonely. I could tell from its eyes. They are the windows to the soul, you know?"

Eoghan beamed down at me. "You are brilliant, Caelen."

My cheeks flushed at his compliment, and I tried to turn away from him, but he held me in place. "I mean it, Caelen. You are always surprising me with your ability to face death head on and come out on top."

"I am nothing special, Eoghan," I mumbled, mouth suddenly void of any moisture from the nerves coursing through me. Pulling my gaze away from his, I stared down the charred ground behind him. My heart was racing again as I tried to gather my thoughts. Heat pooled in my core at his words, but for once in my life, I was speechless.

"Every time you look at me with those eyes..." Eoghan mused, his featherlight touch coming under my chin to pull my attention back to him. His golden eyes swam with emotion as he continued to speak. "Every time you open this smart mouth to argue with me..."

His thumb traced my bottom lip, pulling at it slightly as he went. I stopped breathing as I watched him explore me with just a single touch. Power laid on the pad of his finger, and a gentle hum rolled through me at the contact. It was exhilarating. The trace of his thumb continued downward, sending a streak of energy to surge beneath my skin as he went. I was positive he could hear how nervous he was making me.

"It makes me feel alive again, after so many years of feeling so dead inside. I have been lost to the darkness, and I had accepted that my fate would forever lie in its clutches, but you, sweetheart, have guided me out of that place. I have denied myself the simple pleasure of living for centuries, and now I could never imagine living in a world that didn't hold you in it."

"Eoghan," I breathed out as he leaned down, lips tracing the column of my throat. My mind wandered to where else this might go if I gave in to him, but reality slammed into me as I remembered that we were under the influence of Fírinne magic. He would never have admitted to this if we were not forced to reveal our true thoughts and it felt as if water had just doused the flame of emotion coursing through me leaving only sludge of ash in its wake. Tears collected in the corners of my eyes. "Stop."

Eoghan immediately stepped away from me, putting a good amount of distance between us. I turned back toward the flags and walked on shaky legs toward the black one. The white stitched snake seemed to taunt me in the wind as it slithers through the fabric. I locked my jaw, teeth grinding together as I forced the tears to stop. I would not cry in front of him. No, I would save my weeping for later when I was alone, and I could fully feel the pain that was overtaking my body.

I reached up, ripping the flag from its pole, before turning back to Eoghan. He was transforming into a shimmering mist as the flag's magic transported him out of the arena. I looked up at the sky, and found the beautiful red dragon soaring above. My hand gripped the rough material of the flag between the pads of my fingers. There was one thing I knew for certain in this moment. This ancient piece of fabric was going to be my undoing.

Chapter Forty
Caelen

I handed Lochlan the flag as I walked past him, my fingers going limp against his chest. His hand shot out, catching the fabric just before it dropped to the ground. Our team had come in first and I was too numb to celebrate the victory. Buzzing filled my senses, blocking out the voices calling my name. I shoved my way through the gathering crowd.

The world around me felt as though it was moving in slow motion. Glancing back over my shoulder, my eyes met a pair of hazel ones. Their intense stare stole the last bit of air in my lungs. Fire burned my insides as I continued to hold his gaze. The heat crawled up my throat in the most delicious way that made me want to turn around and collide with him, damn whoever saw. Turning away, I let the sea of Sìth surround me in their race to congratulate their Crown Prince.

"Spill anything exciting to the General?" Soren's voice purred from the darkest corner of the hallway, conveniently blocking my escape from the madness behind me. I turned my gaze on her piercing one. She was leaning up against the brick wall, one leg kicked up to balance her. She twirled a dark piece of hair around her finger. "Don't tell the others, but I am glad that I wasn't forced to endure the magic of the Fírinne. Axiom has sunk his canines into me more times than I care to share. The feeling of burying the truth down is painful no matter if you are the under the influence of magic or not."

I watched her carefully. "I didn't have any secrets to reveal to General Montros. I am an open book."

"You're not." Soren chuckled. "But Eoghan can read you like you are one. Makes you wonder, doesn't it?"

"Wonder what?" I sneered. Soren raked her eyes down my body, and I resisted the human urge to squirm under her scrutiny.

Her gaze traveled back up to mine. "Don't act like you are unaware of your bond. The ink on the palm of your hand symbolizes it. Why do you think Cashel kept so close to my side in the Games? You did not just make a pact with the flag, but with the one who had marked it in the first place. I knew it wasn't the Prince the second I saw how Eoghan watched you at the opening ceremonies."

Bile rose in the back of my throat as I took in her words. Eoghan had lied to me, told me that I had been marked by the flag's magic, not his own. I took a shaky step back. "What does that mean?"

"It means his magic has intertwined itself with your very essence. Cashel and I have trained our minds for centuries for the moment I agreed to him being my Scíath. Cashel is my bonded protector. It is his duty to keep me safe, not only during the Games we play, but for the rest of my eternal life."

"Do these protectors often fall in love with their bonded?" I asked, voice shaking with emotion. Soren cocked her head to the side, a ghost of a smile tracing her lips as she dissected my question.

"It doesn't happen often, but it has in the past. Being a Scíath to another is a very intimate bond that can be driven largely by emotion, if not trained correctly. Many have found it hard to separate the emotions of love and duty when first taking the bond. I did."

Turning on my heel, I left the female behind me, not giving her a second more of my time. My boots slammed into the dirt path toward the exit. Pushing through the iron gates, I landed in the grasslands. My hands gripped down on the blades, pulling them from their roots. Hot liquid burned the back of my throat as I vomited on the ground in front of me. Tears burned my eyes again as I choked back another wave of nausea.

Eoghan didn't care for me, and Soren had just confirmed it. The revelation of the bond just added insult to injury, because I was smarter than to let myself be ruled by my emotions. He had played me like I was a stupid fool of a girl who had never been touched by a male before. My mind whirled around as the memories of every word the General had ever uttered to me rushed through my mind. He had drawn me in slowly, knowing that he was bonded to me. I turned my hand up and glared at the dark ink marking my pale skin. If Eoghan wanted to play games with me, I could play them better. And there was nothing deadlier than the wrath of a serpent ready to strike.

Chapter Forty One
Caelen

Every bone in my body felt like jelly when I finally made my way into the castle's gardens. I knew I could have asked to be transported back by Lochlan or Gideon, but I didn't want to explain why my face was splotchy from the sobs which had wracked my body in the grasslands. I curled my hand around the iron gate to the gardens, but movement caught my attention from the corner of my eye.

Stepping back slightly, I watched three figures gather around the stables. None of them moved to venture into the structure. Instead, one bent at the knees and shoved aside a pile of hay to reveal a cellar door. The crouched figure turned to check his surroundings, and I plastered myself into the shadows of the garden walls. Once satisfied they were alone, he reached out a single hand to press it against an orange painted symbol. My stomach dropped as it began to glow, clearly displaying the scorpion symbol of the rebels.

"Come on," the figure's gruff voice called out to the other two before stepping back and pulling open the marked door. A set of torches lit the exposed stairs. I didn't dare move closer, afraid the three rebels would notice my presence. They descended into the glowing stairwell, leaving the door open behind them.

Staring at the opening for a few moments longer, I crept forward. My toes traced the edge of the cellar, debating if I should follow them. It would be an incredibly stupid move, but I never claimed to make the smartest of choices. I could practically hear Eoghan's nagging voice screaming to turn around and run as far as I could from here. Rage heated my skin, and before I gave it another thought, I silently descended the stairs.

I pressed my spine against one of the dirt walls on either side of the staircase. My breath created a cloud in front of my face as the chill of being underground grew. The sounds of arguing could be heard on the other side of the wall as I made it to the final step. I froze in place, keeping as still as possible to ensure I was not found.

"He isn't coming," a deep voice yelled out over the rest. The tone was familiar, but I couldn't place where I had heard it before. A crash of glass hitting the ground made me jump in place. I slapped a hand over my mouth, suppressing the sound that had threatened to slip out. Breathing through my nose, I trained my ears back on to the male's voice. "What do expect from the King's errand boy?"

My brows pinched together in confusion. Who in Lochlan's court was close enough to his father to betray them? The sound of footsteps coming down the stairs slammed my thoughts back into reality. I was a sitting duck with nowhere to hide. Turning toward the room full of males, my face met the broad chest of one.

"What do we have here?" A hand gripped the nape of my braid, ripping my head back to look into his green eyes. I let out a screech, the awkward angle he had my neck in making it impossible to get away from him. My gaze locked on the red-haired male I had once held a threatening blade to. There was a deep purple bruise tracing the underside of Commander Tavish's eye, but his green eyes still glowed with disdain. I sucked in a breath as he leaned in. "Hello again, mortal champion."

Tavish pushed me back into the room he had just retreated from. I landed on my backside and tried to maneuver away from him, but his knuckle clipped the left side of my jaw. Pain ricocheted through the bone and blood filled my mouth. Another blow came before I could recover, this time finding its mark on my temple. I cowered, pulling both arms over my head to try to protect my face. It was a mistake, as a steel toed boot connected with my ribcage. I coughed out, bright red splattering over the floor and mixed with the dirt, making a muddy paste.

A hand gripped the back of my neck again, hauling me to my feet. I could no longer see Tavish as he slammed me against a large oak table in the center of the room. My cheek pressed into the surface, and through the black dots that were dancing in my vision, I could see a group of males staring at me with hungry eyes.

Tavish stroked a hand down my spine as he leaned over me. I could feel the sharp angles of his hips digging into my skin. A fractured sob broke through my lips as the commander began to speak again. "She is a pretty thing… just needs to be given a lesson in respect."

The males in the room began hollering, but I couldn't make out all they were saying as blood pounded in my ears. His hand traveled farther down, fingers tracing the edge of my pants. I tried to squirm away from him, but his iron grip over me made it impossible. I closed my eyes, waiting for this nightmare to be finished, when a guttural growl silenced the commotion.

"That is enough, Tavish."

I let out a shaky breath, the fear that had just held me captive slowly dissipating at the sound of a familiar voice. The commander's hand paused, resting on my hip. His fingertips dug into my skin so hard that I knew dark purple welts would be visible tomorrow.

"Here to spoil our fun?" Tavish's voice was venomous. There was the sound of shuffling feet before the commander's hands were ripped away from my body. I sucked in a shaky breath, letting the coolness of the wood table seep into my heated skin. Peeling my eyes open, my stomach dropped at the sight.

Eoghan had Tavish by the throat and pinned up against a wall covered in parchment paper. Why was Eoghan here? Had he followed me down into the cellar? If that were the case, why were none of the rebels phased by his presence? They appeared relaxed as they watched the general of the king's armies squeeze their commander until he was turning a dull shade of blue.

"Lay another hand on her, Tavish, and I will sever it from your body." Eoghan's voice was a deadly whisper. He leaned into the male, their noses brushing they were that close. "And then I will rip your heart from the chest and watch as the life fades from your eyes."

Tavish gulped, his throat bobbing under Eoghan's hand. The candlelight flickered in and out as the power that Eoghan had kept buried deep inside rumbled to the surface. A power that I begged to see unleashed on the male under his hold. Eoghan squeezed tighter. "Do we have an understanding?"

"Yes," Tavish croaked out, voice barely audible. Eoghan ripped his hand away from his neck, letting the male drop to the ground as he gasped in ragged breaths.

"Get out," Eoghan growled. No male had to be told twice as they scrambled from the bunker. I lay where I was, every inhale sending a sharp pain shooting through my ribs. Eoghan whirled on me, his normally bright hazel eyes now the same dark ones I had seen on the night we met. "Would you like to explain to me what you think you are doing here?"

Chapter Forty Two
Caelen

Eoghan's eyes blazed with an animalistic glint that made heat pool in my core. I forced a deep breath in, hissing through my teeth as a dull ache pulsed through my body. Placing both hands on the tabletop, I lifted my cheek from its surface. My heart pounded rapidly as I continued to watch Eoghan. It appeared he was no longer breathing. His eyes tracked down my body, taking in every bruise that was beginning to bloom on my skin.

"Me? What are you doing here?" I glared at him. Eoghan didn't move to respond to me. A dark chuckle slipped through my chapped lips. "If it's because you think you made a grand gesture saving me from him, save the speech. I know about the Scíath bond."

The muscles in Eoghan's jaw ticked as he clenched his teeth. I peeled my gaze from his, hanging my head as the world around me began to spin. I could hear the shuffle of boots coming toward me, but I couldn't bring myself to see if Eoghan had left the bunker. A haunting trace of a finger brushed under my chin and lifted it up until I fixed my eyes on Eoghan's golden ones.

They swam with an overwhelming sadness, one that came from years of disappointing the ones you loved. The same one I knew filled my own often.

Eoghan wet his lips before speaking. "Not even Lochlan knows of the bond. How did you come about this information?"

"Soren," I whispered, letting the syllables slowly roll off my tongue. He nodded once, hand coming up now to cup the side of my face. I concealed my nerves with a steely look. "You lied to me again. I thought for once…"

"Say it, Caelen." Eoghan leaned forward, face hanging directly over my own. "Swallow that pride of yours and finally say what you have been hiding from."

I pushed away from his touch, standing tall to tower over his bent form. "I thought, for once, I was going to be able to trust someone because you saw me! The real me. Not the beast I reveal to strangers, but the one who has tea with the male she swore to herself she would forever hate. I thought once you apologized for stealing me away from my lands that I could finally give in to this."

My hands waved between the two of us as I screamed. I knew no one could hear us underground, and Eoghan would never utter a word about this to another soul. A flood of hot tears rolled down my face. "But I was wrong again. I am an obligation to you, and that is all I will ever be."

"You," Eoghan began, voice was rough as he forced the words through clenched teeth, "will never be an obligation for me, Caelen. I am very familiar with the burden of duty. My entire existence has been built on the idea of serving another without question. But what I feel for you is not that."

Our heavy breathing mixed in the silence as I absorbed his words. Biting my lip, I shook my head. "You are mistaken. You don't feel anything for me, Eoghan. I am not someone capable of being loved. You can only be poisoned by me if you get too close."

"Then I would gladly drink every last drop." Eoghan's admission rattled something deep inside me, and on pure instinct, I was launching myself across the space between us to close it.

A low growl reverberated off my lips as his captured mine, glass shattered onto the ground as my hand swiped a crystal glass from the table. I climbed onto the tabletop as his hands landed on my hip, his harsh fingers digging into my skin. My fingers threaded through his hair, yanking and pulling to get him as close as possible. A deep groan emitted from him, the sound enveloping me in warm desire. Eoghan yanked me toward him, causing my knees to drag across the rough surface. A breathy gasp slipped from me as his lips trailed down the length of my throat.

Each kiss felt as if they were brushing against a different cord of my soul. My skin burned as he grew closer to my chest. A moan slipped out as the flick of Eoghan's tongue traced the burn lines that my necklace had left behind. The cold remnants of saliva caught onto the air, making my head lull back. I reached down, pulling at him by his dark hair to bring him back to my mouth.

Eoghan gripped the back of my head, fingers knotting in the hair at the nape of my neck. He tugged, pulling me away until I was mere inches from his face. I did not resist him as his other hand trailed down my front. The rough pads of his fingers danced over the fabric covering my pebbled buds. I was completely at the mercy of this male, and for once, I was more than alright with that. I tried to shift against his hand, wanting him to stop teasing me with the featherlight strokes.

Eoghan paused. He forced me to make eye contact with him. There was a feral glint that flashed across his golden eyes. Every inch of my skin was on fire, its relentless building in a tight knot in my core. I could feel the slickness pooling between my legs as he leaned closer to my chest. Eoghan's heated breath brushed up against my skin as he spoke. "Such a needy little beast."

He peered up at me through his lashes, examining my reaction as he toyed with the buckle of my leathers. Eoghan reached down to my thigh, retrieving the blade he had gifted me. The metal glowed under the firelight of the room. I stopped breathing as he brought it down, dragging the coolness across my collarbone. In one swift motion, he tore through the leather, exposing my breasts to him. I arched into him as he dove down, taking my nipple to his mouth. A panting moan escaped from me. His iron grip held me in place as I writhed underneath his tongue as he sucked and nipped. I could feel his hardness press into my leg, and the thought of me bringing him to this point sent another wave of desire washing through me. Eoghan caught my gaze again before biting into my skin. The coolness of blood rushed to the surface, and I cried out, letting the pain mix with pleasure as his tongue lapped up the droplets. Light kisses soothed the stinging skin.

My hands followed the planes of his chest, taking in every divot and curve that he had honed from years of battle. He moved on to my other breast, not wasting any time in worshiping it as he had to the first. My fingers looped into the ties of his pants, but a strong grip stopped my movements.

"Sweetheart." Eoghan's gravelly tone pulled my attention back to him. Lust danced in his gaze. "Do not tempt me any further."

"What if I want to tempt you?" I mused, lashes dipping lightly as I tried to blink back my clouded thoughts. My heart hammered loudly in my chest. "What if I want you to claim me in every way that you can think of?"

"I want nothing more than to do that." Eoghan stood, bringing me back from my suspended state and close to his face. My lashes brushed up against his cheekbone as I tried to regain a normal breathing pattern. He dragged a knuckle down my burning cheek. "But when I take you to bed, I want you to ache for me."

He leaned in, a ghost of a kiss dancing across my lips. I moved to close the gap again, but the hand that had just been stroking my face latched around my throat, holding me in place. "I want you desperate in the same way I am for you."

I opened my mouth to respond to him, ready to tell him anything if it meant he would let me feel that small amount of pleasure that had just washed over me, but he captured my lips, swallowing the words from my tongue as his danced with mine.

Eoghan pulled away, bringing both hands to the side of my face to hold my stare as he spoke. "For on your body, I will create a manuscript, so you will never forget who you belong to."

Chapter Forty Three
Lochlan

Report," Blaine, my father's lead advisor, called out. He had his head propped against his hand, a bored look on his face as he stared down the solider in front of him. How young were they allowing these males to be conscripted? I eyed Eoghan with a questioning look, but his brows were pinched together in the same way as mine. I could feel the irritation radiating off him as he counted all the ways he could enact punishments on the soldiers ranked below him that had sent a child to give report.

"Rebels have been spotted in outlying villages. They have been slowly moving toward what we assume is the castle." The boy soldier's voice shook slightly. His hands gripped down on the parchment so hard, I was concerned it was going to deteriorate under the pressure. He shoved the crumpled sheet down in front of Blaine. "But they are unlike any other rebels we have seen before."

"What, have they donned a new wardrobe?" Sylas teased from the other end of the table. I glared at her, but she paid me no mind. Her legs were tossed up onto the table, barely even looking toward the solider. She picked at something under her nails. "Maybe a funny hat added to the uniform?"

"Sylas," Blaine warned. She flashed him a wicked smile, which only earned her a playful wink. I didn't understand how someone who could cause so much mischief could also have the oldest advisor wrapped around her perfectly polished finger. Blaine's gaze hardened as he turned back to the boy. "Continue."

"They appear to be in a trance-like state, sir." the soldier's voice was an octave higher. "Eyes glazed over, and no matter how many times you try to kill them, they keep coming back at you."

Eoghan placed his elbows on the table, leaning in. "Are they able to be killed?"

"The only one killed was from the tip of a golden arrow straight through the eye."

Blaine nodded. "Leave us."

The boy did not need to be told another time as he fled from the room. Blaine's eyes stared straight ahead at nothing. I scrubbed at the scruff growing on my chin as his distant voice spoke. "Someone or something is using ancient magic to conjure the Fear Gorta again."

"There is no possibility that it is her again, is there, Blaine?" I called toward him. His eyes snapped to mine. Seona had used her ability to clip lifelines and tie them to her own to suck the life from her most loyal followers until they were shells of creatures. She was the wielder and commander of an undead army. It was easy to win when your soldiers did not perish on the battlefield. Instead, you could stab the bastards in the chest until their hearts were hanging from your blade and they would still keep coming for you.

"I will never say it is impossible for the Second Sister to rise back to power, but I would imagine if that were the case, her queenliness would step out of hiding to warn us," Blaine grumbled, arms crossing one another. I nodded toward him as he stood. "I must go report the findings to Elara and your father."

Blaine bent his head in respect before exiting the room. I gripped onto the edge of the table, the wood cracking slightly as my fingers tightened around it. Sylas stood, beginning her standard pacing, as she did after each meeting. My shadows followed behind her in a dark cloud, their wispy tendrils brushing up against her white hair.

"It seems I need to instruct that more archery lessons in the camps be conducted." Eoghan's joking voice pulled me back to him. I stared at him in horror. Out of everyone, I thought he would be more upset at the mention of the Fear Gorta. After what Seona did to him, I don't think I could ever stomach the thought of taking one of them on again.

Sylas stopped mid-step, eyes going wide as she took in his tone. "What has you so cheery?"

"Nothing." He chuckled at her, and I scanned his relaxed form. Tiny pink scratches littered his neck. Eoghan stood and leaned over the table. "We have dealt with Fear Gorta before, and from what I just heard these ones are easily killed with a good blow to their eye socket."

"Let's use the term "easy" lightly here, Eoghan." Sylas rolled her eyes at him. Pulling out the chair directly across from me, she slumped down into it. "Maybe Em and Theo can enlighten us about their time with the Sisters. Surely one of them knows how Seona created her monsters."

"Don't," I gritted out. "Leave the Twins out of this one. I want to monitor their movements, see if this is just a small group of rebels playing with magic they are not equipped to wield, or if we have a bigger mess on our hands."

Sylas nodded. Her eyes scanned Eoghan the same way I did just moments ago. A wild smile spread across her face. "Why does it appear that you were mauled by a wild beast? Perhaps one with long brown hair and a ruby necklace?"

Eoghan snarled at her. Sylas licked her canines in a taunting way, blue eyes glowing with nothing but trouble only my Second could conjure. Eoghan leaned across the table, the maps and parchment crunching under the weight of him. Sylas didn't shrink into her seat as the room's light dimmed. "Come on, Eoghan, release all that pent-up magic. I have been dying to play with something for days."

"If you two must go after each other's throats, can you take it outside?" I asked in a bored tone as I lifted my hand to let a lone shadow weave in and out of my fingers. Sylas slumped down in her seat, pouting at me for ruining her fun. "Sy, I need you on the ground. Find anything you can on these undead rebels."

"Shame, my gown for the ball was spectacular." Sylas perked up at my command. We both knew there was no ball occurring, but she refused to agree to anything without mocking me.

Eoghan snorted at her comment. "You always wear that

Gods-awful yellow dress. Lochlan should really gift you a new one."

"And what do you think the mortal would wear to a ball in her honor?" Sylas teased. Eoghan reached out, swiping to get a hold of her, but she pranced out of the room. Before the door shut, her voice called back, "Or maybe we should be asking what she wouldn't be wearing at the end of the night."

Chapter Forty Four
Caelen

Does it snow here?" I asked Eoghan. The chill of winter was due to show any day now, and there was a part of me that missed waiting for the first snow fall to stick to the ground as a child. Eoghan turned away from the large map hanging on the bunker's wall. We had taken a liking to hiding away here the past few days, but neither of us had pushed the other to discuss what we had done in this very room. How Eoghan's lips had made my skin buzz until the early morning hours.

"Yes." Eoghan smiled at me. I twirled a single pin that would normally mark a location on a map between my fingertips. He stepped forward, plucking it from me mid-spin. "But, the snow rarely sticks to the ground this close to the castle."

I slumped down at the fact. My eyes wandered around the small bunker. There were propaganda posters pasted to the walls, their bright orange symbol smeared across in a rushed manner. Not one looked the same as I took them in. My mind wandered back to the males who had attacked me. "You never told me why you were down here? Or why Tavish is conspiring with the rebels against Loch."

Eoghan's booming laugh echoed off the walls. "Conspiring? Caelen, no one is conspiring against Lochlan. We are trying to infiltrate the rebels from the inside. I can't very well send Sylas into their ranks."

"She would destroy them all for the fun of it." I shuddered at the thought. As much as I liked Lochlan's second, Sylas terrified me. She could cut me into ribbons without so much as batting an eye. And what was worse is she would enjoy it.

Eoghan leaned a hip against the table. "Well, yes, but they would also know who she is. Tavish is overseeing who is coming and going into their ranks for me. He gathers the information and I relay that to Lochlan."

"So, I'm not harboring a rebel?" I winked at him.

Eoghan brushed a curl from my face. "No, but if that is your taste in males, I may be able to point you on the right direction."

"My taste in males?" I giggled, face already burning red with the words that were about to spill from my mouth. "I think you are well aware what my type of male is."

Eoghan simply winked at me, turning back to the map. Tiny red pins littered the parchment's surface, indicating where the rebels had been spotted recently. A shiver traveled down my spine as I let my mind wander to what Sylas might reveal when she returned.

"Have you ever known someone who was turned into a Fear Gorta?" I blurted out. My eyes widened at my question, and I stammered, trying to apologize for being so forward, but no words came from my open mouth.

The muscles in Eoghan's neck pulled taut at my question, and I knew I had overstepped. I shrank down in my seat, wanting desperately to disappear. His voice was deadly quiet when he responded. "Yes. She entangled herself with Seona and that cost her life."

"I'm sorry," I breathed out. Eoghan dropped his head, letting it hang in defeat. I was on my feet and in front of him before my mind caught up to my movements.

Devastation coated his features, and I felt like I was choking on the sadness that surrounded him. Taking his face in my hands, I drew his attention to me. "I am sorry you lost her, Eoghan."

"She would have loved you." His comment was barely audible. I smiled at him, letting him take his time to get this off his chest. It was clear that it had been eating him alive for a long while and I was honored to be the one to take on this heartbreak with him. "My sister Jemma was quick witted and incredibly bright. Lochlan always joked that if she wanted, she could take the crown from him just by outsmarting him. I warned her that standing by Seona would only bring her downfall, but she was stubborn and loyal to a fault."

Eoghan's voice shook, eyes glazing over as he dove deep into a memory that had long since been buried. "Jemma left the camps one night, and we hadn't heard from her in weeks. There was a breach in the wards that night. I had been on patrol when I came upon her."

Tears streamed down his face. I ran a soothing hand over his cheek, catching them under my fingers. Eoghan reached out, resting his hands on my hips, and holding on as if I were going to dissipate like smoke. He drew in a breath. "It wasn't my Jemma. The thing looked like her, but its eyes didn't hold the same light they once did. They were glassy, the green dull, and I could barely stomach looking at the sickly gray hue her skin had taken on. She was one of Seona's mindless soldiers, but it was a message for me. A reminder of what she was capable of if we continued with the fight against her."

Silence hung in the air for a moment as Eoghan's eyes finally met mine. "That night, I had to put a knife in my baby sister's skull."

"She would have killed you, Eoghan," I said, my mind not fully able to wrap itself around having to kill your own blood. I would sooner die than have to make the decision Eoghan had made. Eoghan gathered my hands in his, pulling them away from his face and laying a kiss on each of them.

"Promise me something, Caelen." Dropping my hands, he combed his fingers through my curls, tilting my head back so I had no other choice than to look at him. "Cut my heart out if they capture me and turn me into one of those mindless soldiers."

"No." I tried to pull out of his grip, but he held strong, not letting me hide from him.

"I mean it, sweetheart. If I am taken and return a different male than the one standing in front of you, cut my heart from my chest. It belongs only to you now."

Theo stood across from me, eyes watching my every movement as I pulled another book from the bookshelf. Lochlan had volunteered the male to help me look into the lore of Fate

Spinners. So far, we were coming up with nothing that we didn't already know. Every text described Spinners as creatures that had the ability to wield the past, present, and future of every living thing. But there was no guide on how a Spinner tapped into their power.

Turning around, I threw a sneer at Theo. "Do you hate me just for the hell of it?"

Theo flashed a predatory grin. "I do not hate you. I can see what the future you will bring to the realms."

Laughing, I threw out my hands with a dramatic flair. "And what do the powers above say I will bring to the realms?"

"Nothing. That is the problem with your path, it is never certain," Theo hissed at me. He twisted around, slamming the same book Lochlan had first showed me when explaining what a Fate Spinner was onto a stack of books we had been going through. "Don't you find it odd that you come into our realm, and then suddenly creatures of Seona's are beginning to appear."

"Are you accusing me of something, Theo?"

"Don't make me laugh." Theo glared at me. He flipped open the book. "I think Seona has crawled out of whatever cave she has been hiding in because your power is calling to her."

Theo flipped the page, finger coming down on a piece of text. "Here."

"I hate to break it to you, witchling, but I wasn't taught to read the old language in my schooling," I mutter toward him.

He rolled his eyes at me, finger following the text as he read. "To unlock a magical relic, the chosen bloodline must channel the power within. This will break the restraints."

"Or I could just smash it on the ground." I smirked at his annoyance. "I don't even know why you are entertaining the idea. I can't unleash this on the world. Not only is Seona's power in here, but a God is trapped in this thing."

"I know," Theo mumbled.

I blinked at him in disbelief. "What do you mean, *you know*?"

"Demios is not quiet, and since you have not been entertaining him, any time we are in the same room, he is chattering away with my sister. I think Em thinks he has fallen in love with her."

"Well, I wish them a very happy life together." I snorted at the statement. Theo cracked a slight smile at me. Gasping, I pointed at him. "Did I amuse you so much that you smiled?"

"Don't get used to it, little mortal."

We sat in silence for a long while, only the sound of embers crackling in the fireplace filling the room. Theo was engrossed in the ancient text, every so often taking notes on a piece of parchment paper. I spun the necklace between my fingers, the familiar pulse of power flowing through my body.

"You won't be given a practice run if we ever need to unlock that." Theo's voice filled my ears. I flicked my gaze to his and nodded. "But to unlock the relic, you will need to cut your palm and grasp the necklace in your hand. Make sure you are focusing all your energy on breaking down an invisible wall, brick by brick. You will know it is working if the relic burns your hand, but do not release it until you feel the necklace's glass crack."

Nodding numbly, I repeated the steps in my mind, memorizing every one for a day I hope would never come. Tilting my head toward Theo, I asked the question that had been nagging me since he began reading. "If you cannot see my future, why are you helping me?"

"Because the path I do believe in does not include you dying in the final task."

Chapter Forty Five
Caelen

A blood-curdling scream jolted me from my sleep. I shot up, eyes trying to focus on the danger that was waiting for me. In the darkness, Coira leaned into Lorna as sobs shook her body as they came. Light from a crack in the door shone into the room. It was partially blocked by Ainsley, who was frantically whispering to someone on the other side. I threw the blankets aside, stepping onto the cool floor. Dread filled the pit of my stomach as I made my way toward Ainsley.

"What is going on?" I called out to her. Ainsley turned large eyes brimming with tears to me. Her mouth opened and closed, words not coming to her in her panicked state.

"Caelen." Eoghan's voice called my attention to where he stood in the doorway. His own eyes were bloodshot, and I could tell that he had been crying recently. A lone shadow slithered into the room, wrapping itself around my wrist. My heart began to beat rapidly, panic overtaking all of my senses.

"Where is he?" I gasped out. The floor seemed to be ripped out from under me as I tried to catch my breath. Eoghan was speaking to me, but I couldn't hear him over the buzzing in my ears. I pushed past him, not caring if I didn't know where I was going, my body was running on pure instinct.

Eoghan followed behind me as I bounded down the stairs, the nightgown I wore swished against my thighs as I went. My bare feet skidding on the marble floor, sending me tumbling into the wall. Catching myself, I looked back toward Eoghan, who motioned for me to follow the hall to my left. The shadow on my wrist pulled me along down the corridor, almost as if it were trying to drag me faster to Lochlan. Time slowed as I made it to a pair of black doors, people rushing in and out of them in a frantic flurry. I pushed past a female carrying a pitcher of water as I entered the room.

Laying in the center of a large, quilted bed was the Prince. His normally pale skin was now almost translucent against the deep maroon sheets. His chest rose and fell in labored breaths, lips coated with the bright hue of fresh blood.

I choked out a sob, tears pouring down my face as I stared at my friend. My legs shook before they gave away entirely, knees hitting the hardwood floor below me. The sting of the fall was nothing compared to the sharp pain that was cracking my heart in two. Falling to the side, I caught myself before I could topple all the way over. There was a distant screaming that was bouncing off my skull, the female's wails driving a knife in my heart. It took me a few moments to realize that the female screaming was me, as I looked up to see every eye in the room watching me. Arms scooped me up, pulling me into their chest as I continued to weep.

"Come on, sweetheart," Eoghan whispered into my hairline. He carried me from the room, and down the hall until we had retreated into another room. I kept my head tucked in his chest as he sunk down on a mattress, settling me between his legs.

"What happened?" I croaked out and braced myself for the worst.

He sucked in a heavy breath as he tried to keep his emotions at bay. "He was poisoned. We don't know how it slipped past his taster."

"Loch has his own personal taster?" I asked, a hysterical laugh bubbling in my chest that I couldn't stop.

Eoghan didn't seem fazed by my hysteria, continuing on. "Every royal has a taster. It is to ensure this does not happen."

"Is he going to be okay?" I whispered, turning my head so it rested against his chest.

Eoghan looked down at me, placing a single kiss on my hairline. "The healers are confident that he will recover, but they are unsure when he will wake."

Gulping down another wave of tears, I closed my eyes and focused on matching my breathing pattern with Eoghan. "He shouldn't be alone in there."

"I promise he is not alone. Lochlan has the best healers in the realms working on him right now." Eoghan inhaled deeply. "Right now, the best thing we can do for him is rest. We will visit him in the morning."

I nodded numbly, but allowed the darkness of sleep to slowly pull me under.

Four days. That was how long Lochlan had been unresponsive, lost to a poison induced coma. All but the one shadow that was wrapped around my wrist was gone. I had barely left his bedside other than to bathe and change my clothes. Food had felt impossible to get down when Eoghan brought it to me. I picked at a bread roll, tiny crumbs littering my plate.

"What's going through that mind of yours right now?" Eoghan's watchful eyes scanned my face from the chair next to me.

"What if I fail?" I turned to gauge his reaction.

His eyebrows knitted together at my question. "Fail what, exactly?"

"All of it. The Games, keeping a relic of ancient power away from Seona if she ever comes for it. I am not a savior."

"Lochlan and I would argue that you are much more than that, Caelen. You do not give your selflessness enough credit." Eoghan reached out, resting a hand on my thigh.

I slapped it away, standing from my chair as I spoke. "Selflessness or self-preservation?"

A groan of pain filled the room, causing both Eoghan and I to spin around to Lochlan. His dark eyes were watching our interaction, a small smirk tracing his lips. "Why can't you just stop for once in your life and see that you cannot control everything, Caelen?"

"Loch." I launched myself at him. My arms wrapped around his neck in a tight hug. "I am so glad you are awake."

"Caelen," Lochlan coughed out, and I pulled back slightly.

"Sorry." I smiled sheepishly. Lochlan peered over at the pile of books sitting next to him.

"Have you been here the entire time?" He eyed me suspiciously. I nodded, and a bright smile broke across his face. "You see that, Eoghan, she does care. You better watch out, I might steal her from you."

He winked at his best friend, and a soft giggle emitted from me. I pulled away, stepping off the bed and sitting back in my chair. The next hour was filled with updating Lochlan on all he had missed, which wasn't much, but it was just good to hear his voice. A pained look flashed across Lochlan's face, making Eoghan stand from his chair and retreat from the room, mumbling something about getting a healer.

"You look like death," I joked as Eoghan disappeared around the corner.

Lochlan pushed himself up on the mountain of pillows behind him. "I am Death, Caelen."

"No, you're not." I shook my head at the male. "Death is brutal and unyielding in its path of destruction. You, my dear Loch, are too lovely of a soul to cause such pain."

"It sounds as if you know death personally." He smirked at me.

I flashed him a wicked smile of my own. "Very."

Eoghan soon returned with the healer, and I excused myself from the room. When I reached the threshold, I gripped down on the handle and turned to look back at the Prince. "I really am glad you are okay, Lochlan."

Exiting the room, I pulled the door closed behind me, but

the sound of Lochlan's hushed words stopped me in my tracks. "She has found herself sulking at the fact that this occurred, has she not?"

I could hear Eoghan scoff at him. "Of course she has, and to think she complimented you."

"You heard that?" Lochlan questioned. There was the sound of shuffling before he spoke again. "I think what she was alluding at, Eoghan, is that she herself is the one who is brutal and unyielding."

"Caelen does not give herself enough credit for how much she cares." Eoghan's voice cracked. "She reminds me of Jemma in that way. So brutally stubborn, it drives me insane."

Lochlan chuckled. "The Gods have tested you with Caelen, and I think you are coming out on the winning side this time."

"Indeed, brother."

Chapter Forty Six
Caelen

Lochlan would not compete with us in the final task. His condition had improved but the healers wanted to take a cautious approach to his healing. In light of the news, the Elders and each of the realm's current rulers had come to the agreement that one realm would forfeit their designated task to ensure the crown was secured swiftly. Having the fate of their lands hanging in the balance of a magical game of capture the flag gave opportunity for another attack to occur. In the end Lochlan's father agreed to allow the Cogadh realm control the course of the final task.

I shifted back and forth as my nerves creeped to the surface. The Elders wanted to make a big deal of the final three champions and that meant announcing each team before they were dropped into the arena.

"Would you stop that?" Sylas snapped at me. She had been in a foul mood ever since she arrived back at the castle this morning. I planted my feet in place, not wanting to set her off.

I sucked in one last breath before the iron gates separating us from the crowd swung open. Theo gave me a slight shove, propelling me forward. I staggered through the arena's threshold, gulping down my breakfast that threatened to come back up as the crowd roared with approval. Hundreds of eyes stared down on us, all of them waiting to see if the mortal champion would let the crown slip through her fingers and damn them all.

A light touch brushed up against the small of my back. Eoghan leaned down, his hot breath tickling the inside of my ear. "Do you feel that? The power that is circulating through this place?"

I nodded, not trusting my voice to not betray me. He was so close I could feel his lips turn up, "It is all for you, and I'll be damned if you don't drink in every last drop."

The General's lips traced the pulse point just below my ear, whispering against my skin as he pulled away. "Let them grovel at your feet. I will be once we are through with this."

Rolling my shoulders back, I drank in the vibrating power that Eoghan had spoken of. The surge gave me a boost of energy as I strutted forward, my team behind me. We arrived in the center of the arena, and I could hear my name being chanted in the distance. A single orb of light shot from the dirt as each member of my teammates gathered in a circle around it.

"We win this together," I screamed over the crowd.

"Together," Eoghan agreed.

Sylas's bright teeth shined under the glowing light. "I wouldn't want it any other way."

"Well, if Sylas is going down"—Embryss shoved her shoulder into the blondes— "then I am going with her."

"By obligation, I guess I will agree to your terms," Theo grumbled, but I could see the playful glint in his eyes. In unison, we lifted our hands and placed them on the orb. It flashed three times before we were pulled into its clutches and spat back out in the middle of a raging heat.

***

Sand covered every inch of the landscape. I could feel the relentless beat of the sun stealing the sweat from my pores and tightening my skin. My tongue fell heavy and dry in my mouth as I searched for some form of relief, only to find nothing. The desert heat had taken anything wet and replaced it with stale, dry air.

"We should start moving," Theo stated, his hands tracing the handle of the hatchet on his back. "There is nowhere to hide here, unless you want to start digging your own grave."

"No one's digging anyone's grave," Eoghan scolded him. He peered down at my wrist one artfully carved eyebrow ticking up in a questioning look. "It stuck around even after Lochlan woke up?"

The dark shadow which had swirled around my wrist since the night of Lochlan's poisoning was still locked in place. I shrugged. "It likes me, and it feels like we have Loch with us."

"Come on, you two," Sylas's voice called to us. I turned, following the trail of boot prints in the sand to find them. Sylas, Theo, and Embryss were halfway down the hill when the ground began to shake underneath us, sand rushed around our feet in a landslide, burying our feet in place. We were being swallowed like quicksand. I reached out, and grabbed a hold of Eoghan's arm to steady myself. The earth settled for a few moments before a large creature shot from its surface. Sand whipped through the air in a hazy explosion; I covered my eyes in my best effort to shield myself from the assault. The dark gray and white scaled snake arced in front of Sylas sending her reeling back. Its mouth opened up, showing off rows of razor-sharp teeth, fading away into nothing but an endless black pit.

"Is that—" I sputtered, words disappearing from my tongue as a second head protruded from the snake's mouth where it's tongue should have been. The second head's black eyes snapped down to where Sylas, Embryss, and Theo stood, a murderous glint shining in them. Sylas slowly reached behind her back, drawing her weapon. The staff was a long metal pole that curved in opposite directions of each other to make two sharp points at the end. She spun it once above her head before striking.

The snake dove back down, head slamming into the sand to avoid Sylas's assault but the end of the weapon clipped its scaled skin. A spray of black blood rained down above us.

"Watch its tail," Theo called up to Eoghan as he advanced to assist Sylas.

My eyes scanned the ground, mistaking the shifting for the end of the snake. In this desert, it was near impossible to track. A haunting rattled skittered through the air like the beckoning call of death before I found the cause. It shot up, menacing spikes protruding from the hardened scales of the tail. Eoghan and I both moved together, racing away from it as it swung down. Sand rained down around us like an explosive seeking its target, the texture assaulting my lungs and eyes.

I stumbled around blindly for a moment, relying only on my ears to predict the beast's next move. But all I could hear was the battering force of wind, and a squealing whistle before the snake's tail whipped toward us again and rattled the ground at our feet.

I risked peeling my eyes open. With the furious glare of the sun and the sand dancing through the air, the world around me had become a haze of color and shapes. I reached over, pulling Eoghan's sword from its place on his back before swinging blindly behind me. The blade slammed into one of the spikes, slicing it down the middle. Yellow liquid oozed from the wound, and I gagged at the repulsive stench that consumed the air.

Eoghan yanked me back by my leathers, "Don't get that on your skin. A Beithir's poison will eat away at any surface it comes in contact with."

Just as promised, the yellow poison pooled onto the sand's surface and began to cave in. I scrambled forward after Eoghan, my ankles sinking in the deep sand as we raced up the newly formed sand dune. My heart thudded rapidly in my chest as the horrifying feeling of being pulled back by the earth's invisible force overtook me. A scream ripped through my lips as I fell, arms flying up to try and grasp onto anything that would save me from the free fall. A hand connected with mine, stopping my descent with a harsh tug.

I locked eyes with Eoghan, as a ragged breath rattled down my entire body. He smirked down at me, "Don't worry, I got you sweetheart."

"Just pull me up before that thing comes back," I hissed at

him. Eoghan chuckled once and then hauled me over the edge of the hole. I grumbled under my breath, "You made that look to easy."

He ignored my comment, and held out his palm face up for me like he wanted me to hand him something. I looked at him with a wild look, "What?"

"Give me back my sword," Eoghan snapped, urgency coated his words, with his eyes on Sylas as she boosted Embryss up and over the snake's long neck. I turned my gaze down to the never-ending crater that was behind us. Eoghan pulled his attention away from what was happening below us, "Caelen, now."

"The thing is…" I shrank down slightly as his eyes burned, alight with anger.

"You dropped it didn't you?" Eoghan shouted, his hands raising in an annoyed gesture, "That's just perfect Caelen."

"Oh, I am so sorry, I didn't protect your precious sword with my life when I was falling through the earth!" I yelled back at him. Eoghan rolled his eyes, frustrated words lost to the wind. Shoving past him I continued toward our three other teammates, leaving him to fume behind me.

Embryss now appeared to be riding the Beithir as it whipped her around. The quick movements didn't appear to faze the witch as she maneuvered herself around the wide neck to of the snake catch its stare. Their eyes leveled in a brutal exchange of power and the creature fell limp, slumping into the ground. A wave of sand propelled from its beastly size. I had half the mind to react quick enough and cover my eyes from the onslaught of sand.

The desert fell silent.

Blood pumped in my ears, in tune with the erratic beat of my heart, I squinted through the light until my eyes adjusted once again. I was greeted with the image of Embryss heaving for breath as she straddled the Beithir. She looked every part the warrior that burned inside her as sand settled around her.

"Now," Embryss snarled. Her typically sweet tone a thing of the past as she held the Beithir in her clutches. Sweat gleamed on her skin, and sand marred her cheek as she lifted her head in our direction; her hair a flurry of color as it whipped through the wind.

Theo stepped forward—his hatchet raised in the air above his head as he positioned himself directly in front of the snake. He slammed it down between the Beithir's eyes. A sickening squelch rang through the air as the weapon embedded itself into the scales. I flinched away as Theo ripped the hatchet from the body of the beast and repeated the movement. I watched in silence as he hacked away again, and again.

After a few moments of silence, I turned back to the scene in front of me. Sylas had a wicked smile tracing her lips as she stared down Theo. A drop of black blood dripped from the tip of Theo's nose as he returned the weapon to its home on his back.

Embyrss's chest heaved up and down as exhaustion from subduing the creature came over her. Sylas snapped her eyes up to the female witch, concern twitched at her brows as she breathed. "You okay, Em?"

"Yes, it has been a long time since I have had to use that much power to—" Embyrss's tired words cut short when the whizzing sound of metal soared through the air.

A scream ripped through the space around us.

A large iron staff embedded through Embryss's stomach. Blood seeped through her leathers. Her body slumped sideways, sending her sliding off the Beithir. Sylas and Theo leapt forward at the same time, getting to the female as she clattered into the sand.

I turned to see who had thrown the weapon, and my eyes locked on Axiom's deadly ones. A bone chilling sweat split down my spine as he wound his arm to throw another staff.

"Get down!" I yelled. The weapon sliced through the air toward Eoghan and I. We both hit the ground, the force knocked the wind from my lungs. I began to crawl, sending sand everywhere as I did.

"Here." Eoghan held out a silver dagger.

I looked at him, confirming what he wanted me to do. He nodded once, and that was all it took for me to stand. I flipped the dagger in the air once, twice, before catching the weapon and chucking it across the desert. The metal sparkled in the air, sending a spiral of rainbow color over the sand, before hitting its intended target. Axiom gurgled, grappling at the blade stuck clean through the middle of his windpipe.

Blood poured out of the corner of his mouth as he sputtered and clutched the handle with fumbling fingers. His teammates stared wide-eyed at him as he hit the sand in a heap of himself. When they turned their gazes on me, I raised an eyebrow at them and held my hand out for Eoghan. He didn't even have to hand me the second blade before they were running away from the scene. I had just taken down their champion with a single dagger.

"You are enjoying that too much." Eoghan smirked at me, and I just tossed him a wink in response.

My feet slipped through the sand, landing me abruptly in front of Embryss. The blood had drained from her deep brown skin, turning her ashen and sickly. Her chest heaved in pained gasps. Theo held her from behind, his hands painted with the blood of his sister.

"You have to go," Embryss's light voice commanded. She had mustered up as much conviction as she could manage through her faltering voice. I stared at her with wild eyes, and began to protest, but she cut me off. "Once you venture farther into the arena, the Elders will pull me from the Games and get me to a healer."

"That is a gamble Em," Sylas mumbled, her shaky hands caked in blood as she pressed down around the staff in a desperate attempt to slow the bleeding.

Embryss grunted, "Theo and I are the last of our bloodline. They wouldn't risk it. Besides, if you have your hands on me, they will for certain rip us both from the arena. They are probably itching right now to get you out and look at that."

I turned toward Sylas. A nasty bite wound enveloped her pale shoulder. Black inky veins were sprouting from the two puncture wounds, indicating poison was seeping into her bloodstream. It didn't look far from infecting her entire body.

They stared each other down, eyes glossy and glazed with unshed tears, gleaming in the sunlight. Sylas glared up at

Embryss, pushing down hard on the wound she was tending to. Embryss squeaked out in pain, a wicked smirk turning Sylas's lips up

"Stop being a brat, Em."

Theo turned toward Eoghan who was hovering behind me. He dipped his chin behind us, "Take my sword with you, but don't let the little mortal lose this one."

I could hear Eoghan step away from us before returning and setting a hand on my shoulder, "We have to go. Em is right, once we are far enough away, they will pull them."

"We said we would do this together," I said, voice wobbling with emotions.

"That was before that brute stabbed me." Embryss tried to laugh, but a painful sputtering shattered what was once a melodic sound. I blinked slowly at both Theo and Sylas. Their faces paled like they were going to be sick as Embryss's condition worsened. She winked at me. "Don't worry, little mortal, I will show you more of my tricks another time."

Blinking back tears and swallowing a harsh breath against my throat that grated like sandpaper, I nodded and rose from my crouched position. Eoghan guided me away from the three of them, but Sylas called back to me. "Remind them what happens when you underestimate a mortal, Caelen."

Chapter Forty Seven
Caelen

Sweat formed a thick layer between my skin and leather armor. My hairline was soaked and sweat beaded from my forehead to the tip of my nose. I swallowed against the sandpaper that lined my throat, and licked my tongue against the roof of my mouth. Every aimless step we trudged through the sand solidified the gnawing feeling in my gut that we would be stuck here for eternity. I kept my gaze mostly to the shifting sand under my feet in an attempt to hide them from the vicious sun, relying heavily on following Eoghan's large footprints, as I trailed a few paces behind. But then he stopped abruptly, and I met the stone wall of his backside headfirst. His reflexes were swift as he reached an arm behind himself to steady me.

I lifted my heavy-lidded eyes to find what had made him stop. A cave jutted out from the desert, its mouth wide, and black, calling to the entrance. The walls were lined with jagged rocks and the air flowing from it was cool against my sweaty skin. I could hear the sound of water dripping from the stalactites hanging from above.

"You have got to be kidding me," I groaned, knowing we would need to travel into the cave's darkness to find the flag. Eoghan ignored my complaints and made his way into the jaws of the cavern. I followed close behind him, keeping one hand firmly gripped on my dagger, and the other traced his backside to help guide me through the dark that I knew he could see better in. Stupid Sìth vision.

The screech of a winged creature sent me stumbling into Eoghan. He whirled around on me. "Watch your step."

"Don't be a brute," I growled, words coming through clenched teeth. Shoving my shoulder into his, I traveled around him. Darkness be damned.

"I'll stop being one when you stop being so stubborn," he grumbled behind me. I ignored him and ventured forward. The roar of rushing water echoed off the jagged walls of the cavern and consumed every inch of my body, urging me to pick up speed. At the end of the path, the cave's walls split apart, arching into an entrance covered in thick moss, leading to a glorious waterfall. Its sparkling water fell from high above until it crashed against the lake below us, sending mist around it. The smell of damp soil filled my nose, and I inhaled deeply, letting the moisture of the room soothed my aching throat. The azure water seemed to glow against the mossy bank, but the center faded to a pit of black, hiding whatever might lie beneath the surface.

I stumbled down to the water's edge and fell to my knees, cupping water and pouring it over my head. It streamed like ice down my body, and I gasped, welcoming the discomfort before repeating my actions. Instantly my body is soothed and I forget about the brutal desert outside, lost in the magical reprieve of the cavern.

"Look." Eoghan's finger pointed toward the slight wave of a flag behind a break in the falls. I grinned, the overwhelming feeling of joy taking over my senses.

Pure elation filled my veins, and a new sense of power thrummed through my body. I felt alive again, as opposed to the sluggish heap of skin and aching bones. This feeling was overpowering. As I looked back at Eoghan, I felt as if a weight had lifted off my shoulders. This was it. The last task.

And the flag was in reach.

There must be some sort of sick twist to this, but after all we had endured outside, maybe this truly was the end. I didn't spare another thought to it.

I jumped to my feet and threw my arms around Eoghan's neck, pulling his lips down to mine. This felt right. They brushed against mine in surprise before taking control of the kiss. We moved passionately, stroking each other's mouths as relief surged through my body. His fingers grazed the underside of my jaw, caressing the delicate skin as he cupped one side of my face and dragged me deeper into him. His teeth latched down on my bottom lip, pulling at it for a moment. I groaned, but as soon as the sting of his bite appeared, it was gone, and his lips were traveling away from mine.

Eoghan's arm wrapped around my waist and his deft fingers pressed into the base of my spine, anchoring me to him. His head dipped down column of my neck, and I had to resist moaning out loud when his lips met my pulse point. Bolts of heat sparked in my lower abdomen, and the bones in my body disappeared. I went limp against his chest, earning a chuckle from the male above me. He knew that he had me in the palm of his hand as he worshiped me, and I would willingly sacrifice myself to whatever Gods to stay here forever.

"We have to stop," I whispered, not sounding very convincing as Eoghan's trail of kisses made their way to the center of my neck. He licked up my throat and I couldn't hold back the gasp that slipped from my mouth. The sound reverberated off the cave walls, mixing with the roaring water behind us. My toes curled in my boots as liquid heat pooled in my core.

"Well, isn't this an interesting turn of events?" A female's voice broke me from my haze. I would know that familiar taunt in her honeyed tone anywhere.

Both Eoghan and I's eyes snapped toward Freya. She leaned against the arch of the wall looking just as disheveled and sweat stained as myself. A feline smirk tweaked the corner of her lips. Kicking up a boot, Freya let the heel of it rest against the rocky surface. "It seems your Prince's reign is going to come to an end tonight."

I whipped my head to look toward the water, just as a male took his first dive into the lake, gliding across the surface, closer to the bottomless out in the middle. Water rippled in waves, crashing against the bank, from the force of his stroke. Ripping myself from Eoghan's grip, I didn't hesitate to leap into the water. It was like a sheet of ice gliding over my face as I dove under before the tip of my nose broke the surface, sending a cool gust of air over me. I gasped in as much air as I could before diving back under and propelling myself forward. The male was only inches ahead of me. I could feel the vibrations of his legs as they kicked through the water.

We broke the surface at the same time. Our eyes locked, his own gleaming with a taunting challenge. The spray of the waterfall washed over our faces. In a normal circumstance, I would have relished the cooling sensation, but it took only a split second for the male to gather air in his lungs and dive back under. I scrambled, slamming my body down into the force of the falls. The water pushed me down and my lungs screamed for mercy. I managed to break through the savage force of the current.

My hand landed on a slick surface on the other side, and I pulled myself onto it. I raised myself to my full height squaring my shoulders. He did the same, towering over me even from the other side of this little island. We moved in time, like we were performing a twisted kind of dance, staring each other down as our shoulders heaved heavy. Water pooled at my feet. He was the first to rush forward, eyes going slightly glassy as they locked on to my necklace. I stepped away out of his path, sending him almost careening over the island's surface.

"Come on, Freya," Eoghan's voice sliced through the air, sounding so cruel and taunting from behind the rush of the falls. "You know you always wanted to spar with me. If you play fair, I will go easy on you."

"Fair? Who said anything about playing fair, General?" Her voice was venomous.

The heavy pounding of my opponents' feet drew my attention. I pulled my dagger from my thigh and swiped out. The tip caught him on his temple, but that didn't stop his rampage as his hands wrapped around my throat. I watched blood trickle from his wound, time seemed to slow as his brutish fingers tightened and I choked on my own tongue. The force sent both of us tumbling to the ground. The sounds of clashing swords faded into the background as I clawed against the male's hands. His thumbs dug into the center, pressing down hard against my windpipe. Black bled into the corners of my vision as it blinked in and out. I was certain the last thing I would see was, the murderous glint of the male's eyes shining down on me.

A crack in the earth's surface drew his attention away from me. Twisting limbs shaped an intricate web around each other, creating a thick vine. Luscious green leaves, sprouted haphazardly, covered the thorns hidden under them. The plant shot down, wrapping itself around my ankle before yanking me from the male's grip, dragging me ruthlessly across the rocky surface. My head slammed against a rock and my vision blurred from the impact. A scream tore through me as I was lifted in the air, left to dangle limp by the ankle. I swiped and jabbed at the thick vine, but it was holding me too far from itself for me to land a good blow. Blood rushed to my head, roaring against the thump in my ears. My lungs contracted, stifling my breath.

"As comical as your efforts are…" Freya's voice called out to me. I craned my neck to see her dripping form. Her auburn hair slicked to the sides of her face in stringy pieces, her eyes blazed, making her look wild and unhinged. I snarled at her, eyes frantically searching for Eoghan.

"Where is he?" I growled, my tone feral I couldn't even recognize it my own. Freya shook her hands in front of her, tiny water droplets splattering across my face.

"The General?" Her gaze met mine, a wicked glint flashing across it. "Drowning in his own blood."

A choked sob broke through my lips. This was it, the moment I had always known would come. Lochlan would lose his crown. I tried to catch my breath, but I couldn't get enough air in my lungs to calm the panic flowing through me. My heart cracked in two at the realization. For the fact that just minutes before this, I had thought we had won. The flame of my elation had been snuffed out, leaving the foul taste of defeat on my tongue. We had overcome all the obstacles that had stood in our way, but that wasn't the case.

Eoghan was dying alone on the other side of this waterfall, and I was soon to follow him. There was nothing I could do to help him; I couldn't crawl to his side just to lay there, and feel him in my heart just once more. I closed my eyes, praying to any of the Gods that they would find it in their power to protect my sister from the impending war that stalked along the horizon of tomorrow.

"You didn't think she could kill me that easily, did you, sweetheart?" His voice called to me like salvation. Eoghan's voice. Thick and heavy, smooth like finely aged whiskey. I would know him blind, by the sound of his commanding footsteps alone.

My eyes tore open finding Eoghan without fail. The shirt of

his leathers was ripped across the front, revealing the golden inked skin underneath. It was the first time I had gotten a good look at the markings, he was completely mesmerizing—with a body carved like an ancient statue of a God long since forgotten. I couldn't pull my gaze away from the marking resting just above his heart. It was the same dark ink that marked my palm.

A tug on my wrist pulled me back to reality. Lochlan's shadow was spinning, growing darker with each turn before it shot out toward the vine gripping onto my ankle. It slithered through the air, growing in size as it went. Large fangs elongating from the unhinged jaws of the shadow serpent before it clamped down on the vine. The green tendrils released me, sending me plummeting toward the ground. I braced myself for impact, but my body landed in a heap in Eoghan's arms.

"Miss me that much?" His bright smile hovered over me.

I shoved out of his arms. "Now is not the time for your teasing!"

Freya screamed out in anger, and I turned just in time to duck under her blow. It landed its mark against Eoghan's chest, but she did not continue her attack on him as she advanced toward me once again. I dodged another punch, and this time my spine made contact with Eoghan's as he maneuvered away from Freya's male counterpart. We moved in sync, turning in a circle as our opponents circled around us.

"I think now is the perfect time," Eoghan grunted out. I kicked my foot out, the heel of my boot landing on Freya's abdomen. She buckled slightly, but recovered in time to miss my punch. My fist sailed through the air, momentum causing me to wobble. "Stop resting on your heels."

I shot him an angry look over my shoulder. "Are you really coaching me right now? Don't you think it's a little late for that?"

Freya had resorted to digging in her weapons belt, deciding hand-to-hand combat was not working in her advantage. A dark whip unraveled from her palm, the metal buzzing with magic, sending shock waves through the air as she snapped it.

I sprang away from her first strike. The tip of the whip slammed into the ground, sparks rained across the space. I hissed inwardly as they caught my exposed arm. Eoghan shoved the male forward, sending him sailing through the air and into the lake. I waited a moment to see if he would resurface, but he never did.

"Answer me this." Eoghan stalked around Freya, his eyes trained on mine. The female spun, aiming the weapon at Eoghan this time. It missed him by a mere inch, and he snarled at her, kicking her legs out from under her. She crashed to the ground, her body contorting over jagged rocks, with a sickening crunch,

I jumped forward, hands wrapping around the base of the whip and ripped it from her hands. The power surged from the weapon into my skin, sending a delicious hum coursing through my veins. Eoghan watched as I wound the whip around Freya's neck, pulling tight to cut off her circulation. She struggled in my grasp, hands clawing at the metal digging into her throat. After a few more moments of struggling, she went limp in my hold.

"What could you possibly want to ask me right now?" I heaved out a heavy breath. The adrenaline from the fight was already starting to wane. I could feel myself growing weak as

I stood, wavering on unsteady feet. I was running on my last fumes, the adrenaline that had once brought me to life, fading away.

Eoghan's gaze left Freya's crumpled form, coming up to examine me further. "Why did you kiss me before she interrupted?"

The toe of his boot nudged against Freya's leg slightly. I gaped at him. "That's what you were thinking about while I was fighting to keep us in these Games."

"No." Eoghan scanned my body. "My mind wandered into other more nefarious corners."

"You" — I pointed one finger at him — "are unbelievable."

"Duck." Eoghan's eyes widened, pulling at his weapons belt.

"What?"

"DUCK," he commanded me. I crouched down quickly, recognizing the intense look of the general. My head was barely out of the way when the knife sailed over me. The kiss of metal brushed past my ear, clipping the side as it went. The thud of a body hitting the ground sounded behind, and I turned to find the male from earlier with a knife embedded in his eye socket. Blood dribbled down his face like tears.

Eoghan rounded my shaking form, plucking the knife from Freya's male counterpart's face. "Well, if you were going to be impaled, I would like an answer from you."

Straightening back up, my legs felt like jelly underneath me. I panted heavily, thinking back to my actions. Why had I kissed Eoghan? It wasn't something I had planned to do; no, quite the opposite. My time in this realm was coming to a close, and I knew when I left, there would be pieces of my soul left in the people I had grown to love here.

Love.

The word felt foreign on the tip of my tongue when coupled with my feelings for Eoghan. I was positive my feelings had not bloomed into full blown love, but I still cared deeply for the male in front of me. Stepping forward, I moved onto the podium, where the flag that had gotten me into this mess waved in victory for me.

"Truthfully…" I turned to look down on Eoghan, his brows knitted together, waiting for my response. "I kissed you because it felt right to do so. I don't have to, nor do I want to try to, justify it to anyone. These Games have proven to me that my life is too short to not act on the feelings I have."

Reaching out a hand for him, he stepped forward, lacing his fingers with my own. Eoghan grinned like the devil ready to corrupt his favorite angel, blinking slowly. He gestured with one hand at the flag. "Take what is rightfully yours, sweetheart."

The pit of my stomach swelled with nervous energy as I turned back to the black flag. My fingers traced the underside of the fabric, letting the magic soak into them. The red glow of my necklace filled the cave, bouncing off the falling water as it pulsed three times.

"The mortal champion, who turned out to be the key to the realm's destruction has come out on top." Demios's *sultry voice filled my ears. "Take me home, Spinner."*

In one swift motion, I ripped the flag from its pole. The magic engulfed Eoghan and I, a glittering gold cyclone of stars swirling around us. Closing my eyes, I soaked in the victory. That was, until I peeled them back open, and the severed head of the king swung back and forth between the black painted fingers of a female lounging in the ruler's throne.

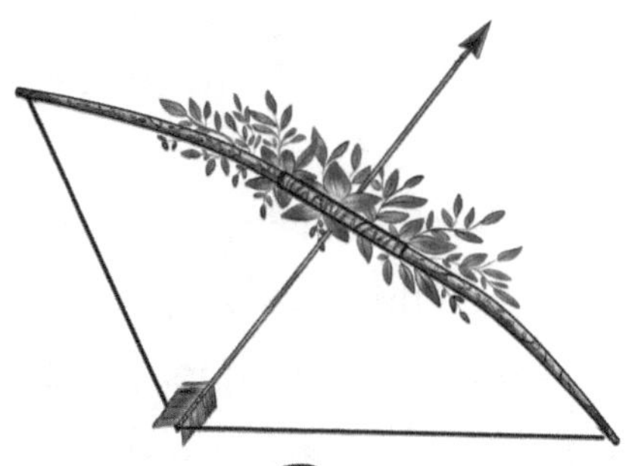

Chapter Forty Eight
Mairead

Thick tendrils of smoke billowed out of the cauldron in front of me. They wrapped around my light curls, tugging at the ends as they went. I caught the wary look of Kol, his blue eyes darkening as the smoke built.

"Aunt Lennox told you not to go poking around in this," Kol called over the bubbling liquid in front of me. I snapped my eyes up to meet his, watching as he cowered at my stare. It wasn't often that Kol would back down from me, but on nights like this, he knew not to cross me. Especially not tonight, when everything was riding on this one moment. If everything went according to plan, I would see my sister for the first time in four years.

When Caelen left me, I was a meek girl whose worst moments were losing my favorite ribbon to the wind. Then they came and stole her away. He stole her away. I gritted my teeth as my mind faded to the dark-eyed prince whose arm bares the mark of my last attempt to reach Caelen. I couldn't wait to rip his throat out with my bare hands, and watch him bleed out for the pain he put me through.

"We can't give up on her." I turned my gaze back to the smoke. Kol stepped behind me, arms snaking around my middle. I leaned back into him, letting his familiar touch soothe my racing heart. "Do you think she is going to show?"

"It all depends on the results of tonight." His lips brushed against my ear. I sucked in a shaky breath before nodding. Blue lightning flashed through the sky as I tried to calm my heart rate.

The cauldron bubbled rapidly before a single parchment flew into the air. I pushed away from Kol, leaping to catch the note as it made its descent. The thick paper was still hot from the magic that clung to it. Green writing was scrawled out across it as if someone was in a rush.

Meet where the mortal champion obtained the first flag. - S.

When I turned to show the note to Kol, I noticed that we were no longer alone. A male with deep auburn hair that hung down his back in a loose braid was holding a blade to Kol's throat. The blood in my veins went ice cold as I watched him struggle with the Sith—his green eyes challenging me to make a move against him.

"They do not lie when they speak of your beauty." He drew in a deep breath, taking in my scent as the wind picked up around me. "I can't wait until you sing for me."

Chapter Forty Nine
Lochlan

The Second Sister had returned long ago, donning a different face than the one I had grown accustomed to. Elara had been a ruse, a disguise for Seona to hide behind. She was a snake concealed in my garden, waiting to strike when the moment was right. My stomach rolled in time with each sway of my father's severed head. His glassy eyes were filled with terror in his final moments. She had no mercy when cutting him down.

Flexing my bound hands, I ran through my options of attack. Each one was quickly shot down by another obstacle. My legs were beginning to grow numb under my body weight as we waited for Seona's true target.

The crash of limbs against marble rang out in the throne room. My mortal champion had won it all, but I wished she hadn't. I would gladly give up the crown to keep the power hanging around Caelen's neck away from Seona. A guttural scream fell from her lips, shaky hands coming up in horror at the scene in front of her.

"I don't think I will be needing this." Seona's red painted

lips pulled at the corners as she leaned down to roll the head in Caelen's direction. She leapt back, landing in Eoghan's lap. He held her close, eyes blazing with a deadly anger that he directed toward Seona.

The Second Sister stood, letting her raven hair tumble down her back. Under the candlelight, it held a blue tint that shined as she shook it from side to side. She let a dramatic yawn slip through her lips. "Why does everyone look so shocked to see me?"

Seona stepped down the marble stairs, her gown flowing behind her in crimson waves. Caelen gasped through angered breaths. "You…you killed the King."

"Yes." Seona quirked a brow at her. "I did do that, didn't I?"

Caelen growled at the female who merely tsked at the girl. With a snap of her fingers, four guards appeared, hanging on her every word for a command. "Bring me the girl."

Caelen was ripped from Eoghan's arms. He roared in anger, but two guards held him back by his arms, preventing him from reaching her. I smirked as my mortal champion unleashed the wild beast that she had been known for when first arriving in this very throne room. Her legs kicked erratically as she arched against the guard's chest. He grunted as she landed a blow to his chin. Obscenities spilled from her lips as the male tossed her onto the floor directly in front of Seona. The scene looked like a thing from my nightmares as the Second Sister stared down the mortal standing in the way of having her power back.

A black tendril of smoke around Caelen's wrist caught my eye as it swirled in a constant loop. I narrowed my gaze at it. The damn thing liked her more than its master. My shadows had yet to make their appearance again after my bout of poisoning. It all made sense now. Seona had been growing everything she needed in her private gardens to kill a royal.

Senoa's hand came down, backhanding Caelen and sending her toppling over. The sickening sound of skin hitting skin range through the room. But Caelen did not cower to the sister, instead she snarled, turning her murderous gaze on her again. Her hand traced under the necklace, tugging at the chain until it snapped in half. She held it up, the red pendent gleaming under the candlelight. "Here. This is what you want, right?"

"I want much more than that, Caelen," Seona hissed at her. Her hand shot out, latching onto the underside of Caelen's chin and forcing her to look directly at her. I tried to lunge forward, but the guard standing to my right shoved me back down and held me in place.

Caelen's eyes glazed over as Seona plucked and weaved through her entire lifeline. A whimper slipped from Caelen's lips as she dove down deeper, ripping every memory from its place and storing them for later use. Seona finally released her, throwing Caelen down like she was nothing. A wonder-like sheen overtook her as her eyes flicked between the struggling General and the gasping mortal.

"By the Gods…" Seona's voice was breathy, as if she didn't quite believe in what she saw. "You love him."

"No," Caelen denied, tears rolling down her rosy cheeks. Eoghan flinched slightly at her tone. He was a fool if he believed Caelen had not fallen for him. Or maybe she was the fool who could not see it?

A hysterical laugh broke through the silence from Seona. "You can't deny it, I saw it. I felt how he made you burn with desire with just the brush of his lips. It won't last—love never does. And then you will be like me, bitter and power hungry because power is the only thing that can fill that hole in your chest."

"But he isn't the one you would die for." Seona leaned down to Caelen, spinning her around until her chest was pressed against Caelen's spine. An iron grip locked the two of them together. "Why don't we bring her in? She has been singing beautifully for us. Maybe she will give you a taste of her song too."

Caelen struggled against Seona, a shattered cry pouring out of her as an auburn-haired male dragged in a bound female. A light sack covered her head. The male slammed the small female into the ground, making me cringe as the sound of bones crunched under the weight.

"Remove the hood, Desmond." Seona's body shook with sick excitement as she waited for Caelen to break. Desmond reached down, ripping the sack from the female's head. I sucked in a ragged breath as I took in the beauty in front of me. Her disheveled blonde hair hung limply around her face. The ends were curling in as sweat and mud caked them.

Blue eyes matching her sister's caught onto mine and a savage growl rolled off her tongue. Mairead Elliston narrowed her gaze on me. "Hello, Prince Lochlan."

A wicked grin pulled at my lips as I scanned her figure. Her tattered gown was dirty and torn up the side, landing just below her hip bone. I winked at her once, bowing my head in respect. "Hello, pretty little *Songbird*."

Chapter Fifty
Caelen

A new level of hell was unveiled as I took in at the trembling figure of my sister. She was staring Lochlan down with a deadly lethalness that should have him cowering under it, but instead he was looking at her like she hung the stars in the sky for only him.

Seona hummed in my ear, "I guess I am not the only creature to want to hear the little birdy sing."

"No," I gasped out. My eyes locked on Eoghan's. He pulled against the guards again, shaking his head at me. I was going to give in to this tyrant and he knew it. His lips pulled back in a snarl, but the pleading words continued to pour out of me. "You can have the necklace."

I battled against Seona's tightening grip. "You can have anything you want, just please let her go."

"No," Mairead shouted across the room. Desmond stepped behind her, a dirty hand slapping over her mouth. I began to shout, but Seona gripped the sides of my cheeks, quieting me as she pushed inward on them.

My crazed eyes watched as Lochlan fought against his restraints, trying to get to Mai in any way he could. When he came to the conclusion that he would not be able to escape the bonds holding him down, he spoke out, voice poisonous as it spilled from his lips. "Remove your hand or I will remove it from your body."

Dark shadows leaked from him, coating the marble floor. I swallowed as the power that emanated from him suffocated me. Lochlan's shadows halted, waiting for the command to strike.

"Enough," Seona screamed. She stood, shoving me back down on the floor. I landed painfully on my side, fingertips scratching the surface as I heaved out ragged breaths. Seona tsked, her looming form hovering over me. "She can go when you return to me what is mine. Release my magic back to me."

My shoulders shuddered at the request. Lifting my head, I met the bloodshot eyes of Lochlan. He sent me a simple nod, giving me the permission to implode the realms if it meant some of us were going to make it out alive. I stood on shaky legs, my hand coming down to retract my dagger from my leathers. I sliced down the center of the mark. Eoghan released a pained groan, and I looked up at him in concern. He gritted his teeth, but nodded for me to continue. I dug the dagger deeper, letting the blood rise to the surface before I clasped the necklace in it.

A burning heat began in my palm, radiating though my entire body as the overwhelming pulse of power rippled through me. I channeled all of my energy into the necklace until I could feel it cracking under my pressure. Blood seeped into the fractured glass, and I could feel Demios drink it in greedily, taking my life source for his own. Then it felt as if the world fractured in two, releasing a burst of energy through the room. I fell forward, hand dropping the necklace as it rolled onto the floor in front of me. Red smoke poured out, rising in a cylindrical shape before slamming into Seona.

Her eyes glowed the same crimson color now, as she breathed in a shuddering breath. My stomach dropped as she lifted one single finger, beckoning Eoghan forward. He moved without hesitation, eyes trained only on her.

"Eoghan," I pleaded, as he walked past me with no acknowledgment. My heart shattered at the dismissal, a sensual smile came over Seona's face as he arrived in front of her. The same painted nail that had held the Kings skull dragged down his chest before her hand lashed out. It dug into the roots of Eoghan's long brown hair. She tugged it back, forcing him to his knees in front of her. I let out a warning growl, causing Seona to smirk in my direction. "Let's see what you can truly do, mortal champion."

My heart hammered as she placed her other hand against his chest and a golden light began to glow from under her palm. Lochlan was shouting, but I couldn't hear what he was saying as Seona slowly pulled her hand away, a beautiful golden string drawing out of the center of Eoghan's chest. She secured it around her wrist and leaned down to speak into his ear. "Do not kill her, General, instead hold her over the edge of death's threshold and bring her back to me."

In a flash, Eoghan was lunging for me. I scrambled backward, but his hand latched onto my ankle and pulled me back. I kicked out, the heel of my boot connecting with the underside of his chin. Eoghan's head snapped back, and I got to my feet, sprinting away from him.

"Caelen, your knife. Use your knife!" Lochlan screamed. I patted the pocket of my leathers where I usually kept it, but terror consumed me as I realized it was laying on the floor across the throne room. Eoghan was advancing on me again. I had never bested him in training, and now he wasn't going to hold back. His fist slammed into the side of my head. I staggered back, tiny black dots dancing in my vision.

Eoghan's foot swept out, knocking me from my feet. I landed on my back, air leaving my lungs. His second punch came down, but I rolled out of the way. The blow cracked the marble flooring next to me.

"Eoghan," I screamed at him, pleading that whatever bond we might have had would awaken if I begged hard enough. He punched down again, but I dodged it. "Eoghan!"

"He can't hear you," Seona taunted. Her fingers stroked the golden thread. "He doesn't even know who he is anymore. All he knows is me."

I threw an elbow into his gut. Pain radiated down my arm as I slid across the floor on my belly. My fingers grazed the wood of my blade, but Eoghan was quicker, snatching the weapon from me. He ripped me up by my hair, my body pulled taut in an awkward angle.

The sting of the sharp metal dug into my throat. I choked out a sob, hands coming up to wrap around his wrist. "Come back to me, Eoghan, and I swear I'll love you until my final breath.

Let me tell you every day until you are sick of hearing it. I just need you to come back to me."

The blade loosened slightly, and for a moment I thought I got through to him, as his golden eyes soften. His lip quivered slightly, and I sucked in a breath of relief. The feeling was short lived as Eoghan leaned down and snarled in my face. Seona waltzed toward the two of us, her lips pursed in a pout. "That was beautiful, but no matter how much you plead, he will forever be mine."

I closed my eyes, hot tears streaming down my face, and I felt like my heart was being splintered into a million tiny pieces. The sound of an explosion in the hallway pulled Seona's and Eoghan's attention away from me. I kicked back, driving all the energy I had left into forcing my heel into Eoghan's kneecap. He buckled under the blow, dagger clattering to the floor. I scooped it up before sprinting over to Lochlan.

Uncontrollable sobs pooled from my lips as I cut through the bindings on his wrists. Once he was free, he shoved me in the direction of my sister. "Go, quickly."

My feet skidded across the floor to Mairead. I rammed the wooden handle of the dagger into Desmond's temple, knocking him out as he crumpled to the floor. I bent down, freeing Mai quickly and helping her stand. We crashed into each other, arms tangling in a desperate hug. Behind her, a duel had begun between Lochlan, Eoghan, and Seona. Flashes of gold mixed with shadows in a brilliant dance.

I shoved Mai toward the door. "We need to leave. Now."

She nodded, not arguing the fact. I turned back toward Loch, his attention focused solely on Seona that he didn't see Eoghan coming up behind him. A jagged piece of shattered glass in his hand as he raised it behind Lochlan's back. I pulled back, letting my blade sail across the room.

Time slowed, as it spun in the air, each second ripping a part of my soul from my body. It embedded in Eoghan's left shoulder, sending blood spraying across Lochlan. The shattered glass dropped from his hands as his eyes met mine, a flicker of recognition as he took me in. I shook my head, not wanting to believe it. Lochlan threw up a wall of darkness, blinding Seona from coming for him, and we raced toward the door. Turning once more, my heart stopped as Lochlan's shadows slipped and I could see a glimpse of Seona pulling Eoghan's face down to hers. His lips moved against hers like they were lovers running on borrowed time and I was just another female who had warmed his bed for a moment.

CHAPTER FIFTY ONE
LOCHLAN

Mairead Elliston would not be underestimated. She stood hovering over a war table, a map spread across the surface. I watched her scan the landscape, drinking in the information. A mortal male stood behind her, his hand resting on the small of her back. Caelen had launched herself at him when we arrived in camp, muttering out the name "Kol" as she held him in a tight hug. Now she sat on a stool next to her sister's, eyes void of any emotion. I could see the bruises beginning to bloom on her face from the fight with Eoghan, but I wasn't sure she was even feeling the pain.

The flaps of the tent flew open, revealing the smiling face of Sylas. I gaped at her for a moment, not sure how she managed to waltz into a rebel base camp. She winked at me. "Did you think little miss ray of sunshine over there discovered our realm by herself?"

Caelen turned toward Mairead. "You were communicating with Sylas?"

"Yes," Mairead mumbled, finger tracing the line of a river.

"Why would you risk that?" Caelen leapt up, slamming her hands against the tabletop. "I left to keep you away from all of this and you go seek it out?

Mairead whirled on her sister. She was only a few inches shorter than Caelen. Her eyes glared up. "I am not the baby sister you left in that cottage. You will speak to me with respect, Caelen. Do not question my motivations to try to get you back."

"Hey." Kol pulled on her arm, but she shrugged him off.

"And you," Caelen sneered at him. She stepped around Mairead, shoulder slamming into hers. "I left Mai thinking you would take care of her. Not to warm your bed when you are lonely."

"Enough." A new voice rattled the structure of the tent. Its command silenced Caelen's crusade against Kol as her fury zeroed in on the tall figure that entered the tent. The male had a long scar that stretched across the left corner of his hairline to just under his right eye. Dark hair peppered with age was braided down his back. His gray eyes caught mine as he dipped his head toward me. "It's been a long time, nephew."

My brows shot up. "I think you are mistaken. I do not have any family."

"You did," he pulled a chair that sat near the table. The wood scratched against the dirt floor. "I would reckon I was your mother's favorite brother. Even if I was her only brother."

"Eamon," I breathed out, "you are supposed to be dead."

Eamon chuckled, "It will take a lot more than the wrath of your father to kill me."

Turning my gaze away from him, I swallowed down the

sadness that was creeping into my throat. Eamon cleared his throat, "I am sorry for your lo-."

"Why are you here?" Caelen cut him off. She scanned him, taking into account every piece of jewelry that adorned his body.

Multicolored gems sat in a metal setting on his fingers, and a single feather earring hung in his right ear. He was dressed in a pair of dark silk pants paired with a button-down cotton shirt that was left open, showing off his tattooed skin. She stepped around Kol and her sister, sizing up her prey. I smirked at her actions, knowing that if Eoghan was here, he would be grinning at the wild beast Eamon had summoned.

"I am here to help," Eamon leaned back as he watched her reaction.

"If you were here to help, why have you been attacking innocent villages? And playing with magic that Seona wielded over her army?" Caelen snapped at the male. Eamon paused, wetting his lips, as she slammed hand down and towered over the male. The smirk that toyed at his lips made it appeared as if the newcomer was entertained by getting under her skin.

Eamon shook a finger at her, "No, you have the wrong group. That group is an outlier. We never supported attacking the courts or villages. We simply get lumped in with them and their actions."

Caelen leaned down, face coming level with him. "Then what is it that you stand for?"

"Seona six feet under, for starters," he barked out a deep laugh, "but our fight is against her currently. The rest can be discussed at a later date."

Caelen nodded, "And what is your grand plan then?"

"It is quite simple. If you want to stop her, we must speak with the one who chained her the first time."

"The First Sister?" Caelen narrowed her gaze on him, "Arable has not been heard from since the final battle. She could be dead for all we know."

Eamon reached out, fingers dancing along the edge of the flame of a lit candle sitting on the table. His voice dipped low as he spoke, "Girl, if she were dead, the very surface you stand on would cease to exist."

The night had grown cold. Mairead and Kol had retired to their tent, leaving Caelen and I alone. Her eyes watched the flame of a candle waver in the wind. One of her hands rested on my homelands, thumb absentmindedly stroking back and forth against the map.

"There is still hope," I whispered to her. Caelen's eyes snap up to mine. "Eoghan. He isn't fully lost to us."

"Maybe not now," her voice was void of emotion, "but Seona will tire of him and send him back to us. And when that happens, I will have to carve his heart from his chest. Just as he asked me to do."

I shuddered at the thought. Her eyes traveled back to the candle. "Don't try to reason with me right now with tales of hope, Lochlan. This is real life. You do not get to reset time when mistakes are made."

Her words hung in the night air, causing a bitter taste to settle on my tongue. I nodded once at her, but she was back in her own mind, eyes wandering across the realms as I slipped from the confines of the tent.

The night's wind swirled around me as I ventured through the camp. My feet carried me forward, mind still reeling from the day's events and all we had lost. I rounded a set of tents coming upon a figure standing in front of my own. Her blond hair whipped around in the wind as it picked up speed. A flash of electric blue lit up the sky, casting a glow over the female's face as her hungry eyes drank me in. We were only mere steps from each other. I leaned back into the heels of my shoes, the thumb of the hand which had been stuck by the same force brushing across my bottom lip as I stared down the figure.

She cocked her head to the side, gaze traveling across my marking until it flicked up to meet mine again, "It appears you have something of mine."

A wicked smirk pulled at the corner of my lips as I stepped closer to Mairead Elliston, towering over her small frame, "So it does, Songbird."

END OF BOOK ONE

Turn the Page For

An Exclusive

First Look At

Book Two

in the Scottish

Folklore Series

CAELEN

Dark crimson poured between the divots of my knuckles. The sensation was the only thing that could break the numbness coursing through my veins since Eoghan was ripped away from me. My soul ached, and as hard as I tried to feel some semblance of him through the oath, there was nothing there.

"The sun hasn't even risen yet, Caelen." Lochlan's deep voice rumbled through the training field. I landed one last punch on the weighted bag and craned my neck to see the newly crowned King with no throne to rule upon. His hair was disheveled from sleep but his dark eyes were alert and trained on me. "Were you able to rest at all this evening?"

"No," I said dryly. Sleep brought the nightmares and the screams that never truly left me. I returned to the bag, ready to get back to taking out my aggression on something other than Lochlan or Mairead.

"You need to rest Caelen. I left the sleep–" Lochlan's words were cut off by the glare I threw in his direction.

"I don't need a sleeping potion, Lochlan," I growled out to him. The sleep aid only seemed to trap me within the terrifying scenes in my mind each night, leaving me more drained than if I had not slept at all. I rotated to face him fully. "Was there something you needed, Loch?"

His eyes watched me with pity. "He wouldn't want you to be killing yourself to feel something, Caelen. Eoghan would have wanted you to–"

"EOGHAN WOULD HAVE WANTED TO BE ALIVE!" I screamed the words that had been eating their way through my soul. Lochlan's eyes widened. They swam with questions that refused to slip out into the heavy silence that was beginning to suffocate us both.

"None of us are going to let you be a martyr," he said, his voice cracking at the end.

I sighed, tears begging to sting the corners of my eyes. "I can finish this if everyone would just let me."

Lochlan stepped forward, tendrils of his shadow power that he typically contained so well starting to creep around in him in dark waves. "And let a piece of you die in the process? What good would that do for any of us, Caelen?"

"If you are going to give a grand speech on how my life is important to people, then just save it," I hissed and turned back to the weapons rack to pull out a dagger. The cool metal stung against my heated skin as I let it settle into my palm.

Lochlan's shoulders slumped, the anger that had radiated from him suddenly dissipating. "I can't help you if you don't talk to me, Caelen."

"It hurts too much to talk, Loch," I choked out, tears finally deciding to fall in heavy droplets down my cheeks. "Doing anything hurts now. Every time I breathe, I feel as if I am being suffocated by her again as she ripped him from us. So unless you have some magical way to get the Eoghan we know back, I don't want to talk about my feelings. Ever."

"Because a part of you will always blame me for this pain? Blame me for bringing you here in the first place? It was me who gave the order to rip you from your perfectly ordinary life and make you play in the Games." Lochlan's voice shook with emotion. "Though you will never admit that out loud."

Planting my feet, I kept my back to him. "I don't blame you for any of this. I blame Seona and her twisted version of revenge. Why do you think I stayed? You gave me an out–told Mai and I that we could go back to our village, but we stayed because you needed us. Why else would I be here?"

"We all know your quest for revenge against Seona is only a mask to avoid having to face the feelings you are burying deep down." Lochlan's words had me whirling around to face him. His eyes blazed with fury. "Eoghan is still alive. And deep down, you know it…but you are too afraid of him becoming himself again because then you would have to face him now as the monster you've become."

I stared at the male, unable to deny the truth any longer. A strange mixture of anger and sadness bubbled in the pit of my stomach until I couldn't contain it any longer. I flipped the knife in my hand to grip the handle and threw it across the ring toward the target behind Lochlan's head. An anguished cry broke through my lips, my knees hitting the mat underneath me as I began to sob uncontrollably–the floodgates finally breaking.

Strong arms collected me in their embrace, drawing me into their warmth. I gathered Lochlan's nightshirt in my hands, pulling him closer as he whispered soothing words into my hairline. His shirt muffled my tearful voice as I begged with the oath to give me any hope, "Please. Please come back to me."

Lochlan's hold tightened as I waited for a tug, a light, or anything that would tell me that the oath was still intact. But nothing came.

Acknowlegments

Sometimes, the universe brings someone into your life that you didn't even know you needed, and then the next moment, you couldn't imagine your life without them. For me, that is Elijah. My Anam Cara, the Aelin to my Lysandra, and the reason this book was dusted off the shelf. Thank you, Elijah Selinsky, for believing in me and this book even when I couldn't imagine it being published. I will forever be grateful for your friendship, support, and the memories we have created on our adventures! If you can manifest 'Dear John' as our surprise song, you can do anything, bestie. Also, everyone can thank her for Lochlan having a POV. It would have been a damn shame if he didn't whisper that to her on a random Tuesday night!

Mom and Dad, thank you for supporting my dreams and encouraging me to never give up on my passions.

Kaleah Hickey, the third to our chaos trio. I can always count on your hilarious one-liners to bring me out of my funk. Thank you for supporting me and always helping me make my writing better! You make me a better writer every single day. Chapter 42 and your favorite girls will always be owned by you.

Thank you to my fabulous alpha, Faye Ruble. I am sorry I made you cry on Facetime, and for the tears I will inflict in later books. I hope Lochlan continues to climb the book boyfriend list because he always aims to please, hun. I am so grateful for your support and feedback!

Thank you to my fantastic beta readers: Calley Martin, Zoë Achor, Cindy Geyer, Khyla Gryer, Sarah Bunning, Kaitlyn Kelly,

Ari Reeseman, and Melyn McHenry. I am incredibly grateful for your feedback, funny comments, and help in making this book into what it is today!

And to you, the readers! Thank you for all of your love and support this past year! I had the chance to meet so many of you at events, and talking about my books with you has been the highlight of 2023. Your overwhelming support for this book has saved it from being shelved again many times, and I hope you loved this band of misfits as much as I do.

Allison Aldridge is an Arizona native who currently resides in Georgia. With a love for all things that have to do with storytelling, she continues to be an active member of the online book community. When she is not writing, you can find her watching hockey with her family or talking about her newfound fictional crush that has appeared in her life on her social media accounts. Allison graduated from Arizona State University with a Bachelor's in English with a concentration in Literature.

CONNECT WITH ALLISON ON:
Website: www.allisonaldridge.com
Instagram: @authorallisonaldridge
Tik Tok: AuthorAllisonAldridge
YouTube: www. youtube.com/ allisonaldridge